Parallel Universes of Infinite Self

Frederick E. Dodson

ISBN: 1-59526-654-2

Printed in the United States of America by Llumina Press

Library of Congress Control Number: 2006908630

Foreword

This book contains advanced viewpoints for the multidimensional human being of the 21st century. Shared within are mysteries of self and reality that have not been published before. As such, it is a jewel. If you treat it with consideration and appreciation, it will treat you with consideration and appreciation. The specific style of teaching or applied philosophy is abbreviated RC, which stands for reality creation.

Table of Contents

1

Go for the Real Thing

This book is dedicated to the spirits who believe life is meant to be magical and fun. It does not see you as a small, insignificant, cowardly, needy human being, but as the multidimensional, infinite, and eternal being that you are. This book's primary purpose is to reawaken your sense of fascination and awe towards life. Its secondary purpose is to shatter rigid belief systems and habitual ways of seeing and focusing on things. Why? Not to invalidate the societal structure in which you comfortably reside, but to support your return to the radical self-responsibility and *vast open-mindedness* of a spiritually mature being. With all the presuppositions you have gathered about life, you will hardly be able to dive into the unknown and learn something new or experience the *vivid freshness* of infinity. As is typical of the human condition, some ways of seeing things have become stale, to say the least. Even if your convictions and conclusions were useful at one time, doesn't it get incredibly dull to think the same things over and over and over—to perceive things from the same vantage again and again and again? But, as nothing can be added or taken away from infinity, the belief systems we shatter will not be lost. You can pick them up and reassemble them later if you need to hold on to concepts, or if you get scared of the joyous enormity of it all. Nobody is forcing you to have too much fun. Expanding awareness, in the original sense, means seeing, feeling, perceiving, noticing, experiencing, and doing something you have not seen, felt, perceived, noticed, experienced, or done before. It's as simple as that. If this is what is happening to you, you are using this book the way it was meant to be used.

If I were asked if this book is any good, my honest answer would be, "It depends who's asking." Reading is a two-way street; it is not only about the information, but also about who is reading and why.

What is the reader's attitude? A truly open-minded reader will neither immediately dismiss what doesn't match his preconceptions, nor immediately embrace what does match them. Be neither the automatic naysayer nor the fanatic yea-sayer. Read slowly, contemplate what was read, and give yourself time to play with the ideas. In this so-called Information Age, much emphasis is placed on collecting information in a browsing, unfocused, random, breeze-through manner. Once the info is processed, its, "Okay, got it. What's next?" That approach will not do for this book. If you want to learn something new that will benefit you beyond your expectations, slow down and actually get interested in what is being said. Consider and re-consider. Put it to the test. Look at it from more than one angle. In the context of this book, unapplied knowledge is no knowledge at all. Place emphasis not on information, but on experiencing joy. If you are not having any fun, what's the use of the knowledge? Application does not mean hard work. Let me put it this way: What is the difference between reading, talking, and intellectualizing about red wine and actually drinking it? Those who have substituted information for experience haven't really tasted it. Actually taking a sip of wine equals experiential-learning and lets you feel different. Go for the real thing.

2

Self-Responsibility

The primary audience of this book is the ever-expanding New Age, human potential, spirituality, magical, self-help, pop psychology, and "you create your own reality" movement. It is these longing and curious souls that I would like to reawaken to the subject of self-responsibility.

While the people of this movement have grown out of the limitations of materialist science & atheism on one hand, and religion, cultism, and submission on the other hand (thesis and antithesis), some still bring the baggage of old ways and ideas into the new paradigm and planet we are creating. Many readers are already familiar with self-responsibility, but for the magic in this book to work, we must expound on it. While I encourage the New Age movement, much of it still operates under lack, infantile wishful thinking, and neediness, rather than identification with the infinite self.

I have been teaching the "you create your own reality," mental and emotional technique and meditation for more than ten years and have witnessed how many approach the teachings as something that will fix it for them, but without you none of the techniques are worth a dime. They get their energy from you. They get attention, importance, belief, and time from you. People take part in programs, courses, meditation retreats, and workshops to get better or feel better. They say they want a better job, more money, lasting relationships, better sex, a soul mate, health, a good-looking body, enlightenment, an out-of-body experience, lucid dreams, or to break limitations. They want these things because they hope it will make them feel different. A higher state, more energy, and greater well-being are the goal of these desires.

Paradoxically, and quite ironically, feeling better is not the goal of my work, but its prerequisite! Well being is not the goal; it is the starting point. Without energy or enthusiasm to start with, none of it works. This is funny and kind of tragic, because the people most desperate for certain things will be the least likely to get them. People who visit my workshops out of curiosity, but in a state of general well-being will get the results—they'd also get them without my workshop.

Infinity (all that is) is attraction or correspondence-based, which means, "like attracts like." This means that lack will produce more lack, and success will produce more success. As long as you need something outside yourself to make you happy, as long as you have a long list of conditions to be met and circumstances to change, you are a slave of the world, and as a slave, you will not experience magical results. If you say, "*When* I have money, vacation, meditation, this book, this file, this knowledge, this job, this partner, this statement by my colleague, I will feel better," you are wearing life the wrong way around. A mirror (life) will not smile before you do. Circumstances will not change before you do. Unfortunately, most people have been conditioned to this viewpoint. Maybe it's also the viewpoint you hold. If that is the case, now is the time to reconsider your approach. These people can easily be duped, conned, and exploited. All one has to do is find out what they desire (lack), promise to deliver, and one can do anything one wants. As long as you are needy, as long as you shy away from self-responsibility, you will rarely feel fulfilled, except for the occasions when one of your cravings is temporarily met. You will forever be running after things, instead of having them run after you. The former is the way of the slave, the latter the way of the wizard. Things are, of course, not bad in and of themselves, but the world cannot give you anything of lasting value. It can only reflect what you give yourself. The wizard does not want to have more, but *be* more. He knows that when he stops chasing the world, the world starts chasing him. Here's a word of advice: Regularly spend a certain amount of time becoming silent and relaxed until you find happiness within yourself in the here and now—independent of the ever-changing conditions and circumstances of the world. Find well-being independent of objects, people, and events. This single piece of advice will boost the quality of your life in ways you may not yet suspect.

Spirituality, New Age philosophy, and the knowledge of existence beyond the limits of bodily form and its five senses can be a breakthrough, an inspiration, but it can also be a limitation. It becomes a limitation when you substitute teachings and techniques for self-responsibility in daily life, first-hand common sense and intuition—your own inner authority. Some resemble a person standing by a lake where a child is drowning; he has to consult his tarot-cards to decide what to do. Truth is not a path followed, but one created by your own footsteps. Follow another's path, and you become the other, not yourself. Dependency on outside sources and teachings is the number one mistake I have observed in the New Age scene. In other words, it is not going to be a guru, teacher or technique that ultimately forms your experience, its going to be you, the "I am," the "*youniverse.*" This is not said to discourage you from considering outside viewpoints, but to encourage you to consult the wellspring of your inner knowledge before you consult others. The answers are not always out there, but very often, in here. When you make something outside more important, you are presuming that you do not create reality, but an outside authority who knows more than you do. This is an invalidation of your infinite nature and the surest way to cut yourself off from your intuitive and common sense. The prime source of reality is not rules, concepts, behaviors, teachers, masters, or gurus, but you. Yes, go ahead, ask questions and gain different viewpoints, but do not become dependent on them. You are a sovereign, individual, unique, beautiful, and very powerful being, and it is silly to assume that others have access to more of the infinite resource than you do.

3

The Nature of Infinity

Highways of the Soul

Take the concept of parallel worlds, as known in physics and science fiction, bring it down to earth, and apply it in every day life to change your personal reality. Here's a simplified analogy of how parallel universes apply to you:

Imagine hundreds of highways, side-by-side, stretching before you. While these highways lead to or come from destinations, the highways are the ultimate destinations. The starting or ending point of a highway contains an experience similar to any other point of the highway. Each highway represents a unique life experience. Each represents a different version of you. Each highway contains experiences, props, people, sceneries, backgrounds, and emotions that are distinct and different (although on some, there may be similarities). Each time you make or change a decision, you change direction. You may move forward, backwards, to the right, to the left, to the side, or even switch to another highway altogether. From the viewpoint of infinity, these highways are not actually beside each other. Nor are they stacked on top of each other. From the viewpoint of infinity, they all take up the same space at the same time. They're not even linear, but for practical reasons, and in an earthly context, let's see them side-by-side, representing different versions of you.

Some of you are on highways containing experiences and leading to destinations that you like; some of you are on highways you dislike. Most highways are a mix of both. Some of you are moving very quickly, others are moving slowly, enjoying, or enduring the scenery. Others are sitting at the side of the road, having stopped to take a break, to be silent and contemplate their experience on their highway or which highway to take next. Others are sitting on the side of the highway because they don't know where to go. Others stand at crossroads, facing a decision about the further path. Too many still walk or drive down their highway in the mistaken belief that it is the only highway that exists or the only highway they are able to take. Some have a low-quality highway they don't enjoy; some have a low-quality highway they do enjoy. Some have a high-quality highway they enjoy; some have a high-quality highway they don't enjoy. The variety of experience is infinite and fascinating to onlookers.

The parallel universe concept, as applied to the self, holds that the multidimensional, infinite, and universal aspect of you is experiencing *all* highways simultaneously, and has traveled, is traveling, and will travel all of these variations. This oversoul version of self not only travels on all the highways, but also creates highways on which it and others travel. You already exist as many different versions of self, even though you (the limited version of you) may only be aware of one reality, one version of you. The reason for this limitation is simple: Were you to perceive all highways simultaneously, you wouldn't be able to focus on, learn from, and enjoy a single highway properly. When you decide to travel Highway A, another version of yourself is simultaneously deciding on Highway B. The version of you that would have decided on Highway B actually does exist—in a parallel universe.

A short version of the analogy, as in which science resolves the concept of parallel universes: Imagine you travel back in time, to before you were born. You meet your mother. Startled by your sudden appearance, she has a heart attack and dies. You've interfered in the natural timeline and killed your mother before you were born. This would mean that you were never born, which would mean you never built a time-machine with which you could travel back in time and cause your mother to have a heart attack, which means you were born, after all, which means you did travel back in time and shock your mom, which means you weren't born, which means you didn't travel back in time…etc. You get the picture. The way science solved this paradox was by postulating parallel time-tracks: One in which you were born, and one in which you were not.

The concept of a parallel universe is easy to grasp. Up to now, the many worlds theory has been kept in the realm of science, physics, and science fiction. Science still struggles with proving or disproving it, and science fiction still places it far from ordinary experience. I invite you to apply this concept to your personal reality, your everyday life, and your own spiritual expansion.

The physicist Hugh Everett III first created the Many Worlds Model in 1957, based on concepts formulated in the Copenhagen School of Physics to explain certain anomalies of quantum mechanics. Quantum mechanics acknowledged that the observer of an event is not independent of the event, meaning that observed phenomena behaves according to the expectations of the observer. The many worlds model goes a step further by proposing that with each observed event, reality splits into different, non-intersecting realities, while the observer remains a special case. Everett's work is now widely acknowledged by leading physicists. Meanwhile, physicists also acknowledge what spiritual mystery schools have been teaching for ages: The observer is not a special case, but splits just as the observed reality does. The observer is connected to the observed reality. Furthermore, the various parallel worlds are not non-intersecting or autonomous, but can intersect and produce overspills or bleed-through into other realities. In the moment an event is observed, the very act of observation not only creates the event, but a split in which one version of the event is perceived and other versions seem to fall away. However, they do not stop existing; instead, they retreat into their own parallel reality with their corresponding observer. The versions of reality that do not manifest here manifest elsewhere and are as real for their observer as your version is real for you. In plain English, this means there is no reality without its corresponding observer, and there is no observer without its corresponding reality. Reality-version and observer-version are always connected. Every reality comes with an observer and every observer comes with a reality. It also means that there are an infinite number of realities you do not perceive, but which are just as real as your current one, taking place, and are accessible by you, because they are also you. This means you don't really have to create these realities; they already exist. You merely have to become the version of yourself that corresponds to the desired reality.

Parallel Reality Surfing

Life becomes even more interesting once you realize there are many versions of yourself and millions of options that await you. The hundreds of highways already in front of you may be called your destinies or paths of highest probability. Which highway you choose is a matter of free will. Even if, from a limited viewpoint, your choice is reduced to only a hundred paths, that's still more than most dare travel. Do you feel the breeze of fresh air now that you're aware of how many options you have? Does the breeze turn into a thunderstorm of fascination when I tell you that your infinite self has actually traveled all of these paths and you can link to any of these versions of reality and experience them just as fully as you experience your current reality? The only catch is that you have to forget or lose one reality to fully identify with another. That is the reason you act as if your current reality is the only one. We do that to focus in detail rather than be swept away by the chaos of infinite possibilities. We limit ourselves to focus in detail on one aspect of being.

The version of yourself that went to the right, the one that went to the left, the one that went straight on, the one that dropped out of school, the one that married, the one that didn't marry, the one that went to Hollywood and failed, the one that went to Hollywood and succeeded, the one that became a vet, the one that became a bank clerk, the one that became a professional soccer player, the one that invented a new perfume, the one that divorced, the one that had children, the poor one, the rich one, the one that was both, the one that was neither—your infinite self has experienced every and any variation of being.

And, since your essence is infinite self, so can you. In other words, the all-that-is universe is one with everything. You are one with the all-that-is universe. Therefore, you, too, are one with everything and have access to it. As the limited world self, the immersed or already identified self, you may be aware that your life might have gone another direction had you made other decisions, but as this world-self, you have probably not been aware that these other versions of you existed and could be entered. Do you remember that desire you had as a teenager to go a certain way? Perhaps you ended up not going that way. Well, another self did and is living that life right now. The ability to become this version, whenever you want, is installed in your consciousness.

The key to this ability is your sense of identity and the attributes the identity or world self uses: intention, imagination, belief, attention, emotion, communication, and action (or behavior or body sense). You needn't control these aspects separately. Instead, a single shift in identity-awareness (I am...) will shift sublevel aspects automatically. From where you stand, you can first view and explore other timelines, choose between them, and then enter these reality-scapes by identifying with them. This means taking on the viewpoint of that other version of you, a person who is already enjoying that reality. This is not done by visualizing, affirming, goal setting, trying, working, achieving, or performing a ritual. That is what is taught in New Age philosophies, but it contradicts the idea of taking on the viewpoint of the one for who it is already real. If you were to take on that viewpoint, you would no longer need to desire, wish for, hope for, affirm, aim for, or visualize the reality—because you *are* it. In this sense, while we might be talking about things familiar to you "create your own reality" readers, the approach is entirely different. The reality you are in may be the most familiar, but it may not be the most fun. Just because it is solid, normal, and factual does not mean it is where you are damned to remain.

An easy way to gain preliminary access to alternate self-versions (before choosing one) is to ask yourself how your life might have progressed had you made another decision or non-decision. As your mind follows the probable flow of events from that decision onwards, you are already in energetic connection to a parallel reality. You are not yet in it, but touching it. Yes, simply by directing attention somewhere, you are already connecting to it. Putting attention there is the first step of reality surfing.

Another way to view parallel universes (before choosing and entering one) is through night dreams. Night dreams are often invalidated as unimportant, but when they are not processing garbled information of the day's events, they often show parallel existences of self—often featuring similar people and roles as your waking reality but from other backgrounds, circumstances, or scenarios. Night dreams offer an opportunity to explore parallel universes of self before committing to one of them. The same thing can be said about day-dreams or imagination.

Another way of becoming aware of parallel worlds of self is by noticing rare and unusual events, out-of-line occurrences, or strange coincidences. Timelines (highways, parallel realities) that closely border your current timeline often generate spillovers or crossovers to your current timeline. Events that don't seem to belong to your daily routine are spillovers from parallel realities. Were you to stay with these events rather than returning to your habitual path, you would start moving towards the alternative highway.

What we call "desire" is actually a spillover from a parallel reality version of you already experiencing a certain reality. Desire is indicative of two things: That you are separate from the version of yourself who is already experiencing a reality you prefer, but also that this alternate version is not too far from you in terms of probability. You can't want anything that doesn't already belong to you. That's the good news. If you didn't already contain the potential to experience it, you would not want it; you wouldn't even be able to think about it. You needn't feel nostalgia or remorse over dreams never fulfilled because they have been fulfilled and can be re-accessed. You are anything you can imagine, and once you understand how to shift consciousness so that you correspond with what you desire or your desire corresponds with your innermost beliefs, you will become a very magical person indeed.

Access to another version of yourself begins by returning to a state of no identity, a non-conceptual consciousness, the zero-point of infinity, the realm of the pure "I am," the observer, the witness who is not identified with anything, the one who is nothing and nobody, and at the same time, everything. Don't identify with a new reality while still identified with an old one. Becoming "identity-less" is not as complicated as it may sound. The infinite identity-less self is accessed in deep inner silence in a specific type of meditation. From point zero, you start receiving (not creating) various versions of self. Then you enter the viewpoint of the preferred version, not looking at it, but *as* it, and experience the joy you would experience as that person. This is a matter of focusing attention in a certain way. Often we don't suddenly shift realities because we focus in a similar way day to day. Reality surfing is much like taking on a film role and behaving according to the script. Before the procedure is outlined, let's loosen your definitions of reality.

The Eye of Infinity

In the beginning, in the end, and in between and beyond, there was, is, and will be, infinity. Infinity is all that is, and it contains anything and everything anyone can imagine. Infinity is infinite, eternal, and multidimensional. Nothing can be taken away or lost from infinity, and nothing can be added; it already contains everything. It always has and always will. Infinity is something-ness, nothingness—both and neither nor. Infinity is also holographic. This means that any part of infinity contains the whole. Imagine cutting a picture in half, and instead of getting half a picture, you get the whole in a smaller version. Such is the nature of infinity. Within the infinite context, there are a limitless number of finite contexts, finite universes within universes within universes. These universes are limited viewpoints infinity inhabits temporarily—eyes of infinity. Each of these finite contexts contains the whole of infinity holographic. Let's get to how this relates to your personal reality and reality creation:

Infinity is one with any reality and the realities you desire. You are one with infinity. Therefore, you can also be one with any reality.

The Eye of the I

Infinity splits itself into many different viewpoints or "I ams." Each viewpoint is a part of infinity and separate, individual. To make a long story short, you come from the creator containing all the potential of the creator, but also have a relationship with the creator because of your separateness. From your original "I am" viewpoint, which is only separate once you split several more viewpoints, "I am this," "I am that," "I am also that." Each word inserted after the original "I am" allows you to incarnate into a reality. Each reality you incarnate into has a context—limitations or game rules. Which realities you create depends on the context. The journey of the soul is an adventurous and exciting one. One might incarnate into a universe, lose oneself in it, and within that universe, incarnate into another one, and another one, completely losing track of the original source of the journey. But since the connection to infinity is never broken, the source can never be entirely lost.

In RC terms, consciousness equals infinity. Consciousness is all there is, and consciousness creates worlds and worlds within worlds. In RC terms, the three most interesting aspects are consciousness (infinity, all that is, the universe, God, the field) and the world-self (ego, identity, self, individual, persona) and the relationship between the two.

There Is No Separation between Identity and Reality

Consciousness is not within the body, brain, or mind. Between observer and the observed, separation always allows something to be observed. You can observe your body and your mind; therefore, you cannot "be" them. The reason we have difficulty knowing who we are is that we are that. The eye wasn't designed to look at itself. Consciousness is not limited to the body. Notice how you can let your attention expand beyond the boundaries of the body or your immediate surroundings. Although you may have been conditioned to the viewpoint that you are "in" the universe, in RC terms, the universe is in you. You may believe there's a small me in a big universe, but it's the other way around. There is no separation between "in here" (me) and "out there." This separation is a construct of consciousness built for the game we call life. For reality-creation coaching, this has many implications. One of them is that identity and reality are synonymous. What you see and hear in your surroundings is within you, part of your body. It also means that a change of identity implies a change of reality. *You see the world not as it is, but as you are.* Life doesn't happen to you, but through you. Truth is not a path you follow, but one created by your footsteps.

The Mystery, the Magic, and the Miracle

Where have all the mystery, the magic, and the miracles gone? You have no doubt pondered this question a few times. If you are missing these three M's in your life, it's not because life is dull. It's because most humans look at things from the same viewpoint and keep seeing the same things. Coming to the same mental conclusions day after day does indeed make life appear boring, but the change you are looking for is not a change out there; the change must be made on yourself. As a rule of thumb, boring people are often bored. If life is especially dull, repetitive, or boring let it teach you about yourself. I don't blame you for becoming this bland, I don't blame you for the tedious routine you call life. You have developed this viewpoint because you have bought into or agreed to certain ways of looking at life, and these ways are not only very uninspiring, but also counterfactual. You have been taught that:

Everything is as it seems, when, in fact, *nothing is as it seems*
What you see is real, when, in fact, what you see is an illusion
Imagination is unreal, when, in fact, imagination is the very source of reality
Everything is known, when, in fact, you are surrounded by the unknown
Things are this and that, when, in fact, they are not
I have to do this or that, when, in fact, you don't have to do anything
I know where I come from, when, in fact, you have not the slightest idea
I know who I am, when, in fact, you don't

There are two ways to re-inject wonder and awe into your life:

- Seeing what already is in a different light, from a different perspective
- Going into the unknown

The first way means becoming aware that there is more to things and people than meets the eye. Nothing is as it seems; nobody is as they seem. What is the world of the known? What is "reality" to the average Joe or the scientist or to someone focused so strongly on this world they live in denial of everything else? What is this 0.000000000000000000000000000000000000000000000000000 000000000000000000000000000000000000000000000001% of the whole that people call reality? Well, if you'd visited as many places in the world as I have, you would notice that it isn't much of anything. Much more important is what goes on between the spirits (humans) inhabiting it. I've driven a car on all parts of the globe, and everywhere I go, I see the same things—structures and objects (buildings, cars, roads and materials), landscapes and nature (trees, grass, waters and mountains), animals, and people. If you think about it, that's not too much, is it? Is that all there is to reality? Is that really all there is? If that were so, life would indeed be unbearably dull, but there are still the things that people do. An amusing place to witness how limited many people are in their horizons is to look at dating forums in the internet, in which people describe their activities and hobbies. People spend a lot of time sleeping and working. In modern western society, working often involves going to an office cubicle and sitting in front of a screen. In their free time, what do they do? Many sit in front of other screens—the TV, a movie theatre, or the computer. Others eat or drink, going to restaurants, cafes, or pubs to do so. Others might go into nature and walk around, play sports, or visit other people. Yet others may have sex. Very few do something creative or spiritual. Even fewer go into the unknown, perceiving or doing something not done before. Once you reawaken your infinite self, even commonplace things and places will become interesting again; you will notice that there are unlimited versions of a single event. When you enter a café, there are many hundreds of ways the café can be experienced.

Most activities are directly connected to survival (sleep, eat, drink, work) or pleasure (distraction from the fight for survival). Is this all there is to reality? A bunch of buildings, cars, screens, and people struggling to survive? You have to be kidding. As far back as my childhood, I realized that this was not going to be my reality. Is it going to be yours? If not, remember: *You don't see the world as it is, you see the world as you are.*

To keep you enslaved as an idiot, unaware of most everything, there are only a few concepts in which you must believe. One is that the outside world is separate from consciousness. You must believe that what happens out there has nothing to do with you. You must believe that you are a small being in a large universe. As you will find out on this journey, this is not true. Your body and the world are within you, not the other way around. Hard to grasp? Hard to believe? An analogy might help: when you dream at night, you think you are observing a dreamscape separate from you. "I am here, and there is the landscape of my dream." But when you *wake* in the morning, you suddenly realize that the whole thing, the dream and all of its characters and events, were a part of your psyche, taking place within you. The same thing applies to waking life. You think, "I am here, and out there is the world," but once you *awaken t*o a higher reality, you realize that "out there" is a part of your consciousness and it was created by you.

Vibratory Universe

Everything is energy, the very same energy. Everything is one. That is the nature of infinity. At the same time, everything is different, separate, scattered. Infinity is everything and nothing. For practical reasons, we can say that everything is energy vibrating in different frequencies, manifesting in different densities. Some readers will be familiar with this concept. Ice, water, and steam are the same energy manifesting in different densities, ice being the most dense (slowest vibration) and steam being the most subtle (highest vibration) manifestation of the same energy. Likewise, body-mind-spirit, or matter-thought-soul are different vibratory densities of the same thing. This means that concentrated thought can condense into material form. The first separation from infinity is the "I am" (consciousness). The second separation is the "I am this" (soul, energy, identity). The third separation is "I am this and that" (body, matter, physical existence).

Contrary to popular belief, the denser forms and realities, what we call "physical reality," are contained within the less dense realities. Consciousness is the source of physical reality. The body is within the soul. Belief or thought precedes experience. Think about these statements. They contradict what you have been taught. If you imagine a dozen concentric circles, the circle in the middle will be physical reality. It is contained within the less-dense reality (some call it the fourth dimension) and so on. The circle surrounding the middle circle is, in this sense, the source of physical reality. Consciousness is the source of reality. Consciousness causes what you experience as reality.

You exist in two states: As identity, an individual soul, an "I am," and as the whole, infinity or the infinite self. Everything is one, and you are that one. The tiniest part of a hologram contains all the information of the whole hologram; you contain all the information of the universes and are connected to all that exists. Nothing can be added to or taken from infinity; infinity already contains everything. This implies that your very existence is proof that you have always existed and will always exist, and that what does not exist has never existed and will never exist. There is no such thing as non-existence, so relax—you will never die). You will exist, in various forms, forever. You exist as a being aware of itself, with free will and access to everything and anything that exists. You are infinite; the rest is changing.

4

Reality Creation

The Law of Correspondence

The law of correspondence is also called the law of resonance or the law of attraction in other RC teaching systems. It is the single most powerful working principle of infinity. It works in all realities, on all levels, at all times, in any number of variations, and in obvious and sometimes not-so-obvious ways. If you understand one thing about life, let it be that there is no thing that operates independently of what you believe. The law of correspondence means like attracts like, you can only experience what you are, what you give is what you get, vibrations attract like vibrations, birds of a feather flock together, and what you put out is what comes back. If you want something in life—anything—you have to be someone who corresponds to it.

You notice vibratory correspondence every day. When you wake up in the morning, feel lousy, and begin the day lousy, you may experience mishaps throughout the day. Notice how it accumulates. The rich become richer all the time. People who talk about sickness all the time fall ill. Someone attacking another is attacked himself. Someone who is fascinated by horrifying things soon has bad things happen to him. Someone gives up needing a partner (and starts corresponding to one) and a partner suddenly shows up.

You attract things according to who you are (which is indicated by what you think and feel). If you feel overweight, it is impossible to attract ideal weight on a long-term basis, no matter how many diets you try. If you feel poor and behave poorly, you cannot attract money. Understand that law of correspondence never sleeps; you may become a bit more interested in the quality of your emotions, reactions, and output.

People don't like acknowledging the law because that would mean they've attracted all kinds of undesirable things. They go on to invalidate themselves: "If I am the attraction-creator of all these things, why did I create this shit?" They believe that agreeing with RC-concepts means agreeing that one is worthless and stupid, but that's not the case, because most things are not created intentionally, but automatically, because you didn't understand the rules of the game. Admitting to your creatorhood does not invalidate you. You are the only thing you have, and invaliding yourself invalidates life, the universe, and everything.

It may have begun with a tiny thought. You gave that thought attention, and it became a consideration, and then it became a normal-sized thought. It got bigger and accumulated similar thoughts. This huge thought then attracted emotions and energies. It became even bigger and started interacting with people and events. In a positive and negative sense, the more you have of something, the more you get. Since infinity does not recognize anything as negative, the way your world self means it, any experience is of value. Not every small thought manifests immediately because it is neutralized by other thoughts before it is born into magnetism. Even charged thoughts don't necessarily manifest soon because of the buffer of time experienced in the dimension of being. This buffer allows for an extended period of sifting, choosing, considering, and deciding to get what you intend to be manifested straight. A small thought indicates and opens the probability of a reality. Continue to focus or involve yourself with it; it will be your absolute reality, no matter what the current circumstance appears to be.

Consciousness creates everything you want and everything you don't want, whether you are aware of what you desire and resist, or not. This duality provides balance in this dimension. Things you are neutral towards (neither desiring nor resisting) are not created/attracted. Everything you are afraid of and everything you intend wholeheartedly shows up eventually. Since most people's attraction/creation is chaotic and unstructured, most things neutralize before physical manifestation occurs. One dimensional tone above ours, feelings and thoughts manifest immediately. On a physical level, there appears to be a time-buffer in which a thought is shot into infinity by an activating emotion, then time passes, and finally, physical manifestation boomerangs back. The process of reality creation is confusing and nearly incomprehensible because we send so many contradictory intentions that we don't know which reality is the result of which intention. We even forget we sent them.

As obvious from the word "correspondence," the process of RC is a two-way street, a dialogue. It does not only involve sending a wish list into the universe, but getting into correspondence with infinity. It does not only contain a desiring, intending, or attracting part, but also an allowing, receiving part that lets infinity create. It is the job of the world self to intend and the job of infinity to create, and then again your job to allow or receive. *Allowing* means being receptive enough not to try to create the reality yourself, but to allow the magnificent intelligence of infinity to find a way to correspond with your vibratory signal, allowing what you intended to flow in. This is directly connected to your feeling of self-value and of being happy to be yourself, independent of circumstances. This goes hand-in-hand with letting others be who they are, granting the same validity to them, and thus granting reality to be what it is. When you know you can attract whatever you want, you don't get upset about others or circumstances. You are not here to repair what is broken, you are not here to convince others of your path—you are here to express your own path. It is not your job to force the world into conformity or sameness. Instead, you appreciate the diversity. Rather than fighting others, you choose people you like being with. By fighting something, you make it part of your world. Conformity is stagnation; diversity is creativity. Having different opinions needn't be a cause of pain and struggle; it can be a cause of fascination and laughter. Working to get others to agree with your reality means working on conformity, on bringing the infinite unfolding of creation to an end rather than furthering expansion. Giving validity to any viewpoint is paramount for the survival of the human species. If you don't grant freedom of speech to people you dislike, you don't grant freedom of speech at all. Allowing is more than tolerating, because tolerating implies that you don't really appreciate what it is you tolerate.

"So should I allow things and people that are negative?" some might ask. The question implies they haven't understood the law of correspondence, which states you needn't experience anyone or anything you personally dislike. Release your reaction and interaction with what you no longer desire. Re-focus on what you cherish, and such events and people won't even enter your field of perception. You'll be at a completely different party. You attracted anyone who enters your field of reality. Only if you don't understand that you attracted it and there is a good reason or pay-off, might you be annoyed by it, but knowing the event flows from you by law of correspondence, you might be able to appreciate the person or event in a new light. It's impossible for others to enter your world if you haven't invited them by vibratory resonance (desire or resistance). You are unable to perceive or experience anything that doesn't match your vibratory state. When you know you create it, or more precisely, attract it all, you don't worry about who and what shows up, because you realize you can attract better anytime. Someone who understands RC fully will no longer need walls, borders, armies, wars, or prisons, and will no longer criticize those who do—because he needn't have anything to do with them anymore. If a bomb explodes in your neighborhood, killing hundreds, you need not be affected by it if you are not in vibratory resonance (fear, belief) with it. For some readers, such claims sound outrageous; if so, take responsibility for your limited worldview. I have been in disastrous situations without so much as a scratch while others were bruised, injured, hospitalized, and even killed (never their "self"; the self does not die). This is not a boast, but an attempt to make a point that what happens to one is no coincidence. You are free to attract the reality you want, you are free to enter parallel realities, and there is no "out there" unless you invite it through your innermost intentions. When you release your urge to control others and circumstances, and find yourself to be the source and cause of the circumstances you tried to control, you will see that you can make the world a better place by making yourself a better person.

Reality Creation

From the viewpoint of the infinite self, contrary to popular New Age belief and motivational psychology, you don't actually create reality. Within infinity, everything already exists and doesn't have to be created. This doesn't mean you can't experience the appearance of creating something that wasn't already there, which is one of the soul's favorite games. Likewise, you can't get rid of any reality, either. In an infinite context: Where would you want to put it if there is no such thing as "outside infinity"?

A very helpful analogy: A television does not have to create the program it wants to receive; the program already exists and is broadcast through the airwaves. All it has to do is tune in to the appropriate channel to receive the desired program. In exactly the same way, you do not have to create the reality you desire, because it already exists. You may not perceive it because your consciousness is not tuned in to reception of the reality. By synchronizing or aligning your own vibration to the vibration of what you want to perceive or experience, infinity filters out the reality that matches your vibration. You will not necessarily get what you want; you will get what you are. Your vibration or reception-channel is comprised of what you believe to be true about yourself and reality and by what you feel. What you feel is determined by what you believe and what you believe is determined by who you define yourself to be. There is always something in which you believe strongly. And what you truly believe does not have to have anything to do with what you think you believe. When you emanate a certain vibration, the universe can do no different than reflect a copy of that back to you. Everything you experience is a reflection of the vibrations (emotions, beliefs, identity) within you. With what you experience, you can make conclusions on what you really believe to be true. If you do not like the show the TV is broadcasting, you don't beat the TV set or drive to the TV studio and threaten its employees. You switch the channel (change focus).

The way most people practice reality creation contradicts the law of correspondence; it is the path to failure. By trying to *make something happen*, they incorrectly assume that first something out there has to change before they change. They have to become the vibration that corresponds to what they want to experience. Reality must be received within. You can have anything you want as long as you already have it. Every identity (observer) lives in a corresponding parallel reality that is already manifesting on some level. The identity statement, "I want success," does not fully correspond with the reality "success," but is removed, slightly separate. It corresponds a bit more with the reality of success, but having to make a statement about it means it is not fully correspondent to the reality of success. Imagine saying, "I am breathing." You wouldn't really do that too often, because breathing is common, easy, and familiar. When an identity becomes as common as breathing, you are corresponding to a desired reality.

The five levels of Reality Creation are:

Level 1: Behavior/ Action
Level 2: Emotions/Feelings
Level 3: Beliefs/Thoughts
Level 4: Reality Models/Core Beliefs
Level 5: Identity

Identity creates models of reality. Models of reality create beliefs. Beliefs create emotions. Emotions create behavior. Altogether, they create reality.

An analogy:

Action: Building a house
Emotion: The builders of the house
Beliefs: The blueprint of the house
Identity: The architect of the house

Most people believe it's the other way around. They believe, "if I do this and that, then I can feel this and that, then I will believe this and that, and then I can be this and that." In the context of pure, physical, 3-D reality, it does work this way. "If I study law (action), I can be a lawyer (identity)." In the 4-D reality of consciousness-as-cause, one would first take on the identity of the lawyer (identity), automatically attract information on the subject (beliefs), feel like it (emotions), and then act on it and from it (action).

The first level of change is the level of action and behavior. Someone wants to change, release, or experience something so he tries to change his behavior or doings. This is the foundation of conventional therapy or coaching. If you do not address the source of the behavior or action (causes 2, 3, 4, 5), it will take discipline and repetition to make the change. Changing level one has a retroactive effect on the other levels, but changing the levels above one has stronger effect because they are the cause of level one. If a relatively strong emotion is operating on level two, the old behavior will eventually resurface. Some actions taken on this level actually reinforce the undesired reality when performed out of undesired emotion, or in an attempt to get rid of a reality. In this sense, many actions taken are to compensate for undesirable creation on the causal levels. The only actions that would be remotely beneficial (from the magical point of view) would be inspired action and acting-as-if (acting from the viewpoint of a desired self). If an ugly house is being built, it is better to change the builders and craftsmen (emotion), or even the blueprint (belief), than rearranging the blocks of the house itself.

In self-improvement practice, it would be advisable to operate on level two feelings and emotions. Everything we do is driven by what we feel or want to avoid feeling. If you change a feeling (vibratory energy) successfully, a few dozen behaviors and actions will fall away effortlessly, gradually, naturally. This is why basic reality creation coaching mainly operates on this level. An emotion, however, can also be used as an indicator to level three causality, as a servant pointing to a belief or thought-pattern one could release. The primary methodologies applied in transforming emotions are a) to give up labels and resistances and fully feel them until they have played out, b) relax the body, or c) gradually upscale one's state (described elsewhere in this book), or d) discover to which belief the emotion points. If the builders of the house (emotion) continue to do a bad job on the house, it might not help to fire them and employ new builders; you may need to change the blueprint, plan, template, or instructions (belief).

Level 3 focuses on changing thoughts and beliefs. One can release, change, or improve unwanted emotions, but if the belief or thought that creates them is not addressed, the emotions may reoccur. Improving emotions works as long as one uses methods that improve one's emotional state. Quit using the methods or be confronted with a certain situation, and they bubble up again because the causal belief is intact. Repeating the emotional improvement can have retroactive effects on levels three, four, and five, but by handling one belief on level three, dozens of emotions and emotional associations can change for the better. These changes tend to last. Advanced methods of coaching and magic prefer to operate on this level. Belief-changing methodologies range from up-scaling techniques (reviewed later) to reframing, or imagination, methods.

Level 4 is that of the reality model, or Meta model, also called core belief or primary intention. This belief is of a different quality than a level three belief. Level three beliefs are thoughts that one is half-aware of having. Level four beliefs are inner convictions that one is identified with to such an extent that they aren't even viewed as reality-creating beliefs anymore. They are glasses one wears and sees through, but never sees. Level three is a thought, while level four is a template, an imprint around which hundreds of beliefs and thoughts accumulate. A core belief is often hidden by secondary beliefs, adopted when a person was unable to think properly or was driven by survival instincts, such as childhood traumas or shocks. The reality model is like a map for understanding life. It's like a first impression that sticks. In the course of a lifetime, an array of secondary beliefs is collected around the core belief to complement, sustain, confirm, and complete that core belief. If one can detect and change a single core belief, dozens of level-three beliefs, hundreds of emotions, and thousands of behaviors and attitudes can disintegrate. Radical and speedy changes are possible on this level. This is why few people dare touch it, why many dare not question their most fundamental knowledge and suppositions about the world. The changes may be too much. But if you take good care of yourself when operating on this level, you can achieve fantastic success. One of many ways to discover core beliefs is to see what events are manifesting in your life. If something similar is happening in your job, your love life, and your health, it will lead you to a core belief. Having a new blueprint of the desired house will make it easier for the universe to correspond to what you want. Of course, if the architect (identity) is no good, the blueprints will be mediocre.

Level 5 is the level of identity. These are definitions about who you are, who you want to be, who you don't want to be—your roles in life. Some schools of spirituality and magic operate on this level. One spiritual tradition defines the self as something bigger, more powerful, multidimensional, infinite, and godly. Another spiritual tradition tries to dissolve any identity and past timeline connected to it to achieve the enlightenment or god-consciousness behind it (When all is removed, what is left is the truth). A third line of schooling replaces undesired roles with desired roles. This resembles method acting, except that instead of changing for a movie, one changes for life (which, in a sense, is similar to a movie). Change the self and you change all the reality definitions, intentions, beliefs, emotions, and behaviors that go with it. Reality restructures around the new identity and gradually adapts to the new self. At this level, we enter parallel universes. One reason people resist operating on this level is because they lack trust in self and immortality, believing something bad can happen or that protection is needed. Survival instincts fixed into the body seem to interfere with this level of work. This book will present gentler ways of going about changing versions of self.

From the viewpoint of infinite consciousness and in light of the many worlds theory, RC is not about manifestation at all, but about synchronization or alignment with the preferred version of self. We needn't create outer conditions, as these are merely reflections of our identity and its beliefs. Change your identity viewpoint, and the backdrop of reality changes. Sure, you can change circumstances a little, but only within the limits of your viewpoint. In RC, then, there are only three factors: infinity, which creates everything effortlessly and magically (planets, landscapes, bodies), the world-self (a version of yourself), and the relationship between the two.

"I create reality," the motto of the New Age movement, is mostly spoken in the mistaken supposition that there is a separation between "reality" and "I." Where this self-imposed separation is in place, an effort of personal will is necessary so that reality delivers, proves, makes happen. If you allow yourself to think in a more advanced mode, you realize that the "I" that creates reality and reality itself are the same thing. In light of this, your RC practice not only becomes magically efficient, but concepts such as "manifestation" and "waiting for manifestation" become silly, if not outright neurotic. You can imagine whatever you want, right now, and you can be willing to believe in what you imagine, right now, and because you enjoy something as real right now, and not in order to have it happen, infinity will reflect that vibration. Physical manifestation is not your business but infinity's—more efficient than world self. Those who are not aware of their infinite self try to manipulate the outside, as if it were separate from them. Waiting on evidence of improvement equals being a slave because one has forgotten that one is the cause of out there. We can't create anything we view as separate from us. That's why the best things happen when we are not busy trying to get them.

Magic will not fix it for you, because you are that magic. Be the improvement you want to see in the world. There is no path to success or peace—either you are or you or not. The shortcut to creating reality or attracting your heart's desire is *being the version of yourself that is already experiencing that reality*.

Some readers might now say, "Ah, okay. The method is 'acting as if.' I got it." But acting as if something is real is still removed from it simply being a reality. One still presumes something is not completely real. Rather than acting as if, try, "I embody this reality." This goes along with acceptance of what is, of course. Once you enter a new reality and fight old things that come up, the fighting implies that you still believe in the old reality. How you react to the old reality determines how long it will take your new identity to be reflected out there. Fighting what you don't want is the same as agreeing with it. Being without resistance resembles being like water. Water flows with what is; it resists nothing, so nothing resists it, and it naturally and quickly flows to its destination—without trying. The reality synchronization is wholehearted—no holding back, no "let's try it out first and see if it works." Once you know what you want, dive into it, and begin at the end. Don't concern yourself with the why, when, and how; begin at the end, and stay there. That's all there is to successful RC. Infinity takes care of the rest.

5

The PURE Technique

The PURE technique is that around which the entire book revolves. While this book contains plenty of exercises and information, the PURE technique is at the heart of parallel reality surfing; no other exercise it is necessary. PURE stands for *parallel universe reality emulation*; it is the vehicle with which we suggest you shift your personal identity and the corresponding life you call reality. It will allow you to shift into the actual parallel realities. While knowledge and use of the practice would suffice for you to enter and experience any reality you desire, this book was written to ease your protests of these outrageous claims.

The PURE Technique

1. Define a reality you would like to experience

Find something you want to be, do, or have, that you feel is accessible to you. You must be willing to live up to it. If you don't know what you want, define something you no longer want to experience and make its opposite what you want. The desire may be vague or specific.

2. Relax into zero-point (be silent)

Before receiving a new something-ness, we return to nothingness. Call a time-out, sit or lie down, close your eyes, and become silent and relaxed. Ignore any issues or problems of the outside world. Ignore any factual evidence of things unwanted. Gently and gradually, allow wants, needs, have to's, shoulds, coulds, and woulds to fade away. Breathe gently. Gradually allow judgments, labels, expectations, concepts, knowledge, opinions, definitions, and reactions about everything to release. They may still exist, but they are no longer relevant to the silence you experience. How to do this? You don't do it. You stop doing anything except observing and noticing. But observing and noticing is not even something you have to do, keep, or hold because the observer is always present, anyway. Behind the clouds of the mind lies a clear sky of awareness, ever-present, ever silent. So while things may come up in the mind, they are noticed with the same neutral ease you would observe clouds in the sky. This does not have to be created. It happens naturally when you rest into silence and allow yourself to become open, unhurried, and receptive. Once an ocean of silence is experienced (and this may take from a few to many minutes, depending on your willingness to release your resistance to the here and now), simply enjoy it. Zero-point means you are in neutral observer mode, neither desiring nor resisting. Nothing is being created; nothing is being de-created. Thoughts come and go, but they are irrelevant. You are not identified with anything. Do not advance to step two before you feel completely at ease. Wellbeing is not the goal of this practice, but its prerequisite.

3. Allow yourself to look at the new version of yourself

Once silent, allow an image to appear that represents the version of yourself that is already experiencing the desired reality. This is not so much visualization in the sense of creating something with effort or concentration, it is more a relaxed receiving of something already available or nearby. No effort of will is used. You are not merely imagining something or opening to possibility, but perceiving a version of yourself that already exists in a parallel reality. You are becoming aware of someone already there. Look at the version of yourself for who the desired reality is already real.

4. Enter the new viewpoint

Rather than continuing to look at that version of you as a separate observer, as someone desiring it, enter the viewpoint (energy field) of this person who is already experiencing complete fulfillment of the reality and look *as* the person. As the person, immerse yourself in the reality; enjoy it with natural ease, gratitude, and happiness. Experience the image as not only a mental event, but as touch, tactile sense, and emotion. Do not do this to experience the reality later or to experience the reality in the outside world for real, but to experience the joy of it here and now. You may feel a smile come to your face. Rest for a few minutes before releasing and ending the closed-eyes part of the process.

5. Rest in fulfillment

In the hours, days, and weeks after, simply rest in the new viewpoint, in the fulfilled reality. Don't try to make it happen because you have already claimed it as real. Don't affirm, visualize, repeat, or wait for it. Don't hope for it to come in some future. Because you have claimed it as already real, don't even think about it. Don't ask when, how, or where it will show up. Instead, do what offers itself to you throughout the day. This will involve commonplace activities. Daily life continues naturally, without neediness or lack. Once in a while, you may want to re-feel the body sense of the chosen reality and enjoy what you have claimed as true, but often, not even that is necessary. Furthermore, you needn't act as if the desired reality is manifest, for that implies separation. Simply cease behaving in ways that presupposes it is not already so. You may refuse to ascribe relevance or importance to events that seem to contradict your chosen reality. Such events may come up, but they are no longer relevant enough to interact with them. It may be the way things are now, but it is no longer the way you are. The corresponding physical manifestation will appear when you stop needing it, chasing it, and looking for it, but are instead willingly and lovingly identified with it—not for the sake of making it manifest, but to experience its joy in the here, now, and today.

Details of the PURE Technique

The PURE procedure was described as:

1. Be still
2. Receive and identify with the desired reality
3. Rest in the fulfillment (let go)

In some shamanic cultures, this technique is called shape shifting. Shape shifting involves giving up your resistance towards something and merging with it so that you totally become it—on not only a mental level, but on a whole-body and cellular level. The secret to this lies not in becoming something, but realizing you are already everything and have only to be one aspect of that. Some shamans practiced shape shifting to become trees or animals. They were willing to give up their armored selves and fully unite with something. It involves giving up the belief that "it's only imagination," a belief that separates you from the effectiveness of the technique.

While the already given information will suffice to put the technique into practice, it can be elaborated on and looked at in more detail. The mind loves detailed study, and what follows solidifies the mind's belief. We start by breaking down the second step, receive and identify with the desired reality, into three further steps—see, feel, and be.

See

This step could also be called "decide" or "choose," because you are choosing one image from trillions of options. This image is not so much visualized, but received in silence. Yes, in a sense, it is visualization, but it is much more than that. Visualization implies a purely mental event, while we are not only going for a two-dimensional mental image, but a complete body sense—a virtual reality experience, so to speak. Since the average human's attention jumps about randomly, like a rubber ball, it is necessary to decide what you really want. Otherwise, there will be nothing to focus on because you won't know *what* to focus on. The decision is usually made before you begin the PURE process, before you go into silence, but it can also change during silence. What comes up in silence may surprise you. In general, you will have had an intention with which you go into the process, and this intention will affect what images come up, even if they are surprising. In other words, know what you are beginning the PURE process for, but leave the rest up to receptivity, rather than effort. "See" means that you are looking at something that represents the desire. You are not yet looking as it, but *at* it. You are using imagination to see your desire as three-dimensionally and vividly as you could see your current surroundings. The problem has been that we, as a society, have been conditioned to be better observers of what is than dreamers of what could be. We observe our surroundings and take them to be indicators or evidence of what our life is all about. We are conditioned to look at what has been created and to categorize it as good or bad, rather than seeing what could be created. This places an emphasis on outside creations, rather than creations made by your inner authority. If your current surroundings and everyday reality seem more real, significant, and meaningful than your inner vision, this is the reason you are not experiencing anything new. Pay attention to what you give your eyes—your outer and inner eyes—to see, because what you give the most attention to becomes bigger. By seeing it, you choose and give your desire a form—you give it space and time. Relax and give your vision time to unfold. You are a visual, visionary being, so see it in all its richness, detail, color, and situation. If you want something to be real, you must view it as real. By saying, "Well, this is only imagination," you are invalidating something you claim to want or like. Consciousness does not differentiate between "real" and "imagined," but if you differentiate, calling something less solid and significant, consciousness will bow to it. This is a very important, but often overlooked part of the reality creation process.

Feel

This element could also be the third element of "Be," because identifying with something is accompanied by the body sense of it. Here, we differentiate it from "Be" to point out how a feeling magnetizes a thought. Without feeling or energy, a thought remains unmanifested. Another word to describe this step might be trust. When you feel something in your body, you have no problem trusting in the validity of it. Emotion activates a thought. Emotion creates vibration, which interacts with reality. Feel what you would feel if you were already in that reality. This would include feelings of gratitude, happiness, excitement, love, peace, or ease, but feel does not only refer to emotions, but also your tactile or body sense. Touch the objects and people in your vision; smell or taste them. See identifies you with something. Feel deepens the identification. These are not feelings you have to create or produce, but let in, allow to come up. *This ability is completely native and natural.* Do not view pictures emptied of emotion. If you view something of substance and importance, you feel something while you experience it, don't you? To experience something out there, you first must experience it in here—not for the sake of getting it someday, but for enjoying it now.

Be

You no longer look *at* it, but *as* it. Your viewpoint shifts from observer of the reality to observing *from* the reality. Act as you would act in that reality. See what you do as this person. Observe from within the image. The image is no longer in front of you; you are it. Feel what it is like to be the person. In the beginning stages of PURE practice, notice the shift and difference between the viewpoints of looking-at and looking-as. You might see the same things, but there is a discernable difference in the two viewpoints.

Does "Be" Imply Taking Action?

Most people view action as a cause of reality, but it is not. Only the belief in action makes action effective. Disbelieve a reality, and it will not manifest, no matter how much effort you invest.

Actually, physical action is not a required step of the PURE technique; it only becomes necessary when people cannot release their conviction that action is the cause of reality. Because some people give action and work such authority, the PURE technique does not totally dismiss action, but if you do take action, do it from an aligned point of view. You can do whatever you want as long as you understand that action is the effect of your vibratory being, not its cause. Action is what midwifes the causal energy into physical form, but this is not something you need to worry about because what to act upon will present itself in an obvious manner. If, for example, you have aligned with the new reality of having many new clients and suddenly, many prospective clients contact you by email, the obvious action would be to write back. If you have aligned with the new reality of ideal body weight, and a few days later, you feel the sudden urge to drink a lot of water, the obvious action would be to follow that lead. Because action is not cause, you needn't worry about taking right or wrong actions. In general, after applying PURE, you simply do what's before you to do, meaning the regular daily activities, such as washing the dishes or going to work. As long as you are emotionally aligned, it doesn't matter what you do, unless you do something in complete contradiction or misalignment with your new self—for example, ignoring those emails for weeks or going jogging to lose weight, although you really dislike jogging (if you like it, is an aligned action). Because of your inner position, other things will occur which you may act upon, but you will know to act when they occur. If you act consciously (which is not a must), act from the idea that your desire is on its way or already fulfilled. If, for example, you have entered the reality of I have many new clients, you would probably not take up a credit because of worry about not getting clients. That would be counter-intentional. But you might purchase a new painting to liven up your office; after all, you have all these clients visiting. In RC, if you act at all, your actions are more being, than acting, rather than acting, in order to be. Your actions come as close to reality as possible; it only needs to fall in your lap when it actually manifests. If manifestation is too far from your regular activities, it will be a shock when it does manifest. If you act, act in a manner that invites more of what you manifest. Your acting becomes more joyful, more that of a stage actor or movie actor emulating a reality already true, rather than struggling to achieve a reality not yet true. This is called physicalizing a reality. Rather than allowing physical reality to be a limitation, use it to your benefit. This includes going places you would be going if that reality were already true, or purchasing, handling, renting, or borrowing objects you would be handling. This type of reality-representative-action is by far the most aligned. It represents what I call physiological magic: Getting used to a vibration frequency by copying the habits and actions of the person already living a certain reality. If you want to be the boss of your company, rather than an employee, you complement your vibratory habit by sitting in a boss' chair, looking at the skyline from the boss' office, spending time near the boss—in short, learning what that reality feels like. There is no higher form of magic than learning what a reality feels like. Once you know what something feels like, it is yours.

After identifying with a reality, meaning you go into silence, receive the image, see it, feel it, become it, rest in it, and let go of it, your inner receiver is firmly set on the channel you want to receive.

After that, do not resist the changes that come up. It all belongs; it's all part of the unfolding of your newly claimed reality, no matter what it looks like. The stronger your resistance towards the changes that come up, the longer it takes to take form in the physical. Why this time-buffer? So that not every single thought and notion you have manifests immediately, plunging your life into chaos.

The Basic De-Creation Procedure

If the PURE technique brings about a given parallel universe, the reversal of it must release or de-create reality, right? Yes, true. But if you wish to release a certain reality/identity, the first recommendation would not be to use the following technique, would not be to de-create it, but to choose what you want instead and enter another reality. Why? Because identifying anew automatically takes care of unwanted realities. The following procedure is only for people who believe they need more than that or who prefer to delve into the undesired before they look at the desired. Some people really want to grasp what is unwanted to be certain of what is wanted. An example: What shape shifters practice is shape shifting into the very thing they are afraid of or uncomfortable with. If the shape shifter is afraid of spiders, he becomes a spider until the fear subsides. If he is afraid of the executive of a corporation, he identifies with or shape shifts into the executive, so deeply immersed in being that person that all fear subsides.

Be

The last step of the PURE technique is the first step of the decreation technique. It does not begin with the non-conceptional, deidentified state of silence, but with identification. Here you consciously identify with what you are identified already. As a paving step to this, you may ask yourself, "Which version of me is experiencing _____?" (Undesired reality) The resistance to this identity further upholds it, which is why "Be" involves giving up resistance and deliberately immersing yourself. You cannot consciously identify with a reality (and thus regain creative control) if you resist it. So create it on purpose. Melt in with it. Synchronize your vibrations with it 1-to-1. You cannot let go of something you do not have. Breathe as it. Confront it. Be It.

Feel

This comes up automatically. If these feelings seem unpleasant to you, you are still exerting resistance toward what you created. Resistance means you have not yet allowed yourself to acknowledge you have created it for a good reason; you have not taken full responsibility for it. An interesting question might be, "What could be a good reason for upholding this creation?" Feel it, breathe it, let it be, and live it until you feel comfortable with it. Experience it with willingness and interest. Take it into you.

See

The next thing you do is take a step back from full immersion and see it from outside, as an observer. Rather than having taking a step backwards be a form of resistance, while you are immersed, label the event as exactly what it is; take on the outside observer position. That means, before applying See, while still immersed in it, you simply state, All right, this is_______, and I created it. Then simply observe it, not as the creation, but as the observer. You will dissociate from it by observing without resistance, judgment, or reaction.

Silence

This is where you softly shift from non-judgmental and non-reactive observation to putting your attention on an open loop—no longer giving special attention to the creation. Gently refocus your attention to silence and peace. Once you have fallen back on the present eternal space, you may choose to either end the process or allow a new reality to come up. In any case, after de-creating something, it is recommended you create something new. By de-creating, you have caused a vacuum in consciousness that wants to be filled by something. It is easy to create something new in a vacuum. The only question is whether you create something new after de-creating, or save it for a later date.

After de-creating, you also have the option of repeating the process of de-creation. If you still have the impression there is relevance or significance attached to the old identity, you might want to repeat.

The Alternating Technique

Another brilliant variation of de-creating involves going into a relaxed mode and alternating between the old self and the new self several times. This means you'd look at the old self, then *as* the old self. Then you'd look at the new self, then *as* the new self. Then you'd switch back to the old self. Then back to the new self. You'd switch back and forth several times until one or more of the following two things occur: Relative neutrality (meaning you no longer resist going back to the old self), a deepened sense of choice between both selves, and the impression that you can easily go into the new self. The less you resist the old self, the easier it will be to slip into the new self.

The Alternating Technique: Written Version

Assume it is one year later, and you are writing to someone about what happened in the last year. You are a future self. Write down three versions of the events:

a) A negative version
b) A middle version
c) A positive version

By consciously creating a negative version, you gain conscious control over unwitting, counter-intentional beliefs. By switching to the middle version, you gain insight into what you deem normal or realistic. By switching to the positive, you gain the realization of what you truly want to identify with, and you do so automatically, simply by being aware of it in comparison to the other two options. This is one of the most powerful techniques for reality change you will ever learn.

Further Issues and Details Regarding the PURE Technique

There are no problems with PURE; all you do is rest in the new viewpoint and feeling, period. For beginners, there may be aspects that seem like problems; I address them in this section, as well as how and why the PURE technique works.

The Feedback Loop

What you currently experience as reality could be viewed as a feedback loop of what you formerly believed. The more unaware you are, the more you label this feedback loop as the factual reality. One might consciously intend the reality, "I am rich." This is created 100% on the timeline. If one's surroundings and circumstances seem to provide counter-evidence to his decision, this is merely a feedback loop to old decisions. It is in how one reacts that determines if one is resting in one's new viewpoint, or letting oneself be talked back into the old one. A bank account statement shows the account is overdrawn and he says, "Well, maybe I am not that rich, after all. Here's the proof!" He is leaving his viewpoint and letting an outside circumstance dictate his being (rather than his being dictating outside circumstances). He has just fallen back into slave mentality. It is important to remain poised in the new viewpoint, no matter what outside evidence is showing you. The poor-spirited will use any opportunity to fall back into the old identity. The reality surfer, wizard, or creator will use counter evidence to remind him of his new reality, as confirmation of his new reality. "Ah, here comes evidence corresponding to my old identity. This is a wonderful opportunity to confirm my new identity. Because this is happening, I can adjust my reaction to correspond to my new identity. How wonderful!" He uses the counter-evidence to deepen his new identity. Things are this way for the moment, but it is no longer the way *you* are. Another way to handle realities that seem to contradict your chosen reality is to witness them without reaction. This means not immersing yourself in it, not trying to be rid of it or negotiating with it. These things give the seeming counter-reality relevance. Instead, notice the apparent contradiction or counter-reality as you would notice clouds in the sky. They are there, but they have nothing to do with you. You rest in a new reality and refuse to assign importance to contradicting realities. The inner authority of imagination soon overrides the outer authority of facts, and thus turns imagination into facts.

Projection into the Future

Once you have identified with a reality, you have entered a parallel universe; it is already manifested. You can feel it here and now. The feeling will have to suffice as evidence for now. People's conditioned tendency to project their desired reality into the future only postpones the result. Merely noticing that the factual, physical manifestation hasn't yet taken place does not constitute a problem or counter-belief. What does constitute a counter-belief is thinking that because manifestation is not here yet, you cannot be fulfilled and happy. There's a long way and a short way to reality creation. The long way means writing down the steps to your goal. Then doing those steps. Then achieving your goal. But the goal does not manifest because of the steps you took, but because of your belief that these steps will lead to the goal. This is the path of the mortal. Projection into the future does occasionally work, but sometimes it doesn't and it takes much more energy and effort. In the ways of a reality creation wizard, you are giving jurisdiction to organize, plan, and manifest your desired outcome to infinity, to the all-that-is universe. You bring your goal into the now and get excited about it. Life takes care of the rest. You do not ask how, when, or where because if you rest in the viewpoint of already received, these questions become irrelevant and counter-creational. Your practice is one of nature and ease, without getting all worked up about timing, form, and manifestation. You are not waiting on proof, you are not waiting on fulfillment, and you are not looking for applause. It has already happened. Reality creation is not an expectation of the future, but a memory of the past.

Expectation

Your expectations on the how, where, and when of physical manifestation actually limits infinity's ability to reflect your claimed reality. When releasing an intention to infinity, you know it or something similar will come up. Why something similar? Because the exact mental image is not reflected by infinity, the vibratory signal is; and because infinity uses the path of least resistance, it can only create within the context you are already living, within what you already believe to be true. This does not mean you have to settle for less than your chosen reality; on the contrary, often something even better than intended shows up. Your attention is not on the how, when, and where of a manifestation because as far as you are concerned, the desired reality is already manifested. *You can't be identified with a reality and be waiting on it or expecting it.* It is important that you grasp the spirit of this. Due to the law of correspondence, factual, physical, real-life manifestation will occur, and you are interested in it occurring, but it will not occur because you try to make it happen, but because you are in inner alignment with it. Physical manifestation, and ways and means and timing are left up to infinity, which is vastly more effective. This knowledge releases you from micro-management and teaches you not to disturb infinity by limiting it to how you think manifestation is supposed to occur or where and when it's supposed to happen. Most of the time, it's a surprise, and it's this element that's so much fun. Where would the fun of magic be if you were in control? Believing you have to manage the whole process is a delusion of grandeur, megalomania. This is not to imply that you are not responsible for the creation. You are. But it needs to be clear what parts of the co-creation (between world-self and infinity) you are responsible for. You are responsible for what you radiate.

Deeper Immersion

In RC practice, there comes a point where you rest so deeply, wholeheartedly, and convincingly in your new belief that you don't even think about it anymore. The identity has become your nature—normal and comfortable. Stay true and loyal to this self and reality will start corresponding with it, building around it. While in the beginning stages of immersion, you might repeat the process on a reality and practice remembering the feeling, at an even deeper level, you don't have to care about it anymore. Instead, you enjoy the feeling of fulfillment as the real thing (it shouldn't even be necessary to make the distinction "just as real as the real thing" anymore). Beginners in RC might find it hard to accept that they can achieve everything by doing hardly anything, but they will eventually realize that letting energy in is more effective than getting in the way of the energy flow. On this deeper level of immersion, you might even want to forget the whole thing by shifting your attention to other matters. This is where living in the here and now and going about daily life become important. Rather than impatiently waiting on manifestation, you rest in gratitude. Reality is no longer dictated by the ever-changing winds of circumstance, but by self. Reality is no longer the source—you are the source. You feel the happiness of being alive. This sweet inner happiness surpasses all outer manifestation and material objects. Once this sweet inner love is found, issues of manifestation or non-manifestation become even more irrelevant—through which they paradoxically become even more easily accessible. What you stop running after, stop needing, stop being a slave of, starts running after you. Being the person for whom the reality is already real is the most important part. If there is any hint of looking for it, chasing it, forcing it, waiting for it, demanding proof of it, you are not resting in the assumption of it being fulfilled, but still a slave. The world has nothing to give you; it only shows what you are giving yourself.

Synonyms

In RC teaching, the following words are synonymous and refer to the same thing:

Reality
Experience
Identity
Viewpoint
Fulfillment

Whenever we say, "reality," we could also be saying, "identity," because both are the same thing. There is no reality without a corresponding, observing identity, and there is no observing identity without a corresponding reality. Experience is another word for reality, and fulfillment is a word for the experience of the preferred reality. Viewpoint is another word for identity because identification simply involves taking on the being or viewpoint of a thing.

Miracles, within matters of hours or days, occur when a desired reality is focused without resistance. Infinity is so abundant that you merely have to let in the constant flow of energy. It is hard work not to be part of life's richness. The moment you appreciate something, as in, "I like that," the eternal energy starts organizing more on your behalf. "Beginner's luck" is often due to the way someone lightheartedly desires something—without all the baggage of conclusions, expectations, and need. Repetition of intent or exercise would not be necessary if one would, only once, purely, and clearly, intend without resistance. Your desires are never denied. It is only that they shift too often. A simple example: You find out you like and want a certain car. You feel the appreciation towards it in your inner being; you feel your connection towards it. The law of correspondence starts moving mountains. Then you say, "Well, I don't know if I can afford it," and the flow of energy is modified. Then you say, "Well, maybe I can afford it." Then, "Actually, I don't know if I want this color or that model; maybe I want another one." "Maybe I should settle on something more affordable." "Maybe I should aim higher." By now, you have released at least five contradictory intentions, thus interrupting the work of the infinite field five times. Being clear on what you want is the first step to RC. Blessed are those who find something they would give into wholeheartedly. Infinity is like a copy-machine, in that it reflects your vibratory intentions 1-to-1, granting you free will. What you put out is what you get back. Since getting back happens on a time-line, by the time you get it, you might have forgotten you asked for it. This is what makes life a comedy. RC becomes more obvious, quickened by releasing limiting beliefs, expectations, and resistance. The good thing is that you know when you are blocking, when you are not letting it flow through you. The indicator is your emotional state. Sometimes you are in an unreceptive state. Sometimes, merely improving your emotional state, without intending or desiring anything new, allows all kinds of things you want to manifest. They are already created, waiting to flow into an open receiver. Relax—completely. If you knew what you were capable of, that's what you would do: Relax—completely. And laugh more often.

Exclude and Include

Infinity is inclusive; you cannot exclude anything from infinity. When you try to exclude something, you actually include it. When you try to deactivate it, you activate it. When you try to get rid of it, you include it. If you put 51% of your attention on what is wanted rather than what is unwanted, you would live a life of magic. The wisdom of this book could sink deeper than the ocean and fly higher than the sky. If not, it's just a bunch of words on paper, nothing more.

By excluding things you don't want, such as sickness, violence, shame, guilt, poverty, and so on, you don't feel yourself, because these things do not represent who you are. Noticing these things does not mean excluding/including them in your energy field; actively denying, resisting, fighting, or pushing against them is inclusion. Some people resist things until the things they most hated and were most afraid of start appearing in their reality. Usually, at this point, they have a change of mind and say, "No way," and shift their attention to the preferred. They wouldn't have to wait that long. They wouldn't have to continue until the unwanted manifestation started rearing its ugly head. They could have shifted attention long before that, but some seem to need to go to extremes, to find out what they don't want, before knowing what they do want. At this point, it is more difficult to shift energy because they are (as far as vibration frequency is concerned) still far from their desire. Still, the contrast can be utilized to find out what is wanted. The unwanted can be used to find greater alignment with what is preferred. Rather than letting a desire torment you by upholding it without aligning with it, merge with it, focus on it thoroughly. If you do not take the step from desiring to align with the desire, your self-trust decreases and your beliefs about what is possible decrease.

RC is not merely desiring, but bringing your identity into alignment with that desire. When this happens, nothing can resist your vibration. It doesn't take long to learn this art. Usually, a couple of weeks will make you familiar with the basics and yield results, but it requires a shift of thinking. You have not been taught to flow energy, you have been taught to look at how others flow energy—at what has already been created. You have been conditioned to look at results, rather than cause, and to categorize these results into good and bad. Teach yourself to notice cause (self) rather than result (circumstance).

Notice what you are trying to exclude. That is what you are actually including. Once you notice, you can choose what you want to include. You live in a world of duality, polarity, contrast; it helps you practice free choice. Include what you want rather than exclude what you don't want. You will be astonished at how quickly things move.

The only thing between you and happiness is resistance (exclusion). You cannot control what others include or give you, but you can control what you include and give others; that's the only thing that will determine your vibration. You can attract anything you want if you know how to align your vibration.

Law of correspondence is not about getting, deserving, or working for it, but about finding emotional and energetic alignment by looking at it, remembering it, thinking about it, writing about it, or the short cut—identifying with it. Once you are aligned and united, it belongs to you. It may not manifest right away but it is already irrevocably planted; all you have to do is lie back and rest. You don't have to check on the seed everyday or try to build the plant yourself. If you get out of alignment before it manifests physically (which is highly unlikely, because a planted seed remains planted unless tampered with), all you have to do is get back into alignment using the PURE technique, and it starts rolling towards you again from where it left off when you first abandoned alignment. The time-buffer allows you to remove bugs and viruses (unaligned beliefs) from the creation before they physically show up. You might be manifesting money and notice how you believe having money means losing friends. Thank God, it didn't manifest too quickly. You notice the misalignment, make the correction, and re-start the process without losing friends. The only reason you avoid immediate manifestation is the unwitting and half-conscious disadvantages you attach to manifestation. This space-time dimension is a perfect stage on which to practice RC. If everything manifested immediately, your life would be chaos. Negativity and contrast are very important for this process because they show you when you are putting attention on something that isn't in alignment with the chosen realities. Without them, you wouldn't know the path.

Sometimes you agree with (include) extremely low energy vibrations and ideas because everyone else agrees with them. Since it's the consensus, you agree with it, without noticing how very far it is from your true self. However, nothing forces you to agree with a reality you don't like. In other words, just because everyone else is watching the eight o'clock news to see the horrible events taking place doesn't mean you have to. You could be enjoying the woods, a good movie, or caring for a loved one. The people sitting in front of the TV screen watching atrocities are not contributing to the situation by giving attention to it. You contribute by being your true self—by shining and radiating purity, love, and confidence. One person radiating positive energy neutralizes millions of people radiating hate, antagonism, and fear. This is not just a sweet-sounding New Age philosophy, but observable phenomenon. Negative and positive are not actually polarities balancing each other (as so many teach) but descriptions of vibratory density. In reality, there is no such thing as negative; all is one.

Feel your way through life rather than thinking through it. The energy I refer to is the feeling you feel. Yes, think, too—that's fine—but let feeling be the guiding light. Resistance cripples you, slows you down, and makes you sick. Every time you are in resistance, you are destroying energy, body, and being. Take a deep breath, relax, and you are out of resistance. It is not even desire that is your main task. You have desired enough to fill thousands of years of existence. Desire is not what you lack. The issue is releasing resistance to allow things you desire to flow. Seriousness, dullness, strictness, rigidity are all indicative of resistance. Fun, lightness, success, and appreciation are indicative of non-resistance.

Even if you do know what you want, you don't bring yourself up to speed with that desire. You may state a desire, but the words sound hollow and empty; you feel nothing, and thus attract nothing. You constantly pulse an electronic signal into infinity, but what you say you are pulsing is often not what you are really pulsing. Get honest; get real. Look at your life, and you know exactly what you are pulsing. RC is about being aware of vibratory alignment, identification, and closing the gap between desire and belief. See if what comes to you is not an exact vibratory match of what you have been giving off. It is, isn't it?

Note that it is no more difficult to have something big manifest than something small. Infinity does not make this discernment, you do. Because you do, the small (e.g. parking spaces) may seem easier to manifest than the big (e.g. the Porsche).

While you are trying to solve a problem, you are resisting the solution. Look at the problem, and you start vibrating the same way, and the solution can't flow in. You might say, "Well, shouldn't I face reality?" to which RC answers, "No. Do not face a reality unless it's beautiful and to your liking."

Note that 99% of your reality creation is done before you see a hint of physical evidence of it. Why? Because the world self only represents 1% of the whole self. The world self (what you mistakenly call "me") has amnesia about the rest of it during its incarnation on the planet. Ninety-nine percent of your life is not about physical manifestation but about the path to manifestation. Actual fulfillment or manifestation is a beautiful moment, but it passes quickly. Soon, new desires will come up. The deepest experiences are found on the way to manifestation. If you don't find joy on the path, you won't find it at the goal. Being unfulfilled is the soul's tool for growth in the physical reality. This is why souls forget much of their power when they incarnate. Even if you, as the world self, protest this truth, your whole self (soul) loves this game. Bless being unfulfilled, for it is 99% of your path, your most common friend. Relax and appreciate the here and now. The perfection you seek would equal the end of the path. The journey never ends, change is the only constant, every ending is a new beginning, every death a new birth, every unfulfilled reality sparks a new desire, and every new desire, a new feeling of being unfulfilled. For RC to work you have to change your attitude towards being unfulfilled and start enjoying the path to manifestation of your desires, not only the manifestation itself, which only lasts a few minutes.

You don't perceive the world through your senses; you create with your senses. Your senses (seeing, hearing, touching, tasting, smelling) filter out 99.9999999% of all that could be perceived and only allow you to see a tiny portion that agrees with the dictatorship of our beliefs. Like a TV contains all programs, you contain all realities and merely have to switch the channel to receive something new. This is what PURE does. Once you shift identity, everything changes. Your surroundings may look the same, so you might say, "What do you mean everything changes? I just shifted my viewpoint and opened my eyes, and here I am, still at the same place." To which I respond, "It may look like the same place, but it is not." It's a parallel world. You have entered a new timeline, a new dimension. Your surroundings will start corresponding to that, even if it looks the same at first. Your identity will automatically attract other scenarios, backgrounds, and places. Since the aim is not manifestation but vibratory alignment or synchronization, the outside surroundings are irrelevant, anyway, and your question reveals that you are not properly aligned.

Why do many seem to stick to negative or unwanted things rather than shifting attention? Because they don't accept the negative, they don't integrate it, don't appreciate it, don't own it, and don't use it for their benefit. By denying what is, it is difficult to shift attention to what is wanted. You can't say, "This is unacceptable!" and at the same time be connected to what is good. When you integrate or accept what is, you breathe it in, allow it into your heart, accept it as part of the whole—even as part of the path to your goal. Go a step further by using the negative for the benefit of that goal, and then move on. It is easy to direct attention to what fascinates you and allow it to become bigger and bigger, more real and more solid. In order to create/attract any reality, you have to fall in love with it. The more familiar with it you become, the more you vibrate in sync with it, the more you trust it, the more real it becomes. If you want to experience something, look at it for weeks. Look at it in your physical environment or your mind's eye or in a picture or on TV—there's no difference between the three. Select what you give your eyes to look at wisely, and then familiarize yourself with it until there is no more doubt or fear. Go where it is taking place or lose yourself in the daydream of it. Drink it, swim it, melt with it, merge with it, marry it, act it, purchase accessories that go with it, do what ever it takes to make it an already-real thing. Give up expectations about it, for that type of future-projection separates you from it. To fully be identified with something is different from expecting it or expecting something from it. What you want does not come to you but from you. There is actually no universe sending you something. Only you that is something and you that is not something.

Reaction and Creation

World self believes the world to be the cause and itself to be the effect and thus always lives in a reactive mode. Sometimes it believes, sometimes it doesn't, sometimes it feels good, sometimes it doesn't, and all are dictated by circumstances, facts, and evidence.

Notice the similarities between the words "reaction" and "creation." In a sense, they are opposites. You are either reacting to the world or creating the world, but what you are really reacting to is what you created. Let's say some woman harbors anger. By the law of correspondence, she will attract something about which she can be angry. Someone might call off an appointment, or she might burn a stain into a shirt while ironing it. She gets angry about that thinking that the call-off or the stain made her angry. Actually, she was already angry and now acts as if it's the circumstances that made her angry. Although it may seem as if you are reacting to events, events come up because you have an inner correspondence to it. When you understand this, your reactions become a valuable tool for expansion of awareness, for further identifying with what you prefer. Your reaction to things reveals what you are creating. And it is in that moment that you can change what you are creating. The deepest changes can be made while an undesired event is happening. Unwanted events are a perfect opportunity for a reality shift across the board. One can look forward to such events. The question always is, "How do I want to react to this, next time it happens?" You might ask yourself, "Which version of me is reacting like this? Who sees it this way?" The more important question is how you actually want to react. What must someone believe who reacts with fear every time he looks at his balance at an ATM machine? Such a reaction reveals the creation of need. It is, therefore, at the ATM machine that a person can shift creation to something better. How do I want to react the next time I am standing at the ATM machine and see that my account is in the minus? How would someone who believes in his financial abundance react? The moment you shift your reaction towards the unwanted event to one more at ease, even joyful, reality changes. It's no art to react joyfully to a full bank account. It is an act of wizardry to react joyfully to an empty bank account. By reacting in such a way, the same problem will never happen to you again. If you react as someone would react who believes in financial abundance, financial abundance will follow.

It might be that you intend to change reaction next time, then the next time happens, and you react the same old way because it caught you off balance. You notice how every time your spouse says X you get emotional and angry. You ask yourself, "How do I want to react, instead?" and you enter a new viewpoint in your imagination, a new way of reacting. A few weeks later, she says something similar. Meanwhile, you have forgotten your intention to react differently, and you're in a general antsy mood. She caught you off-guard, and you react in the same way again. This time, at least, you notice it more clearly. You restate your intention to react in a new way the next time, and this time, you really look forward to her saying X because it allows you the opportunity to demonstrate a new you. When X finally comes around again, you notice it, and you remember your new reaction. You react in a pleasant, understanding, or even humorous way. Your spouse may be puzzled at the unexpected response. Since there's nobody fighting against it anymore, you will never hear X from her the same way again. People repeat stuff until it's acknowledged. You have just shifted your reality in a major way. As long as you react to events the same way, they will keep happening, in many variations. This is one of the greatest secrets of life, and it will take care of most of your problems.

Let's take another example: a woman harbors the belief that men treat her badly or that men are unappreciative. There will be a good reason she holds on to this belief—some secret pay-off (as is the case with all beliefs we think are negative), but as long as she does not accept her facts as just another belief, she will filter out any reality that doesn't match her belief and eagerly zoom in on anything that confirms it. A guy doesn't call her back when she expected because he's not feeling good or is extremely busy, but she will think, "Well, yeah, that's how men are!" A man, on the other hand, who tells her how much he appreciates her, she wouldn't take seriously because he does not correspond to the requirements of her belief.

Some people will dismiss this book as nonsense, some will view it as entertainment, and others will view it as therapy, still others, the truth. Although the book is none of the aforementioned, people will adapt it to what they believe. Anything that supports our fixed beliefs we agree with, defend, search out, need. Anything that contradicts our beliefs we ignore, deny, trivialize, misinterpret, or don't even perceive. Beliefs do not only filter our perception, as taught in many psychological schools, but also filter out complete realities. You might recall the tales related by Columbus and others—how indigenous tribes did not perceive certain objects of the Europeans until they were described and explained to them. One tribe did not perceive a captain's ship, only the accompanying small boats. Why? They knew boats, but a big ship did not fit their belief system. A tribe member did not see anything but dots when shown a photograph, until someone explained that the photo depicted humans. Tales of this phenomenon abound.

Any event or circumstance is a door to different versions of that event, depending on the observer. Most people will perceive what the masses have agreed upon, but even among the individuals, the event will be interpreted and experienced many different ways. This means you can experience many different versions of an event, if you want. All it requires is a corresponding observer, a corresponding viewpoint. You have a meeting with someone tonight in a restaurant. You probably have certain expectations about this event running as thought-flashes through your mind. This single event can take place in an infinite number of variations, and it actually is taking place in that many number of variations. Which of these variations you experience is up to you. Grasp the enormity of it. The evening may end up in a fight, in a deal being struck, in an embarrassing "we have nothing to say to each other"; in a one-night stand, in falling in love, in learning something new or in none of the above. What baffles me is how conservative and safe most people keep their events, afterwards labeling them common, normal, or boring, without realizing that they themselves provided the mood, the setting, and its outcome. Understand that the parallel universe offers unlimited versions of your day. An event is only unmovable when you yourself are unmovable. You enter an event with a pre-conceived belief, which acts as an intention that creates the event. The event will not change as long as you keep reacting to it in the same way, often unknowingly intending the same things. We keep a fixed belief on how things are, without noticing the pay-off for that belief, and then we keep the event created by that belief in its place by reacting to it and interacting with it as if it were real. We do this on a daily basis. You won't find a single human being who does not do this, unwittingly, to a larger or lesser degree. Even the most enlightened wizards are not entirely free of presupposing beliefs and their accompanying creations. Neither is the author of this book. I write a book in the belief that many people do not know enough about reality creation. What is the secret pay-off for this belief? It allows me to appear to know more, make money off the book, and be part of a knowledgeable elite. From a higher viewpoint, it's all hogwash. All I have to do is change my belief and view other people as fully knowledgeable and enlightened, multidimensional beings, and accordingly, I would start meeting all kinds of people just like me, especially people who don't need to read my book. But with that belief, I couldn't enjoy writing this book and couldn't enjoy taking on the version-of-self called "teacher." See how far-reaching secret pay-offs are? When you change who you are, everything changes. No matter how convincing the facts may seem, you can change anything, anytime. Nothing is fixed and finished; everything is always in a process of unfolding and flowing. Even the direst circumstances can be labeled as "unfolding to accommodate my desires," and those events will transform into exactly that. A good example of this happened to me about ten years ago. I had been self-employed for a few years and evading paying my taxes. I was terrified of being found out. The day came I wished to reveal myself to the tax authorities. But first, I had to change my viewpoint and beliefs about that revelation; otherwise, it would end in the disasters I so vividly imagined. I created a belief about coming clean, meaning my finances would skyrocket due to my newfound integrity and honesty. I assumed a stance of eagerness to reveal myself because it would make me rich. And that's exactly what happened. I did have to pay a huge amount of back taxes, but at the same time, my income exploded to tenfold what I had to pay. I had used something negative for something positive.

After applying PURE, you are not meant to shift your attention to waiting on a physical manifestation. Nevertheless, how quickly a thing manifests is sometimes dependent on how you react to things that seemingly contradict your chosen creation. If you were truly resting in fulfillment of the desired version-of-self, you would react to the old stuff differently. This means you may use adverse events to deepen your chosen reality. The adverse events only repeat because you react to them from the same point of view. Some newly entered identities or creations even spark adverse reactions to show which beliefs you are still holding that are in contradiction to what you have chosen. So if you enter a new creation by means of the PURE technique and suddenly, only hours or days later, all hell breaks loose, you know you have chosen a reality you are not willing to believe in entirely. The adverse events may either be misused as an excuse to fall back into the old reality or used as an opportunity to define even more deeply, what you now believe. In some instances, the next step after assuming a new creation is not receiving manifestation, but reacting to the unwanted in a new way. You can demonstrate that you no longer fall for the evidence of the old reality, are no longer easily talked out of it, and are no longer willing to eagerly give in to something you don't want. Being a new person in the face of adversity or counter-reality drives home your heart's desire with surprising speed. Without the adverse reality, you wouldn't be able to prove who you now are. Echoes of the old reality can be seen as a test you place on yourself to see if you are ready for what you say you want. Since you are a new person, a new observer, a new being—with a new body sense—there is no reason to let the adverse event convince or prove you are not a new person after all. This gives the circumstantial world more authority than your inner-self. Since you absolutely feel that goodies are flowing your way, you don't fear, fight, or denounce temporary echoes of the old. True belief remains true belief, no matter what. Period.

The Movie Star Process

When you apply the PURE technique, when you shift your attention to desire, you do it for no other reason than that it's fun. You don't to it to get something from the world that you lack. This is what makes the PURE technique work like magic.

The following process is a playful addition to PURE. As with all other exercises, it is not necessary to do more training to be a parallel universe surfer. PURE is sufficient for that. These tools are games or toys with which to experiment. They may deepen your understanding of PURE, but they are not obligatory.

This process invites you to play with the idea of identity and reality. It allows you to view your old and new reality as different movies with corresponding scripts and character roles. Remember that changing identity is the same thing as changing reality; the purpose of RC is not manifestation, but vibratory alignment. You cannot have what you want; you can have what you are. In creating "I want," infinity will reflect a feeling of wanting, not more. You have to be the change you want to see in the world. In this game, you become more intimately and specifically aware of the differences between one version of yourself and a parallel (desired reality) version of yourself.

One word of caution: When shifting reality, do not do this to test the limits of a reality, but to align with what feels authentic and best to you. You are not going to create "I am the president of the United States" just for the heck of it, but align with something you truly feel is within your vibratory reach, something you truly feel you deserve and would be willing to live up to, something your soul might have wanted to experience prior to incarnation. An indicator of something right for you is a soft feeling of joy, love, or excitement. Operating with creations higher than what you are willing to be can have unpleasant consequences. What would it be like to try to jump on a train going too fast? You'd be knocked off or injured. This is not to say that you cannot manifest anything you really desire. If you feel a true desire, then you can manifest it. But some things you will have to work towards gradually—by either becoming faster or making the train slower. The mistake many RC practitioners make is believing they can manifest a desire without changing themselves or losing an old reality. A reality too high for you is therefore not really too high, but something you are not willing to live up to. As an inexperienced youngster, I applied reality creation technique to manifest "I am sexually irresistible to women." I failed to address the underlying motivator of this desire, which was a feeling of insecurity and inferiority and went ahead with the creation. Furthermore, I failed to specify the type of women in which I was interested. The results were a nightmare. It worked perfectly well—unfortunately. Not only did I attract undesirable women I had a hard time getting rid of, but my feeling of insecurity stayed with me and even increased (as it was the emotional motivator of the desire). I could have sensed this was not an authentic desire because I didn't feel much joy while identifying with it. But I chose to ignore the obvious. I solved the issue by defining what I really wanted: A feeling of ease, self-confidence, and light heartedness, not only towards women, but towards men and myself, too. This is not to be taken as, "sex is an inauthentic desire." Often, it is. But in this specific case, it was not. Before defining a desire with which to work PURE, you might want to ask, "Why do I want this?" This will lead you to the underlying desire, which might be something entirely different. Go for what is really you. Or, to quote the Beatles, "The more real you get, the more unreal things get" – in a positive sense.

1. Define your old role

Your old role will contain some aspects you like (and may even keep), and some you no longer prefer. Every self-definition begins with I AM. So if an item asks you to define your gender, you'd write, "I am a woman," or "I am a man." Items that do not apply to you can be skipped. Define the "I am" of your:

Gender
Nationality
Hair color
Looks
Weight
Profession
Friends
Success
Home
Car
Typical emotions
Clothes/ fashion
Favorite food
Favorite color
Voice
Body posture
Body movements
Sports
Walking style
Tone of voice
Body/ health
Spirituality
Sexuality

Status
Handling problems
Communication
Speed of talking
Interests
Sexual preference
Abilities
Ownership
Money
Towards children
Towards colleagues
Towards men
Towards women
Towards customers
As a man
As a woman
Towards authorities
Activities
Personality
Talents
Something good about me
Something bad about me
Talents
Other

In doing this, you have completed an interesting list. Your self-definitions are the source of what you experience in life, even more than your secondary beliefs and behaviors. If you define yourself as someone who is talented, you will attract events and people with which you can express your talent. If you define yourself as having no or little value, you will attract events that prove what a failure you are and you will be abused from all sides. If you have extra time on your hands, try the following additional exercise and ask yourself if aspects of your identity came about through:

a) Free choice
b) Resisting something (example: I am someone with long hair as a rebellion against parents)
c) Fulfilling somebody's expectations (example: I am skinny so men will like me)

In this experiment, you will find what is (your free choice), and what is not, you (identity assumed by outside pressure). Of course, after realizing this, you are free to let go of what you once freely chose and free to choose something formerly bestowed upon you (you might, for example, want to stay skinny).

2. Define the new role

This is the fun part in which you will start touching on alternate realities. Use the list you made in step one to define your new role—who you would like to be from now on. Be specific. Which role do you want in the movie of life? Who do you want to be in all its delicious subtle detail? You might want to add a few "bad sides" or quirks to invoke the reality with more realism.

3. Props

Some will have an easier time accepting a new role if they surround themselves with props. Props are used in film and theatres as background to a character. Props can be objects, places, circumstances, clothing, jewelry, movements, favorite things, mottos and statements, rituals and symbols, and anything that reminds the self of the new role. Enjoy making a list of props that fit the new identity, ones your old identity didn't have. The aim is to purchase things or go places that symbolize the new reality.

4. Practicing the role

What reality has been up to now gets its power and energy from routine behaviors and thoughts where you act as if you had no control. It appears it's easier to follow routine ways of acting and thinking, but that is not true, no matter how often you try to convince yourself. Our play shop proceeds by taking automatic behaviors belonging to the old identity into conscious awareness and teaching the self what it means to be the new identity. We do this by alternating between the old and new identities intentionally until we gain conscious control of both sides.

1. Intentionally behave like your old role
2. Intentionally behave like your new role

3. Alternate between both roles until you feel you exercise enjoyment and control of both and there is no doubt that your consciousness understands the difference between them.

Examples:

You walk the way your old identity would walk, and then you walk the way your new identity would walk. Shift between the two.

You deliberately go to a place your old identity would go, and then you go to a place your new identity would go. Shift between the two.

You intentionally respond to fear the way your old self would, then you deliberately respond to fear the way your new self would.

Here's a secret: Unwanted behaviors that you create intentionally and consciously eventually come under your full, conscious control. Why? Because what you create intentionally, you can also release intentionally. You make yourself the source or cause of the behavior, rather than watching it come up. This makes it easier to allow the new identity.

5. The Holodeck Experience

If you wish to take the whole thing yet a bit further, you may use this add-on to the movie star process. "Holodeck" is taken from the TV series *Star Trek: the Next Generation.* The holodeck creates holograms of three-dimensional realities so that they can be experienced as real. It can create perfect and convincing simulations of any environment, person, object, or situation. In the TV series, the spaceship's crew uses the holodeck for adventure, education, vacation, training, and recreation. They can visit any country or planet and touch or interact with anything they desire. You can use the holodeck as a tool for powerful choreography. Take your chosen identity; imagine a space in which this identity would typically reside, and interact with that space.

Consciousness operates no differently than the holodeck. It creates holographic pictures and projects them into the universe. In this way, the holodeck ritual makes reality more real for you, as long as you don't label the imagination only imagination. Once again, we are not only visualizing, but also getting a real, three-dimensional space, touching it and interacting with it. Your whole being is involved. You have to create the reality before it is created. By spending time in your holodeck, it will eventually gain a life of its own that acts and manifests, on your behalf, anything you put in it. By habituation on an intense experiential level, you will get results. You no longer see two-dimensional images in your head, but three-dimensional images all around you. Visualizations gain density, space, time, three-dimensionality, and physical form. You define a space in which a reality takes place, and you act out your imagination. You train your sense of reality. To give you an idea: Touch an object. Now touch an imaginary copy of it. Alternate between the two until you feel no difference. You put energy into the holodeck with sounds, smells, colors, textures, physical objects, sound, movement, and voice.

Reincarnating While Alive

Using the PURE technique cleanly is the art of reincarnating while you are alive into a parallel reality. Your beliefs about who you were become irrelevant and you enter a new self. For this reason, circumstances become irrelevant, too. Not that you can't enjoy them or be entertained by them, but you no longer base your being on them.

Once you become good at shifting viewpoints and their accompanying body senses, other techniques and methods become superfluous. Techniques are the middleman, but if you can go directly for the intended identity or feeling, which is what everyone wants, you don't really need methods. Strictly speaking, you don't even have to look for limiting or countering beliefs or subconscious patterns, as is taught in other RC systems. Why? Because you enter a parallel reality, in which you never had these beliefs and patterns.

In the first step of PURE, the stillness of being, it can sometimes seem as if more than one parallel world or option is offered to you. To some you will gently say, "No, thanks." One of them you choose and enter as if looking through the eyes of complete and thorough fulfillment of desire. If you find it challenging to change a belief you have harbored an entire lifetime, think how much more difficult it is to walk around with contradictory beliefs and desires all day. Self-contradiction is what makes life difficult, not identity alignment. If you think merging with your true joy is risky, I ask, "What is it to not follow your joy, not do what your heart desires, and not align with your inner peace? Is that supposed to be safe? Not following your true path is the most risky thing you can do, because that's where all the problems come from in the first place. Following your joy creates rapid change, but never to your detriment, always to your benefit. Identifying with a preferred self only takes a few minutes of closing the eyes, falling in love with the new reality, and remaining there effortlessly. Millions of contrary paths, pasts, and issues disappear the moment you shift awareness—shift channels. They are no longer relevant to who you are. For some, this joy may be too much too fast, and they will undertake the shift systematically, which is fine as well. In any case, once you shift a core belief about who you are, something happens. Never does nothing happen after such a shift. Either the desired reality or something better appears inside (and soon outwardly, which is infinity's task), or you are put to the already-mentioned test. Infinity doesn't give you this test; you give it to yourself by holding to beliefs that don't match your chosen world. So whether the reality or a test appears, both indicate successful use of the PURE technique. The test always involves choosing or deciding between an old and new reality. No test would appear if you were identified wholeheartedly, but if it does appear, it is not a bad thing, as it allows you to deepen your resolve as to what it is you want. When a test or choice appears, even if somewhat dramatic, give your loyalty to the chosen reality.

Observing and Being

All of RC or life can be summarized by two states of awareness:

Observing, Looking At, Witnessing, Dissociation
Or,

Being, Looking As, Identification, Association

As observer or witness, you look at something in silence, without reaction or interaction, and are not identified. You are pure awareness, floating above things; you are the sky observing the clouds. Self is not involved in a reality, but separate. When you are identified, you take on a viewpoint, feel a reality, enter a belief, and become one with what you were observing. You lose yourself to the extent that there is no difference between "I" and the object of desire or resistance. You no longer observe it—you are it. This type of devotion and embodiment transforms a mere thought-form into a belief with a powerful effect on reality. First, you watched a movie, and then you became an actor in the movie.

The words "attention" and "intention" reveal the secret of reality creation, the secret of shifting from observer to experiencer or from experiencer to observer. When you put your AT-tention on something, you are observing it, which is the obvious prerequisite for identifying with it. When you go INto the reality, it becomes an IN-tention or a BE-lief. Even more appropriately, you BE-live it, and as such, interact with reality. Attention is the preliminary step and already touches the desired vibratory frequency. Then you intensify attention by going inside it. Seeing something is a soft form of reality creation. Feeling something makes it more intense. Actually being something is the most powerful form of magic. You then are that for the fun of it, not as a strategy to make something happen. Strictly speaking, there is no "out there"; it all happens "in here" – not within the body or brain, but within the consciousness. Nothing significant ever happens out there. You can have anything you want as long as you already have it.

In the same way, observing something without reacting to it de-identifies you from a reality. You may try the following as mediation: Choose a reality you have repeatedly experienced. Let the event well up in your mind's eye, together with the corresponding observer or experiencer. Now observe in silence until you have no further reactions to it. You give up your analysis, labels, judgments, and opinions until there is no concept of it. That is successful de-identification. If you can identify with what you want, you don't need this meditation, but if you have difficulty entering a new being, then first de-identify with the old one.

Some students of RC have difficulty no longer discerning between "out there" and "in here" or between imagination and reality. If that that is the case, and you prefer to hang on to those separating concepts, you might want to see it this way: The seed of a reality already contains the whole reality. If you plant a seed in the garden, it already contains all the information it needs to become a plant. All you have to do is plant it and leave it alone and it will become what it naturally is, given that soil, sun, and water are in place. If not, you might have to add light or water, but this is not a big deal. The seed knows how to become what it is. When applying PURE, you plant a seed. Your work is done. Problems and delays only arise when you dig out the seed to see if it has grown, or start pulling on the first signs of a small, and vulnerable plant to speed its growth or make it bigger. Other problems arise when you plant other seeds next to the original seed. Two seeds will compete and perhaps neutralize each other. This is why it is not advisable to plant too many seeds at once—two or three will do—and not to plant seeds that are, in your mind, contradictory ("I want to have a monogamous relationship" and "I want to be polygamous" would be contradictory). Plant the seed and let infinity take care of the rest.

Another helpful analogy is pregnancy. By an act of high energy (sex), a child was conceived. It is now in the mother's womb. She is pregnant. You would not say, "The child is not real," just because it isn't yet physically manifest, because it isn't born yet. Once you have claimed it inwardly, you know that it is real. It would seem unnatural to try to build the plant or the child yourself. Can you imagine how ugly the plant would look if you taped together parts so that you got something that looked like a plant? Unfortunately, this is what many people think reality creation is. Because it feels so very stupid, they give up the subject and say that reality creation doesn't work. Trust the universal efficiency of infinity. Quit trying to do nature's job. Feel the relief of entering the viewpoint of self for which it is already manifest, the imaginary scenario of "already happened." Don't judge the day by what you reap, but by what you sow.

The Body Sense

One could describe it this way: Body sense creates reality. When identifying with a reality, there is an accompanying feeling to it. The body never lies. It shows you exactly what you are identifying with. It predicts what reality is coming your way. For any reality that you wish to experience, there is a corresponding body sense. For wealth and financial abundance, there is a certain body sense. For being in a romantic relationship, there is a corresponding body feeling. Even for things such as owning a car, there is a corresponding body sense. The body is the gate between subtle energy and physical expression. Having a body sense of something goes beyond the New Age concept of visualization as a separate mental event. Reality creation is a holistic and integral event in which the whole body is involved. So if you want to be the boss of a multi-million-dollar corporation, which body feeling do you have? If you had that body feeling, you wouldn't be thinking about becoming that boss. You would replace wanting, needing, and striving with being. You would take it for granted as easily as you take breathing for granted.

Beginning at the End

Creational magic requires that you begin at the end and stay there. You bring the future to today. You make the goal the starting point. You don't leave a back door open or concern yourself with the how, when, or where of manifestation, but rest in loyalty and solidarity with the chosen self. When you begin at the end, linear time is irrelevant. In this way, we can enjoy the identity today and rest in relief.

This takes persistence. Persistence means to stay loyal to what you have chosen rather than swaying between contradictory beliefs and desires. Persistence does not mean discipline, stamina, or effort, but making a decision within and remaining there.

If you misuse reality creation or the PURE technique to make something happen, you are presupposing it hasn't happened yet. Visualization, affirmation, etc. are not used to make something happen, but to experience it happening now. Using it as a means to an end presupposes that we have to make something appear, which presupposes that we believe it is not yet here. The word "already" is one of the most important words in RC. If you want resources, notice, appreciate, and use the resources you already have. If you want spiritual adventure, notice the spiritual adventure you already have. And if you want to experience a reality, feel it as already done, created, manifest.

Trying to make something happen through an act of will is in complete contradiction to magical RC because it is based on the belief in lack. This principle is often repeated in this book because it is so important, and because so many teachings and books fail to point it out. You let it exist in consciousness to the extent that factual manifestation becomes unimportant. That is true belief. Contrary to most New Age teachings, RC does not utilize affirmations, at least not in the traditional sense. Affirmations are phrases people use to manifest something. They might repeat, "I am rich" a hundred times a day in front of the mirror. But what does someone really believe who does that? He believes the opposite, of course. This is why affirmations rarely work. When they do work, it's often not because of the affirmation technique, but because of the person's belief that something magical will happen. This is why most affirmation techniques lose power after awhile. The person doesn't notice that the energy is not coming from the technique but from him. In RC, we don't use affirmations that refer to the future, as in "I want," "I intend," or "my goal is." Imagine a future self for which the goal is already true. Would he use affirmations to make it come true? Not hardly. Discern between RC and wishful thinking. We will discuss quasi-affirmation techniques later on, but these will have different purposes and effects. Because your creation has already happened, it is accompanied by good feelings, and you leave it alone. You cannot enjoy and wait for it at the same time.

This is why New Age teachings of "expectation manifestation" are not necessary or beneficial when using PURE. When you really expect something, you do not think about it, right? When you deeply expect something, you don't consciously expect it. You take it for granted; that is why it is granted to you. An example: you do not expect the next breath to come. Wouldn't that be silly? If you spent your time expecting the next breath, something would be wrong. The ease and gracefulness with which you take the next breath for granted is the ease with which you claim your new reality. You don't work yourself into a frenzied expectation about it. You've identified with the reality of "I breathe," and it's a normal part of you. You no longer look at it (it least not much); you no longer look for it. Manifestation occurred while we weren't looking, while we were busy with other things. Laugh about your neurotic attempts to use RC, thinking you had to create something already there, easy as breathing. You cannot be something and expect it at the same time. You cannot look at it or for it and BE it, effortlessly.

Put SELF in the center, rather than reality. This will not make you selfish; on the contrary, it will take you to a place in which the generosity of life flows from you and teach you the paradox of being and having.

6

Timelines and Timelessness

Everything you want to experience is accessible at this moment. The present can be your greatest present. The present is the only reality of importance, the only reality in which RC practice occurs, the only time in which happiness can be let in. Everything is accessible immediately, because it is already contained within the infinity that you are. What you call "my life" is an exciting game called "Planet Earth," in which one of the main characteristics is linear time.

This planetary reality is only one of many options you have. You've identified so strongly with the game, you have forgotten it is a game; this amnesia is part of the game. In fact, the game wouldn't be much fun if you were constantly aware it was a game, just as you wouldn't enjoy a movie while constantly thinking, "It's only a movie; it's only illusion." No, you identify with the movie; you allow it to touch you. Maybe you complain about the difficulties, hurdles, and opponents on the game board. But honestly, would you really enjoy a game if you could reach the goal without barriers or challenges? If you've played soccer before, would you enjoy playing in an empty stadium, without a team, without an opposing team, so you could shoot the ball into the goal just like that? I really don't think so. Look at the songs, movies, and stories that fascinate human kind the most—drama, tragedy, heartbreak, violence, disaster, followed by a happy ending—representative of the adventure a soul longs for when incarnating into this dimension. So if you say, "I want enlightenment" or "I want to win the lottery," you misunderstand the purpose of the game. Your soul (higher viewpoint of self) did not want to be where it already was all the time; anyway; the soul wanted to experience.

The concepts before, during, after are traits of linear reality which allow us to experience things in detail. This ingenious set up allows us to forget we are infinite beings. Physical reality is creating by separating and compartmentalizing all that is so that it can be experienced and viewed systematically. "First, I'll do this, then that, and then when that happens I'll do this," and so on. On this level, the past is the source of the present and both are the cause of the future.

But in ultimate reality, you are already all-knowing, all-seeing, all-pervading, simultaneous, and multi-dimensional. You are currently expressing yourself as if you were something less. So you gather knowledge and experience and seem to become more than you were before. Viewed from infinity, this is actually funny to watch. God is a comedy for an audience that is afraid to laugh. God created a rock too heavy to lift, but will lift it, anyway. God split itself into different viewpoints, and you are one of the viewpoints of God.

Everything is already within consciousness, and consciousness is infinity. There is no in and outside—these are linear expressions. The body is inside consciousness, not the other way around. People who talk about "my soul" or "inner self" often seem to refer to something inside their body or brain, or something limited to the space in and around the body. But that is only because consciousness identified with the body as a vehicle of perception and expression in the time-space game. You are not in the universe; the universe, including everything around you, is within you. You are the cause, not the effect. Things don't happen to you, but through you. You are the creator, not the created. You already have access to everything that can be known or experienced, because you are all that.

Growth and learning is a funny illusion. To understand anything being said here, the knowledge would have had to be within you to begin with, otherwise you couldn't imagine or conceive it. If something weren't possible or in your potential, you couldn't imagine it. You cannot imagine something that doesn't exist. All the things you don't think are because they are not within your current reach. The easier you can think a thought, the closer that reality is to you, the more probable it can manifest in the physical. If you want to experience an expansion of awareness and quality of life, all you have to do is express more of what you already are. You will only experience the happiness and abundance you allow yourself. Don't long to have more, long to *be* more.

Within your physical parameters, you may start considering yourself not as a small, insignificant being, but as a royal, shining, beautiful, and unlimited consciousness. When you even start considering it, you start attracting different information and events into your field of experience, which allows you to be more of who you really are. Not to become something you are not, but to show more of your original energy. Your true colors start shining through. Rip the mask of "poor limited me" from your face. I see through it. The frequency at which you vibrate is incredibly dense and contracted, which enables you to forget 99% of who you are and focus on the 1% you show. Loosen your suppositions of who you are, and your frequency vibration increases, which creates a seeming improvement or "getting better." But expanding self does not mean you have to get from "here" to "there," as here and there both exist within you. There is no separation. Rather than looking for enlightenment, be more authentic and unique. Spirituality does not leave physical reality, as many people assume. Physical is not separate from spiritual. This is a common misconception, another way to separate. You chose to be here, and going away, or ascending, is not what the soul's path. To teach this is to induce the trance of separation. The game of life is irresistibly beautiful and has obvious benefits to the soul who understands the game rules. Where would you want to go, anyway?

The more experienced aspect of self ("higher self," if you want to make that separation) does not see this planet as a prison or a dark conspiracy, but loves the game. It wants to forget other realities to create the appearance of starting with a clean slate. It wants to act like it is discovering and learning, and what's most important, experiencing *surprise*—a concept that has little meaning for the infinite self. The benefit of this is the joy of discovery and not knowing what's going to come next. Do you recall situations from your childhood in which you were thrilled you didn't know what was behind the curtain? Isn't it a bit dull to want everything planned and figured out beforehand for reasons of security (fear)? If you say no to joy in exchange for security, the only security you will get is the security of joylessness and boredom.

Take part in the movie willingly. The more you love life, the more it will love you. Paradoxically, the more you love "normal" life, the more you will ascend spiritually. Wanting to get away from here, as many spiritual teachings propose, binds you to this reality even more—all resistance binds you. If you look closely, any reality reveals its magic—even the mundane and profane. Everything is infinity, and as such, a miracle, so there are no common things. By giving into the world in terms of love and interest, you gain power and influence over the game. Being disinterested or antagonistic toward the game will not teach you how to play it well. You can't control a dance partner you push away. Being antagonistic towards the world implies that it has power over you. Loving the world implies that you have power over it. If you want to experience something good, then dive into your situation, without resistance or wanting to get away from it. It is implied that you created this experience, and by giving into it, you fulfill the reason you created it. If it is something unpleasant, the way out of the situation is by going through it, by feeling it to the end. When you resist nothing, nothing resists you.

You do not have to give anything up to become more of who you are. Some suspect that the new, minus the old, is the real you. But actually, it's the old plus the new that equals the full you. Everything is within you, there is no external. Refusing something that you are already experiencing means refusing yourself. This does not mean you have to go through every negatively labeled reality imaginable, but if you are already experiencing it, then dive in and experience what you created for the very purpose of experiencing it. Experience it eagerly and willingly, and it will turn into what you prefer. What you put attention on, you include into your vibratory field. What you try to remove from your vibratory field, you also include. That's why it's impossible to get rid of something. The moment you say, "I exclude this," you are including it. Stop fighting problems. Either dive into them or start loving what you prefer instead.

It is not the aim of this chapter for you to give up the convention of time when everyone else has agreed upon it. This would unnecessarily single you out from your fellow humans. It is okay to make dates, count birthdays, wear watches, and agree to appointments. However, apart from what you discuss with others, you may stop letting time have you, and start having time. No matter what you express towards others, adopt a different view of time—as something more flexible, malleable, reversible, and fluid than you thought. The ancient Romans put bands around people's wrists to indicate that they were slaves. Consider not being a slave of time. This awareness makes it easier for you to change states of being, because you no longer believe the past is the cause of your state. There is no future to worry about and no past to blame things on, because both are in the now. You will gain a sense of freshness, witness the infinite depth of the moment, and have an easier time bringing your desired manifestations into the now, rather than projecting them into a future that will never come. Furthermore, you will learn the secret of changing things immediately and thoroughly—as if they had never existed.

Certain memories repeat themselves because they were recorded when you were more present, awake, aware, and intense than you are currently. If there was an event that was charged emotionally, one that captured your attention or impressed you in some way, you were present in that moment. These events keep repeating until you experience something even more interesting, current, up-to-date, or important. Depending on your state, you will remember different things. Many problems solve themselves. An extreme example: The tornado in front of your house will dismiss the love-sickness in which you were immersed. When you are truly present, really alive, there is no "who am I" or "what are my goals." You couldn't care less. The questioning and pondering world self only arises when you are not feeling well. Postpone your future happiness less. If you feel happy, you don't care about the past or future much. We don't have to do much to come into the living present than release resistance or become interested in what's going on now. If there were an exercise on becoming present, it would involve conducting one of your favorite activities. While immersed, you quit waiting for a better future and simply do what's before you. You forget time, space, and even your surroundings. Your efficiency increases. You behave as an integrated, whole being without fragmenting your reality into pieces in time. In this way, you experience a substantial increase in life energy.

Why is it that for many people, what happened before and what will happen after or later is always more important that what is happening now? Because they are not happy now, and do not know they can transfer their visions, feelings, pasts, and futures into the now. So they escape the now into a past future, which they unfortunately view as separate from "now," so the joy does not become too intense. Teachers who misunderstand the concept of here and now teach that attention should only be focused on the current surroundings, and that this behavior constitutes being here and now. But I wouldn't suggest that being in the living present is only about looking at the current surroundings. Daydreaming with the supposition that the daydream is not real, or not here and now, causes pain. Daydreaming for the sake of enjoying yourself here and now is pure joy.

It is my opinion that enjoying yourself in the present and loosening your definition of time slows the aging process. Being present summons the vibratory power of all times into the now. If you want to see something spooky, notice how people create fragmented, linear time nearly constantly in order to uphold the illusion. Their language reveals the underlying belief in time. Don't criticize it; just notice it. Notice how they regularly refer to a concept that doesn't exist. "I have to wait until—" "I don't have time for—" "Later, I might—" "We used to—" Our language compels us to view time as linear.

What are you waiting for? Waiting is a state of being. It means you want the future and do not want the present; you do not want reality. It implies that both are separate and that you have no immediate access to all that is. That's why you wait. When people are waiting, they do not notice how they could have their attention on millions of nicer things than what they currently have their attention on. The key to happiness is to stop denying the present, give up resistance, and put attention on what is wanted here and now—no matter where you are. Once you notice you are in waiting mode, you are present once again. Some mystics believe that being present for only a few days would lead to the automatic manifestation of your highest aspirations because you are no longer contradicting who you are. Anytime you notice you are waiting, gently re-direct your attention to your present surroundings, the body, or to some pleasant thought. You were in hypnosis, now you are awake. You don't have to keep thinking about that appointment later on in order to fulfill it. Your attention could be anywhere. Why waste this precious moment being impatient?

A note on time management: Some people (not all) find it easier to be present if they have a good, written time management system in their life. Why? Isn't time management and its accompanying prioritization, order, and structure contrary to the flow of single-pointed time? For some, it's not. By handling linear time in an orderly manner, they de-fragment it and gain power over it, rather than linear time gaining power over them. This frees attention that then can be used for the here and now. This is not to condemn concepts such as time management. Of course, if you are thoroughly in the flow, no time management is required, because everything appears naturally at the right time. But for someone still struggling with the basics, putting order into chaos might not be a bad idea.

Loosening the concept of linear time also frees the world-self from the rigid belief in the continuity of reality. The belief in continuity makes certain realities seem solid, unchangeable, and inflexible. People trying to progress often talk about setbacks, in which they feel they have worked towards something for a long time, and not made as much progress as they thought. They suddenly behave like someone they wanted to overcome and don't think they are allowed to behave that way after all they have learned; they suppress parts of themselves that belong to their old version of self. But actually, they are not following linear evolution. Sometimes you experience highs, and sometimes you experience lows. You can access highs and lows anytime. No matter how much you have progressed, you can fall back into your worst version anytime. The good news is, though, as quick as you fall into something undesired, you can access your highest version again. At any point on the timeline, you can experience incredible lows or highs. Even after applying the knowledge in this book, you can access a version of yourself that doesn't understand any of this and makes the same mistakes it used to. Even before having this knowledge, you had the ability to access your highest states. Continuity is an illusion. Every passing moment is another chance to turn it all around. Reality doesn't have to be as it was a moment before, but something completely different across the board—if you decide it is.

Beings from other realms lovingly and jokingly like to call us masters of limitation because we are so eager to identify with realities we don't want. In a sense, our ability to limit ourselves is considered an art form from discarnate viewpoints or viewpoints alien to this planet because our true nature is unlimited. On the other hand, being unable to focus or limit oneself means being unable to create anything. Reality creation implies limitation—a limitation to a specific focus. However, certain limitations that counter our creative power can only be upheld by a series of concepts or core beliefs. One of these core beliefs is our trust in the authority of linear time, in which we have become so deeply immersed that we hardly notice it. Exaggerate your immersion in linear time and you become a reactive idiot that has completely forgotten itself as cause of reality. One forgets one's observer mode or de-identified state of witness, and one's ability to make decisions soon gets lost in a trance or waking sleep. Being this fully immersed in a beautiful reality might be a good thing, but being immersed in something you don't really want is a good opportunity to return to awareness.

The world self sees time as a river flowing from past to future. We sit in a small boat called the present and don't see much of what lies in front of us, being pretty sure that what lies behind us is done. From a viewpoint more congruent with infinite self, time is not a river, but a lake. Time is not a line, but a circle. The present is like a rock thrown into the middle of the lake. Waves ripple out in both directions from this center representing past and future. Each ripple is an event. Looking down at the lake, you see that time exists simultaneously and that each circular wave group represents another time stream of past, present, future and that each one is caused in the now. Throw another rock, and the formations and directions change.

Not only parallel universe theory but also this analogy implies that the complete timeline can be changed right now. Since we chose our beliefs (the rocks we throw into the lake), we cannot only change present and future, but also the past. This may not make sense to a world self who has been educated (forcefully conditioned) to forget the eternal now it knew as a child. Past and future are being created right now, through your current focus. While most would agree that present and future are changeable, it might take some getting used to, to view the past as changeable. Some readers may find the proposal outrageous. Yes, you can change the past. Not just your perception of the past, mind you—you can change *the* past. When you enter a parallel version of self, you might assume you have the same past, but you don't. You are on a parallel timeline, with not only a new future, but also a new past.

Most of us understand that if we change our viewpoint today, we will start remembering things from our past or place different emphasis and relevance on remembered events. But what is being suggested here goes beyond change of perception or emphasis. There are many examples of someone changing viewpoint, belief, or identity in the now, and the past changes accordingly, but we hardly notice it due to our belief in an unchangeable and fixed past.

Have one belief today, and you might be struggling with your parents; change the belief and you might find out you've been adopted; suddenly, the past completely shifts. Shift back into your old identity or timeline, and you will find out that you haven't been adopted after all; that information was a computer glitch. Have one belief and you might remember you were sexually abused as a child, something on which you can blame what you are like today. Change the belief and you might find out it wasn't abuse, or that it was just a dream. Change the belief once more, and you might find that it didn't happen at all. As difficult as it might be for some to grasp, especially with emotionally charged subjects such as sexual abuse, nothing is as it seems.

On a basic level of RC, one might teach that the past is over and in this way, free attention from it. On an advanced level, one might teach that the past is not over, and that it is not even the past. You may dismiss the concept of "past" as irrelevant, or rewrite the past to your liking. Physics has shown again and again how linear time is not real, so why shouldn't this knowledge be applicable to your life? How you think the past was is only how you think the past was. The present is only how you think it is. The future is only how you think it is. With different perspectives, the entire scenario changes. With your current focus, you are creating a version of the past that you unquestioningly believe is the past. Many people, when changing the present or themselves, assume that from this point forward they have changed, when actually they have changed from this point forward and backward. "Now" is the place from which all realities stream.

Remembering something from the past? You are creating it right now as evidence for who you are now. This is important because belief in the past implies that the past is the source, when actually, *you* are the source. Cause lies, not in the past, but in your momentary belief. Your past has nothing to do with what you decide or do not decide to do today. This knowledge is dangerous in that it removes the base of a whole civilization that has always made the past "cause" and the future "effect," rather than consciousness cause and reality effect. "I've had tough relationships in the past, which is why I don't want to give in to new ones." That's a typical example of a false assigning of cause. Past-is-cause thinking will perpetuate a limiting reality. Making the past responsible for something relieves you from thinking and acting.

If there is anything you dislike about your past, you can re-create it. How? By using the PURE technique on a past event. By changing the event, you recall something you prefer, or remember something different entirely. Be writing a script of a preferred past and believe in it. If you get a body sense of that memory, you have changed the past, which again effects your present. By changing the past, you change what happens today and tomorrow. By planting retro-causes, you speed up change here and now. If the past happened differently, the present would be different, too, right? You can do this despite the mass belief in objective time. The seriousness with which one demands, "Yes, but I experienced that, and it cannot be changed!" shows the rigid resistance against one's ability to change facts. Some people would rather be right than change for the better. Some expect reality to change without them changing. But a new reality is always accompanied by recognizing apparent "facts" or reality as "only a belief," releasing it and exchanging the intention for something new.

As you continue to ease your mental grip on linear time, other side effects may occur. Things may happen at just the right time. Moments will pop up in which you can sense the future. Once you understand your emotions as a navigational early alert system, there won't be bad surprises anymore. Precognitive dreams, clairvoyance, and remote viewing become commonplace, rather than strange events that must be trained.

Exercises

If you are accustomed to releasing general resistance, loosening fixed beliefs, or going into deep silence, then no exercise is necessary to make something happen. Being present and loosening the time concept happen naturally, but some will want to consciously play with the idea of stretching and altering time, and for such occasions, you may use the following exercise commands, or invent your own.

Sudden Stare

Focus on something you would normally only view in passing with a sudden, abrupt head movement and gaze, staring at a specific spot. Some people will get a rush through the neck when doing this, the rush one feels when the hypnosis-like routine of everyday life is suddenly interrupted, and one returns to present time. I walk by a vase at which I normally never look. Suddenly, I turn my head and stare at it. I sit at my desk. Suddenly, I turn and stare at the door of my house.

Reality Breaking

Interrupt what you are doing and do something completely different or out of the ordinary, something you have never done before or something nobody would normally do. Start jumping up and down on a leg, sing a hymn, take your kitchen dishes for a ride in a car, or bathe in champagne. The sudden break of routine followed by something crazy signals the following message to self: Reality is not what it was. Reality is what I decide it is.

Past into Present

Remember something nice from the past. Now, while warming that scene back up, notice how the feeling of it occurs, right now, and is a resource, right now.

Past into Future

Notice a situation you will have in a few days. Remember a time you had a similar situation and were successful at it. Transfer that feeling to the upcoming situation.

Future into Present 1

Imagine something nice expected in the future. You are feeling it now; it is happening now.

Future into Present 2

Imagine a wise, more expanded, loving, and powerful version of yourself in the future (ten, fifty, one hundred, one thousand, or more years). If you want, ask this version of you questions and let him/her answer. Or, let this version of you provide guidance. Or identify with this version of you right now. No need to wait a thousand years.

Present into Past

Recall yourself when you were younger. Gently place your attention on this younger version of yourself. Now act as the guiding, loving, and reassuring future self of this past version of you. By giving guidance, advice, or appreciation to a past self, you automatically create a future-self giving guidance, advice, and appreciation to your present self. Grasp the logic of this.

Changing the Past

Apply the PURE technique to remember something you would have liked to have happen in your past. Fully feel that having happened. What was, just a moment ago, a fantasy, view it as your actual and factual past. Then let go of the new memory. Your present will start changing accordingly, but not because you are looking out for it or waiting for it, but because you trust your inner authority and what it is showing you.

Expanded Present Time

Notice something that is moving (e.g. a car). Speculate about where it's coming from and where it might be going. Repeat this with various things until you feel an expansion of your sense of here and now.

Here and Now Drill 1

Remember something unpleasant from the past. At the same time, notice something pleasant about the present. Stay aware of both simultaneously until the past event loses weight, charge, and relevance under the more intense impressions of the present, and you feel an obvious shift in mood.

Here and Now Drill 2

Walk around. Notice that when you look at things, you automatically associate them with things (connecting the dots) from the past. Example: You see a house in Vancouver and you think, "They have houses like this in Liverpool." Notice your inner linking of something present to something past. Also, notice your tendency to think, "I already know this." Then dismiss the association for a moment and look at the object as if you were seeing it for the very first time—fresh, new, amazed, open, and without expectation. Repeat this until you feel a significant shift in mood or vibration.

Here and Now Drill 3

Sit somewhere where you can observe many people (e.g. a café). Spend time watching and observing people, nothing less, nothing more. Do this until you are certain you can learn anything about anyone simply by observation (reading vibration). A feeling of appreciation and humor. A feeling of deep relaxation beyond deadlines or appointments.

Here and Now Drill 4

Take a walk near where you live. But this time, walk in directions you've never walked before, to parts of the place you've never seen or have never taken a closer look at before. Or walk where you have walked before, but see the place with new eyes and an emphasis on different things. Notice how your attention behaves at new places. Notice how new places or viewpoints naturally produce present "being-ness."

Here and Now Drill 5

Completely give in two one of the senses (hearing a piece of music, touching or caressing, tasting totally, smelling completely, or seeing totally).

Here and Now Drill 6

Search out a person in whose presence you feel uncomfortable, self-conscious, shy, or generally unwell. Approach the person who supposedly "sucks your energy," and be in the presence of that person. Take your attention from the story in your mind about that person and focus on their energy-field, eyes, or breathing. Dismiss all past associations and simply perceive the human. Remain this way in silence or conversation until any inhibition, worry, heaviness, or desire to escape has ceased, and you feel well, or at least okay, in that person's presence.

Here and Now Drill 7

Observe a rose. Hold it in your hand. Touch it. Smell It. Identify with the rose, be the rose. As the rose, observe yourself. Then, close your eyes and observe the rose. Hold it. Touch it. Smell it. Eyes still closed, be the rose observing you. Acknowledge that what you perceive as "rose" is electric signals being interpreted by your brain. Without you, without interpreter, there is no rose. Without you, the rose has neither look nor smell, only an electrical impulse. The rose exists within you.

Here and Now Drill 8

You can easily come into present time by shifting attention from the inner dialogue to the body, feeling the body, breathing with the body, sitting or standing upright with the body.

Here and Now Drill 9

Notice something (object, person, place, plant, thought, etc.) and non-verbally say hello to it, acknowledging its existence. If you want, imagine it saying hello back to you. Repeat until you feel a new sense of here and now-ness.

Here and Now Drill 10

Put yourself to a place and time outside of your current surroundings (examples: market place in Japan, Internet café in Melbourne, court of law in Boston, boat in Greenland, etc.). Become present and aware at this place, be "here and now" there and then by looking at the surroundings and touching things or noticing temperature, landscape, and time of day. Repeat with different things until you notice a significant shift in energy.

7

Viewpointing

There are single techniques or practices that are worth more than thousands of words because they deepen an experiential understanding of things that words can't sufficiently describe. The practice I call "viewpointing" is one of them. It is not the only way to exercise shifting into parallel realities, but it is very quick and efficient. The side effects of viewpointing are new realizations, heightened awareness, heightened energy, heightened ability, heightened intelligence, and heightened well-being. I offer a few variations of viewpointing here; choose the one that suits you or try all of them.

The Technique

Look at any object without expectation, in a relaxed, receptive manner for a few seconds or more. Next, look *as* the object. You are no longer looking *at* the object, but *as* it. This means you identify with it, be it, get a real body sense or feeling of being it, and view your surroundings from this new viewpoint. From this new viewpoint, look at the next object. Then look as that object. As the new object, look at your surroundings and choose the next object to look at, then merge with it and look as it. Continue until you experience an obvious shift of energy, feeling, and consciousness for the better, until you can clearly discern between "looking at" and "looking as," and can effortlessly and easily take on any viewpoint or identity.

An Example of Viewpointing

I look at an apple for a few moments. I allow myself to become relaxed, my focus to become soft. Once I have a good impression of the apple, I project my consciousness into the apple, imagining I am the apple, looking as the apple at my surroundings. Once I get a body sense of being the apple (felt in one's own body), I choose the next object (as the apple—you are the apple choosing an object) to look at. As the apple, I choose a tree. I look at the tree as the apple, perhaps noticing the relation between the apple and the tree. Then I project my consciousness or attention into the tree (moving from at-tention to in-tention). I am the tree, looking at my surroundings. And so on.

More can be said about the meaning and results of this technique and how it serves to loosen your identification with the limited perspective of "I am a body" and opens you to the limitless identification of "I am consciousness," but I will mention no more so that you may have your own realizations and experiences. You cannot do too much of this exercise. You might say that you would prefer to identify with your desired realities rather than rocks, cars, and apples, but to this, I respond, "World selves desire is only to identify with a limited number of things they have been conditioned to view as desirable, while the soul wishes to identify with anything, everything, and everyone. In this exercise, you practice becoming one with all of physical reality. In this way, you gain more influence or rapport with physical reality. The least amount of time you spend on it per session would be fifteen minutes, but it may also be practiced for many hours, leading to deeper and deeper states of feeling and energy. You want to assume as many viewpoints as possible, flexing your ability to shift (if you can't even identify with a rock, I doubt you will be able to identify with wealth). Shifting viewpoints is equal to shifting resonant realities. As a side-note, you might already have guessed: Remaining in a viewpoint for a length of time would start attracting that reality. But that is the aim of the PURE technique, not viewpointing. Here, you don't remain in a viewpoint for more than 20 to 160 seconds. The important aspect of this practice is: Getting a body sense or feeling of being something (being able to discern what it feels like to be a tree or a human) and being able to discern the feeling between looking *at* and looking *as* something.

Advanced Viewpointing

This would be the same procedure as just described, except imaginary objects and people or objects outside your current surroundings are included in the practice. You might be a tree looking at a building on the other side of the world. Then you are the building that is looking at a person walking by it. Then you are that person who notices a celebrity. Then you are the celebrity that notices the sun. Then you are the sun that notices the earth. And so on. Have fun with the extraordinary states of awareness you will have on this one.

Turning Expectation and Desire into Memory

Take any desire or expectation you have about something and turn it into a memory. Think or fantasize about it as if it were a memory that has already happened, as if you are a future self, remembering it. See how easily you can become convinced that it already happened. Notice the difference in vibratory feeling of expectation and memory. Expectation feels separate and even subtly stressful, while memory feels like relief. You may experiment with this as often as you want. It is a valid alternative to the PURE technique, a quick route to identifying with something.

Multi-Viewpointing

Choose an object (physical or visualized). Look at it from the front, from the back, from the sides, from inside, from the distance, and from close up.

Look at the object from the viewpoint of a neutral person. Look at it from the viewpoint of a murderer, a child, an alien, a politician, a mother, a guru, a grocer, from the viewpoint of you when you were fifteen, when you were eight, and when you were eighty. Look at it from the viewpoint of a person who likes the object, and one who dislikes it. From the viewpoint of someone who thinks, it’s dangerous. From the viewpoint of someone who finds it boring, and so forth. Look at that same object from many different viewpoints and enjoy all of them. With every new viewpoint, you will perceive the object differently and even perceive things about the object you did not perceive before. Each viewpoint is not only a different perception, but also a different reality. In the multi-viewpointing meditation, you are actually reality surfing.

At the end of the exercise, try looking at it from the different viewpoints simultaneously (without too much effort or concentration). Try to remain in this multi-viewpoint for a bit. This may sound difficult or even impossible, but you'll get the feel of this state immediately, even if you can't hold all viewpoints at the same time. This will produce extraordinary states of awareness, no matter what subject you are using.

Multi-viewpointing is one the most important meditations of this book because it trains your ability to shift reality. Here are some things on which you can practice multi-viewpointing:

- An event from your life (pleasant and unpleasant)
- Any object
- Your home
- Money
- Another person
- The mind
- The body
- Life
- The universe
- All that is

Of course, the meditation requires a bit of time and focus. So what? A single session may teach you more intuitive and specific knowledge than hundreds of lifetimes, consumer goods, or books. Why? Always viewing something from the same viewpoint teaches you to always perceive the same things. If you wish to expand your intelligence, wholeness, and the soul's fluidity, you need to be able to change viewpoints. You can only experience something you are. Shifting your vibratory correspondence to a number of things and topics, enjoying the good, the bad, etc., not only helps you feel more energy, but it's much easier to choose between your preferred viewpoints, rather than being stuck in a single way of seeing things for the rest of your life. Every reality is upheld by some viewpoint observing it. No observing viewer—no reality.

The last part of the exercise shifts your consciousness to a viewpoint beyond all viewpoints. By taking on many viewpoints simultaneously, you automatically identify with the you that was taking on all the viewpoints. Up to now, you perceive yourself as someone with one single viewpoint. In this meditation, you shift yourself to the one beyond all viewpoints. The inability (unwillingness) to take on a certain viewpoint is a stuck viewpoint of the world self and not the viewpoint of source (soul) who is interested in any viewpoint. By forcing yourself not to take on certain viewpoints, you are blocking large parts of reality from being perceivable. Infinite consciousness can take on any viewpoint—the bum, the superhuman, the impersonal, the right-wing-extremist, the left-wing-extremist, the policeman, the god, the angel, the sportsman, the millionaire—a soul can be anything and understand anything. Remaining in a viewpoint for a short time doesn't mean you are creating this reality. It would only start creating itself if you remain wholeheartedly. But by resisting certain viewpoints, you create a problem in your life. Use this meditation as a journey, an exploration, and don't hide yourself from the infinite options and experiences.

Multi-viewpointing emulates the game that the soul has been playing since ages. This simple meditation allows the world-self to remember the game the infinite-self has been, and forever will be, playing. In this sense, enlightenment is also merely a viewpoint. Everything you have ever experienced flows from a viewpoint. Any belief anyone could have is a viewpoint. One will experience according to one's viewpoints. Any experience is valid and beautiful. The game of the soul is to experience. Period.

Why did the soul incarnate on planet earth? To experience a particular kind of surprise that comes with not knowing everything. Forgetting the source leads to surprise; this again leads to fun. It is fun to take on various viewpoints and watch what unfolds for these viewpoints. Being caught and fixed in viewpoints is quite tedious. Nobody is forcing you to remain in a viewpoint. Teach yourself how to change them. Should you ever want to use this meditation for manifesting a reality, choose a viewpoint you love, and stay fixed in that. This limits you, but also allows you to experience something you want to experience.

Variations

Physical viewpoints on physical objects: Walk around an object, viewing it from different standpoints.

Inner viewpoints on physical objects: Shift between observing an object from the filter or viewpoint of various opinions about the object.

Physical viewpoints on inner objects: Remember some event, and observe it from a distance, from close up, from above, from below, and so on.

Inner viewpoints on inner objects: Remember some event and observe it from the viewpoint of various opinions about the event.

A last note: Viewpointing can be practiced in written form, verbally, physically, and mentally. It's up to you. You know why you are doing it and what it is all about: Practicing the art of shapeshifting, being one with everything.

8

Emotions and Reality

Happiness is the Cause, not the Effect

Wellbeing is not the goal; it is the starting point. This is yet another realization that could change everything dramatically. It might be a concept you'd like to remind yourself of every now and then. Your e-motions are energy-in-motion. And since everything in this universe is energy, too, your emotions interact with the whole universe. Your emotions are the language of your soul. They are the body's translation of your energy state. They are the body's translation of what your soul is telling you. They are the body's translation of what you believe and are.

The emotional frequency you put out or radiate is what you get back as real life experience. If there's something that you want in life, be sure that's what you are radiating. If you want more love, check if it is love of others and self that you are feeling. Everything you experience—your surroundings, the people you meet, the events that pop up, the places you go, the things that happen—are reflections of the emotional state you most often reside in. You notice that when you shift your frequency, other things start happening. By changing your vibratory state—your mood, your feeling—reality starts to reflect that feeling. If you want the out there to change before you feel better, it won't work. Feel better before it happens. In other words, you can make more money relaxing in a Jacuzzi than in the rat race of the stock exchange.

Everything you do is driven by emotions, by the desire to feel better or to avoid feeling bad. You believe that if you do this and that, you will feel better. But actually, it doesn't make you feel better, but what you associate with experiencing it does. It's okay and valid to have *things* you associate feeling better with, as long as you understand that the improved feeling does not come from the thing itself, but from your decision to feel better (and linking or associating it to some activity or thing). From the viewpoint of a reality-creation wizard or a parallel universe surfer there is nothing more important than your state of being. Compared to it, all other things are irrelevant. Feeling good is not the end, but the means, not the aim, but the requirement to reality creation. If, for example, you say, "If I work harder, I will make money, and then I can feel good," you are placing conditions before happiness, before having energy. You'd be dependent on work and money for having a good state. Being needy will never create the money you want, though. You have to feel what you would feel if you already had plenty of money in order for it to flow effortlessly. The same principle applies to other issues. Another example: Are you saying, "I feel bad because I am overweight"? Well, this is putting the carriage before the horse. You are overweight because you feel bad. And another example: Are you using techniques of reality creation to feel better? Most people do. The amusing thing is that none of the techniques will work if you don't feel better in the first place. Emotion is the cause, reality the effect. That is why it is necessary to put well-being first. A mirror won't smile before you do. Demanding a mirror to smile first is what you are doing when you demand life to be better before you feel better. The journey you need to take first is emotional, not one of action. If you let circumstances dictate what you feel like, these circumstances won't change. Don't let other people or things—authorities, bank account statements, or the weather—dictate how you feel. Create your own feeling of well-being first, and good things will follow—almost automatically. When you're in the flow, things happen naturally, effortlessly, easily—all of them to your benefit, reflecting the feeling you give off.

Don't even leap to actions and decisions before you've found that sense of natural calm, well-being, or enthusiasm. Otherwise, any decision you make will be colored by lack, because it is from a state of lack that you take many of these actions. If you don't put feeling good first, you will forever be trying to change and control the circumstances, instead of the source of the circumstances—your emotional energy. You will forever be taking actions as compensation to make up for creating bad circumstances with bad emotions. The most basic principle is to put well-being, a good state, feeling well, relaxed, relieved, comfortable, appreciative, enthusiastic, or excited on top priority, before you do anything else—before you make decisions, before you commit to something, before you act. Compensation actions are things you do to make up for bad energy, and these actions cause more bad energy, believe it or not. Inspired actions are things you do that feel good—when you act on opportunities that present themselves after you've given off good vibrations.

The formula on which All Suffering Is Based

There's more to this principle. When you follow your joy, your life's plan, the plan you designed before you came to this planet, unfolds naturally. Joy is your body's translation of your soul's energy, what your soul would love to do. You can either trust that feeling, or not. But if you do trust that feeling and follow it, it will always ultimately end up with what's best for you, and it will always be understood why your emotion told you to follow it. If something feels good or right, it is good for you and produces good results. If something feels bad to you, it is bad for you and produces bad results. It's as simple as that. If something feels good and bad at the same time, if something feels ambivalent, it will produce good and bad results. You cannot expect that something bad will produce good results. Doing a job you do not like, because you want to earn money, will never produce the money you want. Meeting someone, although you don't want to today, because you want this person to like you, will never cause that person to like you. The formula most people use is:

"I have to do X in order to get W."

X stands for something they don't like, and W stands for something they want. Example: "I have to do this lousy job in order to make money, with which I can then enjoy my life." If you break this formula down you get:

"X = W," meaning,

"Bad equals good."

Does that make sense? No. Does it work? No. And yet, much of people's actions are still based on that formula. Think about how this applies to your life. Write about it. Examine it. Find out in which areas you are using this formula. And realize that doing, thinking, and saying something that feels good will lead to a result that is good, and nothing else. What feels right to you does not have to feel right for anyone else. You know best what is good for you, no matter what others say. You are not on this planet to fix what's broken; you are here to experience and share joy. If you lower your own state in order to help someone else, you are not really helping. If you have no energy, you have nothing to give, anyway. This whole universe is based on resonate attraction, meaning that like attracts like. That means you'd have to become like the thing you desire in your life. Primarily, this means to feel like it. To feel as if you have it. It takes one to know one. You can only experience and perceive and know what you are the vibratory energy of. If you want something to manifest in your life, you'll have to say and feel: "I love it, and it loves me." That's a thought or phrase you can cultivate.

Emotions Are an Immaculate Navigational System

Your emotions are barometers, indicators, navigational systems that tell you which way your day and your life are going. Knowing this, you get a fresh, new perspective on so-called negative emotions. Negative emotions are your servants, your friends—navigational indicators warning you to change your course before something unwanted manifests as reality. They do not indicate that something unwanted has already happen, but that something unwanted will occur if you do not change your course. Thank goodness, negative emotions exist; otherwise, you would never know that you were heading for something undesirable. It is paramount that you learn to trust your feelings and appreciate negative or bad feelings as helpers and friends. Learn to read them, understand them, and react appropriately. Would you trash your navigational system in the car when it tells you are going the wrong way? Of course not. You'd be grateful you were forewarned, and change your course. What do I mean by changing course?

Having a negative emotion means that one of two things are not appropriate for you, not appropriately aligned with your life's purpose:

1. A thought, belief, or judgment
2. An action, plan, person, or surrounding

That leaves us with one of only two questions to ask when we are feeling bad:

1. What am I thinking or believing to feel this way?
2. What am I doing to feel this way?

And this leaves us with one of two solutions to the unpleasant emotion:

1. Change your thought or belief
2. Change your action or surroundings

Either way will work. Allow negative emotions to be indicators, pointing at thought-patterns, beliefs, behaviors, or actions that are inappropriate for you or what you say you want in life. Let's say you are working on a project that once felt good to you, but no longer feels right. According to what we just said, you only have two options: To change or abandon the project or to change your thinking. Both options are completely valid, and both will put you back into emotional alignment with your true self. You can change the way you view, think about, believe, or label the project, you can change the parts of the project that don't feel good, or you can abandon the project altogether. Anything that causes relief is spiritually and physically healthy.

You should not get rid of negative emotions. They are the perfect, immaculate, navigational tools that allow you to stay in sync with your soul's original path. Get rid of negative feelings altogether, and you would no longer be able to discern what your soul intends for you. You would no longer be able to choose between what is and is not you. Your life would no longer make sense.

Suppressing emotions or wanting to get rid of them is attempting to destroy your beautiful navigational system. You will not only destroy that guiding light, but also your body and mind. You see, emotion is simply energy flowing through your body. Energy is neutral. When this energy flows through a negative belief or action filter, you perceive this energy as fear, sadness, anger, or other emotion you term negative. When this same energy flows through a positive belief or action filter, you feel this energy as happiness, excitement, relief, peace, ease, enthusiasm, or any other emotion you term positive. In this sense, fear and joy are the same thing, the very same energy, flowing through different filters. Therefore, you are not trying to get rid of energy. Suppressing the energy is suppressing your own true life force. Suppression and resistance will make you tired and exhausted. You want to find out what filter the energy is running through. You want that feeling to be an indicator, to lead the way to the thought or action that is inappropriate. If you suppress the feeling, not only will you suppress energy and joy, you will also not uncover the thought producing it.

The following emotions are indicators that you are following your soul's truest path:

The emotion you call excitement, elation, euphoria, or enthusiasm

The emotions you call appreciation, love, and compassion.

The emotions you call interest, attentiveness, wakefulness, awareness, fascination, admiration

The emotions and states you call relaxation, relief, peace, contentment, calm

There are many ways to use the knowledge you are given here. What follows are a few exercises, but they are not the only ways to apply this knowledge. As you begin to trust your feelings, use your emotions, change your state, and contemplate these things, you will come up with your own ideas. The exercises in this book are optional, meaning that you are not expected to do, repeat, or master all of them. You are given many exercises so that you can choose the ones you enjoy or the ones that fit your current situation. More important than the exercise you practice is the act of practicing itself. Practicing is a conscious behavior and part of the life of a spiritually mature being.

Time Out

The most natural way to improve your emotional state is to call out a time out. This means to ease off, retreat, take a break, relax, become silent, calm down, allow stillness, and give up resistance toward what is. There are many different ways one can take a time out, but don't ask how to *do* it, because it's not about *doing* anything. It's about stopping doing anything—stopping the world, the rat race, being a puppet of your desires, being driven by cravings and resistances, and regaining a sense of control, self-determination, and peace. Time out is actually an anti-exercise. Taking a time out means to leave the movie reel for a moment or two, step back, and gain perspective. It can mean meditation, but doesn't have to. Some use meditation as a tool to do something productive, which perpetuates the rat race. Time out means quitting the habitual flow of things and coming to your self. What is left when everything is removed? Your true self. Time out can also mean to go to a place you will be safe and undisturbed. It can mean to close your eyes and simply breathe for a few minutes, a few hours, a few days, or even a few weeks, depending on the degree of exhaustion you have let life cause you, and the degree of relaxation you need to feel yourself again—to re-orient yourself. Becoming stillness is the foundation from which other things will flow and work. Operating on the tools of this book or on magic from a state of "being driven" will not work. The tools do not work; the craftsman who uses them does. Even needing the tools to feel better is a clear indicator that you have strayed far from who you really are. When you relax into your most natural self, well-being arises, and you are no longer needy of anything. Taking your time out, be it for a minute, a day, a week, or any other span of time, is a self-determined change of pace. This is especially vital when things are not going the way you wanted them to go, when you are feeling down, exhausted, sad, fearful, or angry. These are the best moments, the best opportunities to examine yourself, your life, write down limiting beliefs, replace them with positive ones, meditate, and gain an overview.

Relaxation and wellness are a prerequisite for changing your vibration to any subject.

Non-doing is the opposite of doing and will intensify your ability to *do*. Having come to peace, you will soon find yourself being inspired to *do*, rather than action being a frenzied reaction to worry. Without time-outs, there's not much of a chance you will do the PURE technique, either. You won't be able to relax and concentrate. If you wish to work a lot, or have more energy, you must feel sufficiently regenerated, rejuvenated. If you fail to take time-outs because you feel under pressure, are afraid of the consequences, or feel there are too many unfinished things, you've long passed the phase where it is easy to change your vibe. You are then no longer the master of your destiny, but a reactionary-robot giving in to the imagined pressure of the world. You are fully engulfed in compensatory action and no longer living your true self. Your true self, your eased self, is what comes up naturally, spontaneously, and effortlessly when you chill out. A side effect of silence is that many problems just disappear, without you having to make them disappear. Well-being is not something that has to be achieved, that you have to fulfill conditions for, but something you *relax into*. It is your birthright and most natural state. Most people say, "the suffer," but they are simply suffering from exhaustion. Exhaustion has its roots in believing you must prove something, or struggle or achieve something, or make something happen, otherwise you are not worth anything. This is so very untrue. It does take more effort to feel bad than good, but the most beautiful things don't take any effort at all. Have you noticed how the galaxy, planets, your breath, and your heartbeat are *sustained effortlessly*, without you having to do anything? The best things are free. What you do in your time out is up to you. You can have a massage. Read a book. Watch a good movie. Go for a swim. Go for a walk. Have sex. Have a glass of wine. Or just laze around. None of these things is highly esoteric or has mysterious principles, but they lead you back to who you are more efficiently than any teaching could do. Having the courage to take time outs and turn them into treating yourself to pleasantries means you are demonstrating the power of not running away from the world—not letting yourself be driven and pushed by the world, but calling out, "*No*, this is *my* time out, and I will re-align with my positive feeling of natural self. I will not re-emerge from my time out until I feel better." But it is not to work magic that you take your time out. It is because you are worth it.

Aligning Desire and Belief

One of the deeper secrets of reality creation (which most New Age teachings fail to mention), is that by closing the gap between what you desire and what you believe, you can experience anything you want. Traditionally, New Age teachings tell you that you can have anything you really desire, while others say you can have anything you believe. You are now learning that the alignment of desire and belief, closing the gap actually manifests reality. You cannot have anything you desire, and you cannot have anything you claim to believe. But you can have anything you truly believe.

Write down five things you desire (goals, wishes):

1.
2.
3.
4.
5.

Now write down what you really believe (know) about these subjects:

1.
2.
3.
4.
5.

Example: I desire more money, but I believe I have to work hard for it. I also believe that I don't want to work hard, which doesn't allow me to have any money.

Now, notice the gap between what you want and what you believe. This discrepancy is what causes the most turmoil to your energy vibration. The feeling of relief is the best indicator that you've made a vibratory jump; the opposition of desire and belief causes an energetic pulling and tugging—a strain, tension, and resistance, which is the opposite of relief. There are only two solutions to close the gap and find relief:

1. Downgrade your desire
2. Upgrade your belief

Which of the two is it going to be? Some teach you to give up your desires because it will cause relief and alignment with your true self. Downgrading your desire means setting a smaller, more realistic goal, one that does not strain you or exert expectations. Focusing on a goal higher than what you are willing to believe is like trying to jump on a train that is going too fast. Not only do you run like crazy to get on the train, you face the possibility of being bruised, hurt, and disappointed when you fall to the ground beside the train track and the train disappears into the distance. Downgrading your desire means slowing the train down. Upgrading your belief means speeding up yourself. How do you know when your desires and beliefs are in alignment? You feel it. It feels good. Let's try both. First, re-formulate your desires list, so that it is more of a match to your beliefs. Example:

Desire: I want more money.

Belief: I believe I have to work hard for it. I also believe I don't want to work hard, which doesn't allow me to have any money.

Downgraded desire: I want to find a job.

Now, reformulate your beliefs so that they are more a match to your desires:

Desire: I want more money

Upgraded belief: I believe I can find a job that I enjoy.

By what you feel when you formulate a belief or desire, you will know if there's alignment between the two. And once there is alignment, rest in the feeling of relief. It is enough to rest in the feeling of relief. Enough to attract events into your life that match the new intention. Do not ask for the when, how, and where of the manifestation.

The feeling of being real must be enough proof for now. Infinity takes its own time to restructure according to your vibrations.

Scaling

Some readers want to aim higher and hesitate to downgrade their desires, which is why I offer another, more specific, method to upgrade one's beliefs. You may use variations of this technique, but first try the basic form mentioned in the previous exercise.

Step One: Notice an unwanted emotion: fear, anger, frustration, sadness, or shame.

Step Two: Ask yourself, "What must I be consciously or subconsciously thinking or believing to feel this way?" Write down the thoughts that come to mind. Writing them down makes them clearer, more precise, more conscious, rather than vague, foggy, and ever-shifting.

Step Three: Assume that the thought you wrote down is a Level 3 thought. Downgrade that same thought to Level 2, exaggerate it, make it sound worse, then make the same thought a Level 1 thought. Pull the lever down and create something worse intentionally. Downgrade the same thought to Level 1, making it even worse.

Step Four: Now, create a Level 4 thought. Take the very same thought from Level 3 to level 4. You make it just a little more positive towards what you want to think, but keep it realistic. The Level 4 version of that thought should be a positive thought, but it should come easily, be one you easily believe, one you can easily feel, one that relieves you. If you don't feel a sensation of relief in your body, you have not chosen an appropriate formulation of the thought.

Step Five: Now create the same thought as a Level 5 thought. Make it even more positive. State what you really want instead of that Level 2 thought.

An example: Let's say your original Level 3 thought is, "I am overweight and feel bad about it." You would transform that thought to a Level 2 thought, writing, "I feel fat and unattractive." Then you would take that concept to Level 1: "I feel like a fat pig, a glutton, a wobbly, ugly monster." Then you would choose a Level 4 thought: "Well, I am once again overweight, but I guess I can change that. I'd love to eat more consciously, take more walks." The Level 4 thought must be realistic enough for you to believe—something you *already believe, anyway.* You cannot replace negative beliefs with positive ones you can't believe—positive ones that are too ambitious. You must find and choose a thought that allows you to feel relief. Writing down the thought: "I am not overweight at all. I feel great," might not be an authentic, honest, and appropriate thought. After that, you choose a Level 5 thought, which must also be honest. The Level 5 thought contains what you truly want: "Well, I want to be my ideal weight, eat more consciously, move more, and appreciate my body the way it is." You proceed in the same way for every thought you originally wrote down, first scaling it down to Level 1, then to Level 5. Why would you scale it down first? It gives you more control over the thought itself. If you can scale it down, you'll have an easier time scaling it up. The reaction to scaling it down might be an emotional release or an uncovering of what lies deeper than the original Level 2 thought, or it may make the thought sound funnier or more ridiculous—or both. If you can upscale the thought in written form, and make it realistic enough that you actually feel the thought's effects in your body, you've successfully replaced it and upgraded your emotional vibration.

The emotional feeling will have to suffice as enough evidence of the reality for now. With the buffer of time, things will begin to show up that reflect your new feeling.

Appreciation

Appreciation of things, places, people, or things will melt your resistances and speed up desirable occurrences more than you might imagine. Appreciation, when practiced not for the sake of getting something or manifesting something, but for the sake of love and enjoyment in the now, is the wand of the wizard.

Appreciation (admiration, love, like, acknowledgement) vibrates on a special frequency that attracts positive events—not only the ones you are appreciating. Only what you fear can hurt you. Feeling appreciation while having your attention on something equals channeling higher dimensional energy into physical reality. This does not mean you have to appreciate things you don't like (although that would be an advanced variation of the exercise), but to find things you already naturally appreciate. The more you appreciate, the more you will be appreciated by life, others, and infinity. Appreciation, in this sense, has nothing to do with the pretence of putting on a happy face, but the true and deep understanding and love of things and people. It is irresistible. Ghandi conquered armed men with it. When the command came to fire at him, their hands and legs started shaking. They were unable to fire. Why? Because Ghandi used power, not force. And love is the most powerful weapon out there, not just as a sweet New Age phrase, but a real thing.

Take a walk somewhere and spot as many things as you can that you can say yes to. Ignore anything you would say no to; only notice the things you appreciate, and silently acknowledge, bless, admire, and appreciate them. Your vibratory offering will have increased a thousand fold.

Next, write down things, people, places, cultures, events, memories, thoughts, fantasies, locations, books, movies, music, art, cities, and objects that you appreciate, admire, are fascinated by, like, and want more of. Do not mention anything you don't want. The universe is inclusive, not exclusive. That means you get more of anything you give attention to, whether you say yes to it, or no.

Next, write down a few people or things you don't like. Beside that, write down aspects you do or can appreciate about them. If you can't find anything to appreciate about them, write down how this unwanted person, thing, or event might be of service to you, might help you, could be used or utilized by you for a good purpose, or what you might learn from it.

Remembering the Feeling

There are many ways to focus energy: by looking at something out there, by looking at something in here (meaning visualizing or daydreaming), by hearing, writing, speaking, and doing, or by remembering. In this exercise, simply remember times, places, people, and situations in which you had energy or money or were happy or successful. The moment you remember is the moment you're getting back into alignment with that energy, warming it up again. This will lead to similar things happening again in the future.

Emoclear

"Emoclear" is my word for emotional clearing. This is another way of turning emotional pain into emotional joy. Here's something very important to learn: An emotion does not cause pain. Resistance or suppression of emotion causes pain. What you call fear, sadness, or anger is merely energy in the body, and your resistance towards it is what makes the energy feel like pain. In emoclear, we let negative feelings flow through us. There is no such thing as emotional pain or negative feelings. It is the judgment, labeling, or evaluation of the feeling that makes the feeling bad. It is not the energy itself that feels bad, but the resistance to it. The resistance is the pain. Energy comes up, you habitually and reactively label it as bad, scary, sad, or undesirable, and in that moment, it turns into something undesirable. What you feel is not the energy itself, but something you've constructed over it, some resistance. Transmuting energy into joy means no longer avoiding and resisting it, but letting it through. By doing this, you make the energy useful; you free it up and claim the jewel that lies within. Suppression causes a tension or energy block, which the body then translates into pain. In this light, fear and joy are the same thing. How so? Energy flows through the body. If it flows through an unwanted thought or belief, you experience that energy as fear; if it flows through a wanted thought or belief, you experience the same energy as joy. It then follows that suppressing emotions equals suppressing your own life energy. It also follows that when you remove the unwanted belief-filter or release the resistance, that what you called pain naturally turns into energy, which can be felt neutrally or as joy.

Notice an issue or feeling that has been troubling you. Dive into the feeling, allow it, immerse yourself it, breathe it, breathe as it, give up any resistance, label, opinion, or judgment, explore it, go into it, identify with it deliberately, and let it play out. It will eventually play out. And after it does, you will feel much lighter and probably ask, "Now what?" If the feeling is still unpleasant, there is still some resistance, labeling, or belief that it is not serving you. You might want to ask, "How is this issue secretly serving me?" or let it play out some more. Finally, after it's all flowed through, and you once again feel soft and light at heart, you may define what you would like to experience instead, or even begin a PURE session.

Energy File

What you look at, looks at you. When you look at something beautiful, preferable, or pleasant, your vibratory or emotional energy shifts and changes. If you're in a normal state, it will only take about twenty to sixty seconds of looking at something nice for your vibration to lift. If you're in a bad or difficult state, it may take a few minutes. An exercise I've devised is to collect all kinds of nice, desirable pictures in a file on my computer. On a regular basis, I put pictures of things I like, want, remember, am fascinated by, admire, and appreciate into this file. I look at these pictures when I want to boost my vibration. Sometimes I even play them as a slide show. I also create different picture files for different topics. The titles I put on these files are statements of what I want to manifest. For example, one file reads "Places where I want to play and work." The file contains picture of beaches, mountains, intelligent-looking people, interesting buildings, and locations. Another file reads "Things I want to own," and the pictures are of nice cars, objects, resources, accessories, and so forth. There are many variations of the exercise, but the basic message is, "Beware of what you look at, for that is looking at you." Beware of what you include in your stream of thought and feeling. Learn to choose where your attention and emotions go, rather than being swept away by what the world is offering you. You only experience what you feel. If somewhere near you, a disaster happens, and you have no fear inside you, nothing bad will happen to you. You can only be harmed by what you fear. You can never be harmed when you feel love within you.

Finding the Feeling

1. Write down an issue you want to improve
2. Write down what you really think about this issue. To really feel the thought you are holding, you may exaggerate it a bit.
3. Now write, "I want to find thoughts on this issue that feel better."
4. Now write your list of thoughts. For every thought you write, note if it is a thought that feels:
   a) worse
   b) the same
   c) better

While doing this exercise, stay with the feeling so you have can an intimate understanding about how some thoughts feel compared to others. You will make a few interesting discoveries. You will discover that some thoughts you pretended felt good, actually don't really change your state at all. The thought you thought was better might leave you in the same vibratory position or have become boring because you have thought it so many times. You will also find thoughts you pretended felt better that are actually unrealistic to your current belief system; they exert pressure rather than pleasure. Don't invalidate or analyze the thoughts that feel the same or worse. Keep your intention on finding thoughts that really feel better or relieve you. Sometimes it will take a while until you find the feeling you really want. Take your time. Sometimes it's not done in one day, and you will want to repeat it. There is nothing more important than finding your natural feeling of wellbeing, for it is a feeling with which you correspond in the worlds of your dreams.

Example

Chosen Topic: Time pressure

Intensifying the Feeling:

I feel time pressure.

I feel a retching in my throat from it.

I feel time pressure in my stomach.

I am afraid I won't fulfill expectations.

I am getting old.

Finding thoughts that feel better
(Indicating in brackets what the apparent better thought really feels like)

I need better time management (worse).

I need a vacation (worse).

Maybe I should just admit that I won't make the deadline (worse).

Time is a construct of consciousness (same).

Time doesn't exist (same).

I ought to live in the here and now (same).

I should just take the time I need (same).

Why am I doing all of this? (Worse…tears).

I just want to do a good job (better).

I have all the time in the world (same).

I'll just take the time (same).

Well, I really don't know (better).

Maybe I just want to relax (better).

I have to decide between my husband and work (worse).

I'll decide for my husband (worse).

I'll decide for work (worse).

Both decisions are no good (better…realization).

I don't have to make a decision (same).

I like this exercise (better).

Instead of making a decision, it's time to raise my emotional level (better).

I'll think about something good (same).

I'll think about my last success (same).

I sure put myself under a lot of pressure about time (better).

I already feel a bit better (same).

Well, a little bit better (better).

All I actually want to do is deliver the documents at the right time (better).

I can deliver the documents on time (better).

I will delegate the rest to Susan (same).

I will delegate the rest to Tom (better).

This exercise is done until you feel enough better thoughts to actually have changed your state. Since like attracts like, you will notice how more and more good-feeling thoughts come to your mind that you weren't aware of before. During the process, there will still be thoughts that feel the same or worse, but you can do the exercise until you feel free enough not to worry about them. This can be done with any topic. Your new state of being will turn into reality. This is yet another exercise that has the power to change everything.

Energy List

Take a piece of paper and write down things that you:

Are interested in
Are fascinated by
Are excited about
Are enthusiastic about
Appreciate
Admire
Like
Love
Find beautiful
Find brilliant
Find euphoric

This list may include places, people, desires, locations, artists, colors, movies, books, cultures, teachers, scenarios, situations, memories, ideas, professions, money, health, body, love, sex, spirituality, culture, politics, fashion, music, architecture, paradigms, organizations, or anything that comes to mind.

You have just created energy that aligns with your truest self and higher purpose. There is nothing more important. Even if society, others, or the rational mind may deem some of the things on your list unimportant, they are what your innermost soul enjoys and are thus indicators of your ideal life's path. A movie you get excited about has much more to do with your life's plan than something reasonable that contains no such energy. The truth is not in the next chapter of this book, but on your self-created list.

When you follow joy, bliss, inner peace, and excitement, the right things happen naturally and effortlessly. You learn effortlessly, you remain healthy effortlessly, and money flows in effortlessly. These issues become things you don't have to think about, because you are in your natural vibration of well-being. What your soul wants is not contained in a second-hand recommendation or book, but on this list. Notice how merely considering these things, writing them down, puts you in a state of high energy.

While contemporary society will label not facing the facts as denial, the wizard will label not admitting your true desires as denial. The things on your list needn't have anything to do with what others think is appropriate or even with what you think is appropriate, nor is the list intended as a list of things you have to do or achieve. It merely puts you back in connection with your feelings; it is a list you can meditate on if you wish, a list on which you can daydream. Notice how you didn't even have to meet several conditions before you could allow yourself to feel it in the here and now. You didn't place dozens of things before being happy. What would your life be about if you could allow these feelings to touch you more frequently? What happens to your body sense and body posture? What happens to your movements? What happens to your facial expression? What happens to your memories? What happens to where your attention goes? In what way do your priorities change? In what way does your reaction to adverse events change? In what way does your voice change? In what way does your thinking change? What changes, merely by being aware of what excites you? And what makes you disallow these feelings once in awhile? Your reality is a reflection of your identity and accompanying body feeling. This you can create, independent of what's happening around you. Why not get into the flow now? Because of obligations? Fine. You may continue to fulfill your obligations, but never have so many that you can no longer spend some time each day in joy; otherwise, you are missing the point of life. Don't commit to too many obligations. The ones you no longer feel comfortable with, end in respect and integrity. There are things you used to do because you believed you needed them for survival. Now that you know how to create reality, you no longer need some of these things, and you are no longer willing to pursue them. Drop them. Quit doing what is not good for you. There will be a few remaining obligations, such as paying taxes, but once you spend much of your time in joy, you will no longer feel that as a burden.

When you are in the flow of energy, uncanny coincidences start appearing because you are shifting into parallel worlds. Making the list you just made is only one of many ways to get into the flow. I'll share other ways with you, but I invite you to come up with your own.

Go for a walk. Relax. Perceive something beautiful and breathe it in. Hold your breath for a moment before you breathe out slowly. Repeat this for ten minutes or more. Allow admiration to expand. What do you feel like?

Go for a walk. Perceive something you normally criticize. Observe it neutrally; give up judgment on it. Now notice good, positive aspects of it. Do this for about ten minutes. Allow appreciation and understanding to expand. Afterwards: How do you feel?

Go for a walk. Imagine that everything you ever wanted, all desires and longings, are already fulfilled. Breathe softly, slowly, and deeply, and accept the reality of your vision 100%. Do this for a few minutes. How do you feel?

Consider an activity that you always wanted to do, but denied yourself. Choose something that would be easy to do immediately. Then do it. How does that make you feel?

Go for a walk. Observe another human being. Notice his/her breathing and heart beating. Notice how similar he/she is to you, in that he/she also experiences good times and bad times, and strives for completeness. Allow love and appreciation. If you want, take on the viewpoint of the person; look *as* the person. How do you feel?

Put on a piece of music you love and let yourself be taken away by a daydream of your choice. Combine the soundtrack with a scenario you wouldn't mind having fulfilled.

Make a list of things you criticize about yourself. Put your right hand on your heart and leave it there for the remainder of the session. Look at the first item on your list and ask, "If I truly accepted and loved myself, how would I feel about this item?" Breathe. Notice. Go through the whole list this way. This can also be done with other people, of course. It can be done with undesired realities that you haven't fully accepted. Want what you have, and then you can have what you want. Notice the way these activities make you feel. Notice what they do to your life. Appreciation is the sword of the wizard, and it transforms everything. No darkness can prevail in the light of appreciation.

Although these may seem like many different activities, they all come down to one single thing: Are you following the path of the heart, which is the path of true power, or are you following the path of force, which is the path towards failure? Are you involved with something that represents your highest interests, or are you wasting time fighting something you don't want?

If you object that you don't know what it is that excites you, I will say that you do very well know what excites you, but refuse to admit it, in the mistaken belief that you can't act on it, or that you will be disappointed by acting on it. Where you have identification instead of expectation, there is no such thing as disappointment. Following one excitement may not lead to its fulfillment, but to something even better.

If you object that you have to wait before you can do something you truly love, I will say that those who make the best of what they already have will get more and more with less and less effort.

If you object that what you love is not productive, in the sense of making money, I will say to you that you are gravely mistaken. By doing things you don't love, you will make a mediocre sum of money, always barely enough to survive. If the excuse for not following your joy is security, the only security you will get will lead a mediocre life and your body will die. Period. You can *only* make good money by flowing energy and love.

The Secret Path

We've talked about creating states of high energy, without which reality creation does not work. High energy is the energy needed to create something new. But there is also a second path, an alternative path, which works quite well. This consists of noticing what already contains energy (happiness, interest, fascination, and love), what is already offering itself to you, and then going in that direction. By following this thread of objects and events, you are on the quickest path to your soul's purpose, whether you are aware of it or not. This type of behavior turns life into the most effortless trip you can imagine. It has been kept secret because most souls incarnate, not to have an easy life, but to experience limitation and struggle. If that is no longer your preference, you can follow the secret path. Imagine a cork floating in the ocean. For the cork, it is effortless to stay atop the water. It takes more effort for the cork to be underwater. Once you let go, it pops to the surface automatically. This is exactly what a life without resistance is like. There is no such thing as lazy people, only activities that are not in alignment with ones true self. Following the path of your truest self, following joy, makes you a person of magical charisma. If something—anything—is really you, you notice by what you feel like when you do it. However, the things that are really you change in the lake of time. Attaching to something, although it no longer contains the energy (love, joy) it used to contain, means you have strayed from the soul's secret path. Should you continue to follow that path, the puzzle pieces of your life come together in surprising and graceful ways. Following joy does not necessarily mean that you constantly have to work on your project, career, or finding your soul mate. It can mean that, but it doesn't have to. Following the path before you often involves little things. People tend to invalidate themselves when following something other than that big project, but that big project is not always the thing that feels the best on any given day. And your soul mate is not always the only content of your life.

Instead, we follow the path from moment to moment, hour to hour, and day to day, in gentle steps. In every here-now film reel, in every scene of the moment, you have a variety of options at your disposal, a choice of things to could focus on or do. No matter where you are, no matter who you are, you always have more than one option.

Now, to follow the soul's secret path, or God's calling, all you have to do is choose the option that shines the brightest, evokes the most interest, or contains the most energy, and follow it as well as you can for now. Let's say you take stock of the present moment, and there are five obvious things you could do (of course, there are an unlimited number of things, but you prioritize to five).

Now choose the option containing the most energy, no matter if it seems reasonable or not. Interest and joy are the best indicators of what is right for you. The world-self cannot see the consequences of his actions, but it can feel them beforehand. That's all. You can now put the book aside, because it's not going to get any easier than that.

But what then? What after that? Well, after you've followed that interest, there comes a time you've used up the energy within it, and you find yourself in a new here and now, a new scenario. Then you once again take stock of the present moment, noticing which options lay before you. You evaluate which possibilities lay right in front of your nose, which are immediately available, and then again choose the one that contains the most energy. Once you've determined that (because you feel it), you go in that direction as far as you can for now. You carry this activity or focus as far as it will go and to the best of your knowledge. And there will come a point at which the activity or focus will have played itself out and contain no more energy. When this point comes, instead of invaliding and insulting yourself or questioning your existence, move on by asking yourself, "Of all the available options, which thing contains the most energy now?" There will always be an option that sticks out compared to the others—one that offers itself. Then you follow it, and so forth and so on, to the end of this life.

Energy (in the form of joy, interest, love, peace) is the thread that leads you to other energies and truer life purposes. The secret thread of higher self leads you to things you may not be able to see from your limited viewpoint, but a higher version of you is able to see. It is a signal, an intuition of what path your soul intends to travel. Because of the limited perspective of the world self and nervously forcing its free will, most people ignore and trivialize this signal, instead of following it. The world-self cannot possibly imagine the purpose or reasoning of certain activities, but the higher self, with its overview of many millions of years and timelines, can. This higher self is the playful version of you and beckons you to a life much grander than the one your world-self envisions. Your feelings show you whether you are following this path or not. For anyone asking about his life's mission, destiny, or meaning, that issue has just been answered. It is in the following of the secret path that one's purpose reveals itself.

There is one more consideration to following the path though: Follow it with integrity. What does that mean? All is one, and what you put out or give is what you get. That means you follow the path, you follow your personal excitement—not as an eccentric running amok, but with dignity and respect towards the reality frames of your fellow humans, without harming others. It is possible to follow one's bliss without harming others. What integrity does not mean: Let's say you are in a relationship that has run out of energy, meaning it no longer offers opportunities for experience and growth. Saying, "Well, I will not end my relationship because I feel sorry for my girlfriend" is not what integrity is about. Integrity has nothing to do with the socially indoctrinated and hypocritical views of morals. Integrity means ego-ism in the positive sense. It means doing what is right for you without intentionally or knowingly harming others. In our example, that would mean examining your beliefs before you break up the relationship. If, after you release limiting beliefs toward your partner, you still don't match, you would end the relationship in a respectful and appreciative manner. *That's* integrity.

All these are just words. The fire of love does not burn on these pages, but within consciousness. If it burns high enough, not only will the rest follow naturally, but it will also burn on these pages. In the presence of the fire of love, nothing else is important. Sometimes the thing you would love or that would interest you does not seem to be in alignment to what you think you are supposed to be doing. But things are rarely as they appear. The outside may show you one thing, while intuition, your soul's communication, may indicate something else. Here is an example from one of my coachings:

Coach: Take stock of the present moment. What are your options?
Student: Well, we're sitting in this park. I have the option to go home now and work. I also have the option to sit here and relax. I think I like that option better; it feels better. But there's a third option that I'd enjoy the most. I'd like go over and feed those swans. After that, I'd like to take off my clothes and jump into the water. Silly, isn't it?
Coach: Okay, do exactly that.
Student: I think I'll settle for the second option of just sitting here and relaxing. After that, I should get home to do some work. I need more customers for my business.
Coach: Don't you want to try to follow that hunch your intuition just gave you?
Student: It seems counter-productive to feed the swans and then jump into the water. I don't really need it.

Coach: You think the swans would agree that it's counterproductive?
Student: Well, for them, maybe not. Look, let's call it a day, I really have some important stuff to do.
Coach: Excitement is infinity's signal; it is God's calling and shows you what is to be done, no matter the concerns of your ego. Trust it. Do it.

What happened? Faking reluctance, the student got up with a grin on his face. As he started feeding the swans, a woman joined him, doing the same thing. They eventually struck up a conversation. Then an acquaintance. It later turned out that this woman employed 9000 people, many of which soon became customers of my student. In a few minutes, he had gotten more business at the lake than he would have gotten in three months of work.

It is only when you are not aligned with yourself, not trusting self and life, that this type of behavior is risky or requires courage. If the amount of fear that suddenly wells up is overwhelming, you best not take that path, because the belief in failure is certain to produce failure. You best change that belief before you take that action. We are always faced with two options when an action does not feel good: Change the action or the belief about it. Fear is merely a form of excitement or enthusiasm being resisted in some instances.

Your higher self (a more expanded version of yourself) already knows what your desires are and have been. You don't actually have to repeat them hundreds of times; it knows. Because it knows, it offers certain options that look interesting and that would lead to the quickest fulfillment of that desire, even if it doesn't look like it has anything to do with the desire. It's as if your higher self is dangling a carrot, urging you to go one direction. Once you enter that new space, the next steps are visible, and it eventually becomes obvious how all these things have lead up to your desire.

The prerequisite for adjusting and calibrating your actions, focus, and directions, according to your true interests, is again silence, time out. You cannot take stock of the present moment and feel yourself if you are racing from one event to the next, without consideration. Before entering the next segment of the day, how about taking a short time out and determining what options you have and what day segments you can enter? Not only that, how about giving a short statement of intention for what you want to experience with the next segment of the day? Is it too much to ask to live your life a bit more consciously, deliberately, and perhaps a bit less automatically?

A small-scale variation of this principle: Go for a walk without any specific destination. Notice some object that interests you. Go to it, examine it, feel it, touch it, study it until you've learned a few things about it and your curiosity is satisfied. Then, continue walking, looking for the next thing that captures your interest. Walk from one event/place/object to another and surf the waves of increasing euphoria.

Go for a walk in silent amazement. Recall the amazement you had as a child or you have when you travel to foreign countries. While walking, try to view everything with amazement. Your eyes a bit more wide open, your breathing a bit deeper, your walk a bit more upright.

Go for a walk in silent gratitude. Contemplate all the things you are grateful for, all the things you've received, which you now acknowledge. Relax, become silent, and allow gratitude to expand to the things and people that surround you.

Go for a walk with the assumption that you will experience something unexpected, some surprise. Remain in the feeling that anything can happen anytime and that surprise and the unexpected lurks at every corner—that something new can be anywhere. Assume that life is full of miracles, adventure, and mystery. Notice how this assumption improves your mood.

Amazement + Gratitude + Openness + Appreciation = *an irresistible field of energy*

Options

Look around you and notice the options you have. Of course, every here/now moment contains millions of options and paths you could follow. But let's say you notice only a few—three, four, or five.

If you want, write them down. Now, of these five options that you could act upon, one or two are shining brighter than the others—are more interesting, inspiring, joyful, relaxing, or exciting than the others. Choose the one most interesting, the one you can follow without detriment to others, or former commitments. That's following joy with integrity. Then, act upon that, feel the energy it gives you, and experience it until the energy starts to fade, until you've fully experienced it. Once the interest starts to fade, stop. You will be standing in a new here and now, with brand-new options, some of which you did not even notice before, when you first chose an option. You are now standing in a new viewpoint; you are a different person than you were just a while ago. Now look what options you have. Choose the most interesting one, the one that contains the most joy, relaxation, love, or excitement and follow it. Don't get stuck in something that is no longer interesting, just because it was interesting. Take stock: What are the options you have now? Which is the most interesting? Which feels the best to you? Which can you follow with integrity—meaning without breaking the laws of your country or intentionally harming others? Act upon that; get the energy out of that. If you did it like this for the rest of your life, you'd be following the pearl necklace your higher self, your soul, has laid out for you. This would be the quickest path to your life's plan, the quickest path to higher consciousness, the quickest path to have all you intended to experience.

Fear

What you fear you attract. What you are afraid of has already happened because you are already suffering from it. All choices can be broken down to two choices: The choice for fear or the choice for love.

While most of us know that these statements from pop psychology and New Age are true, they are not necessarily helpful, because fear of fear causes more fear. The topic of fear fills countless books and courses. It drives whole industries, even a whole civilization. Since enough has been said about fear elsewhere, I'd like to offer a few new ways of dealing with it. One of the greatest misunderstandings in human history may well be that fear is the enemy, something to get rid of as quickly as possible. But is life, or even conscious living, all about getting rid of fear? This is the philosophy of cowards. Fear is not the problem, the childish handling of fear, wanting to get rid of it as quickly as possible without actually having to look at the message it is trying to deliver, is. In reality surfing, fear is not a problem but a:

Friend
Indicator
Servant
Barometer
Energy

It exists to tell you that you are, at the moment of fear, not familiar with your cause over reality. Viewing fear this way will lessen fear, but will never make it disappear altogether. Why should it? Why would you want to get rid of your navigational system, which tells you where and where not to go?

Another misunderstanding is that there is such a thing as "fear in general." There is fear concerning something, and such a fear can be handled by psycho-spiritual means. The real problem here is trying to get rid of fear in general. Someone might release his fear of spiders; that doesn't mean he will never fear anything again, but he will no longer fear spiders. The next time he expands his awareness, he will come upon new limits, new unknowns, and fear will arise again. Fear is an indicator that one is expanding, reaching new frontiers.

In general, fear indicates unfamiliarity with something. The more familiar you become with a thing, the less you fear it. Familiarity grows with the attention you give something. One way to lose fear is to become more familiar with what you fear. Another way to handle fear, which has already been mentioned, is to dive into it, immerse yourself in the energy in your body, removing all labels, judgments, and resistances, until you either reach a point where you say, "Okay, now what?" or what you labeled as fear turns into what it was all along: Energy. Another way to handle fear is to use it as an indicator pointing you to some belief that is not in alignment with your desire. Depending on what you are consciously intending, what you fear will change. Without the fear, you wouldn't even notice you are counter-intending. It can also be an indicator of an action, person, or plan not in alignment with who you really are. What the fear is trying to say is "change your course." Once you do change the belief or action, the fear will subside. It has fulfilled its purpose, and it is no longer necessary. Yet another way to handle fear is to re-label the feeling in your body as excitement rather than insisting that it's fear or something bad. Watch what happens to the feeling when you do that. Another way to handle fear would be to go to anger or rage, which is exactly one emotional level above fear. Finding something to get angry about will quickly transport you out of fear and leave you with more power. Yet another way to handle it is to switch focus to something more joyous. Still another way is to confront what you fear—eye to eye with the tiger. And still another way to handle it is to ask yourself what could happen if what you fear really occurred, and then what could happen if that occurred, and so on, until you find what you really fear. And another way to handle fear would be to terrorize your fear by mentally becoming something much worse and bigger than it and attacking it.

As you can see, you have dozens of options of what you can do; you don't have to fall victim to fear the same old way every time. Once fear notices you are no longer its reactive victim, but a player, it won't show up much anymore.

Abusing Fear

This is a secret technique in which you use or even abuse fear, rather than it letting abuse you. You know you attract what you fear. So the next time you feel fear, how about letting that feeling become stronger, and then connecting it to the thought of something you would like to attract into your life.

Transmuting emotions releases them. Transferring emotions, or putting them somewhere else, does not release them, but makes use of them in order to experience certain things. Examples:

Fear of something undesired can be transferred to fear of something desired.

Fear of spiders can be transferred to fear of chocolate (if you wish to release a chocolate addiction).

Doubt in your abilities can be transferred to doubt in your inabilities.

Anger at another person can be transferred to anger about your laziness (if you wish to have more drive).

These are only a few examples of how negative energy can be put to a positive use.

Vibration Too High

There is one type of fear I would like to touch on here: When people are confronted with vibrations that are too high for them, they sometimes react with fear and resistance. Imagine a UFO landing in Aunt Annie's garden. While it may be a higher vibration, it will not necessarily be healthy for her.

When You're in Trouble

When people are in trouble, meaning they have seemingly lost their connection to all that is, they tend to become reactive. When you're in trouble, silence is recommended. Retreat and go deeper into silence. Sit there and allow yourself to be the observer rather than the immersed. Simply observe what thoughts and feelings come, without resistance or invalidation. What is there is there for a reason; allow it to be there. Many experience surprising solutions and relief only by being still.

Assume unconditional responsibility for everything going on right now. Assume that you are the sole creator of the situation, even if it seems that someone or something else is. Consider that the issue is somehow serving you—maybe to protect you from something you imagine is no good for you. These things happen on levels of belief you seem not to notice. Never having money might protect you from being a bad person if you believe that only bad people are financially affluent. You can skip the steps of looking for subtle and hidden beliefs if you simply take responsibility and then go to the next step.

Allow yourself to shift your attention to a better version of yourself. Receive an ideal version of yourself with a different body posture and facial expression. Identify with that version as if the reality you prefer were already true. Feel what it feels like and rest in that feeling.

Playing with Energy

What follows is an example of playful and creative freestyle practice.

Choose something that feels unpleasant (pressure, pain, emotion). Now play with this energy by…

…putting your attention inside it (synchronizing)
…replacing your negative label (that is bad) with a positive one (That is energy!)
…breathing into it
…imagine a color into it (medicine)
…humming into it
…making it worse before you make it better
…placing your hand on it and transferring the energy into your hand, feeling it in your hand instead of where it was before.
…transferring the energy into an object before putting it back in the body
…transferring it into the air before transferring it back into the body
…noticing how the feeling has improved on a scale from one to ten, and how if that improvement can take place, further improvement can take place

Source Meditation

Become aware of the things in your surroundings
Speak to the things in your surroundings
Experience the surroundings as yourself
Relax the body
State an intention. Take a deep breath.
State something for which you're grateful. Take a deep breath.

State another intention. Take a deep breath.
State something you can forgive.
Touch something.
Touch something else.
Notice something you can change. Change it.
Notice something you can't change. Change it anyway.
Move your energy
Focus only on what you can hear
Experience beauty
Demonstrate a positive body posture
Ask yourself, "When did I stop laughing, singing, and dancing?"
Retrieve your spirit.
State an optimistic intention. Take a breath.
Ask yourself, "If I had one more month to live, what would I do?"
Ask yourself, "What could I now admit to myself?"
Smile until you feel the smile.

Naturalness of RC

To demand to learn RC quickly is a sign of the lacking, desperate, and impatient world-self. RC is a reversal of everything you have been taught; it may take a lifetime to comprehend fully. Yes, of course you can have results overnight. But RC is not meant to be learnt quickly—"Alright, got it. What's next?" It is something you deal with for a lifetime, because the law of correspondence operates for a lifetime and beyond. Measuring a shift or improvement in the context of linear time is inappropriate to RC, anyway. Sometimes you are in the flow of it, sometimes you are not—no matter in what phase of the RC journey you are. Dwelling on how long it takes to master it is yet another variation of immersion in a belief in linear time. You can represent masterful RC anytime, and you can represent lousy RC anytime, depending on how resistant or willing you are to take on a new viewpoint. Readiness to take a leap of faith is always helpful in RC. Putting all your eggs in one reality basket will speed things up; putting your eggs in more than one basket will slow things down, but also make it easier. Some people only make the leap when they are in a crisis, but you don't need a crisis to take a leap into a new world.

What's most important is that RC practice remains or becomes more and more natural. Throw off the baggage of knowledge, questions, complications, and rest in your inner joy. Incorporate the knowledge into everyday life without making a big fuss. When something nice occurs, you don't need to label it as totally incredible and weird because that presupposes the belief that RC is rare or unnatural. Don't get worked into a frenzy or cling to certain beliefs. Allow RC to become as natural as breathing.

Many teach that desire is the creative force, or that willpower is the creative force. RC teaches that it is not directly desire or willpower, but willingness and readiness. You may, for example, know there is something you don't want, but on some level, you are willing to put up with it. If you weren't willing to put up with it, you would no longer be experiencing it. Or you may notice there is something you want, but on some level, you are not ready (willing) to experience it yet. A typical example is that of someone claiming to want the perfect partner, but actually being so busy with other things that he/she is not willing to put up with another person. Try the following experiment:

Write down a few things you want.

Write down a few things you are willing to experience.

Write down a few things you don't want.

Write down a few things you are no longer willing to experience.

Only the things that appear on all four lists (on the last two lists as their opposites) will manifest in your life.

Summary

Emotion relates to all other subjects in this book. For example, emotion relates to attention in that what you feel directs where your attention goes. Vice-versa, attention also directs where your emotions go. Shift your attention, and your emotion shifts. Shift your emotion, and your attention shifts. The same thing applies to action, belief, core beliefs, and identity, as explained in the chapter on the five levels of reality creation. What you feel is an indicator of what belief or identity you are viewing the world from, and the identity you assume will reflect a real body sense. In this way, you can use your emotions as the navigational system they were meant to be, rather than suppressing emotions, trying to produce emotions, and all the other misguided habits we've been taught. Rather than creating emotions, use emotions as an indicator of what you are creating. Remember that it is impossible for harm to come to you in a state of emotional elation. It is not easy to get sick in a state of enthusiasm or to have learning difficulties in a state of interest. It is impossible to be hurt by someone you love, contrary to popular belief. Only something or someone you fear can hurt you. Emotions show you the motion your energy is taking. When you understand this, you can easily predict if good or bad things will happen in the next weeks of your life.

9

Attention and Reality

The Miracle of Attention

In reading this, you are becoming witness to one of the deepest, most profound, and most beautiful secrets of infinity. May this knowledge, secret and sacred, be treated as such. May you awaken to a more serene, powerful, and magical version of yourself.

Attention attracts reality. What you give attention to, you become more aware of—you learn more about. What you give more attention to you begin to trust. What you give even more attention to begins to solidify from subtle energy to material form. In this way, your attention directly affects what you experience as "my life," "my reality," "my goals," "my problems," "who I am," and "what I experience."

You have been looking at the world. You have probably been searching in the world. But rarely have you examined the tool with which you look, with which you search. You have been looking at the created world of objects and thoughts—the world of form—without noticing that which perceives and permeates form.

You resemble a lighthouse that is looking for light. Sound funny? Yes, but that's what you resemble. The lighthouse casts its beam across the land and the sea—searching, looking. Its light falls upon various objects. It is looking for light, not noticing that it is the source of light itself. Sometimes it feels cold and lonely because there's not much light to be found out there. Sometimes objects reflect its light, and it gets excited: "There it is! That's light!" Not noticing that it provided the attention—provided the light itself. It might become addicted to some of the objects, which only glow under its attention or light. One day, it finally notices another lighthouse on another island—another lighthouse with its own powerful, bright, shining source of light. And it stares in awe. "I've found it," our lighthouse says. "I've found the light." What it is still not noticing is that it has a source of light itself. It falls in love with that other lighthouse—a love darkened by the fact that it does not yet notice it's own light (although it's using it all the time). Such brilliance and warmth as is coming from the other lighthouse our lighthouse has (seemingly) never experienced. But there's a problem: The other lighthouse's light does not always shine on our lighthouse. Sometimes it shines elsewhere; sometimes its attention wanders to other objects or lighthouses. In these moments, when the other's light is shining somewhere else, our lighthouse becomes cold and lonely—even more cold than before, because now it really knows what being shone on feels like. The lighthouse begins looking for a solution, casting its lights on mentors, therapists, coaches, gurus, in search of light. If they want to make money off the poor little lighthouse, they will never tell her, let alone show her, that she is the source of that light herself. What she has been looking for all these years is what she has been looking with! How interesting is that? And then, one day, someone tells and shows her. But she doesn't believe it quite yet, because she can't see the light within herself. Why can't she see it? Because she is seeing with it. The only thing she can't see is who she really is, because she is looking from the viewpoint of who she really is and can't simultaneously look at and *as* something. But then she goes deep within and looks at herself. And she holds up mirrors. And she reflects on herself. And she begins to realize that what she was looking for was herself. And now that she has found it, her search has ended, and something new has begun. Playing has begun. She now knows with what brilliance she shines, and she uses this to illuminate the world. Replace "light beam" with "attention beam" and you have one of the keys to spiritual enlightenment and high magic. I mean this literally and practically.

One of the most overlooked, yet most important tools consciousness already has is its ability to focus, steer, shift, switch, and remove attention. Yes, what you focus on most does create your reality. What you focus on with your five senses you perceive, what you do not focus on or look at, you do not perceive. Attention determines what you perceive as real. The moment you do not look at something, it does not exist. Does this sound crazy? Don't take my word for it; contemplate it yourself. What you focus attention on first becomes more important, noticeable, and familiar. Keep on focusing, and it becomes more *feel-able*, solid, meaningful, and ultimately, more real. Beliefs are solidified thoughts that have been focused on so long and with such emotion and trust that they start accumulating similar thoughts and emotions and turn into a package of thought-forms we call, "belief," and then later, "knowledge," or "reality." Believing is the result of intense concentration. Once something is solidified into reality, you no longer have to consciously focus on it to uphold it. In a sense, it becomes a subconscious or half-conscious focus. On the other hand, things you no longer focus on start moving into the background, the backdrop of life, losing their relevance to your current experience, losing their importance and solidity until they cease to exist (as far as you're concerned).

Attention is awareness, and as such, the only tool you have that is completely unlimited. That means while material objects, thoughts, and everything else, are limited by time or space, attention can penetrate, surround, travel, and remove itself from anywhere. Your attention can travel anywhere. It has no limits. You are not aware of this because you use your attention in a rigid and similar way every day, which is the reason you experience a similar reality every day—a reality with not too many alterations or change—a reality that seems solid to you.

Attention is what you've wanted from others since you were a child, and you went to great lengths to get it. Attention from others is what you become dependent on or start demanding when you are unable to generate or give attention to yourself.

Having a problem simply means having your attention fixed on something and being unable to release the fixation of attention. Energy (real, measurable energy as in electricity or magnetism) and emotion go where attention goes.

Attention. You can make it travel anywhere, but you can also use it to find out anything about anything and anyone. Simply by placing your attention on something, you find out things you were not aware of before. Attention allows you to learn everything you want.

The attention of most people is not yet predominantly determined or steered by them, but by the outside world. Others control them. They react to impulses, advertisement, pressure, authority, media, schools, circumstances, indoctrination, hypnotic manipulation, and are pulled left and right by their own cravings and resistances. While applying attention exercises, you regain some of your self-determination and freedom. Rather than being the ball, you become the player. Since reality creation is a question of where you put your attention and what you invest attention in, training your attention is one of the most essential things you can do. You are then not working on what you perceive, but on the perceiver. When you train your attention, you are training the source, the cause of life—not the effect. You stop looking for the truth out there and start examining the tool with which you were searching—especially the user of that tool. If the user of the tool and the tool are misguided, the resulting craftsmanship will be flawed as well.

The most basic exercise is to simply focus your attention on something for a given time span. The longer you are able to do that, the more your willpower and self-determination grow. The willpower gained by this practice can be transferred to any other issue, thing, or subject. Up to now, your attention has been like a ping-pong ball; thrown back and forth by the hysterical rat race we laughingly call society. On the one hand, relaxation is required to focus attention, on the other hand, focus of attention leads to relaxation. Most meditation techniques are actually based on focusing attention one way or another. If you strip them from their ritualism, guru-ism, self-importance, and dogma, what actually remain are various methods to focus attention. That's the secret. Never mind all the beliefs, rules, and luggage religions, cults, and teachings bring with them. Cut to the chase and study the nature of attention and you have an all in one package. Focusing attention, no matter on what, will slow the flow of thoughts, calm the restless mind, and bring your energy back where it belongs: resting in the here and now, without a worry in the world. This is your most effortless and natural state. It is completely independent of the material world. It is only by independence from the world that you gain influence over the world. The power to change reality comes not from lack or neediness, but from happiness independent of outside circumstances or people. The mirror will not smile before you smile.

The second way to use attention is by de-focusing, by intentionally not focusing on anything specific. This puts attention on neutral, idle—on open loop. We will be talking about this incredibly relaxing behavior and its various uses later on.

The third way to consciously use attention is by focusing on something with the intention of getting into vibratory or energetic synchrony with it. You may not be totally aware of it yet, but energetically speaking, what you look at is looking at you! Sound spooky? It needn't. You live in a universe in which everything consists of energy. And it's all the same energy, vibrating at different frequencies, rates, or densities (depending on how you want to look at it). By solidifying thoughts, they become denser and turn into physical, material, everyday reality. And one of the methods by which you can solidify thought is through attention. Are you getting this? When you put attention on something with the intention of getting into energetic synchrony with it, you start vibrating at the same rate it is vibrating. Focus on something desired only for twenty seconds, and your energy starts synchronizing with its energy. Focus on something for sixty seconds and you vibrate at the same rate. Focus on something for three minutes, and you start to attract it into your life. This is what happens when you mix at-tention and in-tention. With at-tention, you are at the object; and with in-tention, you are *in* the object—you become the object.

"Does that mean all I have to do is stare at something, and I can have it?" In a sense, yes, that's what it means. If the intention behind the focusing is not counter-intentional, that's all you have to do. Attention will solidify subtle, etheric energy into material, physical form. This may sound highly esoteric and incredible, but it is easily demonstrable. This has been kept hidden for so long that I understand it sounds unusual. You know that when you focus on one thing, all other things retreat into the background. When you focus on a thought for a while, beginning to resonate with it, do you know what happens? You start noticing similar thoughts and feelings—other, additional, thoughts and feelings that vibrate similar to the thought you are focusing on. You start feeling that way. Most people can demonstrate this by thinking about sex. Focus on sexual thoughts for a moment, and notice what emotions and thoughts are attracted. When you focus a bit longer, more feelings and thoughts accumulate. You start feeling it in your body, whether it's something you like or not. Soon, not only more thoughts and feelings accumulate, and you start attracting real life experiences that resonate or match that focus. That's why, ultimately, you will get everything you fear, and everything you love. The law of correspondence doesn't care what energy you are putting out; it will simply reflect it. You will not experience all of it because your attention drifts, and before anything manifests, all the loves and hates you put out will have neutralized each other. But the purer forms of love and happiness, and the purer forms of fear and hatred, will reflect. For now, understand your attention as an electronic signal, and your reality as the feedback from the signal you are giving off.

What follows is your training program on the subject of attention. I pointed out the importance of attention to give you incentive to do this series of exercises. Realize that doing exercises is a form of guiding your attention in a self-determined manner—whether you are doing these exercises or any other practice. Therefore, if you have problems getting yourself to exercise, it's because your attention is not trained, not developed. Saying, "I can't do these exercises because I don't have the discipline" is like saying, "I can't exercise my attention because I don't have the attention." How silly is that? You are doing these exercises because you don't have the attention and you wish to live more of your potential. A few soothing words will make it easier for you: There is no such thing as being lazy or undisciplined. When it comes to things you love to do, things you associate something positive, happy, or easy, you have no problem with discipline. When you are in love with something or someone, you'll do anything, anytime, to spend time with that thing or person. Look at the things you spend the most time on—things that come easily. These things may be beneficial to you or not, but you believe them to be easy or relieving or interesting or fascinating. You don't have to rev up discipline to do them. It's the same with these exercises: They are easy, they will relieve you, they are interesting and fascinating, and you will learn more about life and the universe than everything than you learned in school (school does not teach attention, it teaches on what one is supposed to put attention). Don't force yourself to follow a rigid schedule in which you have to do these exercises. They are optional, not a must. Enjoy them. They are most appropriate when you feel like improving yourself. Understand that attention or focus does not have to mean effort or hard concentration. School and narrow-minded religions have taught that focusing means hard concentration. Look around the room. Spot an object. Notice how it's just there. It's already there. You don't have to concentrate or work hard to keep it there or perceive it. You don't have to attach it or hold onto it. All you have to do is receive. In this case, per-ceive is to re-ceive. Softly. Gently. It's already there. What's the rush? What's the rigidness to which society has conditioned you? Relax. Chill out. All is well and always will be. That's the difference between hard concentration and soft attention. In the former mode, these exercises will exhaust you. In the soft mode, these exercises will heighten your awareness, your enthusiasm, eagerness, energy, and effectiveness.

The Attention Training

How appropriate these exercises are depends, to some extent, on your emotional and mental state when you use them. Some are not appropriate when you are feeling low; some are not appropriate when you are feeling good. Feel and determine this for yourself.

Silence and Serenity

The very first exercise on attention is, oddly enough, about no-attention, about making no effort or putting attention on neutral. Neutral mode, or silent mode is not only the basis of all the following exercises, it is also the basis of life. It is silence without resistance, in the calming of body and mind, that you return to your native state—your natural, effortless state—the state in which connections to higher levels of being (soul, higher self) are allowed to return. The most powerful magic you will create will not be achieved by doing, but by non-doing. You have been conditioned to believe that you can only achieve something by doing something. This is why you run from place to place, person to person, object to object, working hard, trying to achieve something out there that can only be found in here. It is in silence and serenity that many problems fade away. You have also been conditioned to believe that well-being is a goal to be achieved. Nothing could be further from the truth. With this belief, you can be controlled. Someone offers you something by which you can supposedly get happy, and you follow it. But your natural state is happiness. Remember the cork in the water—it will always pop into its natural state of floating atop the water. On of mankind's greatest problems is its inability to sit silently. Silence is from where creativity and new ideas arise.

Isn't this the same exercise as the time out practice in the chapter on emotions? And isn't this the first step of the PURE technique? Is the author repeating himself? Yes, it is. And yes, he is. Now you might want to take this silence to a level deeper. Sit or lie and put your attention on neutral. Give up. Give up want, should, could, need, not-want, intend, plan, and try. Give up knowing. Give up effort. Give up focusing. Just sit and un-know everything. Forget everything you know. Softly observe what is there, without judgment, without label, without expectation. Stop knowing things about what you see in your surroundings. View them for the very first time. Neither fix on anything nor un-fix. See what happens when nothing happens. No need to think anything. If you do think something, allow that, too. Allow everything and anything. You needn't begin attempting to form a thought about anything. Just be.

In this exercise, you have experienced neutral attention. There are only three types of attention and three types of effect:

Attention charged with desire: Creates reality
Attention charged with resistance: Creates reality
Neutral attention (uncharged attention): Does not create reality.

In other words:

When you say, "Yes, I like that!" you are starting to attract it.
When you say, "No, I hate that," or "I'm afraid of that," you are starting to attract it.
When you are in neutral mode, saying neither one thing nor the other, you attract nothing.

Neutral attention (also called free attention) mode is very relaxing, isn't? An intelligence exists, much more vast and efficient than the immersed world-self you call "me"—the infinite intelligence that created everything with effortless ingenuity. You may call it God, the universe, all that is, the source, the field. When you are in neutral attention mode, neither desiring nor resisting, you are not creating anything. It is in this mode that the vast universal intelligence kicks in and does the creating for you. You are connected to this infinite field. It starts delivering experiences in accordance with your soul's highest purpose. This is why, when you spend time out of town, fully in the here and now, or in pure and simple happiness, that things start happening. Coincidences pop up mysteriously. Life changes. This is the true meaning of giving in to God's will or surrendering to a higher purpose. Some mistakenly think that surrender equals weakness or loss of power, when connecting to the source equals ultimate power.

It is also from the zero-point of neutral attention that it is easiest to shift into various charged attention modes (deliberate reality creation). Normally, your mind is so full of junk that it is difficult to hold a pure thought and manifest it into reality. But when you create something into emptiness, into a vacuum, you'll be surprised at how quickly it manifests. Since the thinking process is involved in reality creating, it might be a good idea to first calm the thinking down. A major reason we suppress our creative power is that our thinking is too chaotic, meaning we would create chaotic conditions if we allowed our power to increase. Slow down. Otherwise, you'll have thousands of thoughts that you are hardly aware of, and they'll flash by so quickly you can't view, let alone question or change them. If you remember anything from this section, it should be—relax. Any tension you did not deliberately create is an indicator that you do not trust the goodness, love, wisdom, and well-being of infinity. But infinity is not the stone cold, impersonal nature some shamans would have us believe; it is loving and positive. The polarity of evil only exists in this dimension. There is no real source of darkness, just like there is no darkness-switch, only a light-switch. Relax. Well-being is your birthright. You don't have to earn it. You don't have to wait for it. You don't have to postpone it until conditions are met. You don't have to let your bank account or partner's behavior dictate it. It is yours anytime. And you'll find it when you relax.

The Joker Card

I call this the joker card because you can pull it at anytime, to your benefit. It can benefit you today, in one year, in a hundred years, in a thousand years. It can benefit you for any situation in any given reality. That's the good thing about attention: It applies to any reality. The joker card will always make you more aware, shift your attention to the better, make you feel more in touch with yourself and the truth of your situation, more in touch with where you really want to go. It consists of three simple questions:

Question 1: Where is my attention now?
Question 2: Where could my attention be now?
Question 3: Where do I want my attention to be now?

That's it really. The only tricky bit is remembering to apply the card when it would come in handy. The card will prove to you that you are its sole owner; you are fully responsible for where your attention goes. The past is not responsible. Others are not responsible. Circumstances are not responsible. You decide where your attention goes. If you've reached a level of awareness where you have difficulty remembering such useful mind-tricks, you might want to make a card out of these three questions and carry them in your pocket or post them in your car. To deepen your understanding of the three questions, I'll go a bit into detail:

Question 1: "Where is my attention now?" You could also ask, "Where has my attention been up to now?" or "What have I been thinking about?" or "What is it that preoccupies me?" or "What am I doing?" These questions remove you from the habitual pattern of attention you are in, because you put attention on attention, instead of being immersed in it. You gain perspective and sink deeper into the here and now. Once you recognize where your attention actually is, that's all there is to it. You needn't invalidate yourself for where your attention has been. Invalidating it causes a deeper fixation on where your attention has been. Simply acknowledge.

Question 2: "Where could my attention be now?" You could also ask, "Where could my attention have been?" or "Where could my attention be today?" But the real question is, "Of the dozens of options I have—" No. "Of the millions—" No. "Of the trillions of options I have, where could my attention be?" Allow yourself to realize how habitual, rigid, and fixed your attention normally is. It could just as well be on millions of other things. Becoming aware of the infinite possibilities puts your previous focus into a new perspective. Your attention could be on other topics, other countries, other people, and other events. In this step, you may also allow your attention to wander to things you've rarely thought about or normally don't consider. This releases fixation on your previous focus, disperses attention, makes your previous focus less heavy, less serious, less charged, less important.

Question 3: "Where do I want my attention to be now?" "Where do I want my attention to be today?" "What do I really want to focus on?" Or, "What would feel good to look at or do?" Once you are more aware of where your attention has been and have dispersed it, leaving yourself feeling a bit lighter, you actually determine and decide where you want to put your attention now. Unless what you had attention on previously is charged with heavy emotion, you will find this easy. Shift your focus to something that is good for you because it feels good to you. You know it's something better when it feels lighter when you focus on it. Remember, you are not going to get any problem solved by only focusing on it. Consciousness always needs on example of what is wanted. Focus on what you don't want, and you get more of what you don't want. If you want to solve a problem, focus on what is wanted. Once you give your mind a proper example, it knows what to focus on and soon feels much better.

Attention on Attention

In this little gem of an exercise, you simply recognize attention as your only true source of awareness and support. It involves putting attention on attention, meaning you become aware of what you are aware of. This removes your viewpoint from identification with a reality to the source of that reality. Let's say you're at a gas station, waiting in line, and you start applying this exercise. "Okay, I'm aware that I am bored of standing in line because I've stood in line so many times. I'm aware that I don't expect anything interesting to happen here. Now I'm aware of that blue car over there. Now I am aware that I am judging that car. Now I am aware that my attention is going to a strange smell coming from behind me. Now I am aware that I am speculating about that person over there..." and so forth. Having attention on attention means that you are examining where your attention is going, thus regaining control over your attention.

Shifting Focus

An analogy: You are sitting in a restaurant in a foreign country, where you don't speak the language. So you'll have to point at things on the menu you want. But as the waiter arrives, you start pointing at things you don't want. "I do not want this. And this is bad. That tastes terrible. Don't bring me this please. I'd prefer not to have that." And all the while, you are pointing. What to you think this waiter is going to bring you? He will bring you what you indicated. He will bring you exactly what you do not want. Universal intelligence is like a copy machine that can only respond to what you activate with your attention. You cannot deactivate negative thoughts and emotions, because the moment you attempt it, you are focusing on them, warming them up, activating them. You can only deactivate the unwanted by activating what you want. And since like attracts like, it is much easier to attract more of what you want when you are already doing good, than it is from a state of lack or incompleteness. This is why the rich get richer and the poor get poorer. Things attract more of things that are like them. The rich person is surrounded by proof of his riches; his attention is on it all day, so he will attract more of it. The same goes for the poor. So when you are in unwanted states or conditions, the time will come where you will eventually have to shift your attention to what is wanted instead. Otherwise, you'll just keep producing and experiencing more of the same. Ever wonder why every day seems similar to the day before? Why thoughts keep repeating? Because you use your attention in a similar way each day. While it is true that many people can define what they want by first experiencing what they don't want, it is not necessary to draw out this method. You don't really have to have a car accident before you understand that you want to change your life. Admittedly, many people use this method, but it's not necessary. All you have to do is define what it is you do want. Here's a simple, yet important exercise:

1. Write down things you have been experiencing that you dislike or do not want.
2. For every point on your list, define and specify what you do want, instead.

That's all.

Sense and Sensuality

Many people claim that they are interested in their goals and desires but a closer look reveals that they don't give their desires any attention, credence, interest, or importance. Even people who know that attention creates reality continue to give what they desire little attention or appreciation. Maybe it's because they don't believe it's possible to achieve, but they don't believe it's possible to achieve because they haven't given it any attention. Some people even think they are focused on their desire when they are actually focused on the lack of their desire. There's a very subtle, but important difference between being focused on what you want and being focused on the lack of what you want. Noticing how it's not here yet is being focused on the lack of what is wanted, not on what is really wanted. If you are truly focusing on your desire or goal, then you are focusing on the things you would be focusing on if your desire were already manifest. In order to truly allow a reality to manifest as real, you have to become the reality, melt with it, become ever more familiar with it, explore it, feel it, dive into it—beforehand, already, in the first place, before you have proof of its reality. You have to make it real. Once you are so immersed in the desired reality that you feel it in your whole being, it is only a matter of time until physical reality reflects your energy state.

Yes, attention creates or attracts reality. But there are many ways to focus attention, many specific ways to sensually immerse or lose yourself in something. Some people automatically equate giving attention to looking at something. But the eyes are not the only means through which attention flows. And focusing attention does not only mean focusing on thoughts. There are many ways to energize or charge a reality, intensify attention, and become one with the object of desire. Here are a few ways to focus:

Visual: by looking at, seeing, focusing with the eyes, observing, inspecting, visually perceiving

Audio: by hearing, listening, focusing with the ears

Touch: by touching, handling, caressing, making physical contact

Emotion: by feeling, sensing, perceiving emotional energy

Memory: by remembering, recalling, going back to certain experiences

Verbal: by talking about, talking as, talking as-if, word, writing

Physical surrounding: by being at a place where something is happening, by being at the location

Social contacts: by spending time with people who represent or experience something

In behavior: by how you behave, by acting as if, by mannerisms and expression

Mentally: by thinking, thinking about, imagining, daydreaming, choosing thoughts

In intention: by willpower, by willing, by deciding, intending

In allowing: by surrendering to, giving in to, trusting

Bodily: by moving the body accordingly

In action: by acting on or as if you were sure it has happened or will certainly happen

In pure attention: by moving attention to things that are associated with it or by filtering things out that are associated with it

When you synchronize with any reality, you create it magically. But it's not so much magic; it's simply physics. You may begin to seem like a magical person compared to others once you apply it, because most people haven't been taught how the reality they were born into works. Give it a few more centuries, and mankind will understand how the viewing human is involved in what he is viewing. There is no such thing as a reality without someone to view that reality. Applying any of the above means allows you to focus attention. If you really want to immerse yourself, apply all of them on the same thing. Once you immerse yourself to an extent that you become the desired reality, you do not require any proof because you represent that reality—are identified with that reality—and it will be reflected in real life. You can only doubt something with which you are not completely familiar. Having given it enough attention, all unfamiliarity vanishes.

The Computer Screen Analogy

Start your computer or laptop and look at the screen. This screen represents your life and contains various icons from which to choose. These icons symbolically represent files or programs you can open. These icons are on your desktop (main screen) and lead to many sub-levels. In our analogy, the icons represent the many options you have in any given moment, the many experiential worlds you can enter. Which file or program you open is your choice. You have reasons for the choices you make, but these reasons are also your choice.

Now, without opening any file or program, move your mouse pointer over the icons. The mouse pointer represents your attention. With the mouse pointer, you choose something you want to activate. With your attention, you choose a reality you want to experience. Move over the icons with your pointer and feel the uncertainty. What should I open? What would I like? What is important? What happens when I open it? Can I close it after I open it? People ask themselves these questions when making choices or creating realities. If you put your mouse on one of the options and click once, the file does not open; it gets dark, or is emphasized. This represents focusing attention. Click it twice, and it opens. But let's rewind here for a second: In the practice of reality creation, most people don't even get as far as double-clicking a file, let alone using it. Often, they don't even get as far as clicking it once. Many people are not quite aware that they have the choice as to which file to focus on, or which reality they activate. Some don't even know that any other programs exist! And those who have finally found out that there are other options—plenty of them, in fact—are stuck, not knowing which file to open. "I don't know what I want," they say. Now, to demonstrate, move over the screen like someone who doesn't know what he wants—go here and there without actually opening any of the files. The screen remains unchanged. The few people who do know what they want sometimes do not have the courage to open the file. Why? Because it will change the screen and might open an array of boxes for which they don't feel prepared, or it might disturb the other open realities.

Now, choose any icon on your screen, which, in this analogy, will represent what you want. Put your mouse on it, but don't click on it yet. What you just did represents knowing what you really want. "Do I really want that? If I focus on that, I cannot simultaneously focus on other things. Well, I can, but it might take more effort. Will I be able to close it again after opening it? I don't know. Maybe I'll open something easier—some game program—maybe solitaire…to distract myself. I'll open something I already know, have already done thousands of times, because that's where I feel safe, that's where I feel at home. So I move the pointer away from what I want, back to a distraction program." Sound familiar? Most people would rather open something known but boring than something desired but unknown, unless they know the following for a fact. There is nothing to fear, and you can close any of the files anytime, just as you opened them. What you can open, you can also close. And what you can close you can reopen again. In infinity, nothing ever gets lost. You needn't attach to anything, because you can pick anything back up again. And you can get involved in anything, because you can let go of it anytime. Do you get the spirit of that?

Then there's the case of the person who is so much against a certain program that he keeps clicking on it! Get an icon that symbolically represents something you hate or resist. Being against it will cause you to constantly double click it in your anger. You don't even want to go there; you don't even want to keep warming it up, but you keep double-clicking it like mad, until dozens of it are open on your screen. To get a feeling of this, click on that icon you dislike a few times. "Damn you!" (Click, click) It opens. Click on it some more, but nothing improves; things get worse. You might even click so often and frantically that your entire screen freezes and you're unable to do anything. Now, relax and click it away again.

In front of you is the silent screen of options. There's the case of the person whose attention is so restless, impatient, and tense, that he haphazardly and randomly opens all kinds of icons. Demonstrate that for a second. Open a dozen or so files, quickly, so that they pile up on each other and it delays your computer. Get impatient about the hourglass icon. What you have now is chaos, overload. You will not be able to get involved in any of the programs. This might seem silly, but this is exactly how many people behave. They click too many options, they don't click at all, they have others click for them, or they click on the undesired.

Reality creation teaches none of this. It teaches the following: Look at the screen before you in a relaxed manner. Look at the options you have, at the cards you've been dealt. Choose what you like, what seems interesting or joyful to you. Gently put your mouse pointer on it. This represents deciding or choosing. Click it once. This represents putting attention on it. Double click it to open it. This represents intensifying attention on it. Start working with the program. This represents focusing in such away that you start interacting with it, feeling it, using it, getting to know it, experiencing it. This is how you make it come true. It takes one to know one. You can only experience that which you vibrate.

Now, something interesting: The most important part of this process is not the screen, not the files, and not even the attention. Turn your view to yourself. You. Your identity. The person applying attention. This is where it all comes from. Imagine this person sitting there, just waiting for something to happen on the screen. Waiting for reality to create on the screen. But it's not going to happen without this person.

Something even more interesting: Is there a world beyond the screen? Yes, for sure. Just turn around.

Decide and Focus

Decide what you are going to focus on next. When you've decided, focus on that. Then decide what you are going to focus on next. When you're sure you've made a decision, focus on that. Decide and focus. Repeat this several dozens of times, consecutively, until you feel in charge of your attention, more relaxed, more self-determined. The basic version of this exercise is done with relatively short time-spans of focusing on something and choosing the next thing on which to focus. It could be anything from three to twenty seconds before you make the next decision. In this exercise, make sure you are making a conscious decision before you focus on the next object or subject.

Losing Yourself in the Here and Now

Pick a neutral object, something you neither desire nor resist—maybe the rug, or a curtain, or anything relatively neutral. Examine it. Look at it. Go into detail on it. Notice things about it you hadn't noticed before. Learn something new about it. Discover something that has eluded your attention up 'til now. Become increasingly interested in it. Focus on it until you lose yourself in it, immerse yourself in it, until all boredom and impatience is gone, until you forget schedules, obligations, time, space, and even yourself. Once you experience that state of calm fascination, that high awareness in the here and now, do the same with another object. And then another object. Continue until your sense of well-being, calm, or excitement grows beyond what you formerly thought possible.

No need to worry: Since you are not immersing your focus with the intention of manifesting or emotionally synchronizing, and since you chose something neutral, you will not attract this into your life. What you are doing is similar to what you do when you lose yourself in a good book or an interesting movie. Sometimes you are so immersed in something that you don't even hear the phone ring. This exercise supports you in calming the mind, powering up your concentration, regaining the sense of fascination you had as a little child, regaining devotion and your ability to learn new things. What you are ultimately practicing is the universal method to enter any reality you want, learn anything you want, find out anything you want—simply through attention. It's how a soul enters a universe: It gets interested, it starts focusing, it comes closer, and closer, it goes into it, it loses itself in it (sometimes to the extent that it forgets everything outside of that reality).

This same exercise can be used with something you desire. When doing it on neutral things, you calm the mind and learn concentration. When doing it on a thing you desire, you do it with the intention of feeling more and more of it, of closing the gap between your vibration and its vibration (the gap between desire and belief). Close the gap between desire and belief and anything is possible. The longer you look the more familiar you become with it. The more familiar, the less fear, more trust. The more trust, the closer it comes. After you've gained some positive experience with neutral items, apply the same exercise to things you would like to have, own, or experience. The exercise can be applied to real life objects, visualized objects (thoughts), memories, words, or pictures.

Defragmenting Attention

Step 1: Write down questions you've been asking yourself, or take issues you've been thinking about and rephrase them to questions you want answered. Or simply create a list of questions you'd really like to have answered.

Step 2: Have another look at your questions and rephrase them if necessary, so that they become better, more intelligent questions. Upgrade the questions. For example, if you want to lose weight you could ask yourself "Why am I so fat?" or "Why am I overweight?" But there's a more intelligent question to ask. You could rephrase that into "How can I lose weight?" Or an even better question to ask is, "How can I lose weight and enjoy the process?" Are there any questions on your list that you can upgrade?

Step 3: Answer the questions yourself. Before looking outside yourself, ask yourself questions. Use your intuition, common sense, and your self-determined, spiritual authority to find answers that satisfy you. If you are not satisfied with an answer, think deeper or rephrase the question until you can answer it and feel good about the answer.

Step 4: Now, if you want, address the questions to others. You can also address the questions to your inner coach or higher self. Say the following prayer before falling asleep: "Thank you for showing me that these issues are already solved." (Repeat) Or you can visualize a representation of your higher self and ask the questions. Or you can ask the questions of someone you appreciate and respect. It's up to you. The point is that it gives your attention relief to have unanswered questions answered. Even more power is gained when you can answer them yourself.

Expansion of Awareness

Expanding awareness, consciousness, and perception is simply a matter of expanding attention to places it hasn't been before, or going into the unknown. In a very real sense, it means to perceive, see, hear, think, notice, discover, learn, feel, taste, smell, or sense something you haven't perceived, seen, heard, thought, noticed, discovered, learned, felt, tasted, smelled, or sensed before.

One of my many teachers (I forget who) once told me a beautiful metaphor to bring this point home. It went something like this: "I get lost in a dark cave. I don't know where to go, and I pray and ask for guidance. As my eyes get used to the darkness, a new awareness awakens in me, and I notice that one direction is brighter than the other. So I go in the direction of the light, and I come upon a wall of rock that reflects light. 'This must be it,' I think. 'This must be enlightenment.' But as my eyes get used to the soft light, a new awareness awakens, and I realize that the light is actually coming from a nearby water basin. 'That's it,' I think. 'That must be enlightenment.' But as I approach the pond, my eyes get used to the reflection in the water. A new awareness awakens, and I realize that the light is actually coming from the moon. 'That must be it,' I think. 'That must be enlightenment.' But as I observe the light of the moon, a new awareness awakens, and I realize that the light actually comes from the flames of the sun. 'That must be it,' I think…" And on the story goes.

This beautiful metaphor shows that there is no static end, that the journey of the soul is infinite. It also shows that when you think you finally have it, there is yet another exciting frontier to be discovered. The following exercise may seem simplistic, but it demonstrates expansion of awareness in its original sense, and aren't the most profound truths very simple indeed?

Pick out a single object and softly examine it until you notice five things about it that you haven't noticed before.

Look at the walls, the ceiling, and the floor of the room you are in and notice things you hadn't noticed before.

Look around your neighborhood and discover ten things about it you hadn't noticed before.

Pick out a memory in your mind. Go back to that memory. View it until you notice a few things about it you hadn't noticed before.

Observe another person and notice five things about that person you haven't noticed up to now.

Observe life and notice a hundred things about it that have evaded your attention up to now.

Learn a new word and use it.

Learn a new ability and apply it.

Put two things that are apparently the same (for example, two coins of the same currency and amount) side by side and discover five differences between the two.

Spot ten differences between today and yesterday.

Coming to Your Senses

Did you know there's a beautiful universe out there that you hardly notice? You might be so eager to achieve enlightenment that you don't even notice the breathtaking beauty at hand. You can expand the intensity of your earthly experience simply by paying more attention to the joys of your senses.

For a certain time span, focus your attention only on what you hear (blindfolding would support this focus).

For a certain time span, focus your attention only on what you see (plugging your ears would support this focus).

For a certain time span, focus your attention only on what you feel (deep breathing and silence would support this focus).

For a certain time span, focus your attention only on what you think (closing the eyes would support this focus).

For a certain time span, focus your attention only on what you smell and taste (foods would support this focus).

The purpose of sensory deprivation is to heighten your focus on the thought you've chosen. You will start experiencing life much more intensely.

Charged Attention and Neutral Attention

Attention particles can manifest in three ways:

- Charged with desire
- Charged with resistance
- Neutral (free attention)

Resistance comes before desire. Without negativity, you wouldn't have desires. Desires are created when you begin resisting or invalidating a current condition. Desire is actually resistance against not having, being, or doing something. The more discontent you become, the stronger your desire gets. The cycle of dissatisfaction/resistance leading to desire, leading to satisfaction, is what we call life. Negativity leads to desire, and desire eventually to fulfillment.

This is easy to grasp. Imagine a stick. One end of the stick (A) represents the unwanted condition (what you resist). The other end (B) represents the wanted condition (what you desire). In theory, all you have to do is take the journey from A to B to create reality according to your preference. What most people really do is remain on A, keep drumming up A, keep talking about A, keep thinking about A—although they claim to prefer B. Why? Because we've been taught that we can solve A by focusing on A or by resisting or fighting A. But the opposite is true, because resistance is an even more intense form of focus. The quickest way to B would be to start with B, to have it not only be the end, but also the beginning. It is impossible to reach B when your dominant thoughts, emotions, and vibrations rest in A.

Negatively charged attention means you cannot get your attention off something; you keep thinking about it, fearing it, getting angry or sad about it, or experiencing something as reality. Resistance, denial, creates this type of attention by pushing away or strongly saying no to something. The resistance itself creates a pressing energy beam towards the object or event that is resisted.

Positively charged attention happens when you desire something. When you desire something on a higher level than your current vibratory state, the desire creates a sort of pulling or attracting energy beam toward the object or event of desire.

No matter if your attention particles are positively or negatively charged, they are still condensing a reality in two different ways: Attention particles charged with resistance tend to push each other away, thus creating a pressing beam between you and what is perceived (this is why you feel what you resist as pressure). Attention particles charged with desire tend to attract each other and create an attractor beam between you and what is perceived (that's why you feel a pulling sensation when you desire something). Something that you desire and resist (feel ambivalent about) will create the most unpleasant of sensations: a pushing and pulling beam. Everything you desire and everything you resist will eventually come into your real life experience (unless the positive and negative attention particles neutralize each other before that).

Pressing beams (negatively charged attention) make the energy beam between you and the resisted object longer and press against the object. Take any object and start feeling strong resistance against it. Notice how your body subtly sways backward. Attracting beams (positively charged attention) make the energy beam between you and the desired object shorter and attract the perceived object. Take any object and start feeling strong desire for it. Notice how your body subtly sways forward. Exaggerated pressing and attracting beams will lead to loss of self-control.

Stand in front of a wall and project a pressing beam (resistance) towards it. Notice yourself moving backwards. If the pressing beam intensifies or gets longer, either the wall or you will have to move. In martial arts, you can apply this knowledge to overwhelm others. When someone is resisting you, and you let go of your own resistance towards him, he will lose his balance. If you place a pressing beam between a lightweight and a heavy object—let's say between a tree leaf and a block of concrete, the tree leaf will move. If the block of concrete resisted the leaf, the leaf would move. If the leaf resisted the block of concrete, it would still be the leaf that moved! If you stick the leaf to a skyscraper and let it fight the block of concrete, the block would move. The pressing beam elongates, and the tractor beam shortens. The beam doesn't care which end of the beam moves. The end with the least physical inertia moves. When you create an attractor beam of desire, the object you desire will move towards you if its relative physical inertia is smaller than yours. If you are smaller, you will have to move towards the object. Again, this boils down to the following: To fulfill a desired reality, choose a smaller one, or get bigger yourself.

Identity, or the "I am," is a sphere of consciousness surrounded by various things. The stability with which "I" can keep its place while projecting tractor and pressing beams (vibratory energy) to affect other people, events, or objects depends on the identity's inertia, meaning his conviction of the rightness of his beliefs. If one's own belief is weak, then sending out energy beams (of desire and resistance) will cause the beams sent back to move or shift the identity that sent them out. Deep beliefs have the advantage, in that you can consistently create a certain reality. They have the disadvantage in that you are limited to a certain viewpoint. On the bright side, deep believers are very successful people. On the dark side, they are fanatics.

Desire and resistance resemble the plus and minus charge of electricity. When you want something that is not or do not want something that is, you get negatively charged attention. Negatively charged attention condenses the reality you resist, making it come alive. What you resist will persist. When you want something that is or don't want something and it is not, you get positively charged attention. Positively charged attention condenses the reality you desire. What you love, you get.

The more charged attention is, the more effort you need to neutralize it (regain conscious command over it) and reintegrate it into universal consciousness (dissolve it). If the charge is higher than the effort you invest, attention fixes, becomes locked, or addicted. If it fixes over a longer period, it is abandoned and forgotten (without being reintegrated) and radiates a foulness, dullness, or unpleasantness from sub-aware levels of being. Putting fresh attention on a non-integrated subject would warm the subject back up. This can lead to temporary emotional pain. Putting more attention on the subject will allow it to re-integrate again, though.

Charged attention needs to be neutralized before it can be re-integrated. Until then, it hangs around the "I am" as energy-clouds of impression (called mind or identity). The interaction of the charged attention units is what causes restlessness of thoughts and the vicissitudes of emotions. Emotions are merely indicators of which path you are on—one leading to the manifestation of a desire or the manifestation of a fear or resistance.

There are many ways to neutralize charged attention. One is to retreat to a place where nothing can re-charge your attention. If isolationism is not for you, the meditation, self-examination, and attention exercises that follow will help you neutralize the charged attention of which you've been a reactive victim. Creation is a path into the world, and de-creation (neutral attention) is a path back to the source.

Neutral attention can be delegated by a nearly identity-less “I am,” effortlessly. What’s amusing is that there are states of being in which you have the power to create anything you want, but in these states, you are no longer interested in creating such things. From a charged state and a fixed identity, you might desire fame and fortune. From a light state of almost no identity, in which neutral attention is not so much a beam, but more an awareness and an interface between the non-dimensional infinity and dimensional creation. Only when an identity is assumed, or something perceived is judged or labeled, does attention become a beam. Neutral attention exerts neither pressure nor attraction on what is perceived. No label is added to what is perceived. Nearly no reaction takes place. The information perceived by this silent witness is transferred to universal intelligence immediately. The observer, in a state of neutral attention, is neither attracted nor repelled, but directed by the will of the “I am.” The more neutral attention one has, the easier it is to create and act deliberately.

Exercise: Neutralizing Attention

Both negatively and positively charged attention could cause troubles. Positively charged attention becomes a limitation when you desire something on a higher level than you are willing to receive, a higher level than your own vibratory level. This creates a longing, a craving—desperately wanting or needing—and thus a desire that remains unfulfilled. One way of neutralizing this issue has already been discussed in Aligning Desire and Belief, Scaling, and Releasing Fixed Attention.

The Opposites Technique

Take a piece of paper and draw a horizontal line or scale that goes from minus ten to plus ten. Zero is the point of neutral attention. The minus numbers are points of resistance and fear, increasing to ten. The plus numbers are points of desire, increasing to outright craving at number ten. Write down a few examples of various points at the scale. For example, on minus one, you might have writing tax statements, if that’s something you don’t particularly enjoy. If you’re afraid of spiders, you might have that on minus five. If you’re terrified of heights, that might be minus eight. If you hate certain people, you may place them at minus four. Your favorite meal might be plus one. An attractive person of the preferred sex may be at plus four. Being rich might be at plus six. Your addiction to chocolate may be at plus seven. And so on.

Now, as you know from physics, positively charged energy is neutralized by negatively charged energy, and negatively charged energy is neutralized by positively charged energy. So, as crazy as it may sound, you can neutralize the negatives by projecting positive energy, and vice-versa. Let's say you want to neutralize charged attention on spiders or fear of spiders. You'd start projecting and associating positive things with spiders, visualizing spiders as cute, nice, cuddly, sweet, friendly, teddy-bear-like, tiny, comfy, cozy spiders. At first you'd hit on doubts and resistances. Maybe you'd even find yourself unwilling to do this at first. But as you continue, spiders start moving up the scale—to minus four, then to minus three, to minus two, to minus one, and finally, to zero, to neutral. When you neutralize attention, you feel a great sense of relief; a fear is overcome. Now, if you continue to project desire, longing, and wanting on spiders, it would move even further up the scale, and your neutral feeling about spiders would become a positive one. With some issues, such as pain or war, you would not want to do that. Maybe you wouldn't even want to move such issues to neutral, but you could at least move a painful issue from minus ten to minus three—to ease up on it a bit, so that it did not dominate your attention. Now, vice-versa, let's say you have a craving of chocolate on level seven, and you would like to ease up on that a bit. You would simply project resistance, negative association, on it. You'd start thinking about it as sickening, fattening, about vomiting in connection with spoiled chocolate, poisoned chocolate, unhealthy chocolate, dangerous chocolate, and so forth and so on. Initially, you'd have doubts, but as you continued to focus, chocolate would move down to plus five, plus three, plus one, and finally, it would neutralize at zero. If, after you lost your craving, you continued with this focus, it would actually turn into a resistance towards chocolate. So stop the exercise before that happens. Having it on neutral or even plus one or two is enough not to have your attention field dominated by it. You have just learned the secrets of neutralizing attention, and the usefulness of pressing and attracting beams.

The Camera Technique

Neutral attention is the only type of attention that does not attract some kind of reality. What you say yes to, you attract, what you say no to, you attract. But what you are neutral on, you do not attract. Neutral attention is your point of relaxation. It is also where those people are headed who seek spiritual realms beyond this reality. Zero-point awareness is the gate to realities beyond the world of creation. That's why any issue you view with completely neutral attention, without pushing it away or pulling it to you, will neutralize—another way to neutralize charged issues. Any unwanted thoughts you view like this for a while will naturally evaporate. Neutral attention is similar to a movie-camera on a film-set. Everyone on the film set is focused on one thing or another. The camera is the only viewpoint that sees the film in its entirety and sees everything as it is. The camera does not have any preferences or resistances, and unless it's zoomed, it doesn't focus on anything, but takes the whole picture as it truly is. Neutral attention is the most useful sort of attention. Positively charged attention, meaning attention that is charged with a desire for something, is also very useful, but only when you are on the appropriate level to receive what you desire. Anything you desire, you start attracting. But with many people, it's not the wanting, intending, or desiring that's the problem, but being in a state where one allows oneself to receive what was attracted.

Scale of Attention

Undefined awareness/ universal consciousness/ infinity/ the field

Neutral attention

Charged attention

Fixed attention

Decaying attention

The difference between neutral attention and undefined, infinite awareness is that neutral attention can be contained within a creation.

Zero-Point Meditation

Zero-point or infinite awareness can be reached in the meditative practice of observing without reacting or evaluating. This is an even deeper version of time out and silence and serenity. Close your eyes and observe the stream of thought without being caught up in any of them. Gradually, stop reacting to your thinking. As long as attention doesn't fix, you remain centered, rooted; source, witness and thoughts come and go. When attention starts fixing to a thought, you start flowing with that thought. Imagine a river and a boat. When you sit at the riverbed, the boat floats by and disappears down the stream. That's meditation. Watch the boat a bit longer; walk with the boat along the riverside. That's observation. Get into the boat and start paddling against the stream. That's the struggle of life. Get into the boat and let yourself be carried with the stream. That's the joyride of life. Retreat from the stream of consciousness for a while and be aware; that is peaceful meditation, and it will neutralize charged attention.

Releasing Fixed Attention

You can actually release any unwanted reality by deliberately and consciously focusing your attention on the unwanted reality and alternating between that and deliberately focusing on something else. Switch back and forth between the object, or issue, your attention has been fixed on and that something else (preferably something neutral) until the fixation is released. From the state of neutral attention, put your attention on whatever it is you want and stay there until the desired reality manifests. It is that easy. The releasing of fixed attention can be done in writing, speaking, acting, or by focusing the mind. So if you're doing it in writing, you would describe the problem, then describe an object in the room, then, once your attention is totally there, switch back to describing the problem, and then back to another object, and so forth, alternating many times until you've switched the problem on and off so often that you've overcome it. This will work with anything, but it is recommended to first try it out on issues that are not highly charged (e.g. a headache, an unwanted bill, a slight mishap) before you apply it to harder subjects.

The Depolarization Technique

Any desire you have polarizes you automatically. Anytime you set a goal or state what is wanted, you polarize between the current state and the desired state. This is the A to B stick mentioned earlier. Any goal about being, doing, or having something automatically creates this tension. Tension motivates you to follow the goal. When you reach the goal, the tension disappears; both poles disappear into emptiness. Duplicating the goal makes the whole construct disappear. Polarities merge and are replaced with relief. The structure of any goal or desire is a triad of current state, desired state, and tension. For example, saying, "I want a career change," automatically creates the other two objects: "I am unhappy with my current job," and the tension between the two. Three methods will make the triad disappear:

1. To reach the goal/ fulfill the desired reality
2. To reach/ manifest the desired reality in your imagination
3. To cancel the desired reality

Most people are already familiar with the first method, which they use on a daily basis. The second method involves duplicating the desired result in your imagination, as if you were already experiencing it. If you duplicate it properly, the goals construct will fall apart. Consciousness does not differentiate between real and imagined and feels the same relief whether the goal was achieved in physical or imagined reality. Most people are also familiar with method three. It simply means canceling the desire or goal, deciding it is no longer your desire (without labeling this as a loss or using it as a cause for self-invalidation). These are three viable paths to release tension-energy or neutralize attention.

Sexual energy offers a good analogy to this:

Desire: Sex
Current State: No Sex
Feeling: Sexual Tension

Method 1: To have sex with someone in physical reality

Method 2: Do have sex with someone in Imagination (masturbation)
Method 3: Give up desiring sex (diverting attention elsewhere)

All three methods lead the tension of polarity to fall apart. In other words, if there is too much exhaustion and unhappiness in your life, use one of these three paths to relieve yourself. Reach the goal, or give it up without regret. Get into the state of having reached the goal, reach it, or give it up. Spending too much time in tension may cost too much energy.

What happens to the desires and goals not handled by one of these three methods neither achieved, experienced, nor given up? Nothing. They are still within you and need energy (attention) to be sustained. It takes a lot of energy to have a desire you don't believe in. If you are not able to reach it (mentally or in physical reality), stop acting as if you are. Or experience fulfillment mentally and emotionally. If you do that and experience the relief inwardly, physical reality will respond to the emotional vibration of fulfillment by reflecting new events. Any desire that has not been handled binds attention, decreases your ability to handle life, decreases your self-worth, and can exhaust you.

In this exercise, you will learn depolarization and handling unfinished cycles of creation. An unfinished cycle of creation is a goal you have set that hasn't been fulfilled yet. It is not a goal you have willingly cancelled. These unfinished cycles of creation are still hanging around your energy field, pulling attention. By procrastinating and postponing things, these fields of tension do not disappear. They stack up until they start feeling like burdens. If you wish to experience less burden and tension, finish the unfinished. Define a limited number of more realistic goals (those you really believe you can reach), or bring yourself up to speed with your goals. Only when you are bored by all the peace and emptiness, should you start going for higher challenges again.

1. List things your attention has been on recently. List things that are unfinished. List things you keep postponing. List things you are unable to begin. List things you feel unable to stop doing. List things you have been resisting.

2. Rate each item on your list for importance. Assign 1 to "very unimportant" and 5 to "very important" or any number in between.

3. Rate each item for its current state. Assign 1 to "unfinished" and 5 to "taken care of" or "ideal state" or any number in between.

4. Mark all the important items and the unfinished items. Number combinations such as 5-1, 5-2, 4-1, and 4-2 are your priority items, which take the most attention-energy.

5. Cross out all items that are so unimportant or finished that they no longer require your attention. Cancel them.

6. Review your new list and choose the easiest item to do, and do it immediately. Right now. Without procrastination. Do not continue reading before it is done.

7. Later on, take the next easiest item and take care of it immediately. Do this for the rest of your list. After you are done with your list, make a new list: List desires you have (some items from the last list may reappear). Decide for each desire if you are going to a) reach it, b) fulfill it in your imagination, or c) cancel it. Then proceed as just defined. You will start experiencing more energy than ever before.

Attention and Manipulation

An understanding of the nature of attention can be and has been used on a regular basis for the manipulation of people, mass-consciousness, and perception of reality. In a wider sense, any deliberate use of attention is a manipulation, but what we are talking about is using attention as a weapon. Politicians, media, and advertisers use a few specific techniques. This section does not imply that you are a victim of such institutions. If you do not resonate with a certain reality, if you do not hold fear in you, or if you are aware of these techniques, others cannot manipulate you. This section does not invite you to use manipulative practices on others, as what you give to the world is what you get back. Here are only a few:

Diverting attention: In order to cover something up, attention is diverted to something else. An example: In order to cover up a big lie, I offer or admit to a lesser lie. Attention is focused on the lesser lie, away from the bigger lie. Another example: A politician wants to divert attention from problems in his country or something bad he did, and creates problems in another country. If you want to find out how easy it is to lead people's attention, stop on any street in the city, and look into the sky for a while. Others will begin looking up, too.

Problem-Reaction-Solution: Someone who wants to sell something or have others believe something creates a problem, has others react, and then offers a solution. This technique has the problem and solution coming from the same source without people being aware of it. Examples: A religious cult wanting to recruit followers tests people to reveal (create) their problems. Then they offer the solution. Another example: You visit a dentist. Because the dentist needs more money, he exaggerates the services you require. Yet another example: A government stages a terrorist attack on itself (blaming others) to justify attacking another country. Or an anti-computer-virus company creates computer viruses to increase business.

Mystery Creator: Someone creates mystery in order to attract attention. Mystery hooks attention. If something is presented with a few interesting points, but many unknowns, attention is often sucked into the subject, causing hours, days, or even a lifetime of preoccupation. Example: Someone makes a few remarks concerning a subject, intentionally withholding the rest, in order to get someone interested. Then, information is revealed piece by piece to keep the person on the hook.

Give and Withdraw: Attention is given to someone, and then withdrawn. This is another way to fix someone's attention. Example: A man gives a woman more love, attention, care, and touch than she has received in years. She had been thirsting for it, now it is given. Once she becomes addicted to the attention, he withdraws it, making her run after him.

Television BPM: BPM—"beliefs per minute." Watch any random TV show, and you will notice the show offering dozens, sometimes hundreds of beliefs per minute, most of which you don't even want to have. It is by your agreement and consent that such beliefs become your own or are reinforced. One method to implant beliefs is by enthralling, fascinating, or getting you emotionally charged (by picture, music, color, stimulation) and then offering certain concepts and beliefs. Once you are aware that beliefs don't choose you but you them, this method no longer works. If you are an aware person, you can watch anything you want without it having detrimental effects on you.

Finally, another way is by offering what someone's attention is already on: Someone notices what someone else's attention is on, and offers it (or acts like he/ she can offer it. Example: A salesman who preys on people in desperate need. A flirter who notices what the desired person is interested in, and acts as if he is interested, too.

Again, you don't need to protect yourself from any of this if you are aware of it. Sometimes you will even allow yourself to be manipulated—by a nice person of the preferred sex, for example. Protection implies that you are not the source of reality, but a victim, which you are not. It can, however, be interesting to observe how others let themselves be manipulated.

Daily Intention

If there's only one exercise that you choose to do regularly, make it this one. It's a very simple one, and it is intended to get you used to giving your attention to what is wanted rather than what is unwanted. The exercise involves writing down what you want, intend, or wouldn't mind happening for any given day. It is done on a regular basis. You write down big things and little things, realistic things and unrealistic things. Things you would like to be, do, and have. There's one major rule: Let go of any expectation that these things must happen, or how or when or if they will happen. You are simply intending what would be nice, not what must happen. You don't go through the day demanding evidence. Many of the things will not happen, but they will raise your vibration while you write them down and think about them. Some will happen, mostly things you have written with a light and playful heart, without any pressure. This exercise obscures the differences between "realistic" and "unrealistic." You write down things that might happen anyway, and things that are a bit more far out. The list may be short or long, depending on your mood. It may be done the night before or in the morning. It may contain specifics or be kept general. Write the intentions in past tense. Here's an example of a daily intention list:

Took the car to the repair shop
Got my hair cut
Met someone interesting
Gave Susan more love than she's ever received
Surprisingly got three new customers
I got money unexpectedly
I felt a lot of energy
I had an out of body experience
My cat recovered

Remember: The only reason we keep experiencing the same things is that we keep using attention in the same way, investing it in the same things, repeatedly. If you want to experience everything new, learn to use your attention in a different way.

The Twenty-second Look

Do you recall being a child and having a skin irritation or bad tooth and continuing to meddle and play with it, although leaving it alone would give the most relief? Remember rubbing it until it hurt more? It's strangely appealing, isn't it? Same thing with rubbing your thumb on sandpaper. It starts out feeling pleasant and interesting, so you rub some more, and more, and you miss the point where you ought to stop, and your hand gets bloody, but you continue anyway. This is the way many people handle attention. They say they want less pain and more joy, but keep rubbing it in by keeping their gaze and interest fixed on it.

The twenty-second look is very easy to do and facilitates rapid change. It simply involves looking at various things for twenty seconds—nice things out there, and nice things in here. Nice buildings, cars, people, nature, pictures, nice thoughts, and fantasies. Why twenty seconds? Because twenty seconds is what is needed to start getting into vibratory synchrony with something and feeling it, and because twenty seconds is too short to let doubts and second-thoughts about what is being looked to come up. Some people will notice how things that are focused on too long evoke secondary thoughts (doubts). The twenty-second quickie doesn't allow for that type of stuff. Look at something for about twenty seconds (you don't need a stopwatch on this), and let go. Then either you focus the next thing for twenty seconds, and the next, and the next, and the next, until you get into a very positive flow or you take a break from focusing and enjoy your rapidly changed state. It only took twenty seconds to make a shift; even if that shift is small, it is a nearly immediate shift. If beginning this exercise in an abysmal state, you might need a few extra rounds to get back up to speed with your true self. If you make this simple little exercise your weekly exercise, you will stop looking for negative things to focus on and go for what's beautiful and good. Actually, RC teaches that you don't have to deal with anything you don't like (one exception: things that force themselves into your view repeatedly need some attention).

What you look at grows. This explains why the rich get richer and why making the second million is so much easier than the first. Once one has the first million, one is surrounded by beautiful things and doesn't need to put any effort into noticing them. If you don't have the million, things you dislike and believe you are forced to look at might surround you. Notice that there is beauty for you to look at, anyway. Label your current surroundings in a friendlier manner and use your imagination to fill in the rest. If you don't have beauty surrounding you, you can still claim it in your imagination and get in sync with it there. After you've gained some confidence in being able to move your attention from the unwanted to the wanted, you might go to the next step: Noticing the one who is looking. This is the level of identity from which attention comes in the first place. To change identity goes deeper than shifting attention, because attention flows automatically to the right places, with less necessity of having to shift it consciously.

Scripting

Scripting is the method of writing a movie script to a situation you want to manifest as reality. You are in the habit of looking at what was and what is. Scripting will help you to look at what is wanted and visualize details of your desires. It will help you test the effects of focusing without resistance.

Scripting works to manifest reality when you are not concerned with manifestation, but with writing the script. You don't do scripting in a state of tension, stress, "must have," or "must get." You write for the fun of it, with ease and creativity. For scripting, you simply choose a topic you would like to experience as reality and start writing about it as a story with dialogues and sceneries. It is written in the past tense and taken for granted as real. Take on the viewpoint that you are a scriptwriter and everything you write manifests (so be mindful of what you write). If you enjoy writing, or if writing is easier for you than visualizing, you can script your whole life, you can script specific situations or topics, or you can script instead of writing in your diary (past) or your weekly planner (present). Your only job is to have fun writing the script, the rest is taken care of by the producers, directors, and actors (infinity). If you focus on things softly (without need), without resistance against the negative, and when you are clear about what you want, it comes to you easily. Playfulness, not seriousness, is the magic of reality creation. Seriousness activates dark and sinister beliefs. You may integrate things you know will happen or which you are going to do, anyway, and mix them with creative additions, or you may make up the whole thing. You are not viewing this is "making something up," but actually allowing the keys of your keyboard or the tip of your pen to be magical.

Scripting touches on many subjects, some of which I will only briefly outline. It will show you how rigid, repetitive, and uncreative one's thinking (and thus one's day) used to be. It will also show you that writing about what is wanted, rather than what happened, is a more effective way of clearing the mind. The more you focus on a topic, the more details you add to it, the quicker the energy moves. With some practice, you will get a feel of how you are moving energy and what type of writing moves energy. You will be delighted to notice how things you wrote come about, sometimes exactly as you wrote them. You are the author of your life.

10

Beliefs and Reality

Beliefs attract reality. This is no contradiction to the former chapters, but simply another way of looking at things. You may choose from which viewpoint (identity, attention, emotion, or belief creates reality) you wish to approach reality creation, or you may combine all methods. Beliefs are superior to emotions in that they determine what something feels like. In this sense, they cause emotions. Belief also determines where your attention goes and does not go. You can also view it the other way around: Attention and emotion cause or create a belief, for the more attention and feeling you give a thought form, the more it becomes a belief. It's a two-way street. This is not meant to confuse you. How elements relate and how they apply to parallel universe surfing will become clear to you.

What is a belief, anyway? It is a thought you keep thinking, whether you are fully aware of it or not. Many teachers talk about subconscious or unwitting beliefs being the most powerful because you are not aware of them. But it is not really that you are unaware of them, but that you hold them to be so true that you do not view them as beliefs. In this sense there really is no such thing as unconscious or sub-level-awareness or unwitting beliefs, but only things that appear so real to you it never occurs that it's only a belief, only one way of seeing reality. Imagine that beliefs are like sunglasses. You often do not look at the glasses themselves, but *through* the glasses at the world. While the sunglasses may be apparent for outside viewers, they are only half-apparent to you. You say, "This is what reality looks like," "This is what is real," without noticing that it only looks that way through the sunglasses. However, there's more to beliefs than that: You are wearing magnetic sunglasses, which attract events matching the belief. A belief is nothing more than a thought. You think a thought. And when you think it more often, this thought accumulates other thoughts on a similar vibratory level. When a thought grows big enough, we call it a belief. When a thought starts running on automatic, and is pushed out of conscious awareness, we call it a subconscious belief. A core belief is a fundamental definition, a presupposition of reality, something you term "knowledge," or "truth"—something you are so convinced of you don't even question it. A belief is any thought, statement (which is a verbalized belief), mental image, or definition of what is and what is not. In that sense, anything you think and say is a belief and based on other beliefs. A core belief is something on which many beliefs are based. RC involves recognizing what we thought of as fact as merely a belief we are projecting, and shifting that to a preferred belief.

It is common knowledge that your behavior and actions are driven by your emotions. What is less known, but coming more and more to the awareness of this planet is that your emotions are driven by your beliefs. Beliefs, emotions, and actions form a triad, a triangle—influencing and confirming each other. You believe something, and that creates a feeling. You feel something, and that creates an action. You act on something, experience it, and that confirms a belief.

Most people think seeing is believing. What they say is, "I'll believe it when I see it." Or, "I believe this, because I experienced that." Or, "I am this way because that happened." In the reality creation worldview, it's the other way around. In our view, believing is seeing. First, you have to believe something, then you will see it, then you will experience it. Because you believe something, you experience it. Most people will disagree, but that doesn't change the demonstrable fact that this view of things is more workable and effective. When you experience something bad, there was a thought, a suspicion, or a labeling that came before. Or there was a judgment of it while it happened that made it seem a bad experience. But no two people will experience the same thing the same way. They will experience it according to their beliefs or judgments. The way they label the event will determine how the event turns out for them. Since everything is energy, everything is essentially neutral, neither good nor bad. The way you label events will determine how they turn out for you, no matter how these events turn out for others. On many accounts, I've experienced myself and others involved in disasters or accidents that did not affect us because we didn't believe they would.

What you term "thought," "idea," "opinion," "knowledge," "fact," "concept," "paradigm" is a belief. These are different ways to refer to beliefs; sometimes using these expressions masks the fact that they are simply beliefs. Reality creation acknowledges some fundamental paradigms of existence, but these are beliefs, nonetheless. And beliefs can be changed. In reality creation, beliefs are like cars. They take you from one place to another, but once you no longer like the car, or it doesn't work anymore, you can easily replace it. You are not forced to drive the same car for the rest of your life.

Before we talk about how beliefs are created to attract what you want in your life, let's talk about how to uncover and solve unwanted belief constructs. An important discernment: When we are talking about beliefs, we are not talking about what you think you believe or want to believe, but about what you really believe. There's often a major difference. It's often easier to find out what someone believes by observing his experience than having him tell you what he believes.

The uncovering of limiting beliefs is not to be applied as a witch-hunt. It is often by looking for limiting beliefs that limiting beliefs are created in the first place. This is what many teachings fail to point out. Do not create the belief "I have a bunch of limiting beliefs I need to uncover before I can be myself." Limiting beliefs are only to be looked for when you are in a low or problematic state or experiencing the repetition of a problem. As we mentioned, you are mostly not looking *at* your beliefs but *as* them. That's why it's helpful to write them down. If you write them out on paper, you have an easier time viewing them. Since your beliefs are reflected as outside reality, you can use outside reality to determine what you really believe. You don't have to dig into the distant past to find them. Look around at what you are experiencing, and it's obvious what you believe. Presupposing that you have a bunch of deep, super-subconscious beliefs to figure out or release before you can move on is a very limiting belief in itself. Believing you have to uncover something you don't know is yet another limiting belief. Use the belief techniques in the awareness that what you truly believe is reflected in your daily life and does not need much searching.

Another principle many teachings fail to point out is that there are no such things as sabotaging beliefs. All beliefs are taken on with a positive intent connected to survival, protection, or to enable you to experience something. Presupposing that someone would secretly sabotage himself, as many therapies and New Age teachings do is nonsensical. Every belief has its benefit and its pay-off, and every belief serves you in a certain way. Finding out how a belief labeled "negative" actually serves you is a huge step to releasing that belief. Resistance presupposes you did not create it or did not create it for a good reason. But if you did not create it, you are not going to be able or willing to de-create it. This is where responsibility comes into play. You will be able to de-create something you admit to having created, assumed, or taken over for a good reason.

Releasing Beliefs

If you wish an undesired experience not to happen anymore, you have to find out what you want instead, and apply PURE to it. If that is too simple or quick for you, you may walk the slower path by uncovering the beliefs creating the experience.

First, choose a topic about which you would like to uncover your beliefs. Then, list your beliefs as answers to the following questions:

Question 1: What would someone experiencing this have to believe?
Question 2: What would someone doing this have to believe?
Question 3: What would someone feeling this have to believe?
Question 4: What are my thoughts about this issue?
Question 5: What am I trying to be right about? What am I making others wrong about?

In answering these questions, you write down a list of beliefs. Writing is a more powerful focus than thinking. Thoughts are vague, ever changing, and hardly observable. You have to get it all out on paper.

Next, deepen your exploration of beliefs and start unraveling or neutralizing them by questioning your list of beliefs in the following way (write down the answers as additions to your list):

Question 6: How can I prove this statement true? (This question will eventually lead you to core beliefs.)

Question 7: What is the payoff for believing this? What benefit am I getting for believing this? How is this belief serving me? What can I be right about if I continue to create this?

Once you have the whole list, we can begin to play. I like to write my beliefs, not as a list, but as different circles or bubbles to indicate the thought forms, and then from these circles, I associate beliefs connected each. Any judgment or association to a belief is yet another belief supporting the original one. Now, on this whole list or collection of circles, you will find statements that evoke emotional reactions within you. Sometimes the reactions occur when you rephrase a statement. Anyway, the ones you react to are more in the direction of core beliefs than other statements. If you are sensitive enough, you can actually feel how some thoughts have more weight than others do. It is these beliefs that need to be acknowledged (as regards their usefulness) and then replaced. But if you want to do a thorough job, you will acknowledge and replace all of them. At least, mark ones you feel have the most weight on your reality. You may also want to ask yourself which beliefs were freely chosen by yourself, and which beliefs were adopted from an outside source. If you want to do a little extra, you may number them by the degree of conviction in which you believe them, 10 being "I am totally convinced this is true," and 1 being "I totally doubt this is true." This intermediate exercise will help you desensitize the beliefs even further.

Finally, after you've examined and acknowledged each belief, noticing the connections, contradictions, and relations of these thoughts, it is time to replace them. On a separate piece of paper, write for the core beliefs—or in the long version of the exercise—for *every* belief what you want to think or believe instead. Write down thoughts that should replace the old thoughts. And if you want these new beliefs to stick, write down positive thoughts that are realistic, authentic, and easy to believe.

Creating New Beliefs

Having completed the former exercise, the next step is to take the most important new beliefs and create a thought out of them, a mental image, visualization, a daydream, a fantasy, a visualized representation of that belief. Imagine what your life would be like and what you would be doing if that belief were true. Do not have your visualizations be effortful; allow pictures representing the beliefs to come up by themselves. Once you have imagined, enter the embodied viewpoint of the person experiencing that reality.

The next step is to fill these new thoughts with emotion. Focus on a thought creates a new belief. Emotion activates it, and action grounds the new belief. Do whatever you must to feel joy, enthusiasm, gratitude, or excitement while visualizing the new belief. Do not force or create emotion; allow the emotion to well up because of the imagines you are experiencing.

The final step of creating a new belief has two variations: One for the advanced practitioner, one for the beginner. If you have a deep body sense of your new belief, rest in it, and then let go of it and the whole exercise. You are done. Doing anything further to create the belief presupposes that the belief is not already created. If you truly believe, then you will end the exercise here, go about your normal daily business, and not concern yourself with the new belief anymore. You would not re-affirm or repeat it. Nor would you look for evidence of it. You'd give your attention to other issues. You would take it for granted that your belief sticks.

If you are a beginner in conscious creation or if you have a strong belief in physical reality or believe imagination is not real (one of the most limiting beliefs), you will have to ground your new belief in physical reality, midwife the ethereal energy into form. In this case, we'd be using the belief in physical reality, not as a limitation, but a resource. You do this by taking physical action that represents, symbolizes, or demonstrates the new belief. To do this thoroughly, get out a sheet of paper and answer the following questions:

1. What would someone be doing who really believes that it's already true?
2. What would someone be doing who is certain that this desire is reality?
3. What would someone do who is already living this reality?
4. What actions did you see yourself do in your imagination, and how could you copy these actions into physical reality?
5. What desires will you have when that one is fulfilled?

By acting as if something is already true—dressing that way, going to the places you would, getting things you would, taking part in events you would—by making it your belief, you ground it in physical reality. You have to come as close as possible to the real thing for the real thing to manifest. Even if you role-play it, you are training your body-mind-consciousness to receive it, so that it will not be a shock when it actually arrives. However, the idea of "acting as if" is one step removed from total reality. Don't "act as if," but *as* the new belief or reality.

That is the process of releasing old beliefs and creating new ones. You become aware of the old ones. You then become aware of the beliefs behind the beliefs. You desensitize these beliefs, and then choose what you want to think or believe instead. Activate these beliefs with attention and imagination, then anchor or ground these beliefs by physical action. In your new feeling and behavior, you will notice physical, real-life evidence as quick as within only three days. If you can keep your new vibration, you will experience a complete shift of reality within only three weeks.

I could give you examples of how others have applied this miraculous process to issues and successfully transformed them. I could give you examples of improved financial situations, improved health, improved relationships, improved perception, and improved quality of life. But I will not because the stories I would tell you are not your stories. I want you to find out for yourself, not be pre-programmed, or limited in how to use these tools or what's supposed to happen. Use them yourself and in your own way. The working material is not to be found in this book, but within your own consciousness. Without you, your experiences, feelings, and memories, these tools don't mean anything. They get their energy from you.

After your belief has manifested, with first evidence appearing after three days, and concrete manifestation appearing after three weeks, you can decide if what you received is what you wanted. I'd recommend not re-affirming or re-creating that reality before you've given it a few weeks to appear. Then, after the three weeks are through, you may refine or repeat the exercise according to what appeared. If you said, "I want to meet an attractive partner," and that attractive partner did indeed appear, but without any brains, intellect, or zest, then you will want to refine your belief to "I want to meet an attractive and intelligent partner." If you do all of this belief-work in a playful and exploring way, you will have many interesting, fun times. If you get too serious or needy, don't even begin. Neediness is the opposite of creative flow. If you need something or someone in order to be happy, you are not going to get it. Instead of needing it, love it.

Truly, there is no other reality than what you define it to be. Some people say you have to be realistic. What they are saying is that they give the things that are already created more importance, reality, and solidity than the things that are wanted. They have become observers of the past, of what's been created. If you want reality creation to work, don't judge your experience from what was and what is, but what could be. Don't judge the day by what you reap, judge by what you sow. Don't judge the day by what you get, but by what you give and give off in your vibrations.

I'd like to conclude this chapter with three incredibly powerful exercises that immediately transfer you to the viewpoint of a creator and allow you to release unwanted beliefs.

How does this serve me exactly as it is?

Notice an unwanted condition and ask yourself, "How does this serve me exactly as it is?" Keep with the question until you find a satisfactory answer.

What bad thing happens if the good thing happens?

Note a desire you've had that hasn't fulfilled. Ask yourself, "What bad thing happens if this manifests?" Remain in this question until your heart answers.

This tool is used when you remain convinced that you haven't manifested what you want. The question is not really answered by the mind or world self because it can't imagine there is any benefit in not manifesting a certain desire. The question addresses the heart, which is why you become silent and open before posing the question. Stay receptive after you ask it. The phrasing presupposes that non-fulfillment has some pay-off, protects you from something, secures your survival, or supports another creation. Don't change the wording to "what bad thing *could* happen" or "what bad thing *would* happen"; keep it straightforward.

This question alone can get you into vibratory synchrony with what you want. It requires vulnerability and honesty and is therefore not used very often, and preferably not used on others. Also, don't use the tool if there's no real problem, since using it or any other of these belief tools presupposes that you are not resting in your chosen identity.

Reversing this question can also be a good tool in some cases: "What good thing happens if ____________ (undesired reality) keeps happening?" This question reveals that apparently undesired realities do have a secret benefit, a secret pay-off. If they didn't, the person would not be experiencing them.

Blessings in Disguise

Should challenges or problems come up on the timeline after synchronization with your new identity, do not label these as interruptions of your chosen life, but part of the process. Label them as beneficial tools, servants, and things with hidden uses and resources. Abuse them for your chosen identity, make use of them for your benefit, see them as blessings (perhaps in disguise), and see them as magnificent opportunities to try out your new viewpoint/identity.

Threshold of Believability

You can change core-beliefs with this powerful exercise. You take a reality you desire and define a time-span in which you are 100% sure (belief) the reality will take place or manifest. Are ten years enough for it? Then say ten years. Work back from this defined time, finding the "threshold of believability." What about nine years? Would you also be able to experience that within nine years? Yes? For sure? Okay. Fine. How about six years? Yes? For certain? Okay, let's work back until we find the first doubts coming up. How about three years? Maybe? Aha, there we go. We've found the time at which certainty turns into uncertainty. Let's go back up. How about four years? Yes? Okay, then, let's stick with three years. Three years is the threshold. Now define why you are not sure your desire can manifest by this time. Uncover the belief. Once you have uncovered the reason (belief) why "maybe" it cannot be achieved by this time, formulate a belief that is easy to believe and states why you can make it in three years. Once you've established that and are 100% certain you will make it in three years, you can leave it at that and enjoy your transformation from ten to three years 'til manifestation, or you can start at that point and break it down even further, working your way backward until you reach a new threshold. With your new belief, do you think you can make it in two years? Good. One year? Not so sure? Okay. Why? All right. What can you and do you want to believe instead?

Rightness

Needing to be right is a form of intense conviction, often concerning an unwanted reality. The question is would you rather be right or fulfilled?

Write down a desire you have. Write down your strongest doubt or counter-belief. Then write down why that that is so, why you can prove that is so. This is called mis-creating.

Now write down the opposite of your desire (how you are going to fail). List the strongest doubt you have. Write down why you are right or can prove that this doubt or objection is true. This is called creating.

Penetrating and Releasing Typical Core Beliefs

Become/ penetrate, then dissociate from the following beliefs (in this order):

- What you feel like at the moment
- What you think about this exercise
- A belief that this exercise might not work
- Something you think you can't release
- Your concept of "Future"
- Your concept of "Past"
- Your concept of "Present"
- Your concept of where you are (location)
- Your concept of a body
- Your concept of a mind
- Your concept of who you are (identity)
- Your concept of what a spirit is
- Your concept of what a higher self is
- Your concept of earth
- Your concept of physical reality
- Your concept of birth
- Your concept of being human
- Your concept of how you are supposed to feel
- Your concept that there is something you don't know
- Your concept that there is something you can't do
- Your concept that there is something you can't have
- Your concept that there is something you can't be
- Your concept of what exists
- Your concept of what is still left

What is not a belief?

Everything is a belief, even the belief that some things are not beliefs, but facts. There are different orders of belief that are more factual than others are. A number of beliefs you wouldn't want to view as beliefs or release because they are part of the package you agreed to when incarnating on this planet. They assure your functioning in this time and space and within organized society. Creating the reality "I can fly with my body" might be in stark conflict with other beliefs you agreed to upon your arrival here. And as such, trying to create things like that can cause major disruptions.

Beliefs, or definitions of reality, make up the entire world. They are the concrete on which all reality is built. Things don't just happen; they only work because you agree, believe, or imagine they do. If any higher order of belief can be determined, it's what one might call the "laws of the universe" or "laws of infinity" or "the nature of things." One could say that they are active no matter what you believe. Some examples of such beliefs: You exist, which implies that non-existence is not an option. Everything changes (except for laws of the universe). Reality corresponds with your beliefs. Like attracts like. Nobody can create for someone else. You are responsible for what you create, even if you are not aware of it. You cannot take on beliefs that contradict universal laws. If you don't believe them, the laws correspond with your disbelief. Infinity is ultimately a pure, positive flow of energy, always and forever accessible to you. Your intentions for others are only effective when others allow them to be. Others' intentions for you are only as effective as you allow them to be. What you intend for others, you intend for yourself (as infinity is one). These are some of the higher order beliefs that, at least in our context, cannot be changed by your beliefs.

Apart from these universal laws are a collection of beliefs about the structure and nature of physical reality, which needn't be messed with. Messing with these would be like messing with the system commands of your computer. Example: As long as you live on earth, you may view a tree as a tree. And when that tree has fallen down in a storm, you may view the tree as having fallen down. Anything apart from this obvious appearance is yours to choose (e.g. "that's bad," "that's good," "it's a nice tree," or "I can communicate with the tree," etc.). Of course, it is possible to recognize, "It's only my belief that it is a tree," and de-construct the belief. But why do that? You would be deconstructing the scenery of your planetary incarnation, de-constructing your humanness and body. This may be advisable practice for some far-out shamans, but it's not the purpose for which you came here—which is to enjoy life and all its versions.

Beliefs about Reality Creation

This is a special class of beliefs about RC and its workings, often overlooked. Playing with or shifting this type of belief can change how reality creation works for you. This book is full of this class of beliefs, some of which radically change what people have been taught by other New Age sources. Even some of the beliefs presented in this book may be limiting—from your perspective. If so, you are free to define other parameters of RC. It's all up to you. As the responsible, multi-dimensional being that you are, I assume you would create your own truths, techniques, and ways of handling the mysteries of life. Beliefs about RC can be deepened or released. A few examples of such beliefs:

"I have to release my old beliefs before I create new ones." Now, to some, this belief will be beneficial—to others, not. Any belief can be either beneficial or not. There was a time I deeply believed this, because it's what I was taught at various seminars and workshops. But as I hint at in this book, over time, I loosened my grip on this belief and realized it was not necessary to shift the old before entering the new, but that truly entering the new made the old obsolete.

"My chosen creations take a long time to come true" vs. "My chosen creations come at just the right time." The first statement is a beneficial belief, if you want manifestation to take a long time, but counter-intentional if you want things to manifest quickly. The second statement is a bit better—a bit more released and ideal to many. But even it can become a limitation if it draws your attention to outer manifestation, rather than inner alignment.

Noticing your beliefs about reality creation, many of which you have picked up in books like this one, and shifting them to what you prefer, can be a very rewarding area of exploration. Books, seminars, and CDs on the subject provide anchors or middlemen that help you believe in reality creation. But what they teach does not have to be taken at face value. This trust in an authority outside yourself is a bit irresponsible, especially because many teachings are still colored by viewpoint limitations. There are no limits to your own imagination. You can come up with even better techniques and beliefs and claim them. In my coaching work, I've had people ask me about the inner workings of RC. But the fully developed wizard needn't ask—his own creative authority determines how things work. If someone has taught you that you need to do a hundred affirmations a day, and you believe that, it will work to some extent. But do you want to do that? If yes, fine. If not, you can choose to believe and feel that three a day will do. You can even teach yourself that you don't need any at all, because you eliminate the middleman of affirmation and go directly for what you want by identifying with it. One of my intentions with this book was to change the suppositions of how reality creation works. I view intentions and beliefs as synonymous. Why? Many, when they say, "I have this belief," don't feel responsible for it is they would by saying, "I have this intention." Viewing a reality you dislike as an intention you have immediately presupposes the creator's responsibility—which makes it easer to release, as you can only release what you admit to creating.

Skepticism: A Blessing and a Curse

Skepticism is a blessing in that only an idiot would unquestioningly grin while jumping down a balcony in the mistaken belief that he can fly. Without skepticism, we would not question our beliefs or progress. Skepticism is a curse in that to create a reality, all skepticism must be released; one must immerse oneself with full conviction. So, rather than saying skepticism is good or no good, let's use it for our benefit. Concerning your dreams and desires, give up all skepticism, intellectual reasoning, and hesitation. Concerning unwanted beliefs, counter-intentions, and limiting, or unhappy situations, be skeptical and doubtful.

Core Beliefs

While your reality flows from our deepest intentions and not from superficial considerations these deep-seated and extremely powerful intentions are not difficult to discover. Your deepest beliefs are more easily noticeable when you understand the following:

Consciousness is holistic. It therefore follows that a core belief manifests in more than one area of your life. By looking at one tiny part of your life, you can figure out what core belief is influencing large parts of your life, or vice-versa. This knowledge is extremely useful if some part of your life seems too emotionally charged to handle. Some things may be so charged you are not even willing to acknowledge the reality as a belief or feel anything when trying to connect to a new self-version. But that is no longer a problem. All you have to do is look at a subject that is less emotionally charged, in which you have a similar feeling. That is, if you feel stuck in one area, look at another, smaller area in which you feel stuck. The things you are stuck in are based on core beliefs, and a major, defining trait of a core belief is that it manifests in more than one are of your life. All you have to do is look at the less-charged area, and from that, deduct the core belief. Having released that belief, release all areas in which it is affecting you, as well. You can release emotionally charged issues without digging around in them, but by solving something else, something smaller, you will automatically solve the other.

An example: Let's say you feel stuck in your professional career. Applying the core belief technique, you would look for a similar feeling in another area—for example, in your relationship to your partner. Once you find a similar issue, you would determine which is less charged. You may find that the relationship issue is more charged because you get tired when trying to identify with the preferred self-version, and that the career issue is less charged and you are able and willing to align with a new self-version here. By creating something new for work, you directly or indirectly change the other area in which the same core belief was operating. Not only would your career improve, your relationship would reflect the release of a major belief respective the new identity.

This is good news to people who have been struggling with core-beliefs for a long time, because if one area feels unsolvable, you can achieve results by addressing a similar problem with less emotional charge. By choosing the easier issue and creating a new version-of-self for it, you leave the core belief behind. The areas of your life are interconnected and the law of correspondence doesn't prefer one area to another, but permeates the whole self. Change a core belief, and suddenly, you have access to new information, new experiences, and new people, seemingly coming out of the woodwork to assist you.

Every Problem is a Solution for Something Else

The reality surfer handles problems as follows:

He uses them to his benefit
He abuses them for his goals
He misuses them for the positive
He not only takes the bull by the horns, but rides the bull to better places
He lets the problem serve him

This approach is radically different from that of the teary-eyed victim we see on a daily basis on the front pages of the yellow press, who sees any type of interesting challenge as negative, and invalidates everything that could serve him instead of appreciating it. A specific example: Tim lost his job today. And that's great! Now he has the time to work on things he really loves, and finally has time to allow abundance into his life! Or, there was an earthquake. Thousands of people died. This is the perfect time to cultivate mutual support, world improvement, and appreciation of life. Or, there's been a blizzard. This is Ted's opportunity to increase his pocket money by helping others dig out of the snow. Or, I just lost one million dollars. What a great opportunity to prove that what is lost can be regained! Or, I have a headache. What a great thing—now I can explore my body's behavior, laze around, or even try my self-healing skills. Or, his wife dumped him. Excellent! Now he can devote himself to becoming a better person! Or, I died. Wow. Perfect. This is the time to explore other levels of existence.

How does the problem serve you as it is? For what is the problem a solution? How can you use this problem for the good of all concerned?

The Problem Is the Solution

Here's an even more holistic way to view problems. A problem is nothing more than resistance to a situation. The object or situation is not the problem, but your way of looking at it. When you resist the situation, it becomes a problem, and more problems appear. When you accept the situation, the problem turns into its solution and more solutions appear. Both things are contained within the situation; the difference is viewpoint. Resistance binds you to the issue and lets it persist. Acceptance releases you from the situation and lets solutions come up. As long as you resist a problem, you are resisting its solution.

Accepting something does not mean you desire it or want it to continue. It means you stop giving it energy. Take a problem you are having and sit down with it. For now, give up criticism, invalidation, conclusion, judgment. Become silent. Have a conversation with the enemy; make friends with it. Give up the limited world-self viewpoint and shift into a deeper kind of interest, as if the enemy were a messenger. Listen to what it has to say. Understand the message. If you pay attention a little, you'll notice that the so-called problem is actually a solution for something else. An example: If smoking is the problem, acceptance will show you that smoking is a solution for feeling tense. Then you realize the issue is not really about smoking, but relaxing. Relaxing is the solution you want, and the information was contained in the problem. Every problem serves you; otherwise, you wouldn't be creating it. Having a problem means not having listened properly while life was trying to tell you something. Once you consciously create the preferred you, the problem is no longer a problem. Without resistance, a problem is merely a wake-up call to a better version of you—it's that simple. Follow the wake-up call, and the solution will reveal itself to you.

The Meaning of It All

What is the meaning of life? Life has the meaning you ascribe to it. Other than that, there is no meaning. All that is, or energy, is neutral and behaves according to the meaning you create. What meaning, importance, label, or judgment you ascribe to something (wittingly or unwittingly) determines what that thing will become—if it will be to your advantage or disadvantage. Everything that exists has no built-in, inherent meaning. Infinity is a neutral, empty, impersonal vastness (not to be mistaken with hopeless, senseless, or cold) with which we can play. Everything that exists in your field of perception, everything you see, hear, feel, or experience is like a film prop. You may use these props for the various scenes and dramas of your life. Everything can be of value and service to you. Anything can turn out good, if you allow it. Every person, object, or event can be of positive value. These things do not contain inherent qualities of positive and negative. They are neither good nor bad; they just are. By understanding this, your life becomes even more magical.

Giving meaning to something is another variation on belief/intention. Consider an event, any event. This event has trillions of versions. The moment you label the event, you filter out one version of the event, and it becomes only that for you. Label a job loss a disaster, and it becomes just that. Label a job loss a chance to have something better, and it becomes just that. Nothing forces you to label things the way others label them or the way you have labeled them up to now. Labels are learned, and you can unlearn them.

Due to the conditioning and indoctrination we all pass through, it can seem certain things have inherent, non-arbitrary meanings. This appearance is even stronger when masses of people agree on meanings and definitions. Example: That is a house. Its purpose is to shelter us. I don't mean to get too abstract and question whether a house is a house and what its purpose is. It would be possible to give that definition up and find yourself in a new reality in which those structures are not houses at all, but something entirely different. What we are going for here is to add a more pleasant and flexible dimension to your life by teaching you that nothing is fixed except by your judgments, definitions, and who you are.

Choose an event that happened some time ago. Now get playful and creative and interpret that event from the viewpoint of someone in a terrible mood. Next, interpret the event from the viewpoint of someone in a neutral mood. Finally, interpret the event from the viewpoint of someone in a cheerful mood. Notice how the event changes? If you have difficulty switching from a negative to a positive judgment about something, the intermediary step of "neutral" will help you.

Now observe some event or thing you automatically label negative and ask, "In which way does this thing serve me? How could it be useful?" If you are a bit more courageous, ask, "In which way is this event evidence that my life works and my desires are unfolding?"

Electricity is neutral. It can be used either to burn someone in the electric chair or to warm someone in an electric blanket. It all depends on the interpretation of the one viewing it.

Let's deepen the concept by giving you some first-hand experiences: Observe any object near you. Relax. Now label it as ugly, negative, bad, stupid, dangerous. Keep your attention on the object and simply feel. See what aspects of the object you notice most. Next, label the same object as positive, beautiful, interesting, useful, or nice. Keep your attention on the object and feel. Notice what aspects of it you notice. Next, label the same object as what it is, neutrally. Observe the object and don't label it at all. Repeat this a few times with a few objects. Let it be your next meditative exploration. Some lessons within this exercise go beyond the obvious ones just described. Four basic states are contained in the exercise, and each of them is useful: resistance (negative label), appreciation (positive label), neutral (label as-is), and no-label (silence).

If you wish to demonstrate this to an even deeper extent, try the following: Get two glasses of water that look and taste the same. Have a group of people label one of the drinks negative, disgusting, repulsive, poisonous, bad, old, evil, and dirty for a minute or two. Have someone mark this glass with a small dot of a certain color. Have the group of people label the other drink as positive, fresh, healthy, good, clear, beautiful, tasty, and delicious for a minute or two. Mark this glass with a dot of another color. On a piece of paper, indicate which color stands for which drink. Then have a test-person take a sip from each of the drinks and tell you which tastes better. In a phenomenal 80% of cases, you will have the test-person getting it right—a figure which is beyond any probability.

Let's deepen your awareness of label-magic even more. Look at an object (for example, a book) and declare it important. Give reasons why it is important. Afterwards, declare the same thing as unimportant. Give reasons why it is unimportant. Play around with this with various objects, thoughts, and ideas. Notice how we all create importance and unimportance on a daily basis, and how the importance we ascribe determines where our and other people's attention goes. Think about how this will benefit your business.

Want more? There is an abundance of applications for this knowledge. Observe something you feel obliged to do this week, of which you say, "It has nothing to do with my heart's desire." Now declare that this errand has everything to do with your heart's desire and will even support you in it. Label it as something that "belongs." Then see what becomes of the errand.

People keep asking what things mean. See if you can spend one week of your life without asking questions; instead, give answers. When you notice yourself starting to ask questions like "What is?" or "Why is?" or "What does ... mean?" stop yourself; instead, use statements beginning with "It is" and "It means." For every "why" you hear from someone immediately answer with "Because." The purpose of this exercise is to ease your addictions to outside answers and return to self-determination and the ability to say what something means to you. While applying the exercise, you are no longer the needy searcher, but the one defining what reality is.

If you are asking yourself what the difference between lying and reframing or re-labeling is, here is the simple answer: Let's assume someone has had an accident and is walking around on crutches. A lie would be to say, "Well, he didn't have an accident; he is not on crutches. All is well." Re-labeling would be "Now he's finally got time for things other than football. Isn't that great?"

The world is full of props. But of the props to which you can assign certain meanings, importance, and relevance, some props (objects and symbols) have already been assigned a high degree of significance by our mass-consciousness. You can use the props that are already loaded with energy to your benefit. This is the secret behind the talisman, and the manipulation of people with symbols labeled as significant.

We already assign certain meanings to many things; they have developed a life of their own, and now seem to posses meaning inherently. Most of the time, this brings us joy. We've assigned a good mood to sunshine, and when the sun comes out, our mood changes for the better. But our automatic labels can also become serious limitations, and it doesn't have to be that way. Let's take "what time is it?"

as an example. What meaning does it have if it's seven p.m. and you haven't had dinner yet? What meaning does it have that it's midnight? What meaning does it have that it's midday? What meaning do we ascribe to certain times of the day? In which way can these associations enslave us? In which way can they serve us?

Our reality is made up of many chains of definitions. Sickness means this, and if I am sick it means that, and this has to be done, then this. Change a definition, and you change reality. One way to be without definition is to go into non-conceptual silence without reaction. When you go into silence, you quit labeling things. When you quit labeling and defining things, nothing is created. Where nothing is created, you become that which is beyond creation: infinity, and that's a viewpoint from which it is relatively easy to create something new.

If you want to experience a very nice high, take a walk and label everything you perceive, as it is, without adding any interpretation. Call a house a house and a tree a tree. After a while, you will start feeling pretty high. Do you know why?

You come home, and your house is burning. The negative label would be "This is a tragedy. My life is lost. I will never recover. Why do these things happen to me?" As a side note, it would be even more detrimental to have that label and suppress it. The neutral label would be "My house burned down. This might bring some complications with it." The positive-label would be "My house burned down. That's excellent, because I was starting to feel imprisoned; I was bored and lifeless with it and all the clutter I've been hanging onto for years. I am now free of that burden and can create what is really me. I thank God for this release."

Once someone understands that the label determines what reality he will get out of any situation, and there are millions of versions of one event, he can start playing with labels, instead of buying into one single version of reality. The less trust one has in himself, the more he is going to label something in a way that he can be a victim of it. Watch what labels come up automatically. If the negative label is your first, most honest reaction, then allow it to play out. Verbalize it; don't suppress it. Exaggerate it if you want. Consciously re-label the situation so that it becomes more neutral, and then take the jump to a label that is satisfying to you.

Removing labels (as happens automatically in meditative silence) allows us to experience life directly, without pre-suppositions and definitions. Living life without filters can be an even more exhilarating experience than living it with positive filters. Our constant labeling of the world means that we lose our perception of reality as energy. Automatic negative labels are, however, very detrimental to your reality. Let's assume you've consciously created the reality of a job that is right for you, and you now rest in that field of energy. The day of the job interview comes, and the human resources person tells you that you can't have the job; they are not interested in you. Now, if you buy into this and label this situation as "Well, I failed. I am not getting the job I want," then indeed, that's how reality will start unfolding. But, if in that very situation you can remain calm and convinced that the job is yours, the person sitting across from you will suddenly either change his mind, or offer you another opportunity somewhere else. It's ALL your choice.

There's No Such Thing as Negative

Labeling something as negative is a habitual convention. Everything is neutral energy, and what this energy transforms into depends on our label. As a beginner of RC, one learns to put attention on the things one finds positive—the things one labels positive. At an advanced stage of RC, you go a step further and learn to find the jewel in the negative. This is the opposite of victim consciousness. It is radically responsible, radically source, and radically positive. Creative denial does not mean suppressing or ignoring the negative, but secretly still believing in it—that would be psychological denial. Creative denial means confronting and changing it to something beneficial, something that serves you, something for which there is some pay-off. Everything your soul experiences, it experiences for a good reason. To assume otherwise is to assume that there is an evil force after you. Labeling something as bad implies that you did not create it, for you would probably not want to admit to creating something bad or useless. The reason most people don't want to believe they create their reality is that that would mean admitting to mistakes, because they label many of their experiences as negative and "Why would I create something like that?" When you start realizing that the events you label bad were created and experienced for a good reason—for your growth, experience, and learning—you will have an easier time taking responsibility for them and even making use of them. It's in your evaluation that they are bad, that they do not serve some purpose. Talking badly about an ex-partner, a job, or earlier experiences shows that you do not appreciate the learning experience, which is why it will be repeated in your life.

Good and Bad

A beautiful parable from ancient China makes the point a bit more clear:

A poor farmer and his son lived on a farm, back in the days when owning a horse meant having a fortune. One day, a horse came grazing on the farmer's land. By local law, this meant that the horse belonged to him. His son was ecstatic. The villagers all commented, "What good fortune!" But the farmer remained calm and said, "Who knows what's good or bad?"

A few days later, the horse disappeared, and the farmer's son was heartbroken. The villagers looked on the farmer with pity, but the farmer remained calm and said, "Who knows what's good or bad?"

The next day, the horse returned with dozens of other horses. The son couldn't believe his luck; the villagers were stunned, congratulating him on his good fortune. But the farmer remained calm and said, "Who knows what's good or bad?"

Another few days passed. The farmer's son was riding one of the wild horses; the horse threw him off, and he broke his leg. Agonizing, he cursed the horses that they had even appeared. The father got a doctor and tended to his son. He held him, looked him deep in the eye, and said, "My dear son. Who knows what's good or bad?"

Only a week later, the army came through town to recruit all the men as soldiers. The only one they did not take was the son—because he had a broken leg.

The son represents our reactive self, which is swept back and forth by desire and resistance, forever reacting to circumstances. The father represents the observer mode—source awareness that determines what is good or bad, or makes no determination whatsoever.

11

Imagination and Reality

Imagination would have the potential to create reality if it weren't for how we label imagination (what we believe about it). Early on, we are taught that imagination is *only* imagination and that it does not have much use or value. Okay, some will admit that it is important for art, economic inventions, and creativity. But compared to what imagination is capable of, these are *shallow* remarks. The problem is that we've been taught to differentiate between imagination and reality. Imagination has become a synonym for "unreal." This is tragic, because imagination is not only real, it is the *source* of what most people call reality. The only reason imagination has lost power is because we assign more solidity, reality, importance, significance, and validity to the physical world. Because we assign them this meaning, they appear more solid and real than imagination. Why have we taught ourselves this? To be more focused on this world. To protect us from losing focus. To protect us from our every thought becoming real. This protection is valid. We simply want to loosen it a bit, to allow more experience to flood into our life. There is no difference between the physical matter surrounding you and imagination. There is no difference between an imagined rose and a real rose, except in *your* definition. This definition has imagination appear as subtle energy, and matter as denser energy. Anything you can imagine is real in some sense and on some plane. As long as you keep your definitions of reality in place, your imagination will manifest on some other plane. When properly used, your imagination has the power to influence your everyday life in very specific ways.

Imagination is not only a tool of reality-manifestation; it's more than that. It is can reveal a lot about your personality, your abilities, and next steps to take. Your imagination is there for a reason. Images in the mind don't just pop up for no reason. Use the beautiful tool you have been given. Use imagination as a guide. What is your imagination telling you? Act on it. What is it showing you? Learn from it. The easier it is for you to imagine something, the closer it is to your current vibratory set point. The harder it is for you to imagine something, the further it is from your current state. There is much to be learned from the last two statements, but I will not rob you of your journey of discovery by describing everything in detail. Find out for yourself.

How imagination relates to the other modes of consciousness we've discussed:

Emotion: Imagination can create emotional energy vibration easily. Vice-versa, certain imaginary images are activated by emotion. Practically, this means that if you don't want something imaginary to manifest on the physical plane, don't feel anything while imagining it. Reduce emotional reaction. If you do want to quicken a mental image into physical experience, add emotions such as gratitude, excitement, euphoria, and love.

Attention: The more attention you place on an imaginary image, the more importance, solidity, and reality it gains. The less attention you invest, the less reality it gains.

Belief: Beliefs are created by adding attention, emotion, and a body sense to a mental image.

Action: By copying what you see yourself doing in your imagination to active, physical reality you can quicken a manifestation.

How about taking a week's vacation from the facts and trusting your imagination as real? How about being grateful for something before it happens? What would happen to your life if you made the inner authority of daydreams more important than the outer authority of factual circumstances? Would that be an escapist attitude? No, it wouldn't, unless you label it that way. When you resist nothing, there is nothing from which to escape or distract yourself. If you believe in your dreams, they soon override the authority of outer circumstances and become outer circumstances themselves.

Intensifying Imagination

Imagine a pleasant scene—for example, an ocean beach. Allow it to intensify on the following imaginational modes:

Visual: Have your picture be more colorful, or see more about it. Make the ocean a deeper blue. Notice palm trees in the distance.

Audio: Add sounds. Hear the rush of the waves. Turn up the volume.

Reality: Add more reality to the image by adding dimensional depth, by intensifying your conviction that it's real, by smelling and tasting, and especially by touching and feeling the objects. Let the sand run through your hand.

Emotion: Finally, allow positive emotion to flow through you as you experience the picture.

The whole point of the exercise is to experiment with your imagination. Get to know it; build a relationship with your imagination.

Wouldn't It Be Nice If...

This is a beautiful technique to train your mind to reach for higher thoughts. Spend a few minutes or more beginning every sentence with the words "Wouldn't it be nice if…" Here, you simply speculate on what would be nice, without any expectation that it really has to occur. You are not using this technique as a strategy to make something happen out there, but to feel playful in the here and now.

Little and Big

Infinite self does not differentiate between little things and big things—only world-self does. Thinking that something small is easier to manifest than something big is yet another label. It is a belief about how reality creation works, and you might want to release it, because it's not especially helpful. Little things seem to manifest more easily because we are not desperately pushing, needing, and waiting for them to happen, but approach them in a light-hearted, playful way. Chances are that you have this belief about "easy" and "hard." Try this: If you've been trying to manifest something big for a while, and it hasn't manifested, apply RC technique on something you'd consider easy. Notice how quickly it shows up in your life. That's certainly enjoyable, but it also reveals that you make a difference between small and big. The same efficiency can apply to big things.

Life Is a Dream

RC teaches that the world out there is merely a reflection of the world in here, and therefore a dream, just like your night dreams or imagination dreams. When you dream at night, you often think events, landscapes, things, and people are separate from you, the dreamer. Except when you are lucid dreaming (in which you not only know you are dreaming, but also notice you are creating the dream), the dream seems to be something that you are not deliberately creating. After you wake in the morning, you realize, "Oh, it was all a dream," and you understand that all things in the dream were part of your psyche, within you. While immersed in the dream, the "I" in the dream views all events as separate. The awakened "I" notices that the entire dream and its contents are a creation of its own consciousness. What seemed separate is "within me," and after awakening, you can look at the symbols of the dream to consider their meaning and find out what you were telling yourself. One part of self is immersed in dream action, loses awareness of the overall self that knows it's only a dream, and is observes the action from outside the dream body. But both the immersed self and the observing self are always present. The two versions are the immersed one, who is acting as the dream figure, and the one who is observing the dream self (the lucid dreamer).

And now the revelation: The exact same thing applies to your waking life. This means you can gain considerable benefit from viewing your waking life as another dream. From the perspective of the night-dreaming self, it is. From that perspective, waking life is the dream, and dream-life is real. But both are the same illusion on different levels of vibratory density. In every day reality, we have an immersed viewpoint identified with experience, and an observing viewpoint that is not immersed or limited to the body—not looking as an identity. The embodied viewpoint moves through the world of things, people, and circumstances that seem separate from it. But just as you awaken in a night dream, you can also awaken in waking life and realize "it's all happening within me." You can view the things in waking life just as you would view dream objects and events: as symbols or mirrors of consciousness. Every experience you have, especially those that capture your attention or are emotionally charged, are tools for self-reflection and deeper fulfillment and alignment with the desired self-version. You can see waking life as the dream that it is. This requires you to be lucid in waking life, to take a step out of immersion, gain perspective, be the witness, and perceive the meaning of an event and its correspondence to your inner self. RC is not a one-way street. Once you create or claim something within, infinity will start communicating with you and showing you symbols and coincidences in your daily life. Our beliefs/ identity are how we talk to infinity. The waking dream (events in daily life) is infinity's way of talking to us. Intuitive guidance, pointers, impulses, information—it's all there if you open your eyes. Only the stupid trivialize or ignore the guidance offered. RC is not just about sending wish lists into the universe, but entering into a lifelong dialogue with infinity. This is where being silent becomes of use once again. While you are immersed in the rush of events, you cannot read the deeper meanings. Life is a letter your higher self sends you. What you are experiencing is all about you. Wake up! Nothing happens independently of you. Reality creating is actually reality co-creating; start listening to what your infinite self is saying in response to your creations.

Imagination and Parallel Universes

Understanding parallel universes means understanding imagination as something very different from what we have been taught. A new understanding of what imagination is will open many gates for you. Within RC, the distinction between real and unreal is not made. If any distinction is made, it is between real and manifest. Something has to be real in a parallel universe in order to manifest. Just because you do not perceive it doesn't mean it's not real. Many events are taking place in this world right now that you do not perceive. That does not mean they are not real. There are many programs on TV that you are not seeing. That does not mean they are not being shown. To think of something as unreal just because your specific viewpoint doesn't perceive it is presumptuous. Your world-self experiences only a tiny percentage of all that is at a time. Imagination and desires are bleed-throughs from a parallel reality version-of-self who is already really experiencing something. Someone else is already having that experience, and you are feeling it as a desire. You can only desire something that is already yours. If it weren't, you wouldn't be feeling it, couldn't be imagining it, and wouldn't even be aware of it. The only thing missing now is that you correspond with it one to one, rather than out of phase with it, which is what a desire is—being slightly out of phase with a certain reality. If you were too far removed from that reality, you wouldn't feel any desire for it.

Even the most basic understanding of the Many Worlds model can fill you with appreciation and amazement for the infinite creativity of being. Every split-off reality appears with its own whole history, timeline, and mood, and each of these realities splits again—from eternity to eternity. Do you know why the concept sparks so much excitement and interest? Because it's the "next big thing." From our perspective, it's a future science. After humanity has passed through turmoil, games, and gets bored of the struggle, they will turn their attention to the fun and vastness of being.

When you practice RC, you shift into a parallel reality. The reason your surroundings appear the same is because you have a built-in, protective system that keeps you from shock. It would be possible to open your eyes after PURE and see a completely different surrounding, too, but that would be too much for the majority of beings. The protection system allows the newly chosen world to form slowly and gently around you, so as not to short-circuit your nervous system. Some people, when using PURE, experience sudden uncontrollable jolts of the muscles, the same muscular jolts sometimes experienced when one is falling asleep. What do they mean? They indicate an abrupt or sudden shift in vibration/energy, a sudden shift in state-of-being. In my experience, they are all right to have, but if you don't wish to experience them, go easy, slow down. Understand that when you re-open your eyes after having immersed yourself in a new identity/imagination you are in a different universe. If you remain in it, this universe becomes your main universe.

There are plenty of scientific indicators that an identity shift causes a reality shift, but here is one of the more extreme examples: In researching multiple personality disorders, it has been proven that extreme changes can occur when someone shifts identity. In clinical studies of MPD, people have been seen to lose twenty pounds in a few days, facial scars suddenly disappeared completely, as if they had never been there (or returned when they shifted back), voices, memories, and looks transformed within minutes, and so on. But an identity shift does not only change the body, it changes the experience, as science will someday have the courage to admit. Since the outside world is not separate from consciousness, changing the self equals changing the outside world. In this light, you may understand how superfluous and unnecessarily complicated it is to use affirmations and visualizations to make something happen out there.

You are always at the crossover of many realities. Which direction you take is up to you. The next, better, version of self is already real and available for you to enter. What if you take the wrong direction? That's fine, because you can notice and alter it the next minute. Just as you no longer need to differentiate between real and unreal, neither do you need to differentiate between true and untrue. Instead, differentiate between truth (real) and fact (manifest). Everything is true, but only some of it manifests in your life.

Truth in RC is not the truth of religion, which not only tries to state absolutes to which you must submit, but makes everyone who doesn't submit wrong. It is also not the truth of empirical science, which teaches us to concern ourselves only with what was manifested. RC truth is the truth of identity, the truth of what you feel right now. Over time, facts begin to align to your deepest convictions. Impatience and urgency in manifestation point to the event with which you are not really identified. Self and imagination are the gateways to all worlds.

Remember, whenever you wish to create something, it already exists. What you have been waiting for is actually waiting for you. When you no longer look for the manifestation, but feel it, it comes to meet you. This is similar to flirting. If you give a woman/man attention, and then remove it, he/she moves closer to you. The same principle is taught in New Age as "desire and letting go." Desire is turned into the gratitude of already having received.

This can also be called "non-attachment/non-disinterest." You are interested in manifestation and evidence, but you don't attach to it as if it were something on which you are dependent. Again, this is similar to flirting. You are interested in the manifestation, but you don't attach to it. You meet someone you like. You'd like to get closer to the person. You exchange phone numbers. The excitement increases. You don't call the same evening (attachment, urgency, lack), but wait a few days—let go for a few days. Maybe she won't be able to bear the tension and calls you before. Otherwise, you call after three or four days, and she is interested in seeing you again. Were you to wait too long—let's say a month—it would seem like disinterest, and she will have forgotten you.

12

Action and Reality

The statement "Action creates reality" is not really true, but it's what people believe the strongest. By believing it with such conviction, they make it true. Someone might say, "Well, I will go to the gym and lift weights. I will do it three times a week for eight months, and then I will have muscles." Nearly anyone would agree that this is true, and that the action of training three times a week for eight months created the muscle. And from a purely physical point of view, this seems very true. But what actually created the muscles was the person's belief in the process, the person's decision to be that version of himself. In order to experience a progression on a timeline with its result, the belief was connected to an action. Without those actions, he might not have been willing to believe it would work. Were he to believe he had muscles without having to do anything for it, then yes, he would have muscles without having done anything for it. As unlikely as it may seem to some readers, it is possible to do nothing and still achieve anything. Action only becomes necessary for people who don't believe in belief preceding action. However, for this belief in action to be source of a reality, as deep as it may be ingrained into mass consciousness, does not have to be taken as a limitation to your creative power, but to your creative benefit. As you've come to this planet to live the life of a physical being in a physical world, it is action, movement, doing, acting, and behavior you can use this circumstance to the benefit of reality creation. Attention and intention create reality, but because most believe that action creates reality, that it just isn't enough to visualize your dream, we will agree. While it is the intention behind taking action that determines the result, the action midwifes the energy into form. In the following, I'd like to discern three major types of actions.

1) Action based on fear and urgency. The pay-off is that this type of action is one that people believe will motivate them to act. But this one is the furthest from the reality creation viewpoint. Not only is action deemed necessary, bad consequences result if one doesn't act. This type of action is more *reactive* than active. You are presented with a problem, and then you fall into reaction, or you're working under time or money pressure instead of following your soul's path. Or you're working to fix things that are broken, instead of placing attention on what's good for you. Fear is used as a motivator to action. Many people actually believe that if there is no fear factor, people will not act. While this may be true on a low level of spiritual development, it is not effective if you wish to live a conscious, deliberate, spiritually mature life. The only time this type of action is helpful is when you are in deepest apathy or depression and need a wake-up call, or when you have dozens of unfinished things building up due to your neglect. In these rare cases, action based on fear and urgency is helpful; otherwise, it's just compensatory action. Compensatory actions are things you do to make up for bad thinking, bad feeling, bad reality creating. You attract something unwanted into your life through negative thinking and feeling, and then you act to make up for it, to make it better. This is not very effective, and will, in most cases, cause even more unwanted events. Making important decisions, taking steps, or going into action out of fear or urgency will cause events that create even more fear and urgency. Like attracts like. The more incompetent a political or corporate leader is, the less he assigns tasks based on vision, and the more he assigns tasks based on fear (of an enemy or job loss).

2) Inspired action or action towards your desires. This type of action will create more of the results you want in life. This is the action you take from a positive state, a good point of view—actions that arise from well-being. This can be planned and coordinated action that you take after you've written down a specific action plan or timetable, or it can mean acting upon opportunities that present themselves to you after you've given off positive energy. In the first variation, you set a goal, then you write down actions to it, then you follow through on these actions. This is the contemporary, mass-consensus way of creating a reality. In the second variation, you set a goal or desire, send the energy off to the universe, and simply relax and wait for opportunities to present themselves, and

then act upon them. In any case, you don't act out of fear, but out of joy and inspiration, out of positive expectation that you are heading toward your desire. In this type of action, you actually work and do less. The more energy you have, the less you have to do. Another way to put it: When you're energized, your actions don't feel like hard work or effort. To outsiders, you may appear to be doing a lot, but inside, you are having a great time. Often, action becomes fun when you associate it with personal benefit. Maybe you remember a time you didn't want to go to school or work. You felt heavy and needed plenty of coffee to drag yourself there. Then, something changed. You fell in love with someone at school or work and couldn't wait to get there; you felt energized, forgetting even the coffee because you had to rush to work. That is the difference between inspired action and pressured action.

3) Acting from the viewpoint that something is already real (what some errantly call "acting as if"). This is by far the most magical of actions. In this type of action, you take on the being of the desired reality. You are not acting towards the reality, the goal; you are acting as the reality. You are doing things you would be doing if it were already real. You are going to the places you would be going if it were already real. You are meeting the people you would be meeting if it were already real. You are behaving as you would if you were already in your desired reality. Since the universe of energy is a copy machine that reflects your vibratory being, you demonstrate to the universe what you are, and it will reflect events that match it. Physicalizing a desire means to come as close as possible to the real thing, to bring the real thing into the here and now, into the today—acting it, role-playing it as close to the original as possible. A convincing role-play is not very far from the real thing. This is one way of tuning in.

From a certain perspective, this third type of action may take some courage. But once you notice the magical results you get from it, and get used to it, you will apply it with joy. Here, you are taking the most direct path. If you can be something today, you won't need exercises or patience or proof because you are representing, being, and demonstrating the reality you said you want. You are already experiencing it and no longer have to achieve or follow or create it. Now, to help you differentiate between the three actions, I will share some examples.

Action 1, fear-based action, will rarely yield positive results. Action 2, inspired action, will eventually yield positive results. Action 3 will yield positive and quick results. The difference between Action 2 and 3: In working towards a goal you say, "Ok, I am going to do this, then this, then that, then this and that, and then I can experience this." That's creating reality on a timeline. In working as a goal, you make the end the starting point. You say, "I am going to be this today, and from this being, I will do this and that."

We will look at Michael, Tom, and Sharon. Michael always applies Level 1 actions, Tom always applies Level 2 actions, and Sharon always applies Level 3 actions.

The first desire they want to manifest is to have more money.

Michael buys a book called *Overcoming Your Fear.*

Tom buys a book called *How to Get Rich.*

Sharon buys a book by someone who is rich.

Michael starts working harder, putting in overtime and talking bad about other employees behind their backs—a move he thinks will put him in favor with his boss.

Tom starts prioritizing and time planning his work to become more effective. He starts talking good about his boss—a move he thinks will give him a pay raise.

Sharon finishes her old job and starts doing the creative, self-employed work she always wanted to do, because that would be what she would be doing if she were already wealthy.

The second desire they want is to find the right partner for their life.

Michael starts running after a girl from the office. He doesn't really like her, but he'll accept second best for now, because his self-esteem is not up to speed for more.

Tom specifies his desire and puts some ads on Internet dating forums.

Sharon cleans up her place as if expecting that special visitor, opens a bottle of wine, and puts out two glasses. She dresses up for him. She goes through the motions, acting out a dance with him. To an outside viewer, it might look silly, but she is physicalizing a dream.

The third desire is to hold speeches in front of large groups.

Michael doesn't do anything about this.

Tom goes to workshops to learn to hold good speeches.

Sharon visits good speeches. She goes into the energy field of what she wants. Later, she books a room with many chairs in it. Maybe she even puts foam plastic human figures into the chairs. After preparing materials, she holds a long speech in that room, as if she were really doing it.

These examples should suffice. Michael will get few results. Tom will eventually get results. And Sharon will get very quick and often surprising results only a few days after she ritualized her desire.

Not to overwhelm your belief system, I recommend to you a healthy mix of type-two and type-three actions.

Despite the fact that action is not a source of reality, it is advisable to be well versed in all disciplines and recommended that you exercise your ability to take action. This is especially recommended to people unwilling to believe many things mentioned in this book. If you are not willing to believe in the power of consciousness, then action is your only option. Build your action-muscle. In some dictionaries, the word "power" is defined as "the ability to take action." If your action muscle isn't built, if you have negative beliefs about what action means, like "Oh, action is hard work," or if you shy from challenging actions, you can re-train this ability. Undertaking challenging or difficult actions does not mean acting in a fear-based way. Tackling challenges can be done with joy. Taking the bull by its horns and just doing what needs to be done, rather than running away from it, can be a very liberating experience.

Suddenly Ending Procrastination

Think about or list some things you have been putting off, postponing, not confronting. Something unfinished that needs to be taken care of because it has been dominating your attention or mood. Think of the feeling of relief you'll have when it is taken care of. Think of what it would be like to have it behind you, rather than in front of you. Then, suddenly, put an end to your procrastination and take care of it. Finish it. Do it. Afterwards, notice how much attention is freed. Having unfinished things and commitments sucks attention energy like a sponge. When everything you committed to is taken care of, you are in a state of free attention, with a clean slate, tabula rasa. It is from this state that it is much, much easier to focus on what you want.

Conscious and Deliberate Action

This exercise is designed to change your state of awareness and mood for the better. It is designed to exaggerate a state of complete conscious awareness and completely self-determined action. To begin, announce what you will do next. After you've announced it, do it. Having done that, announce what you will do next. Having announced that, do that. Continue for a while in this manner—announcing, then doing. Announcing then doing. Announcing then doing. Only do what you announced. I say, "I will go over to the window." And I do it. "I will touch the window." I do it. "I will turn around." I do it. "I will sit down." I do it. "I will play with the alarm clock." I do it. This exercise is initially done with small things that don't take long to do—in progression and for at least fifteen minutes. The consecutive repetition allows you to experience a state of self-determination, willpower, and awareness. In the exercise, you only do what you said you would do. You say it. Then you do it. You decide it. Then you do it. This will also train your ability to decide and focus.

The advanced variation of this exercise is to do the very same thing—announce things and do them—but additionally notice moments of insecurity and subconscious or unintended behavior and actions, and to create these deliberately. So I'd say, "I will go to the window." On the way to the window, I notice how I pull up my pants. This automatic action was not announced. So I stop and deliberately, intentionally, announce this action: "I will now pull up my pants." Then I do it intentionally. This frees up the subconscious behavior. Then I once again announce, "I will now go to the window." I go to the window, but arriving at the window, I perhaps notice that I touch the window, without having announced it. So I also deliberately announce and do that. I continue until there are no more automatic actions, reactions, or behavior in the exercise and I feel in complete, conscious control. There will also be phases where you are unsure what to decide to do next. Relax into these until you've made a decision.

The very advanced version of this exercise is to choose a habit you have on automatic, a habit you want to get rid of. Define the opposite of it, what you want instead of that habit. Once you have the two sides of the issue—the bad habit and what you want—you deliberately alternate between doing the old habit, intentionally, and the new, preferred behavior. You repeat both sides until you have full, conscious control and can simply decide which you want to do. This little technique will eventually break any unwanted habit you have. Let's say that every time you speak publicly, you play with your eyeglasses. Instead of that, you want to assume good body posture. You definitely need something to do instead of the old habit. So, in this exercise, you'd hold a speech, alone or for real, deliberately, and intentionally arrange your eyeglasses, and then deliberately and intentionally assume good body posture. You'd do both several times, intentionally, during your speech. If you notice yourself touching your eyeglasses automatically, you'd do it again intentionally, and then immediately switch to the good body posture. The habit will be broken after some repetitions. The reason this technique works so fantastically well is that unwanted habits can only be maintained if you are not fully aware of them. Let's take another example. Let's say you switch on the TV every time you start feeling tired. Ask yourself what you'd like to do instead of turning on the TV when you feel tired. You come up with "Okay, when I start feeling tired, I'd like to close my eyes for five minutes, and take deep breaths," or, "Okay, when I start feeling tired, I'd like to take a walk," or, "Every time that happens, I'd like to read a book." In the days to come, you'd alternate between switching the TV on intentionally when you get tired and doing the other thing intentionally when you get tired. Soon, both behaviors will be under your conscious control, and you can simply choose what to do the next time you feel tired. Next, you can even apply the technique to getting tired itself. You realize "Ah, every time I talk about this subject, I get tired," and so on.

Being and Doing

A friend once said to me, "When something is happening, do nothing. When nothing is happening, do something." I love this phrase, because it reflects the balance between being and doing. Someone else once told me, "The basis of dynamic action is relaxation, and the basis of relaxation is dynamic action." This is so true. If you can't relax properly, you won't be able to work properly, and if you can't work properly, you won't be able to relax properly. Because many people don't know how to identify with being and doing anymore, they feel guilty when they are being lazy or relaxing, thinking, "Oh, I'd have so much to do; I can't just be lazing around." And when they work, they think about relaxing or taking holidays. They neither fully relax nor fully work. I firmly believe you will increase productivity and ability if you learn to fully relax and fully act. Fully relaxing means deep relaxation. While going to the sauna, or the beauty studio, or taking a walk, or doing a short meditation, or watching a movie will relax you a little bit, deep relaxation could mean taking a full day's hike, going into a floatation tank, doing hours of meditation, hours of massage, or hours of being lazy. Learn to relax fully, deeply, and without reservation or hesitation. When you have fully stopped doing, you will notice the rubber band that has been pulled to one side boomerang to the other side; you will be really keen on acting, working, moving. And when you work, how about working with commitment and concentration. Set a day's plan and work so much that you are pleasantly exhausted at night and just fall into bed and sleep. Little children do it. Once they relax, they sleep deeply. When they get excited, they can be intensely active. Learn both side of the coin.

Things you don't have to do

A common misconception of most people is that they have to take care of and do everything, control everything, micro-manage everything. This is a fear-based concept—that life will go out of control, and they can't trust anything to happen by itself. Realize that life will continue working just fine without you. Many things that happen in your life happen by themselves—naturally, automatically. You do not have to control and do everything. You can trust others to do things. You can trust life to take care of things. You can trust synchronicity, which is another word for meaningful, universally orchestrated coincidence, to take care of things. There is an invisible energy orchestrating things, and there is a higher, invisible aspect of you bringing things into your life, a universal manager to whom you can delegate desires. This may be a new concept, but I recommend you try it. Take out a sheet of paper and make two categories: "Things I don't have to do, that the universe will take care of for me," and "Things I want to do." Now, make those two lists, but allow the first list to be longer than the second one. Then put the list aside. The more you get used to this type of focus, the more you trust that many things will take care of themselves, simply because you allow them to, the more you will see evidence of this in your daily life.

Planned Action

1. Write down a few things you want or want to achieve this week. Not things you want to do, but results you want to achieve.
2. Write down why you want these things to happen. What are the emotional motivators?
3. Write down what you are going to do for these things to happen. Your action plan.
4. Write down when you are going to do each of these things; assign certain times for them.

If you are using this exercise for a team, group, or company, assign each action to a certain person.

Now you have an action plan to follow. This plan is not a corset. You can always move the dates of certain actions. You can always change the goals. You can always act on new opportunities. This plan is written for a focused orientation. Don't become a slave to it, thinking you have to follow it the way it is written. That's what stops most people from consciously planning in the first place. They believe that if they don't follow through exactly as written, they've failed. Better not to plan in the first place. Plans are there to give a general direction and focus in times you don't know what to focus on, not as something that must occur exactly that way. Some people find this type of action planning helpful. This exercise corresponds with the Type-2 action mentioned earlier.

Magical Action

This exercise corresponds with the Type-3 action, acting as if something were already true.

Take a piece of paper, and on it, define a reality you would love to experience. Then, answer the following questions in written form:

If this reality were already true:

1. At what places would I be?
2. What type of people would I meet?
3. How would I dress?
4. Would body movements would I be doing?
5. What objects and equipment would I be touching and handling?
6. About what would I be conversing and talking?
7. What interests would I have?
8. What would I be doing?
9. What symbols and things correspond to this reality?

Once you've answered these questions, you have a good idea of what to do to synchronize your energy with the reality you say you want. Be courageous and demonstrate to yourself, others, and the universe what you are. Life reflects you.

Copying Imagination into Reality

This is a powerful exercise when you are unsure what the next steps are or want guidance and inspiration as to which way to go next.

It is also a way to fish for new information from your subconscious mind. Sit or lie down, close your eyes, and come to rest. Build a feeling of peace, joy, or excitement within you. You don't need a reason to feel this joy; just let that inner smile build within you, without using too many anchors or thoughts. Then, feeling this joy or excitement, simply wait and observe what thoughts come up. What fantasies, images, and thoughts does that feeling attract? Take your time to daydream. Observe what actions you see yourself taking in your imagination. Your imagination is not just a vague dreamy thing; it is a tool that supports you in finding your truest path in life. After this meditation, write down all the actions you saw yourself taking in your imagination. You can copy these actions into real life for the quickest and most positive results. Ask yourself how to imitate these actions in real life. Let's say that at your point of highest excitement, a vague picture of a person you knew a long time ago came up. You don't know why, but that's what came when you went into the joy-vibration. The action you could take is to contact that person, even if you don't know why. If that's what imagination delivered, and if it felt good, that's what to do. Trust that your higher self knows what to do, because it has the overview of many lives and existences, the overview of your life's plan. It will feed you with information that you are not consciously aware of in this meditation. See what happens when you act upon what your joy tells you.

I trust that this information, the application, and the repetitive exercising of it will be useful to you for the rest of your life and beyond. Remember, repetition is the mother of skill. If you want to integrate a new philosophy or ability, exercise it.

Creativity

Do something you have done many times in a new and different way.

Show four different ways to walk.
Write down four different ways to reach a goal.
Write down four different ways to have a relationship.
Write down four different ways to do your job.

Do something you can't do

Examples:

"I can't look at my body in the mirror and love it." (Do it)
"I can't enjoy my poor balance sheet." (Do it)
"I can't smile at everyone." (Do it)
"I can't feel awake after only three hours of sleep." (Do it)
"I can't work, watch the children, go shopping, and write this book in one day." (Do it)
"I can't help you." (Do it)
"I can't get myself to practice meditation." (Do it)
"I can't talk about it with him." (Do it)

Change of Surroundings

It is true that wherever you go, you take yourself with you. Therefore, it is advisable to change your self, first, before you change where you are. It is not about where you are, but who you are. You can be miserable or happy anyplace. But it is not entirely counter-intentional to change your surroundings to change your state. Of course, your state does not change because you change your surroundings; it changes because you believe your surroundings affect you. As we've repeated many times, first comes identity and its beliefs, then the factual world or surroundings. Changing your surroundings to change your mood and perspective is more complicated, but it still works as long as you are immersed in the belief of an outside reality separate from you. In this sense, it can be beneficial to get out of town, occasionally.

Fully Conscious Behavior

Doing any exercise in this book is a conscious, non-automatic, self-determined act. It is natural and all right to have many things run on automatic, outside of your aware control. But if the automatism gets too much, you turn from being a player of the game into a pawn of the game and are no longer cause or source of much of anything. The following exercises are designed to be done occasionally, to remind you of what it means to be pure awareness, or conscious cause.

Deliberate Act 1

a) Announce what you will do next.
b) Do exactly that.
c) Continue a) and b) until you are the 100% conscious cause of every act, and feel evidence of your free choice and will. If during this exercise you find yourself doing something you did not consciously announce, stop, go back, and deliberately announce what you did (e.g. brushing hand through hair) before you continue the process.

Deliberate Act 2

a) Write the day's plan. But only write down things you will really do.
b) Do these things.
c) What does it feel like to manifest what you intended?

Deliberate Thought

a) Choose what you will think next.
b) Think that.
c) Continue until full awareness is regained (this can happen after a short time) and you notice you could be the cause of your thinking if you wanted. Note: Don't attempt to actually always be cause of your thinking. Life is much easier if you just let it flow. If you use this, use it only when your thinking has become too automatic or rampant.

Deliberate Talk

a) Stop before you say something and think about what you really want to say.
b) Say it.
c) Continue until you have regained 100% causality over your speech and realize that you are the prime source of your verbal expression.

Deliberate Feeling

a) Take a time-planner and note what emotional state you wish to prioritize each day of a week. MONDAY: Humor; TUESDAY: Appreciation; WEDNESDAY: Attentiveness;

THURSDAY: Inner peace; FRIDAY: Stability. You may also choose a day on which you deliberately practice a negative emotion.

Survival Actions

To survive in physical reality, a few actions are required—breathe, drink, eat, digest, sleep, be healthy, dream. To function in physical reality and have a good time, most of the following actions are required: see, hear, smell, taste, touch, think, feel, act, move, communicate, create, love.

This may sound obvious to you, but all these things are given without you having to do anything to have them. (Excepting those souls that have incarnated without one or two of them. Society invalidates disabilities when actually, it is training a soul gives itself. Others intentionally impose restrictions, such as doing without eating. This only works if the body has become so light and etheric that it experiences physical reality differently. But for most people, these are the given abilities.) In your most natural and resistance-free state, all of these things come effortlessly. Is it not extraordinary that the most important things are already manifested? Any additions are created by your beliefs. What you see, hear, say, etc. is based upon your beliefs of how reality works, but the tools themselves are your birthright.

13

Personal Experiences in Magic

I've read and heard many accounts of magical experiences that go beyond the ordinary consensus of what most people call reality. But what was always the most important to me was not to know about them second-hand, but to experience them myself. In this chapter, I will share some of my personal experiences, not as something I expect you, the reader, to experience, but merely as examples of the trillions of experiences one can have, to inspire you to make your own experiences. While much of this book is based on technique, a few descriptions should help. While I've had hundreds of magical experiences in my life, I have chosen a few that seem significant and appropriate to this book. My experiences in spiritual growth did not progress in a linear fashion, with me becoming more and more spiritual or more and more evolved. Linear thinking is not how magic works. We are already infinite, multidimensional, and all-knowing beings; growth or progression is only an appearance. As quickly as I reach a high level or state of awareness, I may also lose it. And as quick as I lose it, I may regain it. My most intense experiences, for example, did not take place in my adulthood, after I had learned and practiced these techniques. They took place when I was a child and a teenager. Some took place during periods in which I meditated regularly; some took place when I was leading a normal life. Not all of my life is magical in the sense of phenomena outside of the consensual reality. In fact, my experiences wouldn't be as exciting were I not also leading a normal life. I have allowed years to pass before the next big hit, but I also noticed that labeling these experiences as unusual, extrasensory, higher, miraculous, or even magical would make them so—rare jewels of surprise. So, if you wish to experience more magic in your life, you might want to loosen your belief that you are a small human being experiencing something huge, strange, or weird. Ever notice how people label these things "far out" and "unbelievable"? Declaring them strangers, rather than friends, makes them rare. Viewing miracles as a common occurrence makes them a common occurrence.

The Blue-Skinned People

The most magical experience of my childhood involved night dreams I had that were more real and intense than so-called reality. When your night dreams are more vivid, emotional, and real than anything experienced in waking life, it is a truly consciousness-restructuring experience. In my dreams, in fact, I recalled waking life as having a dream-like quality, not the other way around. My dreams mostly involved aliens from other planets and dimensions. In earlier childhood, my nightmares were of being abducted and abused. But from the age of seven to about twelve, I experienced the most beautiful encounters with a blue-skinned race, which were not only in another star-system, but also on another dimensional or vibratory level. These blue-skinned beings looked similar to humans. Many of them had Negroid features (lips & hair), but their skin was a beautiful indigo-blue. They were humorous, witty, and compassionate. I encountered them on a regular basis; they received me on their planet, which, I recall, had an overdose of oxygen. The high level of oxygen made everything seem hilarious. They received me as one of their own, who had somehow gone astray. In the first of hundreds of meetings, they made fun of me for being so serious, sad, angry, or boring. I always awoke feeling elated, powerful, with tears of joy in my eyes. The sophistication of instruction was beyond anything I learned on earth, but I was rarely able to bring all the information over to waking life. While the elation and memory of the blue beings remained throughout the day, the knowledge discussed stayed hidden in my subconscious. The things I did remember drove me to seek out science fiction literature in bookstores as an eight-year-old child. I was looking for an explanation of what was happening to me, and the first time my eyes fell on science fiction in a bookstore, I couldn't stop reading. At the age of twelve, I read books theorizing that the gods were aliens. While this confirmed what I already knew, it didn't come close to the knowledge I gained during sleep. I was taught that I had never incarnated on earth, something I didn't quite understand as a child, but clearly understand today; it explains why I felt alienated as a child. The blue-skinned beings told me that showing me this information would constitute "cheating" by earthly standards. I was taught about many different races of beings and many types of existences. Some of what I was taught by my blue friends has been integrated into this book. The contrast between what I learned on this plane and what I was taught in school did cause problems, however. Although I never spoke about any of my encounters, I couldn't take my education seriously. It started with me questioning my teachers and curriculum. After getting harsh responses, I stopped paying attention in school and was finally kicked out (of various schools) for disobeying. Today, I understand that my rebellion was unnecessary, a reality I created myself. But without it, I would not be where I am today—with more money, knowledge, and joy than those who did not get kicked out of school have. Being kicked out does not mean I remained uneducated. My room at my parents' house contained more books than the local library. Friends made fun of me for having that many books, but I had decided to educate myself, rather than have so-called authorities tell me about reality. Reality isn't remotely like anything my teachers, parents, or the media taught. I thank my blue-skinned friends, who have remained invisible since my childhood, for the alternative education.

Enlightenment

At the age of fourteen, I experienced a state that only a decade later I would learn was called "enlightenment." It was, again, within a sleeping dream state. I had been reading about and experimenting with the concept of "lucid dreams" (dreaming while consciously aware that you are dreaming). One evening, I lay down and focused on a single image, determined to focus on it for hours, or until I fell asleep. I did end up focusing on the image (a white star) for hours, but I did not fall asleep in the traditional sense; I fell into my enlightenment experience. I entered an incredibly vast space, full of stars. On the one hand, I was within the universe; on the other hand, I felt *as* the universe. My fourteen-year-old mind was intact and had difficulty conceptualizing the experience. "Oh, my God," it whispered. "I am God!" I didn't mean it in a blasphemous sense; I was in shock. "I am God," the fourteen-year-old me kept whispering. Suddenly, earthly conditioning kicked in. "Well, not the God, but a god," a phrase I would, years later, reencounter in the movie *Groundhog Day*. I floated through this space and polarities merged. I didn't know whom or where I was, but I felt more blissful and happy than ever before. The feeling of happiness grew so intense that I felt like I was going to explode. It was the most unimaginably intense experience ever had. I woke the next morning, but even in my waking life, things were different. Everything seemed more fluid and bright, and I had difficulty articulating who I was. I walked around in a near identity-less state for a few days, as high as a kite. Although I hadn't taken any drugs, I felt drugged. A rush of energy kept pulsing through my body, giving me thousands of variations of happiness. On the third day of my trip, I placed my hand on a girl's head and healed her headache. I didn't know I could do that, I just did it on an impulse. It was only after a week that I started coming down and reassembling my identity and beliefs. I witnessed firsthand how identity and beliefs are created. Thoughts moved through my mind as if I were in vivid slow motion. Although I did not know what had happened to me, I had an intuitive understanding of what was going on and did not feel as strange as others describing the non-conceptual experience might have been. After this experience, I lost much of my fear of death and powerlessness.

Healing the Hard Way

By the age of twenty-four, I had read a lot about healing oneself. It's not that I had many experiences with bad health. The last doctor's visit I remembered was back in my childhood. On some level, I always believed the body would take care of itself (which it actually does, when you don't interfere with it). But I couldn't seem to get rid of a condition—a nearly constant pressure in my forehead. Sometimes it manifested as a headache; sometimes it was simply a dull pressure around the area of the third eye. Often I didn't even notice it—not because it was gone, but because it was such a normal part of my everyday life. As I became more aware, I realized my smoking and coffee drinking was related my desire to relieve myself of this enduring pressure. I tried various methods, but they did not work. This was new to me, because "magical techniques" had helped many times before. My second step was to the doctor, but they couldn't help me, either. I planned to visit a Caribbean island with a friend of mine, but I had a secondary agenda. I would not return from the trip until that pressure was healed. I made a vow to myself. No matter how long it took, I would return a healed man. I used a willpower technique that I no longer use. It involved repeating a desired reality as an affirmation over and over and over and over again, alternating that with verbally exaggerating any doubts, second thoughts, buts, and objections I had. I was intent on applying this method until it worked. Today, I would probably not use this method because it puts ego-will over the will of the infinite self; it's an overpowering, rather than an allowing. It is healing the hard way and more effective results can be attained without ego-will. But in emergency situations, it will always work—with enough repetitions—not because the method is especially effective, but because your unbending creates a belief that makes it so. Belief in the technique makes it work. On the third day of our trip, I had a fight with my travel partner, and we went separate ways for a few days (no coincidence, of course). I felt sad and remorseful about the situation with my girlfriend, until I realized this to be an opportunity to start my healing. I walked for several hours, barefoot along the beach, voicing my affirmation and exaggerating the doubts as the technique prescribed. I must have spoken the phrase "My forehead feels free, light and good" at least ten thousand times, but nothing much changed, except for the pleasant stillness of the mind that accompanies mantras. I arrived at my hotel room. My girlfriend was not present, so I went to sleep. The next morning, she had left the room before I woke up. I got up, had some breakfast, and vowed to continue my exercise with no breaks, save for lunch and restroom visits. And on it went. By midday, another thousand affirmations lay behind me, still with no change. I continued, for the whole exercise is based on true persistence through willpower. I had sworn to win in the end. I ignored the bikini beauties, steadfastly focused on my healing. In the afternoon the doubts and counter-beliefs I was supposed to voice started running out, so I continued with the affirmation, only voicing counter-beliefs occasionally. The pressure in my forehead remained, sometimes to a lesser to extent, sometimes stronger, but never could I coax myself into believing it had disappeared, although I tried a few times. Often in those hours, I would wonder, "Is it working now? Is it happening?" but the results weren't near what I had come for. Occasionally, I shed a tear for the relationship that seemed to be gliding out of my experience. After dinner, I continued my affirmation walk along the beach, walking way out of bounds of not only the village we were staying at, but away from any place that seemed safe for tourists. The hotel lights lay far behind me. The beach looked wilder, the jungle denser. Around this time, a shift began happening, but to the worse. I entered the dark night of the soul. I couldn't see much, so my mind started projecting fears of giant spiders, scorpions, and crabs crawling in the sand, or colorful, but vicious snakes hanging from the trees, ready to snap at and kill me on the spot, or cannibals rushing out of the woods to invite me to my last meal. I was covered in cold sweat. My fear grew so intense that a few times I was unable to voice my affirmation. My voice became shaky and thin. According to this ancient shamanic technique, there was no giving up; anything that came up inside or outside me was to be treated as a counter-belief. I started exaggerating the fear. The pressure in the head got worse, turned into real pain. It was throbbing with pain, but there was something in me that rejoiced over the change. "Anything different is good," I told myself. "Before something gets better, it sometimes gets worse." Noticing I was approaching a village that didn't seem like a tourist village, I decided to return the way I came. Returning, I began to notice the lights of the tourist village. This soothed my fears sufficiently. I arrived at the hotel after about six hours of walking with one of the worst headaches of my life. The headache was screaming at me to give up the exercise, but I was intent on following through, labeling the pain a test to see how easy I would give up. My girlfriend lay in bed, sleeping. She had left a note on the table saying, "Can we talk in the morning?" I wrote back, "Sure," and lay down beside her, watching her sleep for a few moments before going to the receptionist to get some aspirin. "Am I cheating?" my disciplined self asked while I popped the pill. But the urge for survival sometimes encompasses the will of the ego. In the morning, my girlfriend and I woke arm in arm, as if nothing had changed between us. "I missed you," she whispered. We had the most beautiful sexual experience we had ever had. Funnily, right after sex, we tried to settle our differences, which led to the same thing we were fighting over before erupting again. She finally left the room, slamming the door behind her. I continued my session the same day, repeating my mantra. The pain actually increased. This time, I would not take another aspirin, but allow the pain to be part of the exercise. It felt as if something were breaking apart in my forehead; I would allow this to happen. Finally, in the afternoon of the third day of exercise, something did very obviously break open in my forehead. It felt like my head cracked. Something was freed. I sat at a café table in silent astonishment. Just a few seconds ago, I had been sitting there, whispering my affirmation so as not to arouse attention, and suddenly, without me expecting it, it started working. A feeling I had never experienced before flowed through my forehead. A supernova of lightness, tranquility, and coolness burst forth from my forehead, as if my third eye were opening to another dimension. I sat there watching the process unfold. I quit affirming and just let it happen. I knew it was over. I knew I was healed. The pressure cracked that day and never returned. I had healed something that had followed me since my childhood within three days. Some might wonder about the persistence with which I kept at it, but what are three days and a bit of pain compared to decades? Nothing, really. My self-confidence or my confidence in my power was at a maximum that day and the weeks thereafter. After the exercise, I did not speculate or worry that the issue might return. The experience of the pressure cracking and the ray of energy emanating from my forehead were too obvious not to recognize the event as a healing. Had doubts returned, I would have simply continued the exercise.

Healing the Quick Way

The same evening I was scheduled for an important meeting with a company who wanted to book me as a coach. For me, this would mean working only four weeks and earning money that would carry me through the rest of the year if I were to decide to quit working. I decided to take my bicycle to the grocery store that afternoon. On my way, my bicycle brakes stopped working, and I fell on the concrete. My elbow and right hand were bleeding. The bone of the small finger of my right hand was obviously broken; the bone protruded loosely from the flesh. It was a sickening sight, and the pain was nearly unbearable. I don't know how I did it, but something in me protested, "This can't be happening; I have an important meeting. No way. This did not happen." I stood up as if nothing had happened and walked home, intently focused on nothing ever having happened. When I arrived home, my little finger was still swollen, cut, and aching, but the bone was no longer broken. I continued my tasks, ordered something to eat, and still insisted that nothing had happened. I did not tend the wounds, did not take care of anything concerning the accident, because "nothing ever happened." "I will go to the meeting tonight, feeling refreshed and well. Nothing ever happened." Fifteen minutes later, the swelling and the cut had disappeared; there was no sign of anything having ever happened. The finger was not only completely healed, it looked like nothing ever happened in the first place. I had reversed cause and effect.

Lucky with Expensive Courses

Back in the day, I was usually short on money, I was incredibly lucky when it came to expensive seminars in the metaphysical and motivational coaching field. Lucky breaks happened several times in this context. In the year 2002, I considered taking part in a course called "Life and Enterprise Management," by world-famous coach Anthony Robbins. The course would be held on the Fiji islands and the course, plus my flight from Europe, plus accommodation would cost me about $25, 000. Unfortunately, my bank account showed $1000 in the minus. Nevertheless, I addressed my higher self with the intent of taking part in a good course on some far away and exotic island. The funny thing was that I had just recently returned from another expensive metaphysical course, which had cost me $14, 000. It was called the "Avatar Wizard Course," and it had taken place in Orlando, Florida. Since I had also gotten the means to pay the course and travel expenses by magical means, I figured I could do it again. Intent on visiting the Florida course, I had gotten an offer to translate the franchise book of a company from German to English. I agreed to do it. To get the money in time, I did the whole translation in a week and received $10, 000 for it. Not bad for someone who normally made $3000 a month. Anyway, right after that course came the idea to visit another one. The week, after placing my intention, I held an English course. I asked my students why they were learning English, and they answered, "Because we want to attend an Anthony Robbins seminar on Fiji soon." I recognized this event as something I had called forth. Sure enough, at the end of the week, my English students ask me to accompany them to the seminar as their translator. I would get the course and accommodation free; I'd only have to pay for the flight. Fantastic. There it was. Manifested within a week. I went to the travel agency to find out what tickets to Fiji would cost from Munich, Germany, and my heart sank—$6,000 to $8,000. Cheaper flights were supposedly not available. "Are they crazy?" I thought to myself. I had mind-manifested my desire to attend that course, I would be getting it free, and here was evidence that I could not afford the flight, which was as much or more as the whole course. But I remained intent on finding a way. Soon thereafter, I had the idea to surf the Internet for flights. I could fly to Los Angeles and book my flight to Fiji from Los Angeles. And this worked out well. I ended up paying $800 for a two-way ticket to LA and $1000 for a last-minute flight from LA to Fiji. Sound incredible? Not if the whole universe is on your side. On my first day at the seminar, I translated for the group of Germans. But on the second day, they told me they would no longer require translation and that I could stay to enjoy the course, which I did. For free. Near the end of the same year, I desired to take yet another metaphysical course in Hawaii. And once again, it seemed I did not have the financial means to do it. And once again, the universe proved that one doesn't need money to manifest what one wants. I got a call from someone who wanted to book me on an English course. But he didn't want to do it in Munich or London, where I usually do such courses—he wanted to combine it with a trip to Hawaii. He wanted to stay there for four weeks; I would be his teacher for three weeks. What a coincidence. I could arrange for the one free week to be the week in which the course took place. I practically was paid to travel to Hawaii and for the week of vacation, as well. The course cost a fraction of what I made. These events all took place in 2002, and they all involved getting expensive things free. Now I am in the beautiful position of no longer having to rely on money-miracles, but it was magic that got me in this position, as well.

Timeslip

I've had many occurrences in which time revealed itself as more fluid and malleable than our rigid linear conceptions hint. But the most intense event of all happened on the Island of Malta. I was listening to a recording, which apparently featured extra-low-frequency waves behind a background of white noise. I was supposed to listen to it for one hour to synchronize the hemispheres of my brain. I fell asleep while listening and had the CD player on auto-repeat. After many hours of the white noise coming through the headphones, I was in the peculiar state between waking and sleeping and had the strangest sensation of my mind or energy rotating—quicker and quicker and quicker. The rotation sped up, accompanied by a high-pitched tone. I had the feeling of leaving my body or not being properly attached to my body. I removed the headphones, turned off the CD player, and re-oriented myself in the hotel room. It was a sunny day. This was quite strange because I had started my exercise at ten p.m., when it was already getting dark. Had I really slept all night? I felt disoriented and spaced-out and went to take a shower to ground myself. Back then, I did not wear a wristwatch, but the alarm clock in the bedroom read three o'clock. My expectation was that it should be three a.m., but it must have been three p.m. because it was sunny and hot outside. I went to the reception desk to verify the time. And indeed, it was three in the afternoon. I could hardly grasp how I had slept all night and a large part of the next day without noticing. As far as I was concerned, I had only dozed three hours or so. I did not believe my earphones could have remained on my ears for seventeen hours straight, or that my batteries could last that long. Confusion welled up in my mind. I stepped outside, into a temperature way above that to which I was accustomed. The thermometer read forty degrees Celsius. I walked around in a daze, trying to accept that I had slept seventeen hours. It suddenly hit me that I had missed an appointment for lunch that day. I had gotten to know a French woman a few days before and had arranged to meet her for lunch today! I phoned her, apologizing for missing the date, but she responded in her French accent, "Oh no, no, no, no. It's okay. Our meeting is tomorrow!" Tomorrow? I accepted the schedule, thinking I had misunderstood our date. Later in the day, while reading the newspaper to a cup of coffee, I realized I was reading the same newspaper I had read the day before. I asked the waiter if they had today's newspaper, and he told me I was holding today's newspaper and that they throw away newspapers from previous days. I looked at the day, and it was Tuesday, although in my mind, it was supposed to be Wednesday. I had started my CD, White-noise ELF Meditation on Tuesday at ten p.m. Now it was Tuesday all over again! Had I time-traveled? Had I time-traveled? Had my childhood dream come true without me even being aware of it? I racked my brain for other explanations. Maybe it had been Monday, and I only thought it was Tuesday. It was my mistake, for sure. But I had to know. I retraced my days. Sunday, I definitely remembered because all the shops were closed, and I had to drink out of the mini-bar of the hotel. And it was on Sunday that I told myself I would go Paragliding above the Ocean. And on Sunday, I looked up various offers on paragliding. On Monday, I actually went paragliding. I know it was Monday because all the shops were open again. I went with a friend of mine who shook with fear of heights while acting as if everything was okay. Yes, that was Monday. It was Monday because it felt unique to not begin a workweek on Monday but to continue lazy island life (I had done a seminar on Malta the week before). I traced Monday into the evening. I recalled spending time at the beach with my French acquaintance. We arranged to meet on Wednesday for lunch. That's when I decided I would do meditation on Tuesday evening, the evening spent without her. There was no meditation Monday evening. I was with her. I woke up on Tuesday and spent much of the time idly hanging around at the hotel pool, reading. Later, I retreated to my room to do some writing on my laptop. At around ten p.m., I started using the sound CD to meditate. I fell asleep after about forty minutes. And then I woke up—to daylight—not on Wednesday, but Tuesday. There was now no doubt in my mind that I had time-traveled. So, being Tuesday again, shouldn't I be seeing the other version of myself? But I didn't. That other Tuesday was taking place in a parallel universe. I spent the rest of the day in a pleasant daze over having accomplished time-travel.

Split-Reality

An entirely different sort of parallel reality experience occurred when I had two realities that apparently didn't match playing out simultaneously without bothering each other. Rather than the two parallel realities being experienced separately, they took place at the same time and place. It was baffling. When I was younger, I understood nothing of "What you do onto others, you do onto yourself." This event found me having sex with the girlfriend of a guy to whose party we were invited. I didn't know too much about him, except that he was a jealous type and would beat the living daylights out of me if he saw me in bed with his girlfriend. I probably wouldn't be there had she and I not been slightly drunk and admiring each other at the party. "What about your boyfriend? He could come in any time," I half-heartedly mumbled a few times. "If you don't worry about it, it's not going to happen," she told me. In retrospect, she told me something I would later teach others. But on a deeper level, I did worry. As we were in the middle of the act, her boyfriend knocked on the door. "Tammy, are you in there?" My heart sank. Tamara (Tammy) was in such a state of arousal that she didn't even notice. "It's your boyfriend!" I urged. She ignored me. Looking back, I still don't understand why I did what I did. I said to myself, "What the heck. If I don't worry, nothing is going to happen. Who says he is going to enter the room? Who says he will be angry? Who says this is still his girlfriend?" Uncharacteristically, I let go of all worry and gave myself to the experience—to Tamara. Her boyfriend did enter the room, and we continued as if he weren't there. It was a magical moment, because he didn't even notice us. "Oh, excuse me," he muttered, as if we were someone else. While Tamara and I were interlocked, we watched her boyfriend walk around the room in a hypnotic daze. "Tam?" he called. He opened the closet, apparently looking for her in there. It was as if he could not believe Tamara and I were in bed together and therefore did not see it. A friend of his entered the room and didn't notice us lying there, either, or if he did notice us, he didn't notice who we were. But it got even spookier. The boyfriend, unaware of us, said to his friend standing at the door, "I have a bad feeling about this. I think she was drunk and went off with some guy." Tamara, meanwhile, was behaving even more strangely. She continued to kiss and caress me as if we were alone in the room. Looking at the incident in retrospect Tamara was behaving like a witch who knew something about reality splitting that I didn't. The two boys left the room in search of Tamara. Two hours later, the party was ending; people started leaving. I dressed and joined the party, still somewhat insecure. Would her boyfriend approach me when I was alone? I half expected it. But I was treated as if I had never been away from the party. Her boyfriend took little note of me, just like before the incident. As far as I know, Tamara was never asked about the incident.

The Hollywood Experiment

Not too long ago, I had achieved everything I set out to do. I had run out of desires. I was professionally working as a coach on the topics I wanted. I had the relationship and type of partner I wanted. I was making more than the money I wanted. I was having the spiritual experiences I wanted. Having achieved this much by the age of thirty, I began thinking along the lines of "If all this is possible, what else is?"

I wanted to know how far I could take my techniques and knowledge. I began toying with the idea of becoming a movie star. Before the breakthrough came, I broke off the project because I realized that fame and attention was not something I really wanted, but something I was toying with to see how my reality creation technique worked. But it was easy to get into the vibe of it. I know many readers don't believe such things are easy or even possible. I began by physicalizing my desire. I drove my car to nearby film studios every day, as if I had a job to do. I started reading books written by Hollywood insiders and stars. I started writing a book on how to become a star. I registered at various casting agencies. Two weeks after I started my Hollywood project, I got three jobs in front of a camera—two for advertisement and one for a starring role in a TV movie. At castings and in waiting rooms on film sets, I listened to actors' lame stories of how hard it was to get jobs, how they'd been trying for years and how little money they make. They had bought into a belief I was naively free of, as I was a beginner in the scene and knew reality creation. I also found out that for the movie role, the other actors were making less money than I was. It's really all about beliefs and definitions of what is real.

In order to physicalize even deeper, I traveled across the ocean to Los Angeles and stayed for a few weeks, further identifying myself with the scene. Upon returning, I detected the belief "Well, here in Europe, you are not going to get anywhere near stardom." A friend of mine confirmed. "You gotta live within fifty miles of Los Angeles; otherwise, you're out." I dismissed this limiting belief and re-instated my desired self. One week after returning from LA, a television moderator called me, telling me that he would be interviewing Hollywood stars and was nervous about his English—could I coach him in English? Could I prepare him for his work with superstars? I said yes. I soon found out that the guy would be talking to the big players—Steven Spielberg, Tom Cruise, Angelina Jolie. Remember, all of this started happening only three months after beginning the Hollywood creation. A few other encounters took me further up the ladder, but out of respect for celebrity privacy, I will not disclose them here. I was heading towards my desired creation at breakneck speed, and I had to decide if I really wanted it. I realized that stardom wasn't what I wanted. I love anonymity, and an acting career isn't exactly anonymous. I much prefer the peaceful realm of creative writing alone at my home on my laptop to sitting around a noisy film set, surrounded by other people's verbalized thoughts. I abandoned the project and turned it into this paragraph, which I share with you.

Shocked by the Manifestation

Since my experiences with the blue-skinned people, I had had the romantic desire to have a "close encounter" with a being from outside this planet or dimension. I also desired to see a UFO. This desire was with me for a long time. I finally realized, "Hey, wait a minute. You have all these RC tools. Why don't you just attract that experience?" A few minutes later, I realized I had been keeping the experience at bay because I was actually afraid of it. I felt a rush of fear the moment I understood that the experience was actually available to me. I interpreted my fear as having had too much input of negative scenarios of aliens as popularized in literature and movies. I identified with the version of myself that perceived UFOs as good, and let go of the bad viewpoint. The moment I ended the exercise and opened my eyes, something unusual happened. The air suddenly smelled as if something was burning. I couldn't locate the source of the smell because it was all around and concluded that it had something to do with my reality shift. The days after the shift seemed different in many ways. I felt uneasy. I later came to understand that this had something to do with the fact that I still believed in evil forces and that my desired encounter was on a higher vibratory level than the one in which I currently resided. In the weeks after the shift, nothing happened, and my unease faded. I forgot about the whole issue and gave my attention to other things. Typical for RC, that was when things started to happen (after really having let go). I was lying in bed one night, nearly asleep, when a bright flash in my bedroom had me open my eyes again. I looked around, but saw nothing. Then, to my shock, I saw something that looked like a star in the sky, except it was pulsing or flashing, as if to get my attention. As it moved closer, I could differentiate it from the stars. It wasn't a star at all, but an aircraft hovering in mid-air, pulsing soft, light colors in my direction. On one level, I understood it was benign, but on my most aware level, I lay in bed shocked, unwilling to move, scared. Another rush of fear. The light-ball was slowly pulsing, indicating that it was there. But I only thought, "Uh, look, guys, this might be too early. I am not ready for this. Please."

As soon as I thought the thoughts, the ball disappeared (or flew away—I am not sure which). I felt enough relief to start breathing normally, but I was still somewhat tense. My heart was beating faster than usual, and my hair stood up on my neck. Finally, after sitting in bed for about ten minutes, I relaxed. What was that all about? I thought, not meaning the aircraft, but my reaction. Something I had desired all my life, then it happens, and I want it to go away? My relief turned to remorse, and my remorse turned into resolve that next time, I would do better. In a dream that night, I was prompted to travel to a place called Königssee, a lake crossing the border from Germany to Austria. Having plenty of experience in RC, this is exactly what I did the next morning. I called off my appointments and went on a 180-mile drive to the lake. Once I entered the region, it started raining, which is typical for that place. While in the car, my attention was once again caught by a light ball in the sky. It hovered there and flashed at me. This time, there could be no mistake; it wasn't a star. Although I had intended to react differently than last time, fear crept up my body. My heart started racing, cold sweat beaded on my forehead. Here I was, in one of the most mystical and beautiful landscapes on the planet, witnessing an otherworldly aircraft, and I wasn't enjoying it. "Slow down guys," I whispered. The ball disappeared. Arriving at the lake, there was no sight of the light ball. Fortunately, because it was raining, there were hardly any tourists.

The lake winds alongside the mountains. One side of it is German territory; the other side borders Austria. I had been here a few times before; I have a special connection to the lake—I come here to meditate. I got on one of the tourist boats, which would drop me off at a place somewhat more remote. I was afraid of doing even this, because I understood that the more remote, the more likely my visitors would reappear, but I had made up my mind. I did not want them to get any closer. The thought of it was terrifying. This, of course, contradicted all my apparent desires and taught me that sometimes what we desire, we actually fear. I got off at a stop that featured a lone chapel and a restaurant and walked a path with which I was familiar. I was nervous; everything in me knew I was walking towards my encounter. The dream had been a message, prompting me here. Sure enough, as I turned the corner, there it was—bigger, closer, more impressive—a glowing orb the size of a hot-air balloon of changing colors. Not a flying disc, but a glowing orb. It did not look technical or silvery as my mind had expected, but more like living energy or a sort of fluid. I took a few deep breaths. I was still afraid, but seeing it close up did not heighten my fear, as I thought it would. It seemed to be emanating a calming effect. "Wow. Okay," I whispered. "Thanks for showing up," I said coyly. The telepathic communication that followed was unexpected. "You call upon us with no purpose, except for personal entertainment, and to ease your own doubts. Next time, come with a purpose." I stood there, surprised at the frank and reasonable message. But I understood. What did I expect? Some grand revelation about the destiny of humanity? I thought about asking, "Who are you?" but didn't. Somehow I understood that who they were wouldn't make sense to me and wasn't as important as who I was being, anyway. I looked around to see if anyone else was witnessing this remarkable event; the orb merely hovered in the air. A rush of a well-being flowed into me—a type I can't remember ever having felt; a liquid well-being—and then it ascended and vanished. I was changed. I walked around, stunned, feeling the liquid energy flow through my body—like some kind of super fuel. I traveled back to the shore and home in amazed silence.

Following the Pearl Necklace

There were times I would follow "the Pearl Necklace of Higher Self." I would let go of all plans, expectations, and goals and look at what option in the here and now excited me the most. I would follow that shining light until it shone no more. Then I would take stock in a new here and now and see what option shone the brightest. I would follow that until the energy of the option was used. Then I would take stock, see what options I had in a new here and now, choose the one that seemed most interesting, joyful, or exciting, and follow that. In this way, I was following a pearl necklace my higher self laid out for me, following a path my soul would enjoy. The most interesting or exciting options in any given moment are not always in alignment with the ego's concerns, which is why it can take courage. But following the intuitive path of higher self always results in the highest forms of joy, surprise, and adventure. At the age of twenty-eight, I was hanging around at home, bored to tears and disillusioned at how unfulfilling the security and comfort I had amassed were. I wished to go into the unknown. My soul found this option exciting. Without further hesitation, I packed a two pairs of jeans and some shirts into a backpack and headed to the airport, not yet knowing where I was going. I would decide which flight to take when I got there. Immediately, my mood elevated. I had broken the routine of and was heading into the unknown. Some adventurers might say that my credit card offered all the security I needed. But I had already experienced the world, traveling without money, when I was a teenager. That wasn't what I was after. I simply wished to follow the Pearl Necklace of Higher Self, and act on the impulses my soul sent me. Higher self (the higher aspect of me) knew I was in sync with it, and began guiding me. Arriving at the airport, I had hundreds of options of where to fly. But only while looking at the city of Oslo, Norway did my soul signal "yes." It produced a tingling sensation at the top of my head (crown chakra). So a flight to Oslo, I booked. I had never been there, didn't know anyone there, and had not reserved a place there. But being in the flow of higher self, everything one needs is provided. It sometimes saddens me to see how far people have strayed from their inner authority and power, from their inner coach (higher self)—how fearful they are of the unknown, having to pre-plan and strategize every move they make. And when anything unexpected happens, instead of enjoying it, they nearly have a nervous breakdown. The universe really does provide, effortlessly and efficiently. Once in the flow of higher self, an array of options and coincidences (synchronicities) pop up. As on my flight to Oslo, when I found out I was sitting beside a book author I had always admired. I did not recognize him because I had never seen his picture, only read his books. We got into small talk. I told him I wrote books, and he told me he did to. I write metaphysical books, he writes for intellectuals. I couldn't have been more pleased by the flight. Landing in Oslo, I took the airport train to the city of Oslo. I spent the day walking aimlessly, but blissfully, chose a hotel at random, and fell asleep. My night dream gave me a clear indicator of where to go next. I continued through Norway by exploring the fjords. In the presence of their magnificent beauty, my mind got even quieter, and my connection to my higher self grew stronger. I then flew from Oslo to Cairo, Egypt because the topic of Egypt confronted me three times in a single day. Someone had left a travel book for Egypt on a seat of the boat on which I was journeying. Later that day, I struck up a conversation with an American tourist who admired Norway, but kept mentioning (for no apparent reason) how I ought to see Egypt. Finally, when checking my emails in the evening, the first email I opened was an advertisement invitation to Egypt. The message was clear. Go to Egypt. Landing in Hurgada, Egypt (a typical resort town) with an American passport and no specific destination was a bit complicated. The authorities had an urgent need to know where I would be going. But I didn't know where I was going. They also needed me to be part of a tourist, diving, or all-inclusive vacation group, but I wasn't. I was a lone traveler, without a destination. They finally released me, and I went where I noticed other people going—to the large, castle-like hotel in the tourist town of Hurgadha. Resting there for a few days, two options excited me: Go diving, or visit the pyramids in Cairo, which I had never seen. The urge to visit the pyramids won over, and I joined a bus tour to Cairo, not yet knowing that it meant eight hours in empty deserts. From the instruction I had received as a child, I knew that ancient Egypt was connected to technology and alien or inter-dimensional beings. I understood that the pyramids were not built by normal means, as taught in history class. I was peripherally aware of books that made the same claims, but I never needed to read these books to know what had been shown to me. I knew I would have flashbacks by visiting these sites.

Cairo came as a shock to me after the clean, shining, rich textures and infrastructure of Norway. The current civilization was lower than the civilization that had lived here thousands of years ago. The city was dirty, loud, and vast, but I saw the majestic pyramids hovering above the city in the distance. Despite the distraction of hundreds of beggars asking me for money, I did have the flashbacks I sensed I would have. As the beggars started getting on my nerves, when I no longer had any small change to give them, I started running after them, acting as if I was begging them for money. This amusing maneuver quickly changed their attitude. The flashbacks came as intense visions that differed from normal thoughts or daytime fantasies. What they displayed was a bit eerie because they were so foreign to humanity. The ancient Egyptian civilization did not have much in common with the human journey today. I made notes in a diary and someday, I intend to incorporate my spiritually channeled insights in a book. I became restless. My ego-mind wanted more. It longed for evidence of alien visitation. But no matter how hard I tried, I wasn't given this evidence—not yet. The reason was simple: We can only perceive that of which we are the vibratory match. There could be swarms of discs hovering above me, but as long as I didn't believe I could see them, I wouldn't. I started noticing the beliefs that were actually there: "Everybody wants hard evidence, but nobody gets it. Why should I be the one to get it? Needing hard evidence equals disbelief." And so on. I had even forgotten my earlier experience with the flying orbs at the mountain lake. But what my higher self was actually leading me to—from the first day I packed my backpack and headed for the airport—was my first physical encounter with an alien life form. I had had plenty of encounters on subtler levels, but my mind was ready for the physical being. After a while, I was exhausted of the tourist trail of Cairo-Luxor-Hurgada. I didn't notice that I was no longer following the pearl necklace. The mind figured, "Well, since I am here now, I ought to stay here," but my higher self suggested moving on. It's a common mistake when following the trail of one's higher self: An experience one's higher self suggested ends, but because it *was* good, we think we have to stick to it. The indicators to move on had long come and gone. After two weeks, my mood hit a low point, and with my mood having decreased, I started noticing other things. I got a headache from listening to the dumb animation music down at the swimming pool's tourist aerobic session. Angrily, I started recalling Egyptians in Cairo throwing their trash into the river and other Egyptians bathing in that river. I became edgy, snapping at other tourists, Egyptian staff, and myself. I finally realized I had cut the connection to the pearl necklace, and I meditated for the first time in weeks. The next most exciting option was to meet an outer-dimensional or alien being in the physical. I embraced this feeling and let go. Then I checked out of the hotel and flew home. The funny thing was that I had reached the actual goal I was looking for at my starting point. But without taking the journey, the starting point wouldn't feel like that, nor would it have revealed my secret destination. On the evening of my arrival, I lie in bed staring at the ceiling. I wasn't yet asleep when my body became paralyzed. I couldn't move. Some would say I was in sleep paralysis and dreaming my experience, but I was awake and aware. I nearly panicked because I couldn't move, but I kept reminding myself, "It is all part of the journey." I felt I a presence in the room. This is how the body might react to the shock of an alien entering one's room. If something higher or outside one's belief system shows up, it tends to overwhelm one's system. Higher vibrations tend to bring up one's own fears. The being walked around the corner into my bedroom. It had taken on the appearance of an attractive woman, but I suspected that it had only taken on this appearance to ease my worries. The woman was wearing a violet overall with an undecipherable insignia on her breast. It looked like a spacesuit, but again, I suspected this appearance was taken to offer me something with which I was familiar.

"Hi there," said the woman casually. She looked human, except that her eyes were bigger and her body taller than any human alive. She looked majestic. "Hi," I mumbled. I knew what was going on, but I suddenly felt very humble. "You are paralyzing your body for protection. Your body contains energy gates that are not yet ready to be opened. It stiffens not to be forced to reveal what it wants enclosed. Relax and breathe normally." "Okay." I tried regaining my composure, but the parts of my body that weren't frozen were shaking uncontrollably. Apparently, I wasn't ready for what I had wished for. "I am here because you intended for us to be seen. I am representative of what you allow yourself to see." "Is this what you really look like?" I asked. "It is one form I commonly take," she responded. Telepathically, it was made understood that the form was taken for me but that it also represented a form that the being had in its closet of forms. "In my female expression, I really do look like this, yes," she added. I wanted to ask where she was from, but realized that the actual question was, "Where am I?" I had allowed myself to enter another level of vibration in order to perceive her. I had come halfway to her so that she could come halfway to me; in this way, we could perceive each other. What she said next surprised me. "What you call for is granted, but there is not much use in seeing us in physical form, except to satisfy the doubting mind." This was similar to what I had been told by the flying orbs at the lake. I had insisted it was of great use to me and ignored the comment. "But as a further link on your pearl necklace, it is appropriate," she added, smiling. At that moment, a ray of warmth emanated from her. The shaking stopped, but parts of my body remained paralyzed—only certain parts—for example, the right thigh was frozen, but not the left one; parts of the back were frozen, but not the whole back. "You know I am not part of your people, but your people ask me to take over the task of visiting you." This was something she let me understand telepathically. “Well, thank you for visiting.” It was all I could say. I was in awe; all the questions I might have wanted to ask were simply not there. She smiled. “A few minutes after I leave, you can look out the window and watch our craft fly away. Take a photograph if you want. That will be the evidence you longed for.” Rather than disappearing, she walked around the corner the way she had come. Soon thereafter, I felt she had left the place. The paralysis eased, but my body began trembling, which made it difficult to get a camera and operate it. The object that appeared in the sky was silvery and violet. I took a picture. It sped away at an unearthly speed. A few minutes later, tears came from my eyes. I was still trembling, and I felt genuinely disoriented and alienated. On one level, the effects of the encounter were inspiring; on the other hand, I found it difficult to focus on my daily tasks. She was right. Inviting higher dimensional beings distracts from the earth experience the soul had intended to have before incarnating. In the weeks after, I experienced a few minor body disturbances, such as flickering of the eyes, headaches, and a few rushes of unfounded fear. After about a month, the experience integrated, and I was back to normal (though never quite the same person). The lesson my higher self had been leading me to was to devote myself to the beauty of the earthly experience, rather than trying to ascend or contact something else. Through the pearl necklace, it had taught me that there’s always something behind what I want. First, it seemed like I wanted adventures and travel. But the desire behind that was an alien encounter. And the desire behind that was ultimately more love to earthly life. The circle had closed, and the necklace could be worn.

Parallel Universe Exploration

I was having an intense lucid dream in which everything felt, sounded, and looked just as real and authentic as in my waking dream. In this lucid dream, I was living the version of myself that had become a songwriter. Apparently, I wrote songs for famous singers. The amazing thing about this parallel life was that it revealed information that was true in waking life of which I did not yet have knowledge. I was never interested in the singer Whitney Houston. I did not know she was having trouble with drug abuse. But in my dream, I was visiting her in a drug clinic as someone that would help her make a comeback.

A record company had assigned me to write new songs with her. This was an actual parallel world; I had a complete set of memories from another life and all the details were in place. I was shocked at Whitney's appearance. My dreaming self knew of her condition, but my waking self vaguely remembered her as good looking. In front of me sat a wreck, hardly able to speak, let alone sing songs. I had brought pen, paper, and some pre-written songs with me. We sat down, and she told me "I'm not really up to this, you know." I felt compassion for her and caressed her hands. "Then let's just write or choose songs you will want to sing when you've recovered." She croaked a few lines of a song I had written and looked through my texts and chose a few she liked. "What's the melody of this one supposed to be?" she asked. The meeting continued for what seemed like hours, in a realistic, sometimes boringly realistic, manner. Whitney was not in very good shape. I went looking for a copy machine to copy the texts she had chosen. I left her with the texts and her dark mood and promised to return when she felt better.

The difference between this dream and any other type of dream is the degree of undistracted realism and the complete identity and memories. This was "me," but another me, one that had little knowledge of me in waking life. I had seamlessly entered another waking life. During my stay in this parallel world, I had a vague memory of my other life, for it was the me of my first life that was intruding on and viewing this one. After waking up, I started getting interested in Whitney Houston. I only recalled a few songs of hers from the '80s and a movie. Surfing the Internet, I found out that she did indeed have drug problems, even in this reality. Years later, drug clinics entered this reality as a fact.

Supernatural Abilities

We often hear of people suddenly gaining extraordinary abilities under great stress, pressure, or survival situations. The story of a mother suddenly able to lift a car with one hand to save her baby's life comes to mind. But it is not always necessary to be in a life-threatening situation to have higher abilities. One day, I was reminiscing about my childhood when it suddenly struck me like a bolt of lighting. As a child, I had jumped from buildings and trees without injuring myself! Up to that day, I had blocked this activity from my memory because it didn't fit into the laws that supposedly govern our physical existence. Another reason I hadn't remembered was because, as I child, I did not see this as anything unusual. I recalled all the times I had displayed abilities one might find outrageous. We played Zorro, Hide and Seek, Star Wars; I recall jumping off the roof of a one-story house. I recall jumping out of a tree and hitting the ground unscathed. My memory went on to other unusual events. I actually drowned and lay under water for quite a while before my cousin noticed I was missing and sent a search party into the lake to look for me. I was practically dead. I also recall my parents scolding me for jumping down from high places. They kept telling me, "You are going to break your arm! You are going to break your arm! You are going to break your arm!" This mantra eventually sank in, and one day, I actually did break my arm. After that, there were no more high jumps. The amazing thing is how I had blocked these events from my memory; I was conditioned to believe it was not possible or healthy to do certain things. We all have abilities and potentials beyond what we are conditioned to believe. In this reality, self-limitation is the game.

Twin Peaks Synchronicity

When I was younger, I purchased a complete season of a television show called *Twin Peaks* on video and watched the entire season twice in one week. I had fallen in love with the series and had the desire to immerse myself in it entirely. I switched off the phone, purchased snacks, and closed myself up, watching the series for days in a row. After I had completed it, I watched the whole thing again, noticing subtler aspects of it. This total immersion must have created a vibratory identification with it because all kinds of odd synchronicities (coincidences) started popping up in the weeks after watching that related directly to the show. Something seen on the screen was felt so intensely that it started reflecting in everyday life—in strange and fascinating ways. I first noticed this when I went to the supermarket to stock up on snacks; a women stood in front of me that looked exactly like one of the characters from the show. She didn't look similar but was a near copy of that character. She turned around and smiled at me, as if knowing my attention had been on her. I took my shopping bags and followed her out to the parking lot to have another look. As she drove away, I noticed her car had a sticker of a pine tree—the symbol of the TV series. On my way home, my mind started working on the event. Being familiar with the concept of focus and synchronicity, I deducted that either she had been attracted into my universe, or I had perceived her differently due to my current focus. Only people who have experienced waves of synchronicity themselves will fully appreciate or believe the story. One interruption to my video marathon was an appointment I had at a hotel to meet someone who required coaching. We were sitting on a terrace for a cup of coffee when we heard an owl hoot. The owl is, just like the pine tree, another icon of the series. The person I was meeting was reminded of the series *Twin Peaks* and asked if I had ever seen it. Had I ever seen it? Well, that was all I had been watching in the last days. Nobody had ever asked me about *Twin Peaks* before. As far as I could remember, this was the first time I had talked about it to anyone except my girlfriend. And it didn't stop there. I suspect that because of these two experiences, my belief and therefore synchronicity flow increased. I was looking for correspondences everywhere now, almost to the brink of paranoia. Numbers, names, and symbols popped up that resembled or could be interpreted as belonging to the show. The next thing that happened really hit the mark. Someone I didn't know invited me to travel to Seattle, Washington to coach a company. Searching on the Internet, I saw that they weren't located in Seattle, but in a small town called North Bend. I declined the offer. Maybe I wouldn't have if I'd known then what I found out later. I had been a great fan of the series, but not to the extent that I looked up specifics, or chatted about it. A few weeks after the offer from North Bend, I became curious as to where the show was shot, and looked it up. It was filmed in the area around North Bend, Washington. Synchronicity. The attractor factor had become so intense that I had been invited to be there physically. I mention this story to awaken the reader to the mysterious joy of the interrelation of all things. Back then, I wasn't aware that one of the creators of the series was David Lynch. About five years later, I became fascinated by other works of his, due to their correspondence to my interpretation of the "many worlds theory," and I realized he had also been the creator of that old favorite series of mine.

Moving through Depression

When I was about thirty, after having had many highs, professional successes, personal successes, extraordinary states, travels, experiences, fulfilling relationships, good health, and financial abundance, I became depressed, despite all the things I had achieved. I felt disillusioned with what I had been learning and teaching. I felt burned out, bored, and empty. I lay home for days, not knowing what to do, not knowing where to go, not wanting to speak to anyone. I despised the books I had written and despised RC, which I temporarily viewed as utter nonsense (after having taught it for more than eight years). I was feeling so low and out of tune that I couldn't even get myself to use any of the techniques that I had been teaching and learning. And if I did, they didn't get me out of my state. Nothing got me out of it. I felt tired, fatigued, and dull all the time. Coffee, cigarettes, and sweets were my companions, but not even they did the job anymore. I was crying, sitting around dully, surfing the Internet senselessly, or in my highest states, cursing someone. Deep down, I knew there was still a part of me that wouldn't give up or was at least aware that I was depressed, but not even that part of me seemed sure anymore. I cancelled several coaching commitments because I didn't want to stand in front of anyone in this state, but especially because I no longer believed I could help anyone, or that what I said was significant. I'd had lows in my teen years, but this was one of the lowest states I'd ever experienced. After a few weeks, it affected my health. My muscles started twitching uncontrollably. What was going on with me? I would awaken from some degrading, evil nightmare and find everything grey, meaningless, and dull. I felt extremely heavy during the day; I hadn't smiled in months. Even my sex drive, which could normally get me out of low states, was at zero. I was single at the time, so at least I couldn't get on someone's nerves. Then, one morning, I decided to come clean. I was so low that it wouldn't have any effect at first, but I had to keep moving upwards. I began by lying down and breathing myself through the most horrific scenarios I could imagine. I lay for hours, breathing it all in, breathing it all out. Tears ran down my face. Once, I had to take a break to throw up. After a few hours, I felt a lighter. I distracted myself with some movies and fell asleep. The next day, I continued my cleansing and started using consciousness practice and tools again. I wrote a lot. Used special affirmation techniques. Meditated. I was still quite low, but now I was at least willing to do something. Days went by; I was still in a heavy state and always had a slight headache and nausea. I had one session in which I cried as long as I could. It took forty-five minutes until all the tears were out and I couldn't cry any longer, but I felt a lighter without having to create it. The problem had been that I was trying to create over my depression, trying to make myself happier, instead of letting it come naturally and allowing for slow, linear progression. When I was feeling a bit better, I, once again, understood the issue. I believed I had already achieved everything, which is generally a good belief, but I included "and there's nothing more interesting to achieve." It was as simple as that. I re-aligned to new and higher versions of myself and the phase passed as suddenly as it had come. Only a few weeks later, I couldn't even remember the low phase.

Floating

It was at a time when I was using a floatation-tank and going scuba diving that I had a few remarkable shifts in consciousness. A floatation tank is a sensory-deprivation tank, once used by the NASA for zero gravity simulation, and by dolphin researcher John C. Lilly for experimentation on consciousness. Today, they are mostly used for meditation. One lies in the dark and floats on salt water. Having no sight, no sound, and nothing to do, all that is left is one's self and one's thoughts. I was visiting a floating tank about six hours a week. In addition, I practiced scuba diving, which produces similar sensations. This overdose of floating apparently led to the following experience: As I walked around town, I at first felt sickened by life and overwhelmed by appointments and the things I had to take care of. I was sweating, had a headache, and was generally sick and tired, hopelessly desperate for the peace I had been experiencing on and under the water. I tried breathing, coffee, meditating, etc. to change my mood, but on that day, nothing worked. My dismal vibratory state led to various mishaps. In a parking garage, I got angry at the small parking spaces and hit one of the walls, putting a dent and a white scratch in its side door. Driving out of the parking garage, I accidentally drove onto a one-way street and was stopped by the police and fined a large sum of money. Half an hour later, an important customer called off an assignment, losing me another large sum. My headache increased. I stopped to get aspirin, but the pain did not subside. I longed for a bed in which to lie down and forget the world, but I was in a foreign city. All the hotels were fully booked. Part of me realized that I was on a negative roll and that the frequency I was emanating was attracting all sorts of undesirable events. I tried various techniques to change my state, but nothing worked; I wasn't willing to give up resistance, to calm down. I started cursing the people I saw walking around, having a negative label for every one of them. "Fucking tourists," "Damn cops," "Dumb Arabs," "Dumb Germans" and so on. I couldn't believe the hatred that was coming out of my mind. I started cursing all the efforts I had put into meditating in the floating tank—all for nothing, it seemed. Everything and everyone was suddenly a problem—because I was the problem. In the evening, I smelled of cold sweat. One look in the mirror showed rings under my eyes—rings I hadn't seen the day before. My head was pounding with pain. I had nowhere to go. I was mad at the world. I stopped the car and broke down crying, my head on the steering wheel. I felt remorse over the way things had been going; this day was only the continuation. After crying, I sat in the car staring at a river in front of which I was parked—for hours. I had stopped doing anything. I had given up. Slowly but surely, deep peace was flooding me, but it was not my regular relaxation, not even the centered, smooth feeling I had after floating or diving, it was more than that—and it had come without warning, without technique, without desire. It was like a powerful drug flowing through my veins, not that I had ever experienced hard drugs, but in this instance, I could imagine what it felt like. A rush of energy through my whole being. Tingling sensations all over my body. Inside, I felt shifts of energy, a rearrangement of sorts, as if my skull was turning and my spine reloading. What seemed so remote only a few hours ago was fully present now. "My God, this feels good!" And I hadn't had to go anywhere, see anything, do anything, or take anything. I don't even know how it occurred. Had it been the overload of floating to higher realms that produced my catharsis, bad luck, break down, and break through? Probably. I felt new and energized for weeks thereafter. The tingling sensation was present when I woke up in the morning, rushing through my body in pulses of natural euphoria, and it would be with me when I lay down at night, blanketing me with waves of love and excitement. The scratched car suddenly became amusing—not because I talked myself into it, but because it was. I was reminded that sometimes, before things get better, they get worse.

Another Self-Version Seen by Someone Else

For a time, I was working on getting a black BMW sports car by magical means. I would lie in bed for hours, daydreaming about my experience of driving the car. The car did eventually manifest in physical reality (I purchased it when my income experienced a surge), but what happened before that was quite amazing. A coaching student wrote, in an email to me, that he'd seen me driving on a certain highway in Switzerland. He asked if I owned a black BMW, because that's what he'd seen me driving. I asked him when he had seen me. I told me, "last Thursday," exactly the day I was imagining myself driving the black BMW—also on a highway in Switzerland. The person had seen a parallel universe version of me.

Mutual Dream

I woke up beside my girlfriend; we had been lying forehead to forehead. After she woke, I started telling her the dream I had about being at a location with a flamingo statue. She was able to continue the story because she had had the same dream—not a similar dream—the very same dream, only from her viewpoint. We actually took turns continuing the story of the dream. We had shared a common reality during the dream.

Another Parallel Universe

I teach people that outside surroundings appear not to change at first when applying shape shifting or reality-identification techniques. But sometimes, if one is open to radical change, even the outer surroundings change dramatically the same day you apply the PURE technique. That morning, I had meditated and shifted myself into a slightly different reality. I was scheduled to go to a hairdresser I had been to many times around midday. Upon arrival, I was astonished to find that a brand-new building had been built right beside the hairdresser's place. "How could they build it so quickly?" I asked myself.

I had only been there four weeks ago, and four weeks ago, there was a lawn and a park bench, without any sign of a building or even a planned building. I stood there for a while, baffled and confused. I entered the hairdresser's shop and asked, "When did they build that house?" The staff looked at me incredulously. "Oh, it's been there for a few years, actually. I remember when it was built," said one of them. "It was shortly before Christmas, five years ago." I stared in disbelief. "But wasn't there a park bench and a small grass hill there?" They couldn't tell me or couldn't remember, but they looked at me as if I was mixed up. I could have sworn that only a few weeks ago, the place looked *entirely* different. After getting my hair cut, I went out to examine the place. Behind the building, everything looked exactly as it had before—except for the brand-new building. Finally, I accepted that I had shifted into a parallel reality, and that the building was a good indicator. It was the first of many physical reality shifts I learned to accept, rather than labeling me insane, as the consensus-reality would.

The Invisible Man

I recall playing hide and seek as a child and knowing how to make myself invisible to other kids. I developed a technique in which I didn't even have to look for hiding places, but simply became invisible or merged (shape shifted) into my surroundings. It involved not directly looking at or thinking about the person looking for me, and believing I had melded with the bushes or buildings around me. The kids looking for me would walk past me without noticing me. I can recall at least half a dozen applications of this technique.

Shifting Pain within Minutes

I lie in the bed of a hotel room, unable to sleep because of a nearly unbearable toothache. The hotel is relatively remote, so there is no pharmacy nearby. Neither does the receptionist have any aspirin. If I had a painkiller, I would have taken it without hesitation. I attempted to use some of the techniques I teach, such as "breathing into the pain," but none of them worked. The motivation behind the techniques was resistance, and they only made the pain worse. I tried to focus on something else, like reading or TV, but I couldn't. The pain was so intense that my vision blurred. The pain went all the way from my mouth to my head. At last, I remembered the parallel universe shifting that I teach. If it really worked, it should work now, right? I envisioned another version of me lying in bed. That version of me lay in peace, without pain. That version of me never had a toothache; it didn't need to heal anything. I lie beside that version for a while. As soon as I felt ready, I rolled over into that version of me; I became that version. The pain subsided almost immediately. I don't know how quickly it vanished because I wasn't paying attention to it (after all, I was the version who never had it), but that was the end of the toothache story, and I fell asleep in peace.

14

Identity and Reality

Masking and Unmasking the Self

Where many spiritual traditions seek to unmask the self to find the real selves behind all the assumed selves, reality creation seeks to mask the self—not randomly or reactively, but purposefully. Spiritual enlightenment resembles removing all masks and identification. What is left when you remove everything? What is left after you remove what is left? The true self. The infinite self. Reality creation is, in some ways, the opposite pole, or the other side of the coin. It resembles putting on a disguise for Halloween. Ultimate self is infinite, and while it contains and experiences all identities, it has no identity. It is impersonal and wears no mask. Finding enlightenment can be as easy (or difficult) as ceasing to create anything at all. See RC as putting on a mask to correspond to a certain aspect of all that is, but once you notice how you have taken off the costume, you don't have to criticize yourself for it—simply put it back on. Why people curse themselves for straying from a desired path is a mystery to me. It is a fine opportunity to get back on the path, but the behavior of self-invalidation again implies, "I didn't create it. There are causes outside of me, causes forcing me to take off my mask." The reality creation practitioner will simply put the mask back on, no more, no less.

When I talk about reality creation being similar to taking on a role or a new identity, people often respond with "I couldn't do that. I can't be someone I am not." And that's exactly the reason they will not experience anything new: They so firmly believe, "I am this and that." But RC doesn't teach that one must be something one doesn't want to be. It teaches that if a certain reality is desired, then that is really you, and you can have a deeper connection with that already-existing part of you.

Just who do you think you are? RC teaches only two identities or identifications: world self and infinite self. I have broken these two identities down, separated them into fragments one could theoretically and practically discern and notice. This separation is by no means necessary, but it provides a few interesting insights into an otherwise mysterious realm. It will not hurt to release some of the less fulfilling aspects of identity. In other words, it's much easier when you are not wearing many masks on top of each other. In fact, de-identification followed by re-identification creates the most magic. That is why the PURE technique begins in de-identified silence and proceeds with a new identification. What follows is a scale of identities, with the upper ones more related to infinite self and the lower ones more related to world self.

0. Infinite Self

The aspect of self that contains all, is all, and is none of it, all at the same time. Source.

1. Oversoul

This is the viewpoint that projects itself into various existences, dimensions, parallel universes, spaces, and timelines. To give you a picture: Look at your hand with its five fingers. One of these fingers is your current existence in this time and space. The other fingers are other versions of you in other realms. The hand itself is the oversoul.

2. Higher Self

This is the viewpoint of "I," without further definition. This is the witness, not far removed from infinite self and even less removed from oversoul. In our analogy, the fingers are the identities, the hand the oversoul, and the higher self is one or more of the knuckles. The higher self remains unidentified with these things and events. It can perceive, observe, and witness. It has greater overview and wisdom than the world self. As soon as it identifies with something, it becomes a core identity.

3. Core-Identity

This is one of the fingers of the oversoul—one of its existences. The minimal definition of the core identity is "I am." The core self does not have to be achieved—you are already it. The formula "I have to do X in order to be myself" is nonsensical from this viewpoint. This is the spontaneous self, the child-like (not childish) self, the free self that can easily identify and de-identify with things. This is what you are when you are a discarnate soul. The core identity is aware of all the identities below (on the scale), as well as the higher self, while identities below are mostly unaware of higher aspects.

3.1. Identity

This is the "I am," followed by another word. "I am this, I am that." Identities are made up of character traits, personalities, mental images, beliefs, intentions, and appearances with which "I" identifies its self. This is a clearly defined viewpoint. This is where pure consciousness identifies with physical substance. This is the world self, as distinguished from infinite self. For purposes of examination, identity can be broken into further identities.

3.2. Claimed Identity

A set of traits are claimed by the self to experience a specific reality. Some schools would call this the "ego self." Example: "I am a doctor." When the world self claims an identity, it starts corresponding to a certain reality, attracting situations that match what was claimed.

3.3. Ambivalent Identity

These are a set of traits which the world self sometimes wants to be and sometimes doesn't want to be. As they are composed of desire *and* resistance, what they refer to can seem hard to release. Example: In the morning, you say "I really enjoy being a doctor," and in the evening you say, "I hate being a doctor." Because of the ambivalence and indecisiveness involved, neither manifests fully. The recommended practice for release would be to become aware of the thesis-antithesis nature of the issue and move to a viewpoint above the two (synthesis, core identity) in which neither of the two are fully relevant and both are seen as the same issue. From this higher viewpoint, a new identity can be assumed.

3.4. Resistant and Projected Identity

The resistant identity goes along with the projected identity; they are two sides of the same coin. If you say, "I am a good doctor, and he is a bad doctor," "I am good" is the resistant identity. It was assumed in order to protect oneself or resist something or someone in physical reality. "He is bad" is the projected identity that automatically follows the resistant identity. "I am smart; he is stupid." One side is the resistant identity, the other the projected identity. When pure consciousness or a neutral awareness puts on a mask, one of the things he sees through this mask are things that oppose it. This is how resistant and projected identities are created. It would, however, be possible to assume an identity (mask) without invalidating its opposite. This occurs by freely choosing masks rather than reacting to others or circumstances. The realization here is that both sides are *you.* Although it may be hard to grasp, labeling someone as inherently stupid not only filters out all evidence to the contrary, but also has the effect of labeling yourself as stupid, and will not only attract undesired people into your life, but also the opposite: Someone you perceive as smarter than you makes you stupid in comparison. This is the turnaround when the projected identity becomes the resistant identity and vice-versa. Then it's "I am stupid, he is smart."

4. Unwitting Identity

This is a set of traits that the self has taken on or projects without noticing. You perceive these masks without noticing them. Any of the aforementioned identities can be unwitting (subconscious), and often are.

5. Approval Identity

This is a set of traits you pretend to embrace because they are seen as beneficial. It is a dishonest, fake identity. The approval identity is the same thing as 3.1, but you claim it to look a certain way in front of others, sensing it is not really you. It is called "approval identity" because you claim it to avoid disapproval (or what you fear would be disapproval) and to gain approval (or what you think would be approval) from others.

Identity can be further split and fragmented for detailed examination. We can move it up to levels of God-consciousness and down to stereotypical costume, parasitical, or demonic identities. But the already shown identities are quite enough to gain extraordinary insights and quicken the re-expansion of self.

Comment on Identities

An identity is a defined viewpoint from which life is experienced. It allows the experience of one parallel universe to be distinguished from another. Infinite consciousness, which flows through an identity, becomes attention. The traits of the identity determine which facets of reality attention will flow towards routinely, and which realities are consolidated to physical form.

The claimed identity wishes to assume certain viewpoints and steer attention and efforts corresponding to that viewpoint and reality. It wants to experience.

An ambivalent identity is a package of claimed identities plus resistance, or projected identity. It is an identity that has gotten so immersed in identification it is in the process of disintegration.

A resistant identity does not intend to experience a certain reality (which it therefore will). Its aim is to fight, beat, and overwhelm a projected enemy, and if it can't do that, it will subdue itself and become a victim. The polarization creates an energy field of tension that easily attaches to sadness, fear, and anger. The persistent identity rarely realizes that the projection is himself—it is mostly convinced that the other is the "bad guy." The resistant identity is caught in imaginary scenes with its enemy. The projected identity was constructed by the resistant identity so it could have something to fight.

The easily recognizable traits of an identity are, opinions, beliefs, attitudes, morals, memories, preferences, habits, addictions, emotions, pains, body postures, presence, originality, relative status, relationships, use of language.

Comment on the Relationship between Individual Identity and Group Identity

A strong group identity does not come about by homogenizing individuals (making them all the same). This is a common misunderstanding. A powerful and effective group identity originates when each individual is strengthened in its individuality and differences. That would be "diversity in unity" or "unity in diversity," rather than only one of the sides. Unity does not mean eliminating diversity, but appreciating the differences that each individual brings to the whole. If each individual were to follow his highest joy and purpose, the pieces of the group puzzle would fit together perfectly, without coming into conflict with others. Only by not being himself does he not fit the group. The artificial dichotomy of "left wing" and "right wing" politics takes place on a level where this is not completely understood.

Meeting People You Don't Like

Two things help to keep your energy up when meeting people you don't like: Love and Leave. If you are aware enough, you will recognize the undesirable person as a projected identity and notice which resistant identity you have adopted. In this sense, that meeting allows you to find out more about yourself. Once you notice the resistant identity, it begins dissolving automatically. If you are not aware enough to notice the reflection and change your reaction, you have the option of leaving and giving your attention to things you prefer. Do not watch so much for the energy flowing from others to you, but the energy flowing from you to others.

Meditations on Identity

If you wish to learn more about this or release unwanted aspects of yourself (thus coming into a more conscious connection to infinite self), you might want to apply some of these meditations. I remind the reader once again that the quickest way to solve issues is the PURE technique.

Meditations on Ambivalent Identities

In preparation for working with ambivalent identities and suppressed aspects of self, you might want to try the following experiment to gain an understanding of how ambivalence comes to be:

1. Write down things you used to like, but don't like any more.
2. Write down some things you used not to like, but like now

The process:

Sit in silence and relax into the viewpoint of the non-identified witness. Notice an ambivalent identity—meaning, someone you sometimes like being and sometimes don't like being. Example: "I want to be free; I will end the relationship" and "I want to be connected and stay in the relationship." Notice how both identities exist in different universes with no apparent connection. Once you are aware of the two sides of yourself, start projecting (creating) a beam of resistance on the version of yourself desiring something; afterwards, project (create) a beam of desire on the version of yourself that desires something. Project desire on the version of yourself that resists something, and then project resistance. Then merge both sides of yourself (in your imagination). Then observe neutrally from a higher vantage point, in which neither of these decisions are truly you or truly relevant. After you open your eyes, ask yourself, "Who do I want to be, independent of circumstances?" Identify with that new version of yourself, rest in it, and release it to infinity. Note that you don't have to decide for either of the two viewpoints, but take in a third viewpoint and feel it, and then watch the events unfold naturally from there. Intentionally projecting resistance and desire on both versions of you (which may seem a strange thing to do at first) neutralizes both polarities. You will feel the effects even if you don't fully understand it. The meditation takes about ten minutes per topic.

Meditations on Resistant and Projected Identities

In general, you are aware of one side of the resisted projected identity, while being unaware of the other side. The purpose of this process is to use the side you are aware of to find out what the other side of the coin is. By doing this, the side you are unaware of comes to light and dissolves. A game you see as limiting or stupid is no longer worthwhile and one quits doing it naturally. By viewing the side of which you are aware, you extrapolate the side of which you were not aware. Once you become aware of the other side of an identity coin, witness it without resistance or invalidation for a few moments. Then witness the interaction between both identities and how you create them both; one cannot exist without the other. State, "This is no longer I" and allow yourself <u>to be the identity you want without having to invalidate its opposite</u>. The meditation will lead to relief and the discontinuation of games you no longer want to play.

The process is:

1. Notice the projected or resistant identity, and from that, extrapolate the other side.
2. Witness both sides.
3. Witness the interaction between them.
4. Decide to be what you want to be without invalidating its opposite.

People with whom you can perform the process:

* Someone who causes you to react emotionally

Let's say you see that the projected identity is an angry person. From that, you become aware that the resistant identity is "fearful me" or "also getting angry me."

* Your partner (during a fight)

Let's say that the projected identity is "She doesn't listen to me." From that, you become aware that the resistant identity is "I can't explain myself," or "What I say is not interesting."

* Something you like about yourself that separates you from others

Let's say you notice, "I am so good looking." The projected identity then might be, "They are ugly."

And so on.

Spiritual Version of Handling Projected Resistant Identities

1. Observe reality as you perceive it
2. See this impression as a projected identity
3. Discover or imagine the resistant identity
4. Notice the interaction and separation between both
5. Specify that this is no longer you; choose who you want to be without invaliding something else.

To play a game, you need at least two parties and their interaction. Most people's awareness is limited; they aren't even aware of these three components and believe that they exist independently of each other. But nothing that happens is outside or independent of you. The aforementioned meditation takes you out of the limited viewpoint of A by showing you the viewpoint of B, the interaction of C, and finally the viewpoint outside of it all that realizes that ABC is a single thing.

Observe something. Now notice how this event consists of three things: The observer, the observed, and the observing itself. And all three are one thing.

Meditations on Approval and Disapproval

The pressure of trying to look good and avoiding looking bad, rather than resting in alignment with your desires is the issue. Craving approval and fearing disapproval is a form of dependence on other people. It is based upon beliefs of how you're "supposed" to behave or not behave. In reality, they were conditioned into the child-self that was desperate to gain its parents' attention. "If you're a good boy, you get X. If you're a bad boy, you get Y." This leads to putting on masks to gain approval, praise, attention, or love and avoid disapproval, criticism, or removal of attention and love. A "having to look good" identity leads to you becoming a chess figure in society's game. All others have to do is to push your buttons, and you will behave according to their desires.

A "having to look good" identity has the aim of fulfilling someone else's desires (or what they mistakenly believe are someone else's desires) to gain approval or avoid disapproval. The less attention, approval, or appreciation you give yourself, the more dependent you'll be of others' attention or "chemical attention," meaning alcohol, food, nicotine, or drugs. If other people's desires (or what you assume are other their desires) do not fit your own desires, a contradiction arises. Someone pushes the button of impending approval or disapproval, and you quickly forget the desires or intentions you had, lose poise and start working to fulfill the needs of the other. All of this touches on peer pressure, social status, and expectations.

Most of the beliefs a child creates are based on its reactions to disapproval/punishment or approval/reward of its parents. Just as much as parents are trying to fulfill their child's desires, the child is trying to fulfill its parent's desires, albeit in a more random way. Both parties (parents and child) measure their success by the approval gained.

This is a source of stress. Whenever you experience pressure, it is probably based on a core belief about what someone else is expecting from you. Although circumstances have changed since your childhood, these beliefs are still operating on some level. Since this issue can drag you out of alignment with your chosen reality, it is worth looking at. Resting in your claimed reality means continuing to do so, despite disapproval from others. Saying "no" can be done, without attacking or invalidating him or her, in a soft and respectful way. Saying "no" in a rebellious way implies that you are projecting a belief about what their expectations are. If you do have a need-to-look-good identity, saying no to someone will arise as an emotional reaction and culminate in a fight or argument. A loving, respectful "no," on the other hand, can work miracles. Should the expectations of others become too strong, a change of job or location can be helpful. Fear of criticism and disapproval is detrimental, but addiction to approval and praise can become a problem by which others can manipulate you. When you are desperate for approval, there is something amiss. Becoming aware of these factors and releasing them will reduce stress and conditioned responses and increase honesty, authenticity, and self-determination.

If you'd like a deeper examination of this issue, you may want to try the following process.

For addiction to approval

1. Write down the name of someone who gave you attention or approval when you really needed it.
2. Write down what identity you had to take on in order to gain this approval.
3. Write down what needs you believe this person has that makes you behave the way you do.

Example:

1. Mom
2. A good and decent son
3. "I hope my children are responsible. My son seems to be lazy."

Once you have that down, meditate, and view the person projecting the expectation and yourself putting on a mask to fulfill that expectation. Notice the stress or pressure between the two parties. Notice that the whole thing is your belief. Then release the image. Reidentify with your true nature.

For fear of disapproval

2. Write down the name of someone that disapproved of you.
3. Write down the identity you took on in order to avoid their disapproval.
4. Write down what needs you believe the person has that makes you behave the way you do.

Example:

1. Dad

2. Get good grades at school. Hide bad grades.
3. "I want to be proud of my children."

Once you have that down, meditate, and view the person projecting the expectation and yourself putting on a mask to resist it. Notice the pressure between the two parties. Notice the whole thing as your belief. Then release the image. Re-identify with your true nature.

The Habits of Identity

Habit: Something you do automatically, unwittingly, or half-consciously. In a positive sense: Something that happens effortlessly, almost by itself. In a negative sense: Something that seems beyond your control. An example of a helpful habit: Driving the car (you don't think about every movement consciously). An example of a non-helpful habit: Eating too much without thinking about it or being able to stop it.

Ritual or routine: In a helpful sense—a collection of actions that reproduce results and states reliably. In a non-helpful sense, a collection of habits (or a mega-habit) that seems to be running on automatic.

Purpose of this section: To show you how much of your life is run by habit and how habits are sustained by identity and choice and can easily be dislodged.

Releasing unwanted habits

The key to releasing habits is consciousness or awareness. Habits only seem powerful because they run unwittingly or half-consciously. Once you become aware of a habit as a habit, it's actually not a habit anymore, unless your belief dictates it is. The moment you become aware of a habit you can quit doing it. Becoming aware of it may suffice to dissolve the habit. An example: You become aware that you run down the stairs every day in a way that strains your knees and legs. Once you are aware, you go down the stairs in a more mindful fashion. If becoming aware of and repeating the opposite a few times is not enough, people try to overcome habits using willpower. Raw willpower only works if unbending persistence and hard work are behind it. Otherwise, it will just produce more of the habit and end in resignation. Why? If you say, "I am going to forget about this," that implies remembering. "Not thinking about smoking" implies thinking about it. Most of the time, raw willpower fails and is exhausting. Some schools teach that the elements or building blocks of a habit need to be reversed, changed, or confused and that this will release the habit. This works in that it makes you aware of the habit, but I'd like to suggest other approaches that are more in alignment with allowing.

If you use the PURE technique and align with the preferred version of yourself, you won't be doing anything in this direction. The alignment takes care of unwanted habits automatically. But let's assume that for some reason, you chose a longer path. In this case, I would recommend you consciously reproduce or create the unconscious habit. What you create on purpose, you gain a certain amount of control over. If, for example, I bite my nails all the time and are unable to stop, I would start biting my nails on purpose. Becoming the source of biting your nails implies that you can release it. By making something worse intentionally, you become overly aware of it, so that soon you will say, "What am I doing here, anyway? I might as well quit." By creating something on purpose, you learn that you are creating it, and you gain insight on why you are creating it (pay-off). Maybe the pay-off is a sense of relaxation, which you can then allow without having to bite your nails. There is nothing mysterious about anything you do.

You may want to copy the unwitting behavior then switch to creating the behavior you prefer and alternate the two. You would intentionally bite your nails, and then intentionally put your hands on the table and relax them. You would alternate between the two, back and forth, until the bad habit ceases and you can easily rest your hand on the table. Soon the habit will disappear altogether.

Creating new habits is a question of associating plenty of positive things with the habit you want to create. So if you can't overcome yourself to create the habit of jogging in the morning, but you'd really like to, what you do is connect as many benefits to jogging as possible or list the different ways in which jogging is good, fun, beneficial. Training yourself on this will soon have you addicted to what you previously avoided. Again, applying the PURE technique, none of this is necessary. But since the easiest way is not always the appropriate way, I hint on additional ways.

Mirror World Meditation

Notice something that bothers you. Ask yourself, "Which version of me feels bothered by that? Which version of me wouldn't feel bothered by that?" Identify with that version of you and look as that version.

Everything is a reflection of you. Everything that happens is part of the process. If you want to know what you think about yourself, notice what you think about others.

The Authority of the Creator

How well a teaching or technique works depends on the authority with which you use it. If applied with authority, even the most mediocre methods will be effective in change. If the authority of the creator, which is composed of self-worth, self-trust, self-love, and personal responsibility, is at a low point, even the most brilliant methods will have little effect on the self.

Meditations on Higher Self

On a relatively low level of awareness, your higher self is viewed or experienced *as* God, guardian angels, etc.

On a higher level of awareness, your higher self is viewed or experienced *as* intuition, an inner coach, your soul guide, inner guru—something with which one can communicate.

On yet a higher level of awareness, one doesn't communicate *with* one's higher self but *as* one's higher self. On this level, one recognizes one's higher self as part of oneself, as an aspect of one's self or as one's self, without much separation.

Linearly speaking, on a mediocre level of awareness, this part of one's self is seen as outrageously distant and huge, something to which one must bow down.

But on a normal level of awareness, it is accessible as a higher being, a magical thing. Communicating with it can be as easy as assuming that this part of you exists and beginning a dialogue with it. This higher self reacts to honesty and humor, so keep your conversation straightforward and light. You can ask the god within yourself any question. The questions are always answered according to what you are able to handle. The answers can come when in a normal mood, as symbols, intuition, hunches, dreams, and coincidence. If they come directly and there is no need to decipher them, you are in a high state of mood. Your higher self designed your life, so enjoy it. Before you incarnated onto this planet, you designed the parameters of your life—not the details, but a rough outline (where you'd be born, what you would look like, what vibratory level you'd start with, a few interests you'd have, and a few people you would definitely meet). The pre-incarnate viewpoint is your higher self that is simultaneously aware of incarnation and pre-incarnation, while your world self is solely aware of incarnation. Within the rough outline of your life's plan, the world self exercises free will and can choose to take routes other than those planned. Taking the pre-paved route of higher self (ultimately yourself) is the easiest and most fun, but you can always make it harder. The rough outline can be termed "destiny," although it's flexible. This destiny can, by the power of free will, deviate into many variations. Coming off your chosen path too far, stretching the limits of your previously chosen life, causes suffering and pain. If you don't like the scenery you have chosen, don't fight it. Instead, return to the viewpoint of higher self (in silence) and chose a new path from that viewpoint. That is one way to change the rough outline or destiny despite still being incarnate.

The higher self is always present, in the background, with a soft smile. It never denies a question addressed to it. It never denies a desire addressed to it. The only catch is that you have to notice its guidance. You desire something, but your higher-self, the creative aspect of infinity, has its own way of delivering, which often does not match the limited views of the world self on how something is supposed to be delivered. Since the world-self is unwilling to imagine that event X could possibly have anything to do with desire Y, he/she denies it.

The higher self is you—the version of you beyond the concerns of the world self. The world self may become so immersed in physical reality that this other aspect seems non-existent. Your higher self is the observing witness that is not seduced by the ever-changing winds of desire and resistance. Although it is sometimes overlooked in the noise and chatter of daily life and the mind, its presence is never lost. A few minutes of silence immediately reconnects you to it. Because of its expanded viewpoint, it naturally expresses love, understanding, compassion, and humor. Your higher self follows the path of least resistance, playfulness, and joy. Your world self follows a calculated strategy, seemingly to its own benefit, and becomes immersed in a world of struggle, separation, and duality. It resists and craves; its attention jumps around like a frightened chicken gone mad. It is immersed in fear and rigid opinions and looks for satisfaction "out there." Your higher self gives in to the flow of infinity that governs the unfolding of universes. It observes life with a light touch, abandon, and appreciation. It doesn't judge and knows not of lack, ownership, or need. Your higher self has the ability to act or intervene, but if it does, it is only in the interest of a more comprehensive overview.

The Observer and the Higher Self

When the world self eases or neutralizes charged attention, goes into silence, becomes acceptant, or allows more well-being to flow, it re-connects with your higher self. The observer mode allows one to see reality as it really is, without all the filters.

The meditation of your higher self consists of observing the world from the higher-self viewpoint. This is the same as "silence without labeling" from the PURE technique, except that isn't necessarily done with eyes closed. One silently observes the restless mind with compassion or neutral attention. It has nothing to do with self-analysis or introspection. That would be observing the mind with the mind, trying to figure something out or questioning what is happening. Instead, you observe without expectation or judgment. You are pure, crystal-clear awareness. You may observe the mind conducting its introspection and analysis, but you are not involved. You observe how the world self is thrown here and there by desire and resistance—how it suffers and celebrates, how it goes here and there, does this and that. All the while, the higher self remains soft and silent. You are identified with the ever-present ocean of silence behind worldly events. The meditation needn't be done continuously, but allowed occasionally.

Your higher self will not evaluate situations the way a human does. It may seem as if the advice is not to the benefit of the urgent world self. An indicator that your current life experience is aligned with your higher self is well-being. In this meditation, you may sit, walk, go, work, sleep, eat, talk, meet, be lazy, act, think, and hang around—whatever the world self does. You observe lovingly from that higher viewpoint. You don't have to explicitly identify with that viewpoint; it is implicit in observing without judgment. When losing your poise or the standpoint of observer by being drawn into anger and resistance or craving and needing, you may temporarily lose the channel to your higher self. But once you allow for silence, it pops right back up. An alternative would be to take a mindless walk—walking without aim or purpose but letting yourself be guided by intuition.

If you wish to remain in the viewpoint of your world self, you may have a dialogue with your higher self, acknowledging that you have an inner coach. You may talk to it, admitting to your limitations, asking questions, and being grateful for answers. Then watch out for dreams, intuition, and coincidences. Acknowledge these as valid communications of higher intelligence. Being ungrateful or trivializing improbable coincidences is not helpful. This doesn't mean you have to place meaning on every coincidence. The coincidence itself can indicate that you are on the right track.

Throughout your life, you may want to shift from addressing higher self to *being* higher self. You may want to give up the old definitions of who you are. As what do you define yourself? As a trash product of evolution? That's very different from the beautiful magnificence that you are. How you define yourself determines what you experience.

You may also want to ask yourself what is left of "you" when everything has been removed. One can do this in meditation or go on a retreat or vacation and leave habitual selves and routines behind. What's left after it has all been removed is closer to a higher aspect of yourself, closer to your true nature. Effective meditation retreats do not offer new belief systems and teachings, but create a caring atmosphere in which it is easy to release belief systems.

Extracting Hidden Information from Your Higher Self

Close the eyes. Create/allow a feeling of excitement or joy by intent alone, without the help of images, thoughts, anchors, reasons, or background. When this state is felt, view what images come up without you having to consciously create them. View what images are attracted naturally. What comes up might surprise you. When something does come up, explore it.

The purpose of this special meditation is that high energy can be used to fish for things that were hidden, things the higher self knows, but the world-self doesn't. This can give you information about which direction to go or what could be done next. Rather than creating excitement with images, you create images with excitement.

Exploring the Unknown

Your higher self is nothing you have to achieve; it's what you already are behind all the masks, beliefs, and identities. The thin layer of experience you call reality, which you perceive with your normal senses, is just that: *a thin layer*. Behind it lies infinity and truer versions of you. Access to these is not gained through what is known, but through many meetings with the unknown. On your life's path, it can sometimes be beneficial to leave the known behind you and step into the unknown. In this way, intuition (which corresponds to the higher self) is activated. Since the world-self doesn't know anything about a situation, another part of yourself is called upon that does know about it.

The thin layer of the known, in which you say, do, and think things similar to the day before, will not lead to the unknown. Looking at the unknown inside or outside (there's no difference between the two), you expand your limits and find out more about yourself behind the layer of habit. There's a lot of consciousness, awareness, and energy waiting to be let in. If you label the unknown, change, new things, or strange things as "negative," expanding your consciousness will seem horrifying and activate fear, losing your safety, social status, or comfort zone. Feeling just a little bit of fear when diving into the unknown is natural, though. When the new and unknown occurs, your mind restructures itself and adapts to the new input. The process of restructuring may occasionally cause a little bit of fear, but remember that nothing has to feel or be unpleasant, and nothing is forcing you to label events as "bad." You are the safety that you seek. Safety is not dependent on outer circumstances. Exploring the unknown doesn't have to be stressful; it can be fascinating and energizing. When leaving your comfort zone, you can do it from a platform of inner and outer stability.

Change of Worldly Identity

Changing the worldly identity is one of the paths of the wizard. The true wizard or shaman is someone who has extraordinary abilities in perception, creation, and action. This is because he does not operate from the viewpoint of a personality or identity, but from the viewpoint of the higher self. By changing his identity, the wizard recognizes two basic truths: That he is none of the identities or corresponding realities. He is something much bigger and brighter than a collection of hobbies, surroundings, and traits. Personality is a construct of consciousness.

Extreme Identity Change: This would involve giving up life, as you know it, and building a brand new life. This might include changing your name and profession, leaving your family, moving to another location, giving up your past, and throwing away anything that reminds you of that past. In an even more extreme variation of identity change, you wouldn't even remain in the same country or linguistic area. You'd learn a new language, find a new job, have a new style of dress, a new circle of friends, develop new habits, etc. In a yet even more extreme variation of identity change, you'd abandon your new identity after only half a year and move on to another identity. In this way, you'd travel from place to place and reality to reality, always as another person with another past, another future, and another name. The extreme identity change and the ultra-extreme identity change of course require a depth of self-trust usually not found in modern society. It would also require you trust that you can create any reality you like. If you don't believe in that ability, you wouldn't give up your safety. In this sense, the identity change would be another way to develop your ability to create realities beyond your wildest dreams. Why? Because of all the challenges approaching you when you change identities. Even considering a worldly identity change is courageous, but having understood the lessons of this book, it is actually not that outrageous. The "I" is an artificial construct covered by a thin layer of daily habits that can easily be deconstructed to experience something more refreshing.

Identity-Change Light: As I am sensitive of people's resistance to change and magical abilities, I can say that it's not necessary to conduct an extreme change of the world self in order to have fun and use magic. A "light version" of identity change would involve simply changing or removing a single element of an identity and replacing it with another. This is of interest to two types of people: criminals and magical people. A worldly identity is made up of the following components:

A name
A profession or regular activity
Family, friends, and foes
A place to live
Ownership of material objects
Documents that prove your identity (passport, birth certificate, CV, pictures, etc.)
Things that prove your past (objects, pictures, certificates, CV, etc.)
Languages and dialects
Vocabulary, phrases, intonations, idioms, and ways to communicate
Body and facial appearances
Gestures, mimicries, and movements
Hobbies, preferred places, and regular activities
Character traits and attitudes

Desires, dreams, and goals
Resistances and aversions
Strengths and weaknesses

Changing, removing, or replacing one of these elements can be fun and cause a slight identity shift and the accompanying rush of energy. You could change the name by which people call you, the friends with whom you spend time, or even your enemies. You can change your job or residence. You could change the way you behave and speak. Cults and sects often use methods of de-identification, not for purposes of reality creation, but for indoctrination into their specific belief system. In changing elements of the world self you are meddling with your core identity, which is a mask hiding your soul. This is one of many methods to reconnect to a truer part of you.

Looking into the Unknown

This exercises your curiosity. If you come out of an experience knowing more than you did before, you have looked into the unknown and made it known. Here are a few variations:

Unknown Information: Using the Internet to find out something you always wanted to know or to get new or foreign information.

Getting your eyes used to the darkness: Go into a dark place—a room or the woods, for example. Stay until your eyes get used to the darkness, your insecurity has passed, and you can see things you couldn't before. Afterwards, ask yourself, "What does this exercise tell me about life, expansion of awareness, learning, and looking into the unknown?"

Look behind the curtain: If there is a wall or curtain somewhere, look behind it. If you are meditating and see a fog, blackness, or barrier, look behind it.

Revealing secrets: Enjoy bringing to light the secrets of people, nature, organizations, the body, companies, or whatever. "Nothing can hide from my eyes." Perceiving secrets is easier when you don't keep secrets from yourself. Know yourself well. Knowing yourself implies knowing infinity, because you are infinity. Don't finish this exercise until you have really found out something that was secret.

Secret realities: There are an unlimited number of realities and games. As long as you can't imagine they are happening, they remain secret. Some things happen before your eyes but you can't perceive them because they don't match your belief system. If someone happens to discover a secret reality while he is in the viewpoint of a victim or in fear, the perception becomes a conspiracy, in which someone is trying to keep a threatening secret. From the viewpoint of self-responsibility and loving vibratory resonance, there is no conspiracy against "poor little me," but merely secrets. Were you to expand your attention only a little, you would find that the most interesting things happen. You would find people and beings living beneath the earth, visiting beings from other planets and dimensions, shamans and wizards, interesting organizations, secret corridors, doors within those organizations, and much more.

Beam yourself into the unknown: If you want something new to happen, you have to behave in a new way. Crazy breaks in routine and action or putting attention on something new will facilitate this.

Write yourself into the unknown. Write a topic at the top of a piece of paper. Draw a line down the middle of the paper so that you have two columns. The title of the first column is "Known," the title of the second column is "Unknown." Alternate between writing what you know about the topic and what you don't know. After you have gathered an overview about what you do and don't know, turn the piece of paper around and title it "Known about Unknown," in which you write what you know about the things mentioned in the Unknown column. Repeat the exercise with various topics. If you do it properly, you will gain new insights and experience an increase in intelligence, while more and more of what you didn't know you start knowing. You have access to infinity and all its knowledge. Presuming that you don't know something is a limiting belief. Trying to figure something out presumes you don't know it. Instead, you could close your eyes and intend that you do know, then let go of the meditation and see what comes up.

Leaving the Cycle of Reincarnation

Popular New Age theory and eastern religion teaches that the soul keeps reincarnating. It dies, and then it's born again here. Many events hint that reincarnation is obligatory by failing to mention that it is only an option. The RC viewpoint is a completely different one. Reincarnation is not necessary, nor is it limited to a single planet or dimension. Reincarnation only becomes an option when the soul hasn't fully experienced the games and lessons it wanted to experience. The process is as follows: A soul chooses a life in order to play certain games or go through certain training lessons. It incarnates and is born with a body—not in the body, but with a body. It is born without knowledge of other existences. The purpose of forgetting everything is so the soul can focus on its earthly life without pre-conceptions or distractions, and can develop new abilities. If you were to be set on an abandoned island without help, tools, chauffeur, bar, hotel, etc., you would be driven to learn certain abilities much quicker and deeper. The lessons a soul chooses are often connected to courage and love. If one does not have the courage to follow the path he feels is right (chosen on a pre-incarnate level), he might choose to reincarnate until he finally has the courage. The after-death self normally takes the most intense experiences to the other side. Mediocre experiences, activities, or emotions fade quickly in the afterlife. The moments you helped someone who was really suffering, the moments you fulfilled a personal desire, the moments of very high and very low emotion you remember. They are saved in your soul's individual field of energy. Some souls take so little with them that they reincarnate to increase the radiance of their energy field. Not the wanting to get away from this life, not escaping this life, not wanting to ascend or become enlightened, is the true spiritual path; you will probably not reincarnate after you have experienced that depth of love. This is how you exit the cycle of reincarnation and go somewhere else.

Identifying with Infinity

RC is the art of not believing in lack. The dark empire that rules this world reminds you of lack every day in every way—in the news, in conversations, in schooling, in events, and in the ways it tries to grab your attention. You only fall for it when you are in agreement with it and are unaware you are buying into a belief based on lack.

One way to release the belief in lack is to view the ways of infinity as they show themselves. If you look at how nature behaves, it becomes difficult to sustain a belief in lack. Noticing the thriving abundance and overflow of resources in the universe it becomes silly to believe in a lack of love, wealth, health, ability, beauty, information, knowledge, or anything else. If you ever doubt the abundance and your incredible wealth and power, all you have to do is face the facts of nature as they present themselves. You don't have to pretend or imagine them, because they are ever-present. Maintaining an attitude of lack takes a lot of effort and squinting. Infinity contains everything. That means it also contains you; but it also contains the thing you desire or the solution to a problem. Since you are intimately connected to infinity, you can also be intimately connected to your desire. Whenever you lack, remember your personal connection to infinity and the aspect of infinity that contains the solution to your issue or the fulfillment of a desire. The formula is:

> Infinity and "X" (desired item or solution) are one. Infinity and I are one. Therefore, I and "X" (desired item or solution) are one.

Referring to this logic may not immediately convince you of the reality of what you want, but it will at least render the unwanted unconvincing. By comparing a lack of belief to all that is, you put things back in perspective. In light of all that is, how does the problem appear? The answer is always "smaller." Not entirely convincing. Simply looking at the attributes of life, the universe, and everything, and identifying with them, acknowledging, "I am a part of this," not just with words, but with the heart will turn lack into respect and uncertainty of your limiting belief. Once you are no longer 100% sure of that unwanted belief, you are in a de-identified space, not yet believing what you prefer, but also not totally believing what you don't prefer. You stand between two worlds. It is here that you can choose.

Just one example of using this type of reasoning: "I feel poor, but looking at the nature of infinity, I see it beaming with lush abundance—of stars, planets, people, sand, trees, grass, cars, and all kinds of other things. This massive surplus is given. I must have drawn a circle around my feet, which makes me the exception to this overflow. In light of the nature of infinity and my inherent oneness with it, I can no longer be completely convinced that 'I am poor' is entirely true. Therefore, both 'I am poor' and 'I am rich' is somewhat true. I notice in which areas I am factually already rich. I am rich in knowledge, objects, resources, information, and friends. I am not entirely cut off from the flow." This type of talk is not meant to make you believe something you do not believe. It is not said half-heartedly. It is meant to be looked at wholeheartedly and to put you into a place of uncertainty about your unwanted belief. From there it will be easier to choose a new belief.

Wholeness

You do not always get what you want; you get who you are. It will often not suffice to visualize the desired reality, you have to identify and embody it with your whole being, as if it were factually present. If you want a situation released, you must first release it within yourself. If you want to become one, if you want to be a whole being, you don't deny or resist anything. People sometimes mistake this statement for "I have to embrace the negative." This misinterpretation then becomes something like "I must also become a murderer and child molester in order to embrace my whole self." This is nonsense. When embracing your whole self and everything that is, we mean emotions, mental patterns and things that have already presented themselves to you. We are not talking about going out and actively searching for negative things to embrace. Embracing all aspects of yourself, leads to no longer having to express them outwardly. In other words, the murderer becomes a murderer becomes he has suppressed aspects of himself so intensely that they are manifested. Society, by defining laws and regulations against things, contributes to the suppression and focus on certain behaviors. In your most natural, non-suppressing state, you wouldn't even consider committing inhuman acts or violence. Violence and degradation are not a built-in part of human nature. They are side effects of a yearlong accumulation and suppression of shame, depression, and fear. In a spiritually mature society, laws are not necessary because in their most natural state, humans wouldn't understand the purpose of crime. In understanding the law of correspondence, one understands that what one puts out, gives, or does to others comes back to oneself. One also understands that lying, cheating, stealing, and hurting others is not necessary because one can manifest whatever one wants without hurting or taking away from others. Crime is based on not knowing the law of correspondence or the law of attraction.

If it is love you want, choose to love. If it is money you want, be grateful for the money you have and generous to the world around you. If you want health, you have to represent what health means to you—strength, beauty, vitality. You claim a reality and rest in the corresponding viewpoint—with your whole being, your whole body. If this is not understood, reality creation never leaves the stage of wishful thinking. Asking about manifestation is a hint that you have not wholeheartedly identified with what you want. Occupying the space in which the desire is already manifest makes any question about it superfluous. You believe in your heart's vision so strongly that questions seem laughable. So what is the difference between fanaticism and reality creation? Fanatics try to convince others of their reality (meaning their inner authority is not enough, which again means they are not fully convinced), while reality creators are fanatic, but do not impose their opinion on others. RC is not a mental event, but an embodiment. To give you an idea: Touch some object in your surroundings or have a sip of coffee. Now do the same thing in your imagination to the extent that there is no difference between the two experiences or so that the imagined version seems even more real. Now imagine holding someone's hand. Imagine sucking a lemon. None of these things is physical, yet while imagining sucking a lemon your mouth probably produced saliva. That is how an inner reality produces effects in the outer. When you held that imaginary person's hand, you probably had an accompanying emotion. To every outside creation, there is a corresponding inner creation. This does not only work on the body, but with anything around the body of consciousness. Nothing you perceive is outside you anyway; otherwise, you wouldn't perceive it. Do you feel the difference between touching imaginary water and imaginary sand? If so, you have the ability to create reality. If you don't merely create thought scraps, but experience feelings *with* your thoughts, you are on the path of reality creation. Define a reality you desire. Think about an object the person already living in this reality handles. Handle it in your imagination until you get a body sense that does not differ from the real sense. Then let go of this exercise, because you take it for granted that the object is at your disposal anytime (which is why you don't have to hold on to it).

Understanding what you just did makes reality creation as easy as placing orders. Let's say you purchase something over the Internet. You sent your order with a click on a website, you paid for it, and you know it's going to arrive. Period. Even though you don't actually have the item physically, once you send your order, you know the item is yours. UPS or FedEx will deliver it, and your job is done. Chances are you will tell someone you already have it, although it hasn't actually arrived. You wouldn't start doubting the delivery service because it doesn't show up the next day. You wouldn't order it again after a few hours. You wouldn't look for proof of its arrival. You may be happy that it is on its way, but other than that, you wouldn't even concern yourself with it. Reality creation operates much the same.

When you live in the feeling of your wholeness, you understand that less is more and that the greatest power requires the lightest touch. Force and effort contradict the lightness of touch required to practice RC.

When Reality Creation Doesn't Work

When reality creation works, people often use statements like, "Wow that is unbelievable," "That is really strange," and so forth. Labeling successful RC this way reveals a lot about the beliefs you have about RC. If it really is unbelievable for you, you don't believe that it can become a normal, familiar, and joyful part of life. When reality creation doesn't seem to work, check your beliefs. Saying "reality creation doesn't work" is using reality creation to create a world in which it doesn't work.

Merely noticing that a manifestation hasn't yet occurred is not a counter belief. A counter belief means letting the lack of an outer manifestation talk you out of your belief in the inner manifestation, letting the lack prove that it is not real. If outer manifestation seems to take a long time coming or if you feel that it has not manifested within you, there are a few things you can do:

1. Notice that it hasn't manifested yet and synchronize with it a bit more, repeat PURE—but this time, wholeheartedly.

2. Call for the manifestation of something simpler or smaller and notice how strong you have become as a creator while pursuing the bigger thing.

3. Choose something similar to the desire or a stepping-stone to the desire that is already naturally flowing in your direction.

4. Let go of the whole thing; forget about it.

5. Enter a version of yourself for whom physical manifestation happens quickly.

6. Act the reality out, using props, objects, surroundings, and places from the reality you want to see manifest. Align with it physically to train your body and mind to what it feels like to reside in that reality.

These are only a few of many things you can do if, after awhile, it seems that you are not manifesting. Or you can, of course, give up RC and continue living life as if it had nothing to do with you. It's your choice. Sometimes this choice relieves people. If giving up metaphysics and RC study results in relief, you haven't been using RC effortlessly and naturally. You have been intellectualizing and practicing RC in the head, rather than feeling it with whole-body awareness, and placing work and resistance before fun, play, and relaxation.

Questioning the Unwanted

Notice how in most teaching models, things such as doubt and insecurity have a negative connotation, as if you are not allowed to feel doubt. Not so in RC. There are reasons for doubt. They point to beliefs you harbor and things for which you are not willing to be ready. Furthermore, doubt in unwanted realities is a blessing. Doubt an unwanted reality, and you remove the fixation on the unwanted. When you are experiencing something that you don't want to experience, ask yourself, "Do I really know this? Is this really true?" Asking such questions honestly will cause doubt to creep up. This frees you from so-called knowledge that no longer represents what you prefer and returns you to innocence, to the open mind of a beginner, and from this uncertainty, it is easier to create something new.

The Secret of Success

So what is the secret of success? Let's see if you have been paying attention. Is the secret of success silence, attention, identification, success, or vibration? The answer is, "The secret of success is success." Like attracts like.

Notice that Shift

Spend time noticing the shift into the unwanted. Notice how quickly you can shift into automatic negativism, how easy it comes. Once you notice the shifting point, you have already stopped it and gained an understanding of how easy it is to shift into something better. It's as easy as closing and opening your eyes. Close them. Open them. You are in a new, parallel reality. Simply observing your daily shifts will give you an understanding of your repetitive beliefs. If you can control yourself, you can control any situation. If you ask, "Why do I keep falling back into old patterns?" the answer is because you believe the facts, rather than your dreams. If you ask, "What do I do when others disturb my reality?" the answer is, "Leave them alone."

Mutual Attraction

Reality creation equals mutual attraction. Choose a reality you want to experience and say:

"I love _________ and _______ loves me."

Reasoning

Write down something you want. Write down why you want it. Then write why you believe you can have it.

Translating a Desire into a Belief and a Belief into a Feeling

Make a statement about what is wanted. Think about what the statement would be if your desire were already real. Speak that statement, and then take a long, deep, slow breath. Repeat ten times.

Attention Laser

State a desire in the "I am" form. Write or express the first objection or doubt that comes up. Repeat steps one and two continuously until objections start getting boring and your focus on what is desired comes easy. An example:

"I am happy."

"Yeah, right."

"I am happy."

"Who am I fooling?"

"I am happy."

Not really. I feel quite lost, actually."

"I am happy."

"Why should I be?"

"I am happy."

"No, I am sad."

"I am happy."

"No, I am really sad."

"I am happy."

"I am starting to get angry."

"I am happy."

"I am angry at this stupid exercise."

"I am happy."

"What a dumb exercise."

"I am happy."

"Sure."

"I am happy."

"Then why don't I feel happy?"

"I am happy."

"I am not happy with my job situation, though."

"I am happy."

"I don't know what to be happy about."

"I am happy."

"Well, I am okay, I guess."

"I am happy."

"Repeating it will not make it so."

"I am happy."

"Okay, just a little bit."

"I am happy."

"Well, I do feel something."

"I am happy."

"I can't get my job situation out of my mind."

"I am happy."

"I wish I really were."

"I am happy."

"I don't believe in this nonsense."

"I am happy."

If you do use this method, don't use it to make something happen, but to focus your attention. It is one of the most powerful tools of this book.

Be-Cause

State a desired reality and follow this with "because," stating why you want it or why it's going to happen. Repeat several times with different reasons. The reality will become more tangible and alive.

Four-Way Statement

State a desired reality in the "I" form, then the "He" form, then the "You" form, then the "We" form. Example:

"I am a successful person."
"He is a successful person." (Referring to yourself from an outside viewpoint)

"You are a successful person." (Referring to yourself from an outside viewpoint)
"We are a successful person." (Referring to all parts of yourself)

This technique is not an affirmation out of a state of lack, but as a playful, quick exercise to refresh a desire. Repeat it two or three times per topic, no more.

Detached Interest

"Do I really have to let go of my desired creation?" many ask. Some have trouble with this part of the equation because they think letting go implies no longer being interested in the manifestation. This is a misunderstanding. It is all right to be interested; after all, it's what this whole book is about—reality creation. Letting go, or leaving manifestation to infinity, doesn't mean you don't care about it. Interest and desire are the energies that spark reality creation in the first place. The problem is when interest and desire become too strong—when they turn into needing, pushing, worrying, controlling. Craving something contradicts enjoying fulfillment. The proper formula is detached interest.

Up to Speed with What You Want

Before entering a new self (reality creating), ask, "Am I ready and willing to be what my new reality requires?" What you want wants something from you. We have already talked about how any apparently negative reality has a pay-off (a hidden, positive reason you have been keeping it). Likewise, every desired reality has a price. The price is giving up your old self and the pay-offs of the old self. You may want a good lover, but are you willing to be a good lover? You may want money, but are you willing to act like a person who has it? By being something, you let the reality you desire find you.

Shape shifting

As already mentioned, what we call the PURE technique in this book is called shape shifting in various shamanic traditions. By this standard, you master what you become. This applies to things you want, as we have pointed out, but it could also be applied to things of which you are afraid. In this type of practice, you would shape shift into it. If you are afraid of dogs, become a dog yourself. Yes, this means closing your eyes and identifying with "dog" to an extent that you become a dog, inwardly. Then, the next time your neighbor's dog approaches, recall that identification and see what happens. It's obvious what will happen: Due to the vibratory synchrony that has occurred, the dog will no longer want to attack you, but bond with you. This is using PURE, not with the intention to manifest something, but with the intention to identify with something to gain an understanding of it. Make that clear at the beginning of your session and there will be no chance of you physically manifesting the traits of a dog. This points to another important aspect of PURE—how imagination creates reality. If you fantasize or imagine without the purpose of creating or identifying with it emotionally, it will not manifest. That means don't worry about your thoughts and fantasies. It is possible to fantasize something without manifesting it, simply by not assigning any reality to it (which is what most people think about imagination, anyway). This is the reason our imagination lost power to begin with; we were scared of our thoughts and their consequences.

Why, Oh, Why?

We have been conditioned to ask "Why?" when something undesirable happens. This conditioning can be seen every day. "What is the cause of the problem?" "Why does it always happen to me?" "Where does it come from?" "Who did it?" Asking the cause of problems, however, intensifies attention on the undesired issue, makes it more important than it is, and creates further answers (beliefs) to solidify the validity of that reality. The question also implies that you are not the source, the creator, and that the cause lays elsewhere or somewhere you can't see. Getting us to look for causes of problems is part of the grand trick being played on this planet. Unless you want to experiment as to how you are creating a problem, don't ask "why" to undesired events, but in reference to positive events. "Why do I want that?" "Why do I believe it can happen?" Such questions create supporting beliefs for what is desired. "How can I lose weight and enjoy the process?" is a radically more beneficial question than "Why am I so fat?"

No Final Destination

The truth is not out there. Your soul is not a searcher; it's a player. You will never arrive at a "final destination," so enjoy the trip. Many desire a final solution, ideal state, or enlightenment, but this implies that existence is static, which it is not. It is infinite and eternal, forever expanding, forever defining itself anew. There is no such thing as "now I have achieved it," because once you have, the next exciting horizon comes into view. If that weren't the case, infinity would be pretty boring.

On Looking for Beliefs

Plenty of RC practitioners have made it a hobby to look for limiting and hidden beliefs. They understand that their beliefs create their reality. While this is a valid way to go about RC, it may not be the easiest way, especially when "looking for limiting beliefs" becomes "looking for problems." It might be easier to understand that your hidden beliefs present themselves naturally, in the experiences of everyday life. By what is happening to you all the time, you can easily glean what deeper beliefs and intentions you have. Looking for deep seated, subconscious beliefs, as many people practice it, not only presupposes that you don't know what they are (because they are so deep), but also ignores the obvious effects of your core beliefs manifesting all around you. The so-called hidden beliefs are not hidden at all, but right under your nose. It is only because they remain unquestioned (labeled as facts) that they don't seem noticed.

What's more, your hidden beliefs (if there are any) come up the moment you choose a new reality. Once you agree to something new, you notice what you agreed to previously that contradicts it. This grants you the opportunity to review and let it go or move beyond the prior agreement (beliefs are nothing more than *agreements* about "how things are"). Let's assume you enter a new reality, and later that day an emotionally charged event comes up. That event is the answer to the question, "What hidden counter-beliefs are in my new reality?" It's already revealed; you needn't look further. Why make it complicated when it is so simple? New Age teachings have a conditioning of their own—conditioning people to believe they have to release, dissolve, work with, or de-create that counter-belief. But this act lends the counter-reality or counter-belief more relevance and importance than you'd give it from your new point of view. From your new point of view, you'd merely witness it without much reaction or interaction because you are the version of yourself to which that belief or event (belief and event are the same thing) is no longer relevant. You needn't hold beliefs like "I don't know" and "subconscious or transparent beliefs are limiting me." The best practice is to notice the event or fact as a belief and return to resting in the ideal version of you.

The Cycle of Creation

Let's repeat it again, for all to read:

Negativity (resistance) is there. From this, desire arises (your business). The desire is delivered (not your business, infinity's business). The desire is received (your business).

The cycle, in short: Your will, infinity's will, your receptivity. The third part (receptivity) is the most challenging for people in this age. You have a will, but you must also release your will and become receptive to what you want.

All or Nothing Meditation

1. Look inside yourself and see a nothingness that contains all potential.
2. Look inside yourself and see the entire creation (including the physical universe).
3. Alternate between the two, not staying for more than 30-80 seconds.

Beyond Questions and Answers

1. Take on the viewpoint of someone who has no questions.
2. Take on the viewpoint of someone who has no answers.
3. Take on the viewpoint of a space in which there is no questioner and no answerer.

Meditation

Many limiting concepts and definitions on what meditation is and is not have spread throughout society. That's why this book refers to meditation as "going into silence."

Meditation is based on the following observations:

- During practice, your attention is not pan-determined, but self-determined.
- The inner universe of thought, emotion, and observation gets more attention and importance than the outer universe. This is especially significant as there is no such thing as an outer universe, except as an illusionary reflection of the inner universe. Because people place such an emphasis on this illusory rim of the whole, meditation becomes necessary. Nothing out there can make you happy. It's all in here.
- On a practical level, relaxation and clarity go hand in hand with concentration, learning, creativity, health, and any other type of success.
- Meditation allows a shift from doing to being, and from effect to cause.
- Meditation allows the observation of your creation and an easier shift to what you desire.

The main reason the whole world is not meditating regularly is because they have been deceived on what meditation means and really is. It is not sitting around, being bored. It is not forcing yourself into uncomfortable positions and making futile attempts to stop the mind. Meditation allows for de-identification, which allows for new identification. New identification is not just a change in attitude or perception; it's a complete shift in reality.

The most basic form of meditation is returning to nothingness by simply letting go and doing nothing, by focusing on one single thing, or by observing the breathing. Once nothingness is enjoyed, go for a new something-ness—that is the essence of the PURE technique.

Wishful Thinking and Honesty

The difference between reality creation and wishful thinking (or self-delusion) is: The former implies desire + belief, and the latter implies desire + disbelief (sometimes unnoticed). Lies are a form of disbelief. Saying something that has not factually manifested yet is not a lie if you truly feel and believe it—even if others perceive it as a lie. This is somewhat different from society's definition of a lie, which is why it is sometimes better to keep your intended realities to yourself. Honesty means saying what you feel or believe. The more honest you are, the more your RC powers grow. Why? Because when you know what you really believe, rather than what you think you believe or think you should believe, you not only understand what believing really feels like, but can also shift to a better belief. Not admitting to what you truly believe is the height of self-denial and makes proper RC impossible.

Responsibility Converter

In RC, everything is seen opposite from what you have been taught. The following technique helps you put any issue into an RC context. If you want to use it, choose a problem and the reason you think this problem exists. Then reverse the statement so that the problem becomes the reason, and the reason becomes the problem, adding "I want" to the reason. Examples of this conversion:

"I am overweight because I eat too much."

Becomes:

"I eat too much because I want to be overweight."

"I am lonely because nobody wants me."

Becomes:

"Nobody wants me because I want to be lonely."

"I don't have time for my kids because I am so busy."

Becomes:

"I am so busy because I don't want to have time for my kids."

"I am afraid of my economic situation."

Becomes:

"I have an economic situation because I want to be afraid."

You Can't Have Everything You Want

Let go of the cheap salesman talk of "you can have everything you want." You cannot have everything you want. *You can have everything you are willing to be.* You cannot have something you don't want to live up to. If you think your life will change without you changing first, you are mistaken. This would be like trying to get something for nothing, which is not how the law of correspondence works.

Magical Prayer

Before going to sleep, address a higher source (God, infinity, higher self) concerning something in which you want improvement. Whisper the following words one to three times:

"Thank you for showing me that this issue is already solved."

This prayer is not pleading and begging, but thanking.

The "All That Is" Meditation

Close your eyes and allow your attention to be on all that is—house, family, neighborhood, city, earth, galaxy, universe, thoughts, feelings, moods, plans, things, etc.—anything that comes to mind when you put your attention on all that is. Immerse yourself in that for a few minutes; experience and observe. Allow your attention to expand beyond the limits of everything, using your imagination or feeling. Observe as if there were a defining border within everything exists. Within this border is all that is; outside this border is the undefined. Once you have that impression, whisper: "That is all that is." Then allow your attention to let go of it. Take a deep breath and release all of it on the out breath. After a few seconds, notice anything that is left and repeat the process of expansion and inclusion with any impression that is still left. Penetrate it all, go beyond it, and let it go. Repeat this a few times until you get the impression that everything is empty and your mind is relatively relaxed. But this relaxation and emptiness is still something, so repeat the exercise with what is left. Go beyond blackness and infinite silence, higher and higher. Stop the exercise when you feel on the verge of exploding with happiness.

15

Domains of Existence

Circles within Circles

All is one, but for a more detailed examination, we can split reality into various domains, spheres of existence, spheres of influence, or mega-spaces. Beginning with the space of the individual world self, we can define expanded spheres of influence. You may picture these as concentric circles, in which each bigger domain contains the smaller one. This means the inner circle will not be aware of the circle outside it, but the outside circle will equally be aware of both.

1. Personal Domain

The individual person, the identity, and anything that relates to its existence—body, name, ownership, interests, desires, resistances. This is the realm of the world self. If you define yourself over a body and mind, you are limited to this domain and will have 100% creative control only over this domain.

2. Relationship Domain

The interactions between individuals close to each other—friendships, marriages, family, and love affairs. Following a linear path of initiation, one would normally first gain control of one's personal domain before gaining creative control of the relationship domain. In short, love yourself before you love others. Gaining control of this domain does not mean controlling others, but your reactions to others.

3. Group Domain

Many individuals collaborating or associating with each other for group activities, group goals, and group opinions—companies, clubs, organizations, religious groups, etc. They are temporary or persistent. A group can develop momentum that goes beyond that of an individual world self. On a linear path of initiation, one would gain control of this group after one gained control of relationships. This does not happen by adapting to a group, but by contributing your own strengths to the group and its goals. You can master the group domain as its member or leader—both are effective. Choose groups that feel good to you (resonate to who you are), appreciate differences, be aware of the group's goals, and contribute to them.

4. Society Domain

Large groups of people co-exist in similar geographical spaces and form societies. A society consists of many groups and interests. Together, they form a loose national identity. A country or state is a society domain. You master the society domain by being aware of different societies and cultures and appreciating the ones that are different from yours (e.g. traveling) or by influencing the masses (e.g. by mass media).

5. Global Domain

A planetary system is a global domain. This includes everything within a planet's sphere—societies, ecology, nature, matter, species, animals. Our global domain is called "earth." On a linear path, mastering this level would mean appreciating this planet, acknowledging the identity of the planet itself as a living being, and respecting nature. When you start becoming aware of other, higher, domains, other worlds and beings, it indicates that either you resist the global domain or you have mastered it. If you have mastered it, you will start being able to communicate with beings outside the global domain (aliens).

6. Stellar Domain

The stellar domain is the solar system within the same space-time the world self occupies. The center of this domain is what we call the "sun"; our particular stellar domain contains planets such as Mercury, Mars, Venus, Uranus, Neptune, Jupiter, Saturn, Pluto, and all the accompanying moons. Mastering this domain involves expanding awareness to the different planets, the interaction between them, travel to the planets (with or without physical body), awareness of the life cycle of a star, and being able to identify with the qualities of each planet. This level is mastered once a being has communicated with beings from other planets within our star system.

7. Galactic Domain

Many solar systems together form a galaxy, which has its own life cycles. Stars are born and die. Civilizations expand and fall. Our star system is located at the edge of the galaxy we call the "Milky Way." One has mastered this realm once one can perceive beyond one's own solar system and experience other worlds and their inhabitants.

8. Universal Domain

Everything within the same time-space continuum, operating under the same laws, forms a universe. Our universe contains many galaxies. Even a universe has cycles in which it expands or contracts. Our universe is in the process of expanding, just like our awareness. This domain is mastered when one can expand attention to various galaxies or is able to levitate, teleport, manifest physical objects out of nothing, or can change the laws of space and time.

9. Dimensional Domain

There are many different universes, parallel universes, and dimensions in various degrees of vibratory frequency. One can travel, explore, and experience these multidimensional realities. There are universes in which the laws we know have no meaning. Together, they form what we call the omni-verse. You have mastered this domain when you are able to astral travel, lucid dream, or create parallel universes on a physical level.

10. Totality Domain

The wholeness of all that is—infinity, creative potential, the expanse, the source. While every other domain is fragmented, this domain is one and complete. Mastering this level is true enlightenment. This domain cannot be grasped with tools created by it (mind), but can be touched on in non-conceptual awareness.

Normally, the human perspective would look at the domains down to up, seeing oneself as an individual inside a huge universe. In RC, we view it the other way around; we accept ourselves as the biggest domain—infinity, totality, godhood, consciousness—and we focus or fragment into ever smaller domains of being, without ever losing our totality. To only define yourself as the individual world self would be an extremely detailed focus. Limiting yourself this way is an act of magic that beings in other realms believe is impossible. I once described to an outer-dimensional being what life was like on our planet, and he didn't believe me. He couldn't believe God could limit himself in such a way that he forgot he was God. But it is possible, and we, as humans, are doing it. Of course, writing and publishing books like this spoils the party a bit. But the natural perspective is always the inseparable wholeness of all. This wholeness creates various dimensions, in which one can discern one thing from another. Separation or duality is the beginning of every game, of any dimension. We can stuff this dimension with all kinds of wonderful things, and within this family of things, we can detect or create a galaxy, and within that, star systems. And in order to focus even more sharply, we can detect a single planet. To perceive a planet means to pinpoint your focus in ways unfathomable for many. Once on this planet, we can create further discernments and separations by creating different groups on different levels in different relationships. Finally, we focus the world self and identify with it to participate in this world even more intensely. We could continue doing this, fragmenting ourselves even more—there is no limit. We could fragment ourselves into body-soul-mind, or we could go even further and fragment the mind and soul into the subconscious—higher self, lower self. All these fragmentations are, except for research and focus purposes, unnecessary and even limiting. The more you split things up, the more complicated things get, and the further away from the truth of oneness you go. To be at least a little more defragmented, view all parts of you as one, without separation. The mind is not your enemy, as many teach. The subconscious is not a separate and incomprehensible part of you that controls you. You are not inside your body; your body is inside you. Once you acknowledge yourself as one, it will be easier to view the surroundings of your reality as you and other people as you (reflections). You can re-identify with them without losing your individuality. The myth of losing individuality is one reason a person forgets oneness. Because the whole contains every viewpoint, your individual viewpoint is never lost.

Showing the domains is a way to get a sense of the bandwidth of consciousness, from infinity down to very specific parts called "people." The higher the vibration of the individual, the more interest it shows in higher domains. Knowing about them, having found out about them, takes your attention from rigidity a bit. One's everyday worries are put into perspective. Consider your biggest fear or biggest desire and compare or view it from the perspective of the next more comprehensive domain. Notice how relatively unimportant it now seems. The desire is easier to create, though, when viewed from a perspective beyond it.

I Can't Get No Satisfaction

Imagine a bunch of paper coins or pictures of coins on paper—two-dimensional coins. Imagine someone stacking them in an attempt to get a three-dimensional coin. No matter how many two-dimensional coins he owns, he will never have a three-dimensional one. What does this mean? It refers to people trying to emulate experiences of the fourth dimension (a higher domain of experience) by amassing things in the third dimension. While 3-D experiences such as sex, material gain, and so forth are enjoyable for what they are, they never quite reach the quality of 4-D (what we call inner or spiritual experience). Some people believe they only have to amass enough 3-D stuff, and they will get a 4-D feeling. So they sniff cocaine, have as much sex as possible, collect cars, and gold, but somehow "they can't get no satisfaction." RC suggests another path. It suggests allowing fourth dimensional feeling to flow through you; you become less dependent and needy, and it then becomes more accessible.

Expanded Abilities

By expanding attention to areas previously unfamiliar (aiming higher), you automatically make lesser, closer, or smaller things easier to reach. Reaching for a Level 5 life will make a Level 3 life seem easier to reach. The following section is not meant to put you under pressure or shift your awareness to the unnatural. It is meant to be used playfully and without needing it to work; otherwise, "I am of no value." If none of it works (yet), that is fine. Rest in your natural joy. Once you wish to expand attention, speculate on the following questions.

1. Am I able to communicate with plants?

2. Can I see elves?

3. Can I communicate with alien beings?

4. Can I move objects by mind alone?

5. Can I levitate the body?

6. Can I heal wounds and injuries on the same day?

7. Can I look at past and future lives?

8. Can I travel out-of-body?

9. Can I practice telepathy?

10. Can I experience miracles?

11. Can I remote-view things?

12. Can I access any information I want in the matrix of infinity?

13. Can I stop, reverse, or bend time?

14. Can I sense more than the regular five senses show?

15. Can I experience any other fun phenomena?

Speculating on these things without expectation or pressure expands the bandwidth of your thoughts. Even without immediate results, it should feel good to consider them.
You could make an exercise of answering each question with a passionate "yes, and this is how" or with a passionate "no!" and then check what doubts appear.

What follows are hints on each item. Within your imagination lie better answers on how to achieve things, but you may use my hints to get started.

1. Communication with Plants

This one is simple. Since you are one with infinity, you can relate to anything within infinity. If you take a picture of a plant, take special care of the plant for a week, talking to it, perhaps caressing it, and then take a picture of it a week later, and compare the pictures; you will most probably see a difference.

2. Seeing Elves

Or any other beings, for that matter. Alien life forms are not only outside the earth, but also on and even in earth. We don't see them because we are not tuned in to the corresponding vibratory frequency. The dolphin, for example, is quite advanced, compared to what we call "animal" and can teach us extraordinary things if we are willing to listen. Elves are found in green lands and sparsely populated woods, providing you have a corresponding vibratory frequency. You needn't take drugs to see them. In fact, drugs undermine and even cripple your inherent ability to shift vibratory frequencies. Once identified with the reality of perceiving elves, begin your walk in the woods by noticing what you see out of the corner of your eyes. Elves can be somewhat shy towards humans and rarely expose themselves completely. The only place I have seen elves so far is in Iceland. The reason for this is probably that the consensus-belief in Iceland accepts the reality of elves.

3. Communication with Alien Beings

There are many different beings with which you can communicate; you have to choose wisely. With what quality do you want to interact? You will get what you represent the most. However, alien life forms rarely show themselves if you don't have a good reason for contacting them. They will not show themselves to give you advice on things you could be solving, and they will not show themselves if your level of fear is too high. If there is a lot of fear, and you call for otherworldly beings, anyway, you may attract events or beings you don't like. That's why it's important to remain pure of heart and intent when making contact. Having read this book, you don't need further technique to make contact; you merely need a definition of what is wanted, attention, and identification.

4. Moving Objects by Mind Alone

This ability is not part of the human consensus-reality, but has been demonstrated by a few people on this planet. In fact, reality creation is like moving objects by mind alone because when you start resonating with a new reality, the whole universe moves to accommodate it. Wanting to move certain objects immediately is problematic for the following reasons: a) the objects could also be moved by hand. Infinity chooses the path of least resistance, and if you can turn off a light switch with your fingers, why stare at it for hours? b) The objects in question are often not ones that spark a lot of excitement in the person attempting psycho kinesis. Would you rather spend your energy trying to bend a spoon or falling in love with one of your desires? c) The practice is often aimed at proving mind over matter, and failure often used to prove it doesn't work, when in fact it works very well. Demanding instant results, however, cuts infinity's efficiency off from manifesting what you put out. Despite these problems, psycho kinesis does work with lots of concentration and practice. It involves identifying with an object, then moving as that object, or identifying with someone who can move an object with their mind, or with pure energy (seeing self and object as energy) or identifying with energy hands that can do that. In any case, as a popular movie once said, "It's not the spoon that bends, it's you." Before going on this adventure, ask yourself if it's worth the investment of time and attention. Would you rather manifest something you enjoy or prove something to yourself?

5. Levitating the Body

I am not competent to talk about this area because I haven't looked into it in this version of my life. But from what we know, we can deduct that it is not close to consensus reality and would probably take a lot of practice in de-identifying from "I am the body" and identifying either with extremely lightweight or with "I am consciousness that lifts the body."

6. Healing Wounds or Injuries on the Same Day

Again, RC practices the path of least resistance and this path usually involves going to a hospital or a doctor. There is no need to label contemporary medicine and doctors as "bad," as the New Age movement unfortunately does. If they'd stop separating between magic and contemporary medicine, and stop invalidating other ways of seeing things, contemporary medicine would become much more open to alternatives. There is no such thing as a wrong way of healing. Whatever works is valid. What doesn't work for you may work for others. In addition, you may want to try the following technique. If you can remember it right after you are injured (which is a challenge in itself), try repeating the same movement that led to the injury, but the way the movement would have happened if the injury had never happened. For example, if you cut your hand with a knife, right after that, move your knife to your hand several times without cutting it, or move it somewhere else several times, as if the movement causing the injury had never happened. This quasi-repetition has created miracles for some and quickened healing for others.

7. Looking at Past and Future Lives

In light of the many-worlds model, this is easy. Since there is no fixed past or future, you would be looking at the past or future which corresponds with the version of yourself you are now. So when people go to reincarnation regression therapy, what they are actually experiencing is not their past life, but the past life that corresponds to who they are right now. Viewing any other type of life is a matter of definition (what do you want to view) and attention (giving neutral attention to see what comes up). It can also be done with PURE by identifying with a future or past version of you. Since you are consciousness, you can identify with and experience anything. In RC, you no longer do this to find something out that can solve problems today but for the pure joy of it. So what about the past of humanity? Is there no fixed past of humanity? It will come as a disappointment to some, especially people who have invested a lot of time in researching the past, but no. There are many versions of the past, depending upon who is looking. What does exist, however, are the most agreed upon consensus or probable pasts of humanity. Within our current consensus, there are not too many different pasts, but there are events that most people would agree took place. However, what we are taught in school is not what most souls (us discarnate) agree took place on our consensus timeline. The theory of linear evolution and technological progress over thousands of years is even more inaccurate than other models, so to speak. It would be more accurate to say that evolution did not take place as a line that went from bottom (Stone Age) to top (space age) but as waves, or cycles, with peaks and lows. This means that, yes, of course we had technology and extraterrestrial and inter-dimensional contact in ancient times. Any half-aware being can easily see that.

8. Traveling out of Body

One aspect of you travels out-of-body once the other aspect falls asleep—every night. The aim here is not astral projection, but consciously remembering your out-of-body travels, remaining aware enough to take part in them. This is a paradox because falling asleep involves losing awareness. Out-of-body experiences mean falling asleep while keeping awareness. This is why the OOBE always involves deep relaxation of body and mind, without falling asleep or while keeping one part of yourself awake and aware. If you can do that, without disturbing your sleep cycle, you will have great experiences outside of your body. The out-of-body experience is different from imagination or dreaming, in that you have a clear sense of traveling around and perceiving things outside of your body. It may begin with imagination (projecting a double of yourself that flies and walks around), but soon turns into something different from imagination.

9. Using Telepathy

Just as a few other abilities mentioned here, this doesn't really have to be practiced because it is a natural side effect of expanding awareness. What is involved is empathy. If you feel connected to something or someone, you know everything about it without having to think about it. Practicing telepathy as a strategy to find out secrets of others is actually contradictory to the ability itself, because it presupposes many limiting things: That you are separate, that the other person harbors secrets, which, if you don't find them out, might be to your disadvantage, and so on. When empathically connected to someone, you pick up all the signals of that person, sometimes even specific thought-bites, without having to control the process of telepathy or follow a hidden agenda. Telepathy is natural to you. Trying to control or strategize it presupposes that it is not. If you want to know something about another person, ask or feel the person—identify with the person in empathy. It's as simple as that.

10. Experiencing Sudden Miracles

If you label miracles and magic as strange and unbelievable, you are separating yourself from those experiences. Accepting that miracles are the norm, rather than the exception, will quicken your experiences of them.

11. Remote Viewing

Despite all the programs, workshops, and trainings offered on this subject, you could learn this easily by yourself. Become silent; relax into neutral attention. Now, look at a wall or barrier you can't see behind with your eyes. Now, move attention through that wall to the other side and remain there without expectation or intentional imagining. See what images pop up. Then walk behind the wall and compare your extrasensory perceptions with what is there. This is one way remote viewing can be exercised. Define something you want to learn. Now put your attention there or at a mental representation of the place you want to find out about, but remain neutral and without expectation or much imagination. Wait for what appears. If possible, corroborate your extrasensory perception with what is actually there in this time-space. It may take some practice to get accurate results, but it's no more complicated than that. Attention has no limits.

12. Accessing All Information

This, too, is relatively simple; there are many different ways to do it. You can ask questions to infinity or an imaginary representation of higher self and allow answers, or you can simply ask yourself in written form and answer your questions in silence. Or you can identify with the version of yourself who knows a certain piece of information. Actually, the tools of attention and identification can be used for anything. If you think there is something you don't know, there is always a version of yourself that does know. Enter that version, enjoy it, and then let go. The answer will pop up soon—not because you are waiting on it, but because you can feel it.

13. Stopping, Reversing, and Bending Time

Some of this is already discussed in the chapter on time. You will not be able to do anything that does not conform to your beliefs. Once you loosen your definitions of what time is, what reality is, and how things are in general, you will automatically experience an increase of anomalous experiences.

14. Sensing More Than the Regular Five Senses Show

There is not only a sixth sense, but also a few other senses that the physical human being has. So even within physical boundaries, there are a few new things to discover. One specific sense that has not yet been discovered by consensus-reality science is space orientation. This sense is located in the sinus region of the body and is related to other locations. Some will argue that space orientation is created by the senses of seeing and hearing, but it is not. Were it not for our space orientation, we would see everything in the same space, or one-dimensionally. Another sense is "sensing" itself. This sense can be called "feeling," not in the tactile meaning of touching something, but sensing something. Both animals and humans have this sense. Examples: People sense when they are being stared at, even from a distance. Humans and, to a greater extent, animals can sense when disaster is impending. Some people wake before their alarm clock rings because they sense it. Some can sense the intentions of others. This has been called intuition. Often this sense delivers more accurate information than the other five senses. Unfortunately, society hasn't paid much attention to it.

15. Experiencing Other Fun Phenomena

This was not a comprehensive list. There are many interesting things one can explore or practice. The ability discussed in the last point could be transferred to things like remote sensing or energy sensing. The body offers many miracles that have not been discovered yet, or have only been noticed by fringe groups, such as martial arts experts or long-time healers. The experience and knowledge to be gained in lucid dreaming at night could fill many books. Experimenting with the PURE technique of silent, non-reactive infinity, identification in joy, and then releasing can offer many thousands of years of enjoyable journeys.

16

Movies of Life

The whole movie making and movie watching process offers a near perfect analogy of how consciousness, reality, and life work. The only difference is that a movie is experienced on a two-dimensional, flat screen, while life is experienced on a three-dimensional screen. All other aspects are so identical that one could speculate that "movie making" and "movie watching" are physical reality emulations or copies of what a soul does or how life works.

The circumstances of life seem to have a built-in solidity, which seduces you into assigning persistence and continuity to them. The same illusion is presented as the continuity of an ongoing film. Movie characters, action, and scenery seem to move on the screen in linear continuity because the human eye is unable to perceive the different frames. Movie, projector, and screen are designed to trick the eye into believing in a continuous process by moving pictures faster than it can see. This illusion creates the experience of emotion and entertainment. Attention becomes immersed in the illusion. If it were sitting in the cinema in a de-identified state, thinking, "Well, it's not real, it's all an illusion," it couldn't really have fun. But one look behind the scenes or at the underlying structure and the illusion is unmasked. Unmasking is not preferable for enjoyable scenes, but might be preferable for scenes you don't enjoy. Maybe you've noticed how when there's a movie scene you really enjoy, you focus all of your attention on the scenery, while when there's a scene you don't like, you tend to remain aware of other things—the room you are in, the cinema complex, friends—whatever. Once you do this, the emotion connected to the movie fades. Physical reality, or the three-dimensional movie, causes the same illusion of continuity that makes it seem serious and real. While watching the movie you don't even want to be aware of the background set up because that would spoil your identification (enjoyment) with the movie.

You don't want to know about how every scene was shot separately, maybe even on separate days, and how an assistant responsible for film continuity made sure the objects were put in the same places as the day before. You don't want to walk up to the movie screen and say, "Hey, look—this picture consists of a bunch of dots, not real objects. (Not even the picture is a real picture, but rather a collection of dots that are interpreted as a picture. The dots themselves consist of yet smaller dots, which again consist of waveforms.) Of course, from the viewpoint of the intending observer, the picture is there because he wants it to be there—because it entertains him. He unquestioningly takes it as real. Questioning the whole thing would spoil the fun, but also reveal what's going on behind the scenes. A closer look at anything makes it dissolve and reveal a structurally deeper reality. You can do that with any reality; you can zoom in or out on anything.

The words "real" and "illusion," as they are used here, don't really refer to metaphysical absolutes (as some try to teach), but to domains, or orders of reality. The moving pictures on the screen are real from the viewpoint of the immediate, immersed experience. Looking beyond the obvious to a deeper order, we see it's the film projector, cinema owner, etc. creating the movie. "The only thing really moving is the projector!" the wanna-be enlightened master might say. But looking at an even deeper level, we may find that there are film directors and film producers and actors behind it all. "It's a lie! Producers are behind it!" the wanna-be conspiracy theorist might say. We can zoom in even deeper and see the projector as an illusion made up of particles. So what's real depends on the viewpoint and what one wants to experience. When watching a movie I don't want to focus on the projector or the inner workings of a TV set, but on the colorful creation that it is projecting. Understanding that everything is real and illusion, depending on the viewpoint, you can trade unfavorable illusions for favorable ones.

The analogy continues: Just like the image on the screen, physical reality is a projection (on a three-dimensional screen). Objects and circumstances may seem consistent and solid when you are immersed in them. When you are identified that way, they seem convincing and hard to change or move. But actually, they are not hard to move, you just don't want them to change, just as the movie-lover does not want to become aware of anything other than the movie. And what's especially significant is that the circumstances seem to be independent of the stream of consciousness that creates them, just as the movie seems independent of the light stream coming from the projector. You don't notice the light stream; you notice the picture. You'd only notice the light beam if you were to look upwards. In the dark space of the cinema (infinity), a light beam (consciousness, belief, intention) is used to shoot still pictures (thoughts) at high speed at a screen (space-time, physical reality) which creates a virtual world of movement, drama, mood. The more tragedy involved, the more enjoy it. Most of the time, you don't notice this because you are part of the movie. In playing a role, you forget that the film was originally written, directed, produced, and projected by you.

The movie analogy is to help you, the reader, remember that reality is much less persistent, solid, and real than it may seem. This will keep you out of trouble (unless it is trouble you want). One problem with this knowledge is that it de-identifies people with the world just a bit and de-identifies them with regard to their desires. This is why RC teaches both de-identification and identification—losing yourself to the extent that you don't know things such as the movie analogy. By reacting to events, you make them independent of the observer: they become effect rather than cause. Desirable realities are the only realities with which you want this to happen. Even questions such as "Why do I have this problem?" presupposes that an event is taking place independently of the observer, as if the movie were independent of the projector. You enjoy movies, but do you take them so seriously that they upset you? The screen reflects only what you project, nothing else. The events are so much more elastic, bendable, and fluid than is assumed. Believing in its fluidity will shape its fluidity. Under the hypnotic spell of the movie, you think that solidity and permanence is an inherent quality and get hooked on them. This gives you the illusion of security, comfort, and familiarity, but leaves little space for new things to happen. If you knew how quickly things could really change, you'd be shocked. A complete shift of everything can occur within a few days—even hours or minutes. All you have to do is shift the intention (projection, belief) that is being beamed into the world, moment by moment—an incarnate as a new self. Don't change the screen. Change the roll of film. The belief in the authority of time, space, and events, no matter how convincing, can be deconstructed and replaced with the authority of imagination and a deeper, happier vibratory wavelength. This happens naturally when you slow down the frames of reality (relax) enough that you can discern them and the emptiness or expansiveness between them. This is why meditation or silence is a prerequisite to RC.

Some meditation systems seem to have forgotten what meditation is all about, especially how it connects to RC. We see many people copying eastern meditation practices, sitting around for years in silence, without using this beautiful stillness and expansiveness for reality creation. It is like owning a gold mine without knowing the gold has value. In meditation, you experience the open consciousness that identifies with infinity beyond all created realities. While it is the easiest way to experience eternal lightness, it is also the best place from which to identify with a new self, living in a parallel reality.

A shift in reality always involves a shift from what seems real or "the way things are" to the realization that this truth is only a belief you are choosing right now. Remember when you realized that things weren't really the way you thought they were, but just the way you thought they were. Take a break from reading to recall a moment like that. In these moments, the power of consciousness to make a belief seem real is grasped. The belief makes reality, and the reality confirms the belief. These are rare, wonderful, and magical moments, and it is my desire that the reader have many such moments. "You see," "It's true," "I perceive it," "I told you so," "It's a fact," "That's why it's true," "There it is"—statements like these are humorous when you have learned about belief projecting these realities in the first place. Nobody doubts your experiences. There's a reason you are experiencing something. You believe (intend) something, this intention is projected into the world of facts, you get lost in the projection, you become the projection, and soon you view it as "cause" or "source." One day, you (hopefully) re-awaken and take the intention back by realizing it was always you that projected it, and then you shift into a new intention—rest in it and allow it—and so forth. The movie of consciousness and it's plethora of beauty never ends.

Releasing Persistent Realities

In rare cases, it will seem as if a reality will not shift despite your conscious creation practice. Best practice is not to focus on solving the unwanted reality, but identifying with the one who is already experiencing what you want and releasing the rest to infinity. This practice is recommended above all other practices. In rare cases, it will seem as if this doesn't create the shift. In this exceptional case, you may use the following procedure. If you want to release a medical issue (e.g. alcoholism), don't use this as a substitute for contemporary medical procedures, but a supplement.

You are never really stuck in a reality forever. It could change extremely rapidly (within minutes), rapidly (within hours), or fairly rapidly (within days), but we will assume there is such a thing as a "persistent reality," and we will assume that it takes a bit more to release it. If that is the belief on which you insist, we will accommodate that belief with a more elaborate process. How will you know when you are releasing a persistent reality? It will move on a scale from one (healed) to ten (chronic). Relief is an indicator. Certain events don't pop up as intensely as they used to.

Four-Way Association

Choose a persistent reality that seems not to be releasing. Answer a few questions about the reality by filling in the persistent reality in the empty space.

2. What does ____________ give you? What benefits do you get from it? How does it serve you? From what does it protect you?

3. What disadvantages would there be to release ___________ or do without it, or be to free of it? What bad thing happens if

you quit focusing, thinking, feeling, or doing it? What becomes worse?

4. What would releasing ___________ give you? What benefits would that have? Which new life quality and feeling would you have? What's in it for you?

5. What disadvantages would not releasing ______________ have? How would not releasing it limit you? In what way would your situation further deteriorate if you were not to release it?

Give at least five answers to each. There are at least four possible associations for any issue.

1. Issue = Good
2. Releasing Issue = Bad
3. Releasing Issue = Good
4. Issue = Bad

Without any RC knowledge, people overcome an issue because they wittingly or unwittingly shift their associations from 1 and 2 to 3 and 4. They find more reasons why 3 and 4 are true. The benefits of release or the pain of non-release becomes so strong that they decide to change. As soon as it's more pleasant to release than to hold on, change occurs. This is why many find it easier to stop smoking when the body would otherwise die.

Viewed statistically, many people don't ever really overcome a persistent reality. Plenty of people have tried everything, only to find themselves further immersed in the undesired issue. Statistics alone is a good reason to find yourself able to release a persistent reality, because it immediately transports you into the realm of the wizard that made the statistically impossible come true, survived to tell others, and will be an inspiration to the world. Wouldn't you love to prove to yourself that you are capable of it when it really counts? If you could release that, of what other things must you be capable? Releasing a tough, persistent reality has enormous consequences on your consciousness and life and makes it much easier to believe "I am the creator."

Mixing Up the Mind

Before entering the next state of the process, the stage in which we mix up your habitual associations with the issue, it is important that you love and accept yourself stop invaliding and criticizing yourself for your associations. Labeling the issue as "wrong" or "shameful" is the first major block. The process (fill in the empty space with the issue)"

1. Create intense desire for ________________. (thinking/feeling)
2. Create intense desire for ________________. (speaking)
3. Create intense desire for _________________.(action)
4. Create intense resistance towards ________________. (thinking/feeling)
5. Create intense resistance towards________________. (speaking)
6. Create intense resistance towards________________. (action)
7. Create neutrality about________________. (thinking/feeling)
8. Create neutrality about________________. (speaking)
9. Create neutrality about_________________. (action)

Repeat steps 1-9 until you start enjoying each step.

Example: Alcoholism

1-3 – I create intense desire for alcohol by thinking about how refreshing, soothing, and delicious it is; I daydream about beer, wine, and liquor with devotion and passion. I associate beautiful experiences with it—flirt, sex, relaxation, laughter—I say, "yes, give me more and more. Bring it on. Come on. I need it, right away. I want to be flooded by it. I am drunk with happiness. I am a real man when I drink. Gotta have a beer. Gotta have another martini. Come on." I act out craving for beer—running to the fridge and gulping down a whole bottle in one go, pouring it all over me, sucking on it, licking it, and exaggerating it.

4-6 – I create intense resistance towards alcohol. I imagine a series of gross images connected to alcohol—disgust, resistance, fear, anger towards it. I imagine myself a homeless bum, drinking so much I vomit all over myself, get dizzy, and fall on the concrete busting my head. Beer and sadness, beer and fear, wine and stupidity, brandy and a wrinkled, drooling face—hanging out at the train station with your buddies, smelly restrooms, a cockroach climbing out of the bottle—fantasize until you feel an urge to vomit. Say things like "Beer makes me sick and stupid. It is the cancer of my soul. I've lost my life with alcohol. I am a loser sleeping in station toilets. I reek of booze. I become violent toward ladies. I will spend time in prison." Take a wine bottle and imagine the wine is foul. Drink it anyway and try to feel really sick doing it.

7-9 – Create neutrality towards it: See alcohol as alcohol, liquor as liquor, and so on. Alcohol is simply a drink, a popular one, at that. A bottle is simply a bottle, neither good nor bad. Some like it some don't. Drinking alcohol is fine; not drinking it is fine, too. It's just a drink. Take a bottle and observe it without opinion, judgment, passion, resistance, craving, or anything else. It's simply a bottle. Open it. Smell it. Take a sip without all the associations you normally link to it. Put the bottle back. Maybe you'll have some more, later. Maybe not. It's no big deal.

This was an example of using this process to cure cravings for alcohol, but you may do it with any other issue persistent reality. The process is repeated until you feel no interest in the issue either way. Once you've lost interest, the issue no longer controls you. You can drop it. The process neutralizes fixed energy and ambivalence. Ambivalence often keeps a reality in place. You go through all the variations: craving, resistance, and neutrality. Whether you are aware of them or not, you have three flows toward a topic. Enjoy all three roles. Not enjoying one of the modes indicates protective walls built around the issue. First, you crave the issue like nothing in the world, then you resist it like nothing in the world, and then you observe it neutrally. The first two are exaggerated.

Useful questions when handling persistent realities:

If you were to release this reality, which other construct you are trying to uphold would be disturbed?

From what must you protect yourself?

Do you think you need something else? What?

Movie-Scene Intending

If you like the idea, your whole day can be viewed as consisting of various scenes of a movie. What are the benefits of seeing your day this way? Well, you can take a time-out between segments and form specific intentions for specific scenes that differ from your intentions and creations for the overall movie. A basic cause of automatism and hypnotic trance unawareness in daily life is that you move from scene to scene and segment to segment without taking any time-outs, without putting the movie on hold, and without consciously intending what you want for the next scene. It doesn't even occur to most people that they can actually intend how they want to experience taking their shower in the morning or driving their car to work. They are moved from one scene to another without conscious thought. They drag issues from work home and issues from home to work. The PURE practice is the most powerful practice in this book. Movie-scene intending is the second most powerful practice. It consists of taking many small time-outs during the day to take a breath, to take stock in what's going on, and to define specific intentions for the next scene. When their telephone rings, one might normally slip into reactive mode and jump for the phone without further thought. In Movie-scene intending or segment intending, one would pause and think about the intention for that conversation. One would have many little mini-intentions. Even if they don't immediately fulfill (and according to RC, you ought not to expect them to immediately manifest), your experience of the singular segments or scenes will be radically different than if you didn't intend anything. But even more important than deliberate intending is to take a time-out between scenes, rather than being dragged through the movie as a reactive and unaware being. You do have different intentions for driving your car than you do for meeting your spouse. By movie-scene intending, you become more aware of what these intentions are. If your car-driving intention is "It's going to be hot and sticky and there might be a damned traffic jam," you can intend something better. "Roads will be free, and driving will relax me." With a little practice, the field of infinity will start responding to your mini-intentions. You are not forced to experience everything the same way every day.

Spaces

Infinity and everyday life consist of spaces, another word for what we just called "movie scenes" you enter and leave. You are in a room, a scenario, a building, or outside a building. Think about it. What are the spaces you entered today? How many did you enter? I was in the following spaces today: bedroom, bathroom, living room, street in front of the house, car, city, hotel, seminar room, restroom, terrace of seminar room, street in front of hotel, basement of hotel, seminar room, street in front of house, living room, bathroom, office, bathroom, and bedroom.

The spaces you enter are the movie sets. To see them as movie sets and become aware of them, especially the in-between times (before you go from one space to the next), allows you to intend certain realities per space. It allows you to take time-outs to determine which space will be next, and it allows you to determine which identities you are creating. Every space corresponds to an observing identity (a collection of beliefs, emotions, and behaviors). Example: You feel and behave differently in the privacy of a restroom than in front of customers. Notice the identity-shift when you enter a restroom? People with too many approval identities will experience major shifts of mood when entering the privacy of a restroom. Free from all the masks they must wear in front of others, they finally relax. Knowing this, you will be able to practice the same relaxation in front of others. Compare your being in the bedroom with being at the office at work, and you find out a lot about yourself. You not only find out where you feel better and where not, but also how you can feel better at any location. If you are looking for synchronicities, meaning messages and hints, take a closer look at your space. If the spaces you are in frequently change, this reflects a consciousness that likes to move, flow, and change. An awareness of spaces will improve your choice of spaces or the aesthetics you place in spaces you frequently reside.

The concept of space and environment is a vital part of the time-space dimension and game you are playing on this planet. The physical time-space realm is a huge realm within which many smaller spaces are contained, in which even smaller spaces are contained, in which smaller spaces are contained, just like a Russian doll box. This dimension has some universes. Within the universes, there are galaxies. Within the galaxies, there are star systems. Within the star systems are planets. Within the planets are continents. Within the continents, there are natural and artificial spaces (countries). Within the countries are cities. Within the cities are parts of town, within town, buildings, within the buildings, rooms. Any of these are simply spaces—atmospheres or backgrounds to your experience. They are all defined, bordered, limited, and located somewhere. Every room is a little galaxy, a reality for itself. Everything—even thoughts and events—are limited spatially or in time. Everything has borders/limits. Notice the borders of things because then you notice the thing that has no borders or limits—consciousness, awareness, attention (all three are actually the same thing). What actually goes on in creating reality is that one creates a space (for example, a three-dimensional space), projects that space, and makes a little universe with limits and content, rendering it different from other creations. Then one enters the space and experiences it. When one is finished, one leaves the room and resides in infinity, or creates another room to be experienced. Unfortunately, some enter a space and then become attached to it and immersed in it to the extent that they forget a reality or context outside of the space. Some forget that they even created the room, in which case they remain stuck in the space, in the reality. If they start resisting or fighting, they become even more attached to it, convinced of the reality of the room. Some remember that they are able to create, but they only create within the limited context of the space they are in—which is like creating a room inside a room—the new room will not be bigger than the current one. (This is what happens when someone creates a viewpoint/reality without releasing the ones that oppose it). If you want to release a reality, notice what it borders/limits—where it is, and where it is not, when it is, and when it is not. It's difficult to release things of which you say "always," "everywhere," "never," etc. Since there is no such thing as an unlimited creation (because only infinity, the creator, is unlimited), such words and absolutisms don't really have merit. The only unlimited thing is the thing that perceives all limited things—consciousness. To create reality, all you have to do is enter a space, identify with it, get into vibratory resonance with it, and synchronize with it. In other words, if you want to create a reality, you have to limit yourself. Maybe you haven't seen it this way yet, but reality creation equals limitation to what you want. You limit yourself to a certain focus, a certain way of seeing things, and it filters out everything that doesn't match. In other words, positive realities are created the same way negative realities are created. You enter one room by leaving another. It's difficult to enter a new room if you are not willing to leave the old one. You may be able to take some of the furniture with you, and even the paintings on the wall, but not the entire room. That's why reality creation begins with silence, stillness, emptiness. Not being in any room at all implies that it is easy to enter a new one. If you have collected too many rooms (identities) during your life, you'll have to let go of some before anything new can happen. Do not try to create a new room at the same place the old room is (switching back and forth between new and old focus). It is possible, but creates many destroyed walls.

17

Life Topics and Miscellaneous

The first draft of this book consisted of roughly 1500 pages of material from my reality creation coaching. The challenge was not writing it, but cutting it down to a normal book format. This chapter will contain comments on the topics of money, relationship, health, sex, and politics, but also add short paragraph versions of longer elaborations of the first draft.

Money

Once you have PURE-ifyed yourself on the topic of money, there's actually nothing left to say. Once properly identified with the existing version of yourself that is wealthy, you don't think about money every day, because you have it. You make more out of what you already have and get more and more with less and less effort. You will joyfully do more than what you are paid for, which is why you will soon find yourself getting paid more than for what you did. You will no longer need, crave, grab, and gasp for money; it will no longer be your God. Instead, you will have married money and have formed a good relationship with it. You will enjoy giving and receiving money—neither will cause any reluctance. You will understand that true gratitude attracts money, but only if it is not used to get money. The necessity to lie or cheat vanishes and postponing the paying of bills decreases. You will understand that trying to get something for nothing is not the stance of a spiritual or magical being (as some believe), but the view of a criminal. You will understand that wealth and abundance is not only money, but also material objects, signed papers, resources, and connections. Therefore, you will stop insisting that money only come in the form of bank notes or numbers on an account. You will learn it is much wiser to focus your attention and desires on what you want to do or have with the money than the amount. You will learn that money flows naturally as a side effect of doing the jobs you enjoy most. Money isn't even the important topic anymore. You are an utterly abundant being and can attract anything you want, so why bother with money? Finally, you will understand that ultimately, it is not money you want, but comfort and security. By bringing that feeling into the today and placing it before money, you will attract money easily.

Relationships

The most important thing to know is that yes, you can manifest the partner you want (provided you are willing to be what this manifestation requires of you). Any type of imagined requirement for that can be identified with—flirtation skills, looks, vibes, and so on. The type of partner you attract says a lot about who you are. The partner is the best opportunity to learn more about you. While physical reality is a mirror, your partner is the deepest mirror. Be honest with what you are able to attract at your current level of energy: Notice a woman/man you wouldn't like who wouldn't like you, either. Notice a woman/man you would like, who wouldn't like you. Notice a woman/man you wouldn't like, who would like you. You can forget about all these categories unless you change your vibratory energy. Now, notice a woman/man you would like who would like you, too. That's the way to go.

The number one solution to any relationship problem is assuming that everything your partner says is right, period—from his/her perspective, he/she is! You will solve any relationship issue by not looking at the kind of energy he/she is giving you but at the energy that you are giving him/her. You are not responsible for him/her but toward him/her. You do not have to go into pain when he/she goes into pain; this will not help him/her at all. When you have no resources of your own, you have nothing to give. You don't look at what he/she is creating, but what you are creating. Much more could be said on the issue, but take this one principle to heart and you will have no relationship issue.

Health

Consciousness is the cause of health, not the other way around. If you say, "I feel bad because I am overweight," you are defining the cause of the feeling. In reality, the feeling is the cause of the weight. Change who you are and how you feel and your body will change. How radically an identity-shift changes reality can be seen in case studies of people with multiple-personality disorders. When such people shift identity, they have been reported to loose twenty pounds within a week. Scars suddenly disappear. Amputated arms even regenerate. It's all well researched and documented, but science calls it a riddle and an illness. These so-called miracles occur because of an identity shift into a parallel reality.

Consciousness as cause of health may take one of the following variations or others:

The Placebo Effect – This is the belief of a person in a therapy, medicine, doctor, or whatever. The rituals undertaken, the pills given, or the authority of the doctor serves as anchors to make it easier to believe. No substances or methods operate completely independently of one's belief in them. Unfortunately, scientists have trivialized the infinite power of consciousness by calling it the "placebo effect," as if it were a curious novelty item.

The Justification-Effect – Someone who invests time, effort, attention, and money into healing will often unwittingly justify that by becoming healthy. What is invested is what comes back. It doesn't seem to matter what one invests all this time, money, and attention in as long as it's done with the belief that it will work. The Justification-effect is a variation on the placebo effect.

The Regenerative Nature of the Body – The body has a tendency to heal itself. This process is often disturbed by all kinds of efforts. In these cases, healing occurs despite these efforts, not because of them.

Quickies for Vibratory Highs

There are many ways people raise their energy or get high without drugs. Some study metaphysical arts such as lucid dreaming, breathing techniques, overtone chanting, shamanic massage, dancing, or floatation tanks. Others practice sports, learn scuba diving, or flirt with people of the preferred sex. These and other practices are ways to raise your overall vibratory tone.

But what if you don't want to create the time needed to practice all these arts? Here are some quickies for between times (café, elevator, car, work break, etc.). Choose whichever you like. They will all raise your vibratory level.

* Perceive something distant and breathe in. Perceive something near and breathe out. Continue for a minute or a few until the mind is calmer or your orientation feels steadier.

* Locate the part of your brain called the amygdala (use Internet resources to locate it. If you put your thumbs into your ears and lay your middle fingers on the edges of your eyes, where your index finger naturally rests is the amygdala, which extends from the head's center to both sides. Imagine caressing the amygdala with a feather, softly and gently, until you feel an obvious shift in energy.

* Breathe in deeply (into the abdomen or stomach). Hold the breath for a few seconds. Breathe out very softly and slowly. Repeat until you notice an obvious shift in energy and awareness.

* Start speculating on the good, wonderful, and nice by beginning every sentence with "Wouldn't it be nice if—" Express many realities you would enjoy (without expectation).

* Copy thoughts. Copy each thought that comes up (think the same thought again, intentionally, no matter what it is). Continue until you feel a new awareness or energy.

* List a problem. Now turn the problem statement into a question (a question that, if answered, would be the solution). Turn it into a question you can easily answer. Then answer it.

These are only a few of several thousands of ways to quickly change mood or outlook. You may want to invent your own.

Politics

The realities that politics create don't have to have anything to do with the reality you create. You create and attract that with which you vibrate. The rest of the world could experience turmoil and strife, and you could still live a life of health, happiness, connectedness, love, and creativity. It is only when you give politicians power over your life (by fearing their policies or believing in their influence) that they create your reality for you. If a totalitarian government suddenly came into place in your country, you'd be long gone to another region, having been prompted by your vibratory alignment with something else. For your personal destiny, it does not matter who is in power and who is not.

This said, there are huge differences in government and there are enlightened and unenlightened governments. Most governments, whether left wing or right wing, are based on extreme polarization, things to fear, and enemies to justify their existence. They play a game of "we are right, they are wrong." Whenever you see this game being played, you know you are dealing with an unenlightened government. These governments are a reflection of the level of idiocy still present in the mass consciousness. They are a reflection of us. Once we change, our rulers will change. Whenever you see the game of "We are right, they are wrong" playing, do not fall for it. Both sides will do everything to convince you that they are right. In actuality, they are two sides of the same coin, both part of the problem. As Ghandi said, "You have to be the change you want to see in the world." If you wish to become an activist, do not become an activist against something, but for something. This channels attention and energy in the appropriate direction. Rather than rallying against war or fighting perceived enemies, rally for peace or with groups you like. Fighting will always cause adverse reactions in the enemy. With resistance, you reinforce the reality of the enemy—you make the enemy stronger. People keep saying, "Don't look away from problems! Don't put your head in the sand!" not knowing that it's this attention that keeps the issue alive.

There is only one rare exception: When a social organism has reached an extreme low, beyond the ability to repair itself (which is what it does when it is left alone, when you look away), from an earthly viewpoint, attack may be viable. This is similar to waking a child from apathy. But again, this is extremely rare. It is safe to say that 90% of all wars are unnecessary and unjustified. Worth mentioning, though, is that this planet is not as war loving or bad as it may seem, neither spiritually nor statistically or factually. There has been no time in which more than 5% (or 10%-15% in the world wars) of the earth has been involved in war. The mass media likes to focus on the 5% that is not okay and ignore, trivialize, and filter out the 95% that is okay. Watching the news makes it seem as if war and suffering are a large part of existence on this planet. In actuality, most of this planet is peaceful and beautiful most times. Interestingly, what one focuses on, grows. But no matter how intensely the media focuses on suffering, the positives of the world always outnumber the negatives. This may seem like new information, but it is completely factual. If you respond emotionally, or get angry at these facts, you have been brainwashed into believing the world is a bad place, conditioned into a victim mentality. There is no such thing as overpopulation. Most parts of the planet are still uninhabited and not only barren lands, as some claim. Furthermore, there is no shortage of resources. All one has to do is line up with abundance vibrationally, and resources flow in. And if a group or country chooses not to line up for abundance, that is free choice, and deep within, they know it. It is not your job to teach them otherwise—they know what they are creating. This is why some countries stay poor, no matter how many funds are flowed to them. If anything is done in such countries, it ought to be on an educational level (as consciousness is the source of reality).

A short note on conspiracy theories: The worldview commonly known as "conspiracy theory," in which secret rulers with hidden agendas are duping the masses, is in some cases accurate and in some cases, inaccurate. In general, the mix of higher awareness (reading between the lines, being aware of more) and a "victim" attitude creates the conspiracy theorist. While noticing more of what's going on and being skeptical of spoon-fed knowledge and social conditioning, the conspiracy theorist tends to blame outside sources for evil. Rarely do such people report of positive conspiracies to the benefit of humankind, although they take place all the time. So while there is much more going on than most are told and can see, it is not all negative or evil, and as long as you harbor no fear or hatred, it can't harm you, anyway. Again, there is no enemy, unless you believe there is. This does not mean one should stop looking to uncover secrets. Being unaware of what is going on "behind the scenes," or not being interested in it at all, is one way you can be manipulated. But once you find out what is going on, you needn't fear it as a personal threat. Simply having opened the curtain, you have weakened the conspirators to such an extent that they can no longer keep up their charade. The biggest secret: They cannot harm you when you harbor no fear. Some organizations write books against themselves, displaying themselves as evil and all-powerful. That may come as a surprise, but benefits of publishing an opposing view of one's self is twofold. First, the organization then controls its opposition to some extent, being able to manipulate how far the opposition goes, and second, fear of the organization is built, allowing for more control.

Religion

If anything could be termed a conspiracy in human history, it's religion. Religion conditions people to an extremely limited view. By introducing a few happy, workable, and inspiring tools, followers are collected and seduced to believing the rest of the nonsense as well. Religions prey on the human desire to re-connect to the source. Since the human knows no better connection, he will rest on religion. Of course, religion is not categorically bad, depending upon the vibratory tone of the person interpreting and delivering it. It can have positive effects. But any belief system diverts attention from the nature of belief systems themselves. Most religions are fear based—meaning punishment is predicted to those who disbelieve. This is the case in all major religions. Religious representatives who interpret religions to love-based teachings will have a positive effect on people, not because of the teachings, but in spite of them.

Most religions are originally based on a misinterpretation of extraterrestrial and extra-dimensional phenomena. From an extremely low point of view (linearly speaking), witnessing one's own higher self, or an extraterrestrial being flying around, will be labeled as a god one must bow down to and fear.

Future generations will develop religions, philosophies, and teachings that are love-based, rather than fear-based. One way to evaluate the spiritual integrity of any religion or teaching is to ask, "Is this teaching directing my attention toward problems and things to avoid, or is it directing my attention to what I am capable of and what is beautiful and nice?"

Science

What is called "science" by most people in this version of the world and on this timeline is a limited belief system, just as religions are. It is a bit more progressive than religion, in that it honestly seeks to examine the nature of reality. This is why its fruits have seen progress on some levels. Nevertheless, much of science is still tainted by studying mostly what has been created rather than what creates it and what could be created. While this slows down our progress, it keeps the game alive for future souls who wish to incarnate and explore extreme limitation. For this, neither religion nor science can be blamed. Both systems are our creation—wool we have pulled over our eyes to filter out infinity. Science, one mini-step higher, will involve recognizing consciousness as influential (if not as cause).

Sexuality

For a spiritually mature being, there are no emotionally charged topics or taboos. Emotional charge in any of the topics mentioned in this chapter is an indicator of resistance toward life, and thus resistance toward self and infinity. Sexuality has been tainted by numerous absurd restrictions and taboos, which have nothing to do with human nature. Sexual energy is the same thing as spiritual energy—something the soul enjoys and wants to experience a lot of when incarnating on earth. One could say that the more dulled and suppressed one's senses, feelings, and energy has become, the more extreme activities are needed in order to evoke any feeling. Feeling something is a matter of energy level. If your vibratory energy level is high, a slight touch could make you orgasmic. If your energy level is low, you need pornography, abuse, or compulsive polygamy to feel anything—not that any of these things are inherently negative, of course. The less you feel inside, the more you need outside. Recall your teen years, when merely looking at a bare breast sent your sexual energy skyrocketing? If years later you need violence and overexposure to feel anything, you might want to think about where your energy has gone.

In any case, the only limit to how you experience sex is ultimately in your beliefs about it. You can release those beliefs on your path to greater fulfillment. Sex will be more enjoyable. Later on, you might even be willing to experience states that are even more energetic and ecstatic than sex. Addiction to sex reminds you that you have forgotten these high states. It then seems that sex is the thing. Trust me, there's more out there.

A few examples of typical limiting beliefs about sex: "When you have sex, you waste energy (a belief many really hold true)." "I have to keep it secret when having sex with someone other than my partner." (If you agree on a monogamous relationship, don't have sex with others. If you agree on a polygamous relationship, do have sex with others. It's as simple as that. Remain honest and there won't be a problem in your life.) "Women have completely different approaches and needs than men (only true if you believe it is)." I recommend dropping the baggage you have picked up and look at the whole thing from a fresh perspective. Nothing is what you think it is unless you think it is.

Children

Children develop and prosper most when parents trust them and supply guidance, shelter, food, and love. Anything else is the parents' beliefs imposed on the child. From the other perspective, parents are not responsible for what you choose as your reality. If you have survived, your parents have done an excellent job—what they were meant to do—and their job is finished.

Children are not yet as incarnate in physical time-space as grown-ups. For this reason, there is more to be learned from children then the other way around. A common misconception is that the children are unknowing, stupid, and immature, when children are closer to the source before they are conditioned by the beliefs of this world.

Animals

The benefit of interacting with animals is that humans gain new senses of being and relating to the world. While many animals lack the intellectual capabilities of man, they have abilities we lack, such as here and now-ness, extrasensory perception, and different types of empathy. The negative extreme is the person who becomes overly involved with animals, spending years living with animals without contact with humans. This happens to those that believe they have failed in human-to-human relationships or developed antagonism toward others (and themselves).

Dolphins and Whales

As advanced research has confirmed, dolphins and whales are not lower-intelligence species. They have more intelligence and experience than the human being does. While this is not flattering, and most will fervently resist the notion, it can be of great benefit to know this. Spending time with dolphins, swimming and interacting with them, will increase your vibratory signal, playfulness, and intelligence. One needn't look outside earth to find intelligent life besides humans. Higher intelligence will become obvious to those who interact with them.

Extraterrestrials and Extra-dimensionals

There are more species in this universe than can be counted in a human lifetime. The diversity is enormous. On a lower level of perception one might ask, "Is there other life in the universe?" On the next higher level of perception, one might acknowledge a few negative aliens or evoke fear of some species. On a higher level of perception, one will not only acknowledge a wide variety of extraterrestrials, but also actively invite communication and exchange of knowledge with them. The reason not more are experienced in certain timelines and realities is the vibratory difference in them. "Meeting in the middle," means they must step down a few tones and you must move up a few tones to reach a place in which interaction can take place. The immature behavior displayed by most people is a far cry from meeting them as equals. If you do not feel equal to them, you will not be able to perceive them.

Extraterrestrials are not the only beings with whom you can interact. There are even more beings in other realities, dimensions, and universes with whom you can play. Who you are being determines whom you can access.

Life after Life

For consciousness, there is no such thing as death. Death of the body perhaps, but not even that is perceived as unwanted, since consciousness never views the body as more than a vehicle for this space-time reality. Losing a vehicle may evoke a loss feeling, but it's not the tragedy humankind makes of death. Actually, death is not something to be mourned, but a thing to be celebrated. It marks the return of the individual soul to its native state, and this state is joyful and ecstatic. Life after life is so enjoyable and energetic that there's not much time to grieve about the loss of a body. From this viewpoint, sadness is almost comic. No consciousness is ever lost. If someone close to you has died, you can easily reconnect to that person by giving positive emotion to him or her. The grieving and hurting puts you out of vibratory reach of that person. Not that grief is an inherently bad thing—it is part of the space-time game. But it's very difficult to connect to someone from whom you believe you are disconnected. How is that supposed to work? As for the afterlife, describing it is a whole book of its own, and I will leave the subject to someone else.

Aging

Aging of the body is a natural aspect of linear time. It can be slowed down, however, and it doesn't have to mean degenerating or falling ill and senile. These are phenomena created by limiting beliefs. In order to age and remain healthy and youthful, allow your attention to flow to ages in which you liked the way you were. Recall them, and remain there in vibration. The second you remember a younger age is the second you connect to it on a vibratory level. Take good care of your body's movement and nutrition.

Food, Drinks, and Drugs

Once again, what you believe about body and foods creates more than what you eat or don't eat. If you believe cigarettes are good for you, they will be good for you. If you don't enjoy smoking due to limiting beliefs, cigarettes will kill you. If you believed so, you could eat anything you want without gaining weight. However, due to intensely focused belief in physical reality and pre-programmed beliefs about masses and body-weight, the easiest way is a mix of both—eating consciously and holding no limiting beliefs about foods. Don't listen to what others say you are supposed to eat or what's good or bad for you; let your body feel and decide what is good for you and what is not. If you are in a supermarket and in a relaxed state of being, this will happen naturally. If you feel the body wanting salad, then this salad will be good for you. If you feel it wanting meat, the meat will be good for you (no matter what people say). It's an entirely different story when you are walking around a supermarket, stressed-out, and craving meat or chocolate. This will have detrimental effects on your body. When choosing food, make sure you are not choosing them out of a craving (lack and emptiness) or from what others say you are supposed to eat (not listening to the body), but out of a relaxed state and intact intuition. You will realize that some things that are no good for others are good for you, and vice-versa. If someone shares their beliefs about how bad the food you are eating is, that is their belief; nothing is forcing you to buy into it. Ignoring the body's advice will make you feel unwell after eating. Appreciating its advice will make you feel well.

As for drugs: The motivation behind taking drugs has the most detrimental effect on body and mind. Becoming addicted to substances to experience certain states (which quickly fade) is the opposite of practicing reality creation. While it is good to long for higher states of energy, it is detrimental to believe you need anything outside of yourself to achieve them. It is an extreme variation of the worldview—not "I am the source," but "outside reality is the source." An exception to this rule is taking a drug once or twice in a ritualistic or scientific setting to experience a state to later reproduce it without the drug. This is a different type of motivation, which will yield positive results. The war on drugs waged by society is, of course, the reason drugs are used irresponsibly. Enlightened politics towards drugs would mean legalization coupled with education on wanted and unwanted effects, detoxification methods, and so on. This would cause a temporary upsurge in the use of drugs, followed by decreasing interest (due to education and lack of resistance by authorities).

Presuppositions of Psychotherapy Compared to Reality Surfing

Psychotherapy: The past is the cause of problems
Reality Surfer: The past doesn't exist

Psychotherapy: Attention on problems (talking, remembering) solves problems
Reality Surfer: Attention on desires and intentions solves problems

Psychotherapy: Something is wrong with the client. He is sick.
Reality Surfer: The client is a multidimensional, infinite, eternal being.

Psychotherapy: I am an expert and can solve the client's problems
Reality Surfer: The client can solve his own issues

Psychotherapy: Healing takes a lot of time
Reality Surfer: Healing can happen here and now

Presuppositions of Motivational and Success Psychology Compared to Reality Surfing

Coach: You can achieve anything if you set goals
Reality Surfer: You can become receptive to your desires

Coach: You have to do more for your goals
Reality Surfer: Do less; be more

Coach: You'll make it!
Reality Surfer: I can't tell you if you'll make it or not. That's up to you to decide.

Coach: No pain, no gain
Reality Surfer: Like attracts like. If it feels good to you, it is good for you.

Coach: You have to overcome your fears
Reality Surfer: You have an emotional guidance system that tells you which path is right or not right for you. Fear is a helpful indicator.

Coach: If you do X, you will get Y
Reality Surfer: If you are X, you will get X

Coach: You need an action plan
Reality Surfer: Do what you would be doing if your vision were already fulfilled

Presuppositions of New Age and Spirituality Compared to Reality Surfing

New Age: Address the subconscious, higher self, angels, aliens, guru to find a solution
Reality Surfer: All is one and you are that one. You are the spiritual authority.

New Age: Attention to magic makes money
Reality Surfer: Attention to wealth makes money

New Age: He is radiating negative energy
Reality Surfer: Others have nothing to do with how you feel

New Age: I create reality
Reality Surfer: I am reality

New Age: The world must get better
Reality Surfer: By improving myself, I improve the world

New Age: I search
Reality Surfer: I play

New Age: With this magic ritual, X will work
Reality Surfer: Through me, this magic ritual will work

New Age: I need a healing
Reality Surfer: I can heal myself

New Age: I am a healer
Reality Surfer: We are all healers

New Age: I have to think positive
Reality Surfer: I feel positive

New Age: I have to control my thoughts
Reality Surfer: I feel positive

New Age: I have to ascend
Reality Surfer: I appreciate the here and now

New Age: With affirmations and visualizations, X works
Reality Surfer: Through me, affirmations and visualizations work

New Age: Nothing is important. Everything is good. I don't have to do anything.
Reality Surfer: I choose what is important and good. I am responsible and enjoy actions aligned with my truest self.

New Age: We are all the same
Reality Surfer: We are all different, unique aspects of the one

New Age: I have to love what I dislike
Reality Surfer: I put my attention on what I already love

New Age: Do what you want
Reality Surfer: Do what you want with integrity

New Age: Do – Have – Be
Reality Surfer: Be – Do – Have

New Age: My former lives tell me who I am
Reality Surfer: What I feel like today tells me who I am

Buddhism: Desires lead to suffering. I must give up my desires.
Reality Surfer: Desires are the motor of the expansion of consciousness and the language of the soul.

Buddhism: Life is an illusion; enlightenment is real.
Reality Surfer: Everything is real; everything is an illusion. The differences lie in vibratory frequency.

Buddhism: I want to achieve enlightenment
Reality Surfer: There is no final state, only many enlightenments and trillions of variations on happiness

Buddhism: I have to reincarnate
Reality Surfer: You can reincarnate, but you don't have to. You can also reincarnate somewhere else or remain without form.

New Age: There are 7 levels (or 12 or 18)
Reality Surfer: There are an infinite number of levels, planes, dimensions, planets, realities, universes, variations

New Age: You have to repeat it often enough for it to become reality
Reality Surfer: True, but the short cut lies in simply being it

New Age: There are secret powers enslaving this world.
Reality Surfer: What you fear or focus on can enslave you. What you don't focus fear on cannot enslave you.

Spirituality: I have to be disciplined
Reality Surfer: Life is fun

Spirituality: I practice denying myself worldly pleasures
Reality Surfer: I practice expressing my pleasure

Spirituality: Nothing matters. We give in to the will of the universe.
Reality Surfer: I am fully responsible

Spirituality: Humility is the highest virtue.
Reality Surfer: Humor is the highest virtue.

Sources & Recommended Literature

1. Frederick Dodson / Levels of Energy
2. Frederick Dodson / Lives of the Soul
3. Esther Hicks / The Astonishing Power of Emotions
4. Harry Palmer / Resurfacing
5. David Hawkins / Truth vs. Falsehood
6. Nisargadatta Maharaj / I am
7. Michael Newton / Journey of Souls
8. Michael Newton / Destiny of Souls
9. Daryl Anka / Bashar
10. Elan / Your Power on a Plate (no longer in Print)
11. Philip Golabuk / Field Training
12. Serge King / Instant Healing
13. Anthony Robbins / Awaken the Giant Within
14. Pipin Ferreras / The Dive

About the Author

Frederick E. Dodson, born in the USA 1974 currently lives in London. He loves viewing life from many different viewpoints and putting spiritual knowledge into the practice of everyday life rather than following the 9-to-5 routine of a "steady job". In his twenties he wrote and published 15 books and held many hundreds of workshops, talks and seminars on the topic of reality creation. Lately however, he has retreated from teaching somewhat and only conducts one course a year. He has started viewing "experiencing joy" higher than "teaching others". Why? Because everyone has their own version of the truth and the purpose of his life is not to get others to agree with him, but to have fun. His favourite activities in the meantime include scuba diving, surfing the internet, writing, collecting movies, travelling and lucid dreaming.

If you liked this book and want to learn more, check out my website at www.oceanofsilence.com, www.infinitycourse.com and www.excellencecoach.biz.

Disclaimer

The author is not responsible for effects readers have or allegedly have from this book, just like a driving school instructor is not responsible for his students driving. Furthermore, the information provided in this book is not a substitute for contemporary medical assistance.